THY KINGDOM COME

Book Cover by MiblArt
Interior Graphic Illustrations by Susan Markloff
Map Illustrations by Shepengul (@jlihanks on Fiverr)
E-book Formatting by McKenna Rowell

Library of Congress Number: 2024904009
ISBN: 979-8-9897283-1-2

First Edition 2024

ARIANA TOSADO

For You, Who called and trusted me with this book.

Thy kingdom come, Thy will be done.

CONTENTS

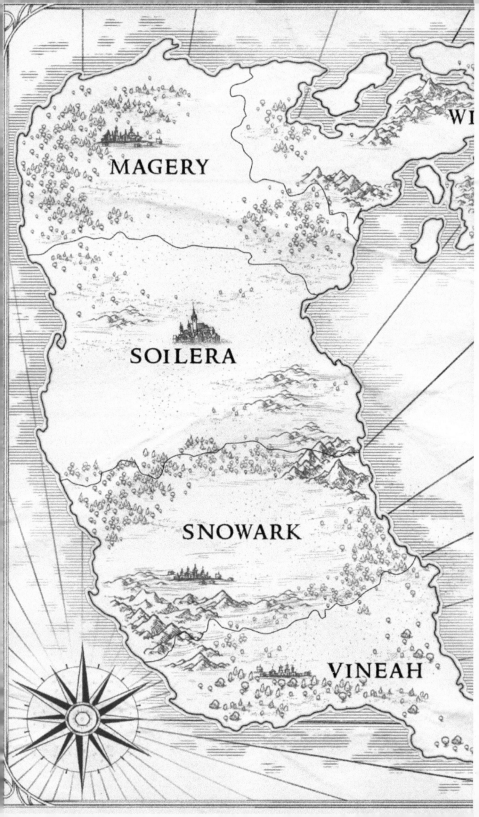

PRONUNCIATION GUIDE

MAIN CAST
Emberly Whitaker – *EM-ber-lee WIH-tih-ker*
Leo/Leon Wales – *LEE-oh/LEE-on weylz*
Zenevieve Lathrop – *ZEN-ih-veeve LAY-thruhp*
Sierra Cathridge – *see-EYR-uh CA-thrihj*
Ambrose Walsh – *AM-brohse WOLSH*
Ezra Everguard – *EHZ-ruh EHV-er-gahrd*
Meredith Prim– *MARE-ih-dith PRIM*
Ithinor Gonzo– *ITH-ih-nore GAHN-zoh*

MONARCHS
Amon – *uh-MAHN*
Cassandra – *kuh-SAHN-druh*
Levi – *LEE-vahy*
Luciana – *loo-see-AHN-uh*
Mara – *MAHR-uh*

KINGDOMS
Lavara – *luh-VAHR-uh*
Soilera – *soy-LEYR-uh*
Windale – *WIN-dayl*
Vineah – *vih-NAY-uh*
Seavale – *SEE-veyl*
Snowark – *SNOH-ahrk*
Magery – *MAY-jree*

CONTENT WARNING:

This book contains mildly graphic violence, near drowning, bloody wounds, descriptions of closing-in walls and great heights, a severe allergic reaction to smoke, the use of tobacco to treat said reaction, and multiple on-screen deaths; and contains themes of depression, suicide, anxiety, claustrophobia (fear of tight spaces), and acrophobia (fear of heights).

TRIGGER WARNING:

This book has mentions of sexual assault, and contains a scene in which a character experiences severe depression and attempts suicide with a dagger. Please read with sensitivity and caution.

PROLOGUE

"YOU WERE CHOSEN"

Emberly

SMOKE INVADES MY LUNGS AND SWARMS THE DARK. The little girl standing on a branch from the tree in front of me comes into focus. Her skin and hair blend in with the night. A white sleeping gown hangs from her body.

She shouts at me, fervently motioning for me to come. "Jump! Now!"

Terror sets aflame every nerve in my chest. I make the mistake of looking down past the branch I stand on: the distance from the ground worsens the tremble in my legs. I beg my mind to return sensation to my limbs to no avail. Even the campfire below offers no heat amidst the icy air and my mind's numbing fear.

My stun swells at the small group of armoured men under me. Their spears and swords puncture the air. Green sashes deck their upper chests, boasting their allegiance to the kingdom of

Vineah. They're shouting at me, the frontmost shaking the tree. Then, they start to climb.

I have nowhere to go—!

"Jump, Ember!"

I look back at the girl. Her curly hair bounces with every motion. The air is growing thicker—dustier. My chest burns. My lungs are locked. My head is throwing me back and forth. The more smoke I inhale, the more my throat closes up.

I—I can't do it!

My body sways.

I can't!

"Emberly!"

My body lulls me forward. I have to jump. I'm going to jump—

With another step, I fall through the flimsy branches.

My throat cages a violent scream as my body hurdles towards the ground. Twigs, grass, and dirt promise to catch me—until a fist-sized rock lands in the centre of my vision.

My heart stops. I squeeze my eyes shut.

A shrill cry jolts me awake.

The familiar cushioning of my bed pulls me out of my nightmare's trance. Elegant cotton sheets and silk covers lie atop me. I gather my rapid breaths, trying to control them. My fingers instinctually rise to the right side of my forehead: the small scar there is as taut as ever. It's my only trinket from that night already half my life ago. Why must that same blasted nightmare visit so sporadically—at all?

Cursed Vineah. Can you at least pick a shade of green that doesn't remind me of vomit?

"Ember!" calls a familiar voice. "It's open!"

The bitter cold of the morning snow radiates across the room. I look up. The ten-year-old girl from my nightmare—now nineteen and already armoured—barrels through the entry hallway of my cavernous bedchamber. The sheer, white window drapes hardly prevent the morning sunlight from blinding me. Somehow, Zenevieve determines that drawing them open is a good idea.

"Of course they're open now!" I hiss, falling back on my mountain of waterbird-feather pillows. I trap myself under the warmth of my covers. "The sun is barely awake, so why should I be?"

"Emberly Genesis Whitaker."

My full name warns me to grant her my attention. She stands at the middle window. There must be extra moisture in the air to cause her shoulder-length, black coils to frizz as chaotically as they do now. She's yet to apply oil to them.

My eyes narrow in cautious thought, meeting her upturned, black ones. I wait for her to start making sense; she clearly hadn't meant the drapes when she said "open".

"Get that fiery mane under control and get over here," she commands, despite being only a year older than me. "There's a portal."

I freeze. *What...? No. No, a portal can only mean that...*

It's a staring contest until I fling myself out of bed. My bare feet never mind the icy, marble floor as I skitter to Zenevieve's side and grip the stone windowsill. The silver kingdom of Snowark rests beyond the snow-dipped palace walls. Beyond that—at the edge of the icy wilderness—is a bright, indigo-lined oval of light.

No... A portal. This is it. This is what the Ancient Mages prophesied about in the Beginning. A portal has opened. But that means...

Not me. It can't be me. I'm not—

"You're the generation running the race," Zenevieve says next to me. "It's you."

I feign a gasp, turning to face her. "You mean—this doesn't happen to everyone?"

She kisses her teeth, sucking air through them, and rolls her eyes. "That won't work this time." Her gaze hardens as she looks down at me. It knows exactly what it is doing as she says, "You were chosen."

I look back out the window. The weight of her words sinks into my stomach: if I've been chosen to run the race to unlock the Last Kingdom, that means I've been chosen to avenge my parents. To avenge all the kings and queens that came before me. If I make it to the end, I will break the death curse that killed them when they bore the next heir—the same curse that will destroy Snowark if I do not bear one of my own.

Someone's made a mistake. The one tainted ruler of Snowark's history? It takes a reserved stupidity to select me for this.

Rest assured: I can throw a dagger and shoot an arrow. I can fight for any other prince or princess to cross the finish line. I can defend. That, however, is the furthest my ability extends; my rule isn't one to be glorified with a crown of ultimate authority.

Ultimate authority... That's right. Whoever does cross that finish line will have reign over all seven kingdoms—including Snowark.

My body tightens with the strain of duty. I must defend. That is why I see the portal at the edge of the kingdom: it is my final call to protect Snowark. Persuade the Last Kingdom's ruler to spare it and care for it. *That* is a destiny I can accept.

I turn to Zenevieve with a hardened resolve. "Get Meredith and Ambrose."

Leo

You can't be too angry with them. They're only following your example, you fool.

At least the rubber adhesive doesn't stick to my fingers as I scrape it off from the metal pump in the courtyard. Covering most of the pipe would have caused the water to spray out in immense pressure when the maids came to collect water. It's an amateur's classic that the castle boys picked up from me.

The same prank that almost killed Ithinor a few years ago. What a fantastic way to thank the man that practically raised you.

A familiar, intense guilt seizes my chest as my fingers freeze. I resist a tremble from them, fighting the same war in my mind yet again. *He forgave you and forgot about it. You were fourteen.*

Besides, the boys didn't even use enough adhesive. The water would have pushed straight through—

Stop that, this is terrible! They shouldn't have done this in the first place.

But they did. And there is no one to blame for that but me. I can barely keep myself in line, forget the castle help. Forget an entire kingdom. Even the scar on my brow is an indelible reminder of that. Not one part of me faults Seavale for its lack of faith in me—but every part of me regrets that I still haven't been able to change that no matter how hard I try, no matter how many years have passed.

I kneel down on the warm sand to ensure that I'm grabbing all of the adhesive. *At least you're improving...*

You hope. How has Sierra stuck with you for the last five years? Ezra is forced to because he's part of the Guard, but Sierra has a choice—

I close my eyes. Even in my thoughts I'm hopeless.

The morning sun beats through the loose linen on my back as I pull the last piece of residue off the pump. Padded steps sound from behind me as I stand. When I turn around, Sierra is running up to me from the front of the courtyard. She's already dressed in chainmail...

She's either decided to train extra today, or something isn't right.

Her pink-toned face is suspiciously flushed, her messy, chestnut bun holding on for dear life as she slows. "What's this?" she asks breathlessly with an arched brow, her hands on her waist.

"The castle boys," I reply, shaking my head. "I was trying to prevent another disaster—but why are you armored?" A wicked possibility grips my mind. "Is Lavara attempting another invasion?"

"No, but there's..." She tautly exhales, gazing at me carefully. Her native Vinean accent almost seeps through her feigned Seavalen one as she says, "A portal is open on the northwest coast."

I drop the adhesive.

It... No, it can't be. If a portal is open, that would mean that I'm... But—no, I can't be, not even part of it! I'm not—

18

I force myself out of my head; I have no time to waste if this is real: "Take me."

Sierra grabs my hand and pulls me down the bush-lined center path of the courtyard. We dart into the stone castle through the wooden door at the end, where she guides me all the way down on the left.

She's nimble, even in her armor.

I smile as we advance onto the steps of the spiral staircase of the pillar. "You're fast in chainmail."

"Ezra's trained me well in his spare time."

A smirk braces my lips. "I'm sure he has—"

"I would focus on your steps before you *trip*, Your Highness," she simpers as we pass the last window until the top floor.

I stifle a snicker as I take the last step up, trying to maintain a steady breath. At least Ezra isn't here to smack the back of my head.

Sierra's soft smile fades as she looks out the window at the top of the tower. "There."

I follow her eyes. A few of the morning ships surround the large island, some of which are docking at port on the east side. Between the houses, huts, and shelters of the kingdom, people are flocking to the northwest edge of the island, straight ahead. Then I see it: on the coast stands a cyan-lined oval of light. It's so bright that it's casting its light onto the sand even in the day.

My stun mixes with my awe, both surrendering themselves. *A portal. It's true. So that's what it looks like...*

My heart hammers a symphony in my chest, threatening to skip every other beat. "This... No, this must be a mistake—"

Sierra holds up a hand in the corner of my vision, drawing

my worried gaze back to her. "When has magic ever made a mistake?" She gently nudges me. "You're the chosen one, captain."

I exhale shakily. That's right: according to the prophecy, it isn't just me who has been chosen to run this race.

That is the only comfort I have as I tell Sierra, "What's a chosen one to a chosen crew?"

Now her lips stretch into a grin, and she brushes a stray bang behind her ear. "What say the captain of the crew, then?"

I look back out the window. Every time I look at the portal, my heart rams against my chest. If I really have been chosen to run, that means that I have more than my current reputation to offer my kingdom. There's more to provide, more to prove, more to be. I could be exactly what Seavale needs, show her that my intentions are changed and true. Even if that means walking through and laying myself down for her sake, for her chance to thrive beyond me—so be it. Someone is meant to lead her to prosperity. That portal tells me that all I have to do is give myself the chance for it to be me.

If even the Ancient Mages believe that I have a chance, I must take it.

"The captain says"—I turn around and take the first step down the stone staircase—"rally the crew."

CHAPTER 1

"ON YOUR MARK"

Emberly

WELL, IF IT ISN'T THE RAT LORD AND HIS MERRY-RATS.
I am sitting on this itchy, indigo-blue velvet in the cold throne room under the cursed weight of this tiara for only one reason: as of early this morning, a matter concerning the kingdom *and* me has finally arisen—and Whiny Winston can do nothing about that.

Unlike how he and his herd rigged the council selection ten years ago. When I was too young to speak up about it. According to this lot, I still am even at eighteen.

The twelve councilmen file into the throne room. Their white shoes echo on the marble floor until they reach the indigo runner in the centre. Even in front of the guards that stand stationed on the sides of the room, Winston doesn't attempt to hide his transparent disdain for the sight of me on the throne. Part of me feels rotten—improper—for sitting up here. It is spite that allows the other part a sense of satisfaction. Above all is a determination to keep Snowark afloat despite the profound stupidity of the men before me. I won't allow Snowark's people to suffer because of my resentment towards the crown.

Whiny Winston approaches in his long, silver robes. His waste-coloured eyes look up at me on the throne—the only time anyone may ever look *up* at me. "Your Highness," he begins in a falsely regal voice. He forces himself to bow, but stiffly and with strain. "The kingdom is alive with notice of the portal that's opened along our border with Soilera."

"So I've been made aware of," I say, matching his tone.

You don't need to remind me that I'm being forced to enter the most terrifying experience of my life.

The crystal chandelier above him illuminates his brown, bald head as he continues. "According to the prophecy of the Ancient Mages, the portals will open for the generation meant to race for the key to the Last Kingdom, which will be ruled by a strong and worthy leader. With the possibility that you are that future sovereign,"—the corners of his mouth twitch with a mocking smile—"should you win the race, it's time you take responsibility for your people. So have the Ancients evidently agreed."

I bite the inside of my cheek. *As if you've ever believed that I have the capacity to rule. You were the one who rejected my initiatives towards addressing the recession three years ago. Now we're still trying to climb out of it.*

"We need you to be prepared," he says, leaning into the words. "We only know that you will be running against the other monarchs. As it's unknown precisely what is to be expected, we remain hesitant in our approach towards the matter; but you must represent Snowark in full regardless."

"Which does not include losing your temper," Moody Myron sneers behind him.

I fight the grinding of my teeth. My hands tighten on the silver armrests of the throne. I know exactly what he wants to unlock in me, but I swallow the key.

"You may put your faith in Meredith that she's done well in teaching me better the last decade," I reply rigidly. "Forgive me, Councilman, but I'll hear no passiveness on a day that demands attention and focus."

Myron slithers back behind Winston. Scorn burns in his muted-green eyes. I despise that they're so similar to mine.

"Forgive us—Your Highness," says Winston with the same strain. "We've assembled the most qualified to guide and protect you. According to the Ancients' prophecy, you are to bring the royal advisor for guidance, who will also serve as your physician. You are also to bring a mage and a knight for protection."

If Zenevieve's isn't the first name to leave your mouth—

He steps aside. The herd of eleven behind him follow. He extends a hand towards the hallway on the east side of the room. "Sir Augustus Milford—"

"No," I say as Augustus steps out from the hall.

His metal sabatons pause at my word, echoing through the air. The councilmen and even guards turn their heads to me.

"I beg your pardon, Your Highness?" Winston asks, squinting those waste-coloured eyes.

"Then you have been pardoned." I smile cheekily as I stand

23

from the throne. "Thank you for your endearing concern, coun-cilmen; but I've already elected a team of my own. Sir Milford, your services won't be needed."

Winston gawks. "I must insist otherwise—"

"So you have. I reject."

I look at Augustus. He stands in the entrance of the hallway, awaiting instruction. "Take your leave for the day, Sir Milford."

"Yes, Your Highness." He bows fluidly, unlike Whiny Win-ston, and then turns out of the room.

He is a fearsome and admirable knight—but I need Zenevieve more.

The councilmen discreetly glare at me as if I were the vile Princess Luciana of Vineah. Only once Winston steps back onto the runner do the rest of the rats follow. "Then," he grumbles, "who does Your Royal Highness wish—?"

"Dame Lathrop will be my protector. Spellster Walsh will accompany us and Lady Prim to finalise his position as the royal mage."

"We agree that Lady Prim shall serve you as usual," Win-ston replies stiffly, "but Dame Lathrop and Spellster Walsh are mere children! They'll only serve minimal protection—"

"Spellster Walsh is only a few months younger than I am, and Dame Lathrop recently turned nineteen." I fight yet another war to maintain a level tone despite his incompetence. "Her age and experience prove that she is anything but a child. May it also please the council to be reminded that it was her bravery and sword at age *ten* that rescued me from Vineah before she had re-ceived any formal training."

I suppress the urge to sneer. *As if you care about my protection.*

You just want to place whatever pawns you can in this race.

Hatred darkens Winston's irises. I know he and his pack wish that Vineah *had* taken me that night. After all, I killed Snowark's true rulers—and they spend every day reminding me as a form of reparation. Unfortunately, that is the one thing I cannot argue them on. The one thing I cannot change nor escape.

I take a ready breath in, my own eyes returning that resentment. "My voice isn't allowed in your council room, Councilman—but we aren't in your council room. We are in the throne room. Here, my voice is what echoes off these walls and seeps into the floor. You rule your kingdom in there. I will rule mine out here. I insist on my chosen three."

He swallows a gulp that pushes his throat far forward. Finally: I've crawled under his skin and stolen *his* authority.

Now I must appeal to his desires to encourage him in my direction: "And should this be the last time I stand in this room, this will be my final order. I should desire it to be obeyed—as an honorary tribute to the princess."

These moments, as few and far between as they are, make each day a little more bearable.

"So be it." He folds his hands and rests them on his distended stomach. "We will send for the members you've requested—"

"Dame Lathrop has already seen to that." I offer my proudest smile.

His tone drops to a familiar, indignant firmness. "So be it. While we're unsure as to how long the race will endure, you will be readied for a week-long journey and formally sent off on the palace's strongest horses at the front gates."

I sit back down on the throne's velvet. It feels a little softer now. In truth, I would almost rather stay here with the council than run in a death race. That is precisely it, however: I was only allowed my confidence moments ago by the fact that I will likely never see this lot again. Though I've earned my victory over them today, there is a chance I may *not* stand in this throne room again. The final victory very well may be theirs. Snowark will be at their mercy.

My glare hardens as the rats turn and file out of the throne room. *This kingdom will never fall into your hands. I will find a worthy ruler before I die.*

"And to think that horses never tire!" Ambrose exclaims in fascination as we trot through the snowy forest. "Though, I suppose the cold eases their strain, such as oil easing the turning of gears, or how water helps us in the same way!"

Zenevieve, Meredith, and I are stuck with the curly redhead's relentless ranting. The journey has already lasted a few hours. I don't know why the portal opened so far from the castle; it's a rather noticeable disadvantage for time.

Zephyr, the palace mage, would have been a wiser choice in terms of capability; but Ambrose is capable enough and also serves my morale relatively well. I've learned how to tolerate his incessant joy over the last five years; he, on the other hand, has almost learned how to fire back when I poke fun at him. The attempts are more amusing than Meredith will allow me to admit.

"What a riveting theory, Rosy." Zenevieve smiles between

us, bobbing up and down on her stallion. Ambrose's red, freckled cheeks match her nickname for him exactly. "What say your thoughts on the mechanics of the waterwheels at Lake Jenara and how they never freeze?"

"Zenevieve," I hiss. Despite my whisper, her name leaves a cloud in front of me. I take extra caution as I lean towards her; my bow and quiver are heavy on my back. "Let the boy spare us a minute, *please*."

She bites the bottom of her full lips with a smirk. With a quick chuckle, her rapidly blinking eyes fall to her gloved hands. "Fine."

Ah. That's why she's encouraged him: he's distracting her. Her smile says otherwise, but now I know that she is just as afraid of this race as I am. In truth, it's somewhat comforting.

Ambrose gasps on her other side. His wide, round, brown eyes land on something beyond Meredith, next to me.

The three of us follow his entranced gaze: a brown bear is walking off in the distance through the forest with us.

Meredith releases a content sigh. "How beautiful..." A signature soft smile traces her lips. "Majestic, aren't they?"

"Until they bite your head clean off," I say, promptly earning a glare from her.

"Respect them and they will respect you," she tells me. "They sense your energy."

Ginger raises his chin, beaming. "Then that one must be happy."

You would never guess that the boy is about to be eighteen.

From a distance, I can understand why the bear is Meredith's favourite animal. Up close, I wonder how quickly she would change her mind.

"And you, Ember?" Zenevieve chimes. Her breath blows past her as we continue forward. "What has your mind?"

I lift my head. The padding under my armour and cloak are scarcely enough to keep me warm. I'm thankful for my velvet gloves. "The same thing that has Whiny Winston's hair: nothing."

Ginger snorts on Zenny's other side. He must quickly regain himself before he can fall off of his horse.

Meredith's voice comes in an all too familiar warning: "Your Highness—"

"I thought we agreed that you'd leave that title in the palace." I meet her hazel-green eyes. They somewhat remind me of dusk in the palace gardens, how many lessons I managed to convince her to hold there.

"It's ill-mannered of you to speak that way regarding anyone of the royal council," she says nonetheless. Her brown skin is spotless despite the scowl, save for the accent marks above her lip and under her left eye. Except for her regality, it's impossible to guess that she's twenty-five. "I understand your feelings towards them, but if you're to become the Last Kingdom's sovereign—"

I lower my voice to all but her. "That word is banned. Use it again and I'll turn around, *Merry*."

She allows a second to pass between us. Her words slow, lowered to all but me. "Don't be a brat—remember?"

I straighten on my horse. The reminder is bitter as always. Nonetheless, it's the only one I obey.

She continues with a tone more fitting for her motherly voice. "Maintain your dignity outside their presence. Then you deprive them of even subconscious satisfaction."

I wish it weren't impossible to be angry with her. Especially when she advises me about stealing joy from the councilmen.

An invisible force pushes back on my horse's next step. The horses are startled, demanding that we quickly regain control of our reins.

"What is—?" I utter.

My mouth shuts at the sight before me. The indigo-lined portal stands metres away. It towers over us and casts a lightning-like beam across the view of the horizon—as if it's barring us from travelling any farther. The blinding brightness of its mouth almost demands that we shield our eyes from it.

"I don't believe it..." Meredith marvels beside me, matching my thoughts. Magic has never conducted something so powerful before; even Ambrose's fireballs pale in comparison to the majesty—and terror—of the portal. I can't help but curse the fact that we are among the prophesied chosen to be the first to travel through one.

Zenevieve's black eyes narrow in thought. She dismounts her horse and cautiously steps forward in the crunchy snow. No invisible wall pushes her back.

"Interesting," she mutters. When she turns around and tries to pull her horse forward, the animal refuses another step. It's almost as if it *can't* go any farther.

"Wait," Ambrose says. He slides off his mare and walks to the front. Waving a hand in front of him, a sheer sheet of indigo magic briefly flutters into existence. Ginger nods before turning to us. "Magic won't let anything through. I think Emberly is the key to move forward."

Lovely. This is where we must dismount.

I feel everyone's eyes, even Zenevieve's, on me as we remove our satchels from the saddles. The weight is almost crushing; I'm the shortest one here. Hence why I enjoyed the horses.

I can't stand this pressure. As if leading them all into a death race isn't enough.

"Is it something I've done with my hair?" I ask in feigned surprise. "I've never worn it completely down before, but surely that isn't so special as to stare."

"It's beautiful, Your Highness!" Ambrose chirps, gripping the brown handle of his satchel over his shoulder.

"Call me that again, Ginger,"—I rest my hand on my dagger—"and Rowena will have strawberries for dessert."

He crosses his arms. "At least strawberries are sweet instead of *bitter.*"

I briefly point at him. "Good one."

"Ember," Zenevieve states, her hands on her waist, "he is about to be the least of your concerns."

Her nervous eyes spare a glance at the portal as she nods to it. My thundering heart pounds against my chest. Meredith is the tallest of us, and the portal stands her height and a half.

There isn't any way around it: we can't bring the horses. Meredith reluctantly commands them home. My satchel rests heavier beside me as I watch them leave and then turn to the portal behind me. Each step is firm and tight as I walk up to it.

"On your mark," Zenevieve tells me.

I match her eyes. Meredith rests a gloved hand on my shoulder, turning me to face her. Despite our last conversation, she smiles reassuringly at me. She's already forgiven me for it. She always does. Meredith knows exactly who I am—I killed her true rulers, too—but at least she forgives me.

An orange glow ignites at the edge of my vision. I turn my attention to Ambrose. His fingertips are ablaze with furious flames. I almost wish I had such power, but mage families are rare; besides, I'm not sure the council would have survived under those circumstances.

"Ready to serve." Ambrose's thin lips beam. Even the plethora of freckles on his face seem to glitter with excitement.

Interesting how the palace boys never harassed him *about them,* I think. Mine are half as much as his and lighter, yet I never escaped such uncreative taunts.

Meanwhile, Arthur smelled worse than the waste in the stables, and Ramses still can't remember how to spell "cat".

I swallow. *I'm still procrastinating.* Zenny is right: nothing I say can prevent the inevitable this time.

I squint my eyes against the light of the portal. Once I step inside, I begin a sacred race we only know one thing about: the Last Kingdom is at the end. That is a worthy prize for the other monarchs. They won't let anyone take it from them. My life will be in their hands once I step through.

I don't have to win. If I can just survive long enough, I can ensure Snowark's survival.

I decide one thing: for this kingdom.

"Let's bring Whiny Winston back something nice," I announce. I'm first to step into the blinding light.

CHAPTER 2

"ALL IS GOING SWIMMINGLY"

Leo

I SUPPOSE IT COULD BE WORSE. SPRING JUST BEGAN, IT'S A *beautiful season for a race.*

If we were actually holding the race in Seavale.

Waiting on Sierra, Ithinor, and Ezra is about to run me into the ground with anticipation. Mostly anxiety. Much anxiety. And it doesn't help that I'm already underground in the cold, humid passageways under the castle.

As if I haven't spent enough time down here.

I release my mounted frustration in a long, shaky exhale, pressing my hands against the frigid, jagged wall. The torch-lit passageway is wide enough to prevent my panic: I can pace, but just barely.

Sierra, you said that you would hurry.

Reality bangs against the walls of my mind, why I'm down

here: to run and likely die in a race meant to break a curse that will kill me once I bear an heir. It's almost ironic.

And if I never have an heir, the curse will eradicate Seavale from the world... There is no winning.

"Leo?" echoes a sweet voice from around the corner of the passageway.

Finally.

I take myself up from the wall and jog to the end of the tunnel on the right side. Sierra emerges from around the corner in her messy bun, a satchel on either side of her. Ezra and Ithinor come behind her. Thankfully, she has my bow and quiver mounted on her back.

They're all here. I exhale a steadier breath. I can breathe a little more easily down here as long as they're here.

Ezra's and Ithinor's satchels bulge with their resources. Collectively, we resemble a group of knights ready for battle, wrapped in armor with swords on our sides and all. Even Ithinor is dressed like the tall, buff man standing next to him, which surprises me. His cyan-blue mage robes are trying to cover it.

Sierra hands me my bow and quiver. I point at Ithinor and grin at Ezra. "You managed to put *him* in chainmail?"

Ezra's icy-blue eyes flash with humor as they meet mine, a brilliant contrast to his black skin. He teases back in a deep voice, "Wouldn't you believe it? Even the elderly can make it work."

"I'm thirty," Ithinor replies dully. His pitch-black curls do help him look younger. Unamused, his sky-blue eyes glance between us. "My robes hide this well, you needn't worry."

It's already been thirteen years since he took responsibility for me... Being the most talented in his class at seventeen, he came to the palace to serve as the royal mage—to help provide a stable life for his parents. He shouldn't have had to become one himself in doing that.

Stop—I need to keep my morale higher in front of them.

"You might enjoy it more than you think," I say, nudging him. "How does it feel to be our *knight in shining armor*—?"

Ezra reaches to smack my head before Sierra hands me my satchel, stopping him. "I don't mean to ruin what may be our last moment of joy for a good while," she says, scowling, "but Leo's been chosen to run in a race against the other kingdoms to unlock some kind of brand-new kingdom, we're about to be last to the starting line, and you're all making jokes."

There goes my last chance of distraction...

"Sharpen your minds and weapons, and focus," she commands. "We know excruciatingly little about this. For all we do know, our weapons will be anything but for show." She glances at me and Ezra, Ithinor nodding his approval. "We understand that, don't we?"

There's a reason my best friend is my advisor. Unfortunately, she advises a little too well sometimes.

I pray that the echoes of the passageways can't pick up my thundering heart. I nod, the weight of reality returning. I always thought I had more time to give Seavale everything I can offer. Now it seems that the most I'll ever be able to give her is my life.

The walls feel that much closer together. *You could have done so much better.*

You'll be twenty years old in a few months. Act like it.

I clear my throat. I can at least make *these* moments of leadership count. "Then let's leave." I turn to Sierra. "Are you sure that you've remembered everything?"

"I've packed as efficiently as I can for the longest journey these satchels will provide," she replies. "Ready whenever you are."

I turn around and scurry down the tunnel. My team follows closely behind, our steps resounding across the stone.

"I must warn you, Leon," Ithinor says monotonously as we reach the end and turn right, "the castle is bound to notice our absence within the next hour."

I quicken my pace as we run down and pass a few more torches. "That is an hour we have to reach the storage basement, run across the beach, and jump into the boat waiting for us on the coast. It should only take us about ten minutes. As long as we're spotted only once we're in the boat, we will be safe."

The sooner we escape, the better. The castle doesn't trust me to be a fitting ruler, and I can't fault them for it—but I definitely do not want those guards to be the ones to escort me to the portal to begin the race. Not only am I all too aware of the kind of "encouragement" they'll try to impart, but I want to show Seavale that I'm doing this of my own accord. The guards will also execute their escort with more patience than we can afford. I don't want to waste time, and I need to run to the start before I can change my mind.

I slow as we approach the middle of the passageway, turning to the wooden door fixed into the wall. It needs a jolt before it opens with a loud scrape, and I motion my team inside.

I know that torches line the pitch-black room; it's foolish to keep them lit when all of the storage material in here is made of wood.

"Ithinor?" I step up beside him, smirking.

He slowly sweeps his olive hand, wrapped with orange waves of glowing magic, over the room. A flame folds to life atop each torch mounted on the walls. With chests lining the perimeter of the room and closed crates scattered across the floor, the four of us focus on the wooden staircase dead ahead.

Ezra steps up first and shoves the doors above him open with a bang. Sierra stands behind him, and he takes her hand to allow her out first. I follow, and Ithinor is last after he commands the torches to rest.

I hear Ezra close the doors with a liberating click. Something is freed in my chest: *No matter how this race ends, I will never be stuck down there again.*

A brilliant-blue sky stretches above us, the air carrying specks of the sea on its breeze. It's a comforting scent, especially when Ezra verifies that we have no tail. We step off of the stone ground surrounding the basement entrance and onto soft, fine sand.

"Brilliant plan, captain." Sierra's smile reaches her green eyes as she looks up at me.

I shrug. "I suppose you could say that all is going *swimmingly.*"

Ezra smacks me on the back of my head. "My father would take offense to that," he teases, resting his large hand on the golden pommel of his sword. "That was his favorite pastime, and you've turned it into the worst joke I've ever heard."

"I wouldn't celebrate yet when the boat stays in our sight and not at our sides," Ithinor remarks flatly next to him, gesturing to the coast.

I scoff as we trudge onward, the sand gradually stiffening the closer we draw to the boat. "Do you even know of the word 'fun', Icky?"

His sky-blue eyes meet my own, and I can practically see the orange of fire threatening me. At least he can't *really* shoot fire from his eyes. I hope.

"You can't leave that insufferable nickname behind in your childhood?" he says.

I run my hand through the top of my hair, the only part that's growing out because Ezra somehow managed to convince me to keep only the sides trimmed. "Until I'm legally old enough to drink ale with Ezra, no."

Ithinor rolls his eyes. "At least the legal age actually matters to you now."

I keep my gaze forward. My mind can't help but add to that sentence: *Unlike a few years ago.* Back when I used the tavern to skip lessons—none of the barkeeps dared to serve the underage prince alcohol in fear of punishment, but I was obnoxiously persistent.

Sierra's words repeat in my head: *That is not who you are anymore.* The fact I'm on this sand right now willingly walking into a race I know next to nothing about proves that.

The tan of my skin comfortably absorbs the sun's warm rays. Twigs stick up from the sand more frequently the farther we walk. Closer to the halfway point, I need to start scouting for hermit crabs buried—or not buried—in the sand. I'm almost tempted to stop; grab an arrow off my back; and fire at the ripe, yellow coconuts growing on the trees on the east side of the beach. I wonder how often I'll have to hunt during this race—

whatever it has prepared for us.

"Aye! The prince has made his way to the south coast!"

My fists clench, my heart dropping at the faraway voice calling from the top of one of the castle's scout towers. He's far away, but not far enough away. To worsen matters, he continues shouting that same announcement to whoever didn't hear him the first time.

"Leo?" Sierra urges next to me, as if she's asking what my mind is deciding: surrender or risk.

No, it won't end like this. I have more to give to Seavale. I've yet to change my mind about that, which means I must do this.

I offer Sierra the same smirk she's seen for the last four years when we're about to break royal boundaries: "Race you."

"And I you," Ezra says in a brilliant grin, sprinting toward the boat with me and Sierra inches behind.

My feet kick up sand with each step I take, my bow and quiver on my back threatening to slow me. It isn't until I crack a twig underneath me that my right side feels empty. I stop and turn around. Ithinor is running with a clan of guards running faster behind him.

I take his hand once he catches up and drag him along with me, which forces his legs to move a little quicker.

"Leon—I can't—run this—fast! The—armor!"

His breathlessness is the most emotion I've ever heard from him.

"Just a little farther!" I shout as I watch Sierra and Ezra jump into the wooden boat on the edge of the shore.

"Your Highness!" a guard calls. He sounds mere yards away, but I refuse to interrupt my stamina and look behind me to verify.

"Stop in the name of the royal court!"

On the bright side, when you die, you won't have to worry about them anymore.

I force my thoughts away as I estimate the distance left with our speed and Ezra's strength. I lock eyes with him. "Push the boat out!"

He turns back around and grips the bow.

"We can't exactly leave without you!" Sierra calls with cupped hands. She gestures furiously for us to move faster.

"L—Leon—!"

Ithinor's gasp erupts the second we step onto wet sand. I finally stop and turn. The guards, even in their armor, have matched our pace. If Ithinor and I don't jump into the boat within the next ten seconds, we'll be captured. But he can scarcely breathe, let alone run.

"Ithinor,"—I grip his arm—"fire!"

With sweat glistening across his forehead, he heaves down a gulp of air before his hand rises against the nearest coconut tree, ten feet away from the guards. Fire climbs its trunk in milliseconds, and Ithinor throws his hand sideways. The flaming tree falls in the guards' path.

I wrap my arm around his waist and his arm around my shoulders. He limps quickly until we're ankle-deep in the tepid sea. Ezra swoops him up and sits him down in the boat, then jumping in and pulling me with him.

I turn my head, breathless. The castle guards have just reached the damp part of the sand. They watch in defeat as we float away, each soldier stopping one at a time.

I turn back around and rest my head against the bow.

"Well—at least our *ship*ment will be on time."

Ezra smacks me on the back of my head again. "I pulled you in and I won't hesitate to toss you out." He slaps my shoulder with a heavy hand as though in congratulations, and then he takes an oar from Sierra and begins to row.

"If you made that," she says, exhaling as she briefly takes her oar out of the water, "I have hope for us, after all."

My breaths pause for only a second as I gaze at her pink face, which is flushing under the sun. Then her words land in my stomach, and I realize exactly what we're rowing to: the portal on the northwest coast of the kingdom.

The realization finally strikes me: what if I'll actually need my bow and sword?

"I won't be able to do this with the armor." Ithinor still pants furiously, taking off his cyan mage robes and revealing the chainmail underneath. "If I'm to have any chance of surviving, I must take it off."

"It will be too dangerous," Sierra tells him, pushing the oar through the calm waves of the sea. It ripples with soft gurgles. "Your armor is all you have to protect you since you have no weapons."

"With all due respect, Miss Cathridge, you aren't understanding the entirety of the situation." Ithinor's robes drop to his feet, and he leans back in his spot. The sun highlights every gleam of sweat rolling down his skin. "The armor is too heavy for me to run in and *live*."

Reluctantly, I reach over and help him slide off his gauntlets. Sierra sighs disappointedly.

Ezra joins her. "I did my best," he says, rowing calmly.

A minute later, Ithinor's armor sits at his feet in the row-boat. Our destination sits a few hours away. I can't help but wonder if, for whatever reason, Seavale's portal was the only one that opened so far away from the castle... Do the other kingdoms already have a time advantage over us?

I swallow. *This is happening.* Out here, we've no choice but to realize where we are going. It takes every fiber of muscle in me to force away the anxiety of us being last to the starting line like Sierra said. The weight of the situation falls like an anchor onto my chest. By the silence and downcast eyes of everyone else in the boat, I'm assuming that my team feels the same way.

Take their minds off of it. Distract them.

"If only we had our poles." I look out at the sea. "I'd love to enjoy a local meal before we go."

"With what fire, captain?" Sierra teases, snickering.

"Ithinor's!"

He only manages to roll his eyes as he continues gathering his breaths.

I look back at Sierra, chuckling with her, and notice again the intensified pink of her cheeks. I lean forward across the boat and reach for the oar. "Let me take—"

She sticks her tongue out at me before sticking the oar back into the water.

I hold up my hands in mock surrender. "I offered."

"Well,"—Ithinor's breath finally slows as he looks at me, a hand resting on his chest as if to calm his heart—"there's your answer, Leon: I do know about 'fun'. And *that* is precisely why I don't like it."

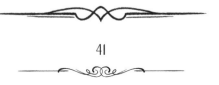

Just as I saw early this morning, practically the entire kingdom has arrived and gathered along the edge of the beach to marvel at the portal. Even upon noticing our boat in the distance as we arrive along the coast, no one steps forward to overwhelm us. They all stay fixed at the invisible barrier between plant life and sand, calling to and shouting at us while we dock. I can't determine if they're thrilled that I'm about to walk into the portal or furious that I'm leaving them with the reputation that I am. And I don't intend on finding out which one it is.

"This is... unsettling," Sierra notes, fixing her messy bun as we walk farther onto shore. "Why aren't they moving forward?"

Ithinor extends both arms, barring us from walking onto the dry sand. He crouches down and waves a hand over it, a translucent wave of cyan-blue that resembles the surface of the ocean glowing underneath.

"This territory is guarded by magic," he says. "It senses Leon and is allowing him by. We're permitted through with him."

"Well, aren't you special?" Sierra nudges me with her elbow. "You're our personal escort."

I internally grimace; should anything take a turn for the worst, I may not be escorting these three to *just* the race.

"But as Sierra warned before we left," Ithinor states, standing, "we've lost too much time to procrastinate any further."

"Let's go," I say before I can hesitate. Ezra smiles in the corner of my vision. "We have everything but time."

We approach the cyan-lined oval of light. It's almost two feet taller than Ezra, which is a terrifying aspect on its own. The shouts and unintelligible chanting of what I know is most of the kingdom erupts twofold as we draw closer to the portal. A border of blue light crackles in a horizontal line as if to prevent anyone from trespassing.

With another ambiguous uproar from the crowd as I step forward, my body freezes. All those people. If I don't win this race—if I pay its ultimate price—Seavale will fall with me. If I don't survive, it will condemn the fate of my entire kingdom.

I don't even know what will happen once I walk through. I don't know for certain what *could* happen. What is on the other side?

"Leo?" Sierra asks. I hear a dozen questions with it.

Right. I don't have a choice.

Don't turn around. Don't turn around.

I step into the portal before I can change my mind.

CHAPTER 3

"BELOVED HEIR, RIGHTEOUS SOVEREIGNTY"

Emberly

BLINDING LIGHT SWARMS MY VISION. I SHIELD MY EYES with heavy arms. When my foot tries to land, it stoops lower than I expect. My eyelids fade from orange to black as my body falls forward. I stick out my hands on instinct, landing on a hard, smooth surface.

My armour jangles upon impact. A few arrows spill out from my quiver on my back with a wooden clatter. At least I'm not the only one sounding a ruckus: my group fall in after me, Zenevieve's and Meredith's armour announcing a clanging cacophony.

I internally groan. My wrists ache with a sprain-like soreness. *Certainly an... experience.*

I rise to my knees, pushing dark-auburn hair out of my face. My gloves did nothing to soften the impact, and I rub my wrists under my cloak. I stare with squinted eyes at the knight on my left and then my advising physician on my right. My mage sits on hers. Meredith's pristine, dark-brown bun has hardly budged; only select hairs have come undone. Zenevieve and I lock eyes. A few of her black coils that just touch her shoulders have found their way into her mouth.

She pulls them out. Her other hand flicks away a piece of my hair that's covering my eye. "That was an adventure."

I scoff. "Concussion, more like." Leaning forward, I rub my forehead. The temperature has tripled, which says little, given Snowark's average day. In the edge of my vision, Ambrose runs his gloved hand through his red curls. Then, my sight snags on the rippling ocean that lingers behind him and Meredith.

Are we...?

We look ahead of us. A couple of groups sit bored in their spots along the circumference of the large, round, white surface. A few more portals of varying colours open. Four people in distinct armour and colours fall from each one.

We're all on a floating platform in the middle of the ocean. *Up in the air. With the sea below.*

I've never seen the ocean; the mountains block the view of the coast the palace is closest to, and I've never been allowed to travel far beyond my four walls. The rippling waves below us, though, taunt me with the distance between us. If I fall off...

As if she's reading my mind, Zenevieve dares to walk to the edge. She reaches out her hand; thankfully, it makes contact with something.

"Glass?" she muses, looking all the way up. "There's a dome over us."

Thank the Ancients.

I step towards the middle of the arena. My knees still threaten to wobble at the mere idea of being in the air. I force my focus onto the other groups: *One, two, three, four...*

There are seven groups total.

The tension in the air is thick: Snowark and Vineah are ever on the cusp of war. Lavara attempted an invasion on Seavale for power and land a few years ago, and the two have yet to alleviate their strains. Windale declared war on Soilera last year after Soilera refused to ally with them in a war on Magery, seeing as Magery lies between them. As a result, Magery was divided: one half tired of silence and wanting to join Soilera in battle, the other desiring their traditional ways of peace—and later forced to join Windale. A civil war resulted; and now they're on the brink of being divided into two kingdoms, if not claimed by both Soilera and Windale first.

On top of it all, Lavara recently proposed to aid Windale in their war in exchange for "military aid". Our scouts in Vineah have detected rumours that Vineah is ready to aid Seavale in case push comes to shove—if Seavale provides them the same assistance "one day".

A hard swallow passes in my throat. Seeing them all in front of me now, the realisation shatters the front doors of my mind: *The entire* world *is on the verge of war.*

It seems as if every monarch is trying to suppress the facts. We all know each other's secrets. We're all wary—except for the groups behind us. They've no trouble orienting themselves and eventually gaining the attentions of their leader.

Zenevieve steps up to my side. "What is this meant to be?"

she whispers.

Meredith gracefully stands. Even her indigo cloak falls with elegance. "It certainly isn't the most explicit start to a race..."

I dare a couple more steps towards the middle of the platform. A careful atmosphere has settled, but curiosity is starting to overcome it.

I remember each monarch's portrait from the book Meredith makes me study the new edition of every two years. My survival instincts remind me to assume that we're all of equal combat skill; we're all roughly the same ages. Prince Levi of Windale is the eldest at twenty-one, Princess Mara of Magery the youngest at seventeen.

My gaze carefully moves to our left. I go down the curve of kingdoms: Soilera is next to us and in, of all things, wooden armour. From their helmets to breastplates to leg coverings.

Your blacksmith—or timber-smith—was playing a cruel joke on you, Princess Cassandra. I would snicker if my legs weren't still wobbly.

The group next to Soilera radiate an arrogance I almost burst out laughing at: Lavara. Prince Amon is dressed in black-plated armour that's lined with red, matching the three behind him. I'm enticed to tousle his slicked-back, black hair. His chin is stuck high in the air like someone has their fist under it.

Certainly a tempting idea.

Next to them stand a group without armour entirely. Instead, they're dressed in violet mage robes with complementary colours.

Magery. Their palette has always soothed me.

They aren't surviving long without armour, though.

I wonder which side of Magery's civil war Princess Mara's group are on, if they've picked one. My question is answered when I realise that they're all eyeing the group next to them. With fear.

Windale.

The Windale group chatter away with each other. They seem oblivious that their enemies are standing beside them. Their tall stance is proud in their white-plated armour lined with gold and light blue.

The group next to them almost pull a doubletake from me: the dark man standing next to the only girl noticeably towers over them all. He must be almost two hundred centimetres tall. He certainly has the biggest build out of everyone here.

I don't realise that my mouth is agape until the back of a rough hand closes it for me. I turn my head. Zenevieve's eyes are also on the man.

She raises an arched brow. "He looks like he could kill us faster than it takes Ambrose to smile."

"Or Meredith to scold me."

"Your Highness," she states behind me.

"See? Faster than that." I turn around to face Meredith. "And I told you to stop that."

"Then stop acting like a princess." She raises her brows as if to challenge my response. She wins again.

I turn back to the tall man's group. Based on his buff build, he is Seavale's knight. There is only one other young man in the group: Prince Leon Atlas Wales. The prince of foolish pranks and an embarrassing lust for entertainment. His reputation alone boasts of his cunning wit and calculating mind. The scar slitting his left eyebrow is even further telling of that.

I should be wary of him if we are to ever meet throughout this.

I'm about to move on when his stare catches mine.

My lips part without my control. His eyes match the blue of the sky above us without discrepancy. They're a startling contrast to the warm tan of his skin and dark brown of his hair that reminds me of Zenevieve's favourite chocolate cake. It's trimmed at the sides but grows out at the top. It's different but—admittedly—handsome. For some reason, he won't look away from me.

Why are you staring at me like I'm your long-lost mother?

He finally takes those eyes to the group between us. Mine race his there.

Oh, curse the stars.

Princess Luciana of Vineah pushes her wavy, auburn hair behind her bronze-armoured shoulder. Her vomit-green–eyed gaze glares at all in front of her. A timid mage in vomit-green robes stands behind her. Luciana's blond knight stands suspiciously close to her side. He's almost as tall as Seavale's but misses a few centimetres. A sombre scowl pulls down both of their faces.

I'd be sad, too, if vomit was the colour that represented my kingdom. If you were trying to imitate the vines and leaves of your jungles, I suggest hiring a new colourist.

What has to be the royal brat's advisor and physician stands short next to the mage. She's scrambling to find something in her satchel. She has to push her long, blond hair behind her ear every two seconds.

That's why Meredith keeps hers in a bun and mine stays just past bust length.

Despite the unfortunate presence of Her Royal Goblinness, my mind reels as my stare sweeps over the platform again. All seven kingdoms stand along the circumference. Each one. We've wars between us all, yet we stand in a circle now.

My heart skips a hard beat: what's next?

Then, it appears in a burst of white magic: a glowing orb the size of Whiny Winston's big head floating in the middle of the arena.

Amon of Lavara sprints to it. His warm-grey hand is first to touch it, but Luciana is a close second. Levi of Windale is third. From what I can see, a red light reflects onto Amon's ashy skin. Green glows under Luciana's tan hand. Levi faces me directly; his colour is too bright to see in the daylight—perhaps yellow. The three glimpse each other in confusion.

"What is this?" Amon asks in a snobby voice, brows furrowed.

You'd be really fun to punch, wouldn't you?

"Maybe this thing... is for all of us," Levi says in an unexpectedly deep voice. His accent is more articulate; he pronounces his "r's" harder. Strange.

He looks up from the orb, briefly meeting my gaze and then Cassandra's of Soilera on my left. She scowls at him, but his stare doesn't change. "Since this race is—well, for us."

"Ridiculous." Amon snickers. I despise that our accents are nearly identical. "The most powerful ruler must be able to activate it. That"—he glances around before a punchable smirk slides to his punchable face—"would be me."

"You touched it first, you idiot," Luciana sneers. "It would have activated then and there if that were the case."

Her accent is similar to Snowark's, but the vowels are more

horizontal—lazier and less proper. Like she is.

"H—how about... together?" Princess Mara of Magery says. Her soft voice struggles to sound authoritative. She steps forward from her group. "All the monarchs do it together."

No wonder she's struggling to keep her kingdom together.

She takes a few steps towards the centre of the platform as though to lead. Then comes Cassandra in her wooden armour.

Brilliant. So I have to touch it, too.

I feel someone's eyes on me before I can take a step. I dare a glimpse in Seavale's direction. With one foot forward, Leon is staring me down.

I regret to inform you that I am not your mother. Being that you're in this race, she's—you know—dead like mine.

"It's all right," Meredith whispers behind me.

I don't turn around to correct her: surely this is entering a trap. Breath regrettably shaky, I shake off Leon's eyes. He follows me to the orb in almost perfect rhythm.

My and Mara's hands touch the glass. The orb warms and swarms with a vibrant array of colours. I look up and share the gazes of everyone around me. We all seem to be daring the other to remove their hand. No one does.

In an instant, everyone's eyes widen before they step back one by one. When I see a sparkly explosion of violet behind Mara directly across from me, I follow suit.

She is looking at something behind me, too, mouth agape. I turn and find a translucent indigo figure floating only a couple of metres away. I manage to suppress a scream as I step back, almost meeting the orb. I can't make out the figures' faces that are moulded by the waves of magic. That doesn't make them any less terrifying.

What are these people?

Everyone is either too stunned or too patient to speak.

"Revered heir," says a smooth, tender voice from the indigo woman. The voice is multiplied by seven, and I suppress a shudder. When I look next to me, at Luciana's green figure, the woman's mouth moves at the same time the one in front of me speaks. "You are a symbol of hope in a time of despair. You bring rain in a cruel drought. You may become the leader your land starves for."

I look at Zenevieve as if for help. She stands between Meredith and Ambrose, who watch the colourful men and women in awe—or fear. Zenevieve, however, meets my eyes with determination. She dares me to step away from the orb, straight through the figure and to my group; she knows that a challenge is the only way I can keep my feet planted here.

I should have never let you know me so well, Zenny.

"We, the Mages of the Ancient Time," the voices announce next, pulling my attention back to the woman in front of me, "bear great news: you have come to bring forth a world that will save yours. They who unlock the Last Kingdom prove that they possess what a uniter requires—that you are the sovereign the United should hold at its helm."

"Uniter"? What are they talking about?

"Since the beginning of time, a curse has stolen your rulers once they bear an heir and threatened your kingdoms should they refuse to continue their lines. You, however, are about to prove yourself as a ruler to break this curse once and for all."

Then why did you create the curse? I scarcely manage to cage the words in time.

"You will face seven stages that represent their associated kingdom. Each stage hides an artifact that will help you overcome its greatest challenge. Once you do, the key to unlock the next stage will bestow itself unto you. Collect all seven keys, and you will form the Last Key. Overcome all seven stages, and the Last Kingdom shall be unlocked."

I can't help but glance away from the magical—and, I realise, dead—woman in front of me. I must catch the others' reactions before they can hide them: there's a unique melancholy to Cassandra's pale face, and I assume it's not from the fact that she's chosen wooden armour. She likely doesn't want to participate in this race for one reason or the other. By the solemn way she casts her brown eyes downward, she wants this to be over and done with.

Leon stands on the other side of Luciana, his back almost to me. Still, I catch the way his head hangs and how his fingers are tapping his thigh armour. Anxious. Calming himself. Perhaps he doesn't believe that he can do this.

Next to redheaded Cassandra is Amon. I must catch a glimpse of him before he catches me; his pride is bound to want to trap any weaknesses he can before this begins.

To my surprise, there lacks even a trace of a smile on his face that I still want to punch. That doesn't mean that his arrogance isn't beaming inwardly, though. Lavara is a proud kingdom. In fact, from the prince's thousand-metre stare, he's likely calculating tactics that will allow him to blaze through this. I can tell because he isn't showing anything outwardly; he wants to be unreadable. Unpredictable. Like he wants to hide what he deems valuable.

I bet my mage can beat up your mage.

That's only a spiteful thought; Ambrose would snap in half if I even startled him.

"Beloved heir," the colourful Mages say, stealing my attention again, "righteous sovereignty, thy kingdom come amidst moral poverty."

A scoff whispers under my breath. *How can they speak so tenderly towards us while sending us to our deaths? Sending us to break a curse they created?*

The translucent Mages gracefully flow apart. Their individual colours rise into the air and then dissipate into nothing. The portals that we used to travel here reopen in their same spots.

The other monarchs and I step away from the orb and turn to face one another. The orb fades away only a second later.

What just happened? Seven dead mages from the beginning of time just spoke to us. I've never seen magic work so... blatantly. Powerfully. Even the portals almost pale in comparison.

Amon stares after every one of us—definitely calculating us now as I suspected he would. Thankfully, I've had years of practice of suppressing anything in my mind. If we truly are meant to kill each other by the end of this, I must keep my mouth shut and observe. I certainly won't give anyone here insight into my mind or mannerisms.

Snowark must still be standing by the end of this. I must convince the future ruler to spare it—no matter who it is.

I don't think I have many quality options.

"For the Kingdom," Mara says, as if she *is* reading my mind. Her tone remains kind. Authority is still severely lacking.

"For *my* kingdom," Luciana sneers beside me. "I've earned my right to this. None of you will steal it from me, especially not a kingdom that can't even agree with itself." Her sharp gaze pierces Mara unapologetically. "I would kill you all now if I weren't severely outnumbered."

You and Lava Man would make a perfect pair—for me to punch.

She turns away before we can speak and walks back to her group. The four of them step into the green-lined portal.

Amon gives a single smirk. "A woman who knows something about war strategy—there's something new."

That's it—!

"Emberly," Meredith calls as my left hand reaches for Rowena.

Cassandra, Mara, Levi, and Leon step back upon my action. I realise my mistake too late, yet pride prevents me from dropping my hand. I glare at Amon. The arrogant dunce merely snickers before walking back to his group. They step into the red-lined portal as though they walk through portals every day.

Only then do I spin around. I'm already the shortest person here; Meredith and Amon certainly didn't help me avoid gazes just now.

I march back to my group. The remaining monarchs' eyes are heavy on my back. "Really, Meredith?" I hiss, finally hearing footsteps spread out across the arena.

"Everyone here is armed," she replies firmly. "Your temper could have begun a bloodbath even *Luciana* wanted to avoid."

The brat's name is wicked even on Meredith's lips.

Cold, Meredith. Ice cold.

"On the bright side, there's something to look forward to,"

Ambrose chimes, fists clenched in anticipation. "We're visiting the other kingdoms!"

"No." I curtly exhale. "If this is meant to be as torturous as I'm fairly certain it will be, we'll be visiting the worst versions of the other kingdoms."

"What do you gather from the others strategy-wise?" Zenevieve asks, resting a hand on her sword's pommel under her cloak. It's too warm to keep them on; I would take my own off if we weren't about to leave.

"Differences here and there," I reply, pulling my gloves farther up my hands. "But they've all the same thing that makes them dangerous: clear, determined motives. Especially the kingdoms at war. Never underestimate any of them for as long as we're running."

Ginger nods firmly. Meredith approves with a soft version.

Zenevieve only bites her bottom lip in a smirk. "If only Winston could see you now." She shakes her head, chuckling at what I have to assume is her imagined response from him.

I hear Meredith's soft sigh in *dis*approval as Zenny nods towards the indigo-lined portal. "Well?" she asks, her eyes quickly blinking in fear again.

I wish she could hear my thoughts: *I'm scared, too. I am.*

I shove my apprehension, doubt, and anger far down my throat. I do not have time to be scared. I have time to get this right once, or I have nothing at all.

For Snowark. To do at least one thing right with my existence. I know I killed two revered rulers—but now is my chance to provide another in their wake.

My heart pounds straight through my armour. Nonetheless,

I step into the blinding mouth of the portal.

CHAPTER 4

"STOP AND SMELL THE CORAL"

Leo

THIS TIME, MY FEET DON'T EVEN LAND AS I STEP OUT OF the portal—yet I stay upright.

Don't like this, don't like this, don't like this—

I try to find my balance in the globe of ocean blue and the light of the portal fades behind me. Then I realize that I'm not falling; I'm floating *in* the ocean.

I can't breathe—!

Wait. I can.

I look down: before I can admire the display of sea rocks below, I find a bubble around my body. A bubble suit molds to my every movement as I gently kick and let my arms suspend themselves in the water. Air surrounds me in a thin layer.

I spin around with extra force against the water to find Sierra, Ezra, and Ithinor all fawning over the same realization as they float. The bubbles even mold themselves over our armor. When I look behind me, it's also around my bow as it hangs on my back.

Thank the Ancients that they're transparent and moldable... It's just like armor; I don't feel trapped.

"Leo," Sierra begins in a muffled voice, pumping her arms and legs to meet me. Her soft features are painted with concern as she swims up a little to match our heights. "Are you all right?"

I take a deep breath as if to test the limits of the bubble suit. The air is clean, pure, even. "I'm... I'm fine—it's just like armor. It's all right."

"Are you sure?"

"Really," I tell her, leaning in to the word. "I promise."

She nods once before turning back to Ezra and Ithinor. "All right... First observation: the bubble suits are letting us breathe underwater."

Ezra's icy-blue eyes widen as he glances at the sword hanging on my side. His voice is also muffled when he says, "The weapons, they'll pop them!"

Curiosity shushes me before I can react. Sierra holds up her index finger and gently presses it to her gauntlet. The bubble bends accordingly. She looks up at Ezra with a cheeky smile.

"They can't be unpoppable," he says, brows furrowing.

"I don't mean to burst your bubble," I muse, "but they *are* magic. So it's possible."

"Leo." Sierra moves her hands to her waist. "Say something like that again and I'll test that for you."

At least Ezra can't smack me underwater; I'll take Sierra's empty threats any day.

"Second observation," she says next, looking straight up at the surface, "look how far down we are. And yet..."

I push down on the water. There isn't any pressure—only resistance from the currents.

Ithinor, on Sierra's other side, repeats my thoughts in his usual, monotonous tone. She nods in agreement, but Ezra keeps a brow raised in doubt.

Before he can speak, Ithinor holds up a finger. "Shouldn't we be moving along?"

Race. Right. Though Princess Emberly had good reason to reach for her dagger upon Prince Amon's remark, that mixes in my head with Princess Luciana's words: *I would kill you all now if I weren't severely outnumbered.* Our chances of survival are definitely higher if we hurry.

"We should." I exhale, my breath hot as it gathers in front of me. I revel in the air that the bubble provides, the cool temperature of the sea. Looking up, I can scarcely see the rippling of the surface, only a lighter blue. "What if we swim to the surface and see if we can do this up there?"

Sierra's lips tighten. "If that were the case, we wouldn't have been given these bubbles to begin with. We're breathing underwater for a reason. The artifact the Mages mentioned must be down here."

I turn around, careful of my encasing. Ahead and beside us, colorful schools of fish travel across the water, shimmering in the rays of the sun streaming to this depth. A mild current pulls me as I swim forward, admiring them. Forests of seaweed sway in the distance. Their leaves dance in the sunlight the higher they sit. Below us sit rocks of all shapes and colors. My arms ache to reach as far forward as they can while I have no boundaries.

I stop swimming and come upright.

"Leo?" Sierra asks behind me.

I know ocean currents; I've swum in them my entire life. The pull I'm feeling right now... isn't a current.

"Do you feel that?" I ask, turning around. "The pull?"

The three of them exchange glances as if tacitly asking each other the same thing.

"There's a mild current moving parallel to us," Ithinor replies. "Is that what you're referring to?"

I hesitate, keeping my gaze away in thought. "No." A faint lull is encouraging me—almost insisting that I come. "The pull forward."

"You feel a pull?" Ezra asks. It sounds as though he's trying to avoid a mocking tone.

"Maybe." I turn back around, facing what lies ahead. My mind reels from the sensation of the underwater waves pushing against my arms and the dryness of the bubble's air. The two sensations conflict, holding my mind with wonder. If I focus on the pull itself, it's guiding us to... the coral reefs.

What is this...?

"Leo." Sierra appears beside me. Her Seavalen accent waivers a little into her native Vinean one as she tells me, "If you feel a pull, follow it. We'll follow you."

"Are you sure?" I ask skeptically, glimpsing Ezra and Ithinor. "It sounds mad."

"We're breathing underwater with bubble suits in a death race for a magical key," Ezra states. "Which sounds more plausible?"

A light chuckle escapes me as I look at Ithinor. He nods softly as if to encourage me to move forward.

Sierra's right: the artifact has to be down here.

"There's a pull," I finally say, looking ahead. "Forward."

"Wait," Sierra chirps. "Could that be the artifact?"

The words pull my head out of the pit of doubt. *Now* the pieces are clicking together: we haven't a clue as to what our obstacle is for this stage. If the artifact is meant to help us with it, finding it will help us realize what that obstacle is. How else are we to find one item in the midst of an ocean if not for something like a pull toward it?

"You're right." I smirk at Ezra as I nod at Sierra. "She *is* bright."

I've known that since I was fifteen, but Sierra doesn't know that Ezra thinks it more fondly than I do.

I don't allow myself their reactions before I start swimming. Sierra's confidence lends itself to me, and I throw myself into the pull.

We maintain a comfortable pace for an hour. Based on our distance from the surface, the bubbles are definitely protecting us from the pressure. It seems to take less effort to push myself through the water because of that. I don't know about Ithinor; but Sierra, Ezra, and I are fulfilling our impossible dream of swimming underwater without needing to come up for air. A peaceful eternity seems to pass before the rocky floor turns into pristine, white sand, which shifts to gardens of dozens of coral breeds. We gaze out at the vibrant red and pink branches, the bulky oranges and yellows, and the domes of green and blue. The sea is an entire rainbow of beauty and fascination.

When I realize that the pull still hasn't noticeably deepened, we rest before continuing at an even more modest pace. Time floats by in the company of each other as the coral beds grow, stretching out farther than we can see. We need to swim more upward to avoid colliding into the edges of the coral. Eventually, we swim across coral breeds that hold two colors in their branches, some even—

Sierra awes breathlessly as she gazes below. "This... this coral... It's *glowing*."

I stop beside her, panting somewhat. Her fair face is even pinker, her cheeks alarmingly flushed. "Are you all right?"

Ezra stops on her other side, brows contorted in concern as she nods. "Tired," she whispers, sighing. "That's all."

"We should rest and pace ourselves," Ithinor replies in the same breathiness. "A race isn't always about who is fastest."

Admittedly, my own limbs are tingling with exhaustion; but the longer we stay here, the more opportunity the other teams have to catch up. At the front of my mind right now is keeping my team safe...

That also means resting so that we can *escape if something comes by.*

"How long have we been swimming?"

Sierra dazedly opens her satchel, mindful of the bubble, and takes out her pocket watch. Her eyes widen, blinking as she swallows. "A couple of hours."

My heart thumps against my chest with an extra hard beat. *Already...? Surely the other teams are already finished with the first stage by now.*

I purse my lips, torn between time and wisdom. "Let's... let's take a break for a few moments," I announce, nodding to Ezra. "Stay on guard. Sierra and Ithinor can stop and smell the coral in the meantime."

Ezra reaches to smack my head, but he hesitates. "I would if I weren't worried about the bubbles," he sneers. "You're still not funny."

I offer a proud smile as my eyes follow Sierra down to the coral beds. I've been diving Seavale's coasts for the better half of my life, and none have captured my attention as these do. They glow so brightly that not even the sunlight can drown it out. The reefs are foreign and enticing—but the ocean can be just as threatening as it is mesmerizing. I remind myself of that every second Sierra spends marveling.

"Just for a moment," Ithinor states. "I'll be ready to travel again shortly."

Sierra briefly glances up at him, staying parallel to the floor and careful to keep herself from the coral's edges. "Allow yourself just a minute of appreciation, won't you?"

"'Appreciation' aligns with 'fun' in this context, as far as I'm able to tell," he replies dully, staying level with Ezra. "And I needn't remind anyone the events of 'fun'—or what you three consider it to be."

A smile breaks out on my lips as I look at Ezra. His gaze intently scrutinizes the waters around us. His hand floats over the golden pommel of his sword sheathed on his right side—as if he can use it down here. He's carefully analyzing our area, but such is his duty; his father wasn't the only reason he became one of Seavale's best.

"Is that...?" Sierra gasps, her eyes widening in fear.

Instinct awakens in me as a colony of crabs the size of Ezra's hand skitters out from behind the coral. Their legs scamper at an alarming speed, claws mercilessly pinching at us.

"The bubbles, they'll pop them!" Sierra exclaims. "Swim!"

Ezra, Ithinor, and I pull the water apart above us to move away in an instant—but Sierra still hasn't come upright. Ezra swims down and reaches for her hand, his fear of popping the bubble seemingly having dissipated. He heaves her up and allows her to swim up past him. I watch in hope as he tries to follow suit—and then see too late a crab just below him reaching up its claw. I open my mouth, but the claw clamps down on Ezra's sabaton. His bubble bursts in a giant, transparent cloud of air.

CHAPTER 5

"WE ONLY LIVE ONCE, AFTER ALL"

Emberly

I FACEPLANT INTO A BED OF FRESH, CRISP SNOW AS WE exit the portal to the first stage. All traces of my tiredness evaporate. The snow bites my skin with icy teeth as my group fall in behind me. They land with a satisfying crunch and clang of metal.

We've definitely begun on Snowark's stage.

I look up. Ambrose rises to his hands and knees next to Zenevieve. Tall spruce trees sit beside and behind them. Ginger shakes a cloud of snow from the top of his red curls. "That's why I still ask my older brother to throw me into the fresh batches of snow!" he says, dusting off his pale hands. "Wasn't that fun?"

The boy is mad.

"I'll toss you back in after supper," Zenny tells him, bopping his nose. She falls back onto her bottom and rests her arms against her knees—something rather difficult to do in a metal suit.

"Let's try not to stay that long," Meredith chimes on my other side. She is already raising herself to her feet with poise and perfect balance. Her delicate, brown hands lightly brush away the white snow from her dark hair. Her pristine bun somehow survived the fall. "We've officially begun a race, my dears."

Right... Not to mention what the brat said just before she left the platform: *I would kill you all now if I weren't severely outnumbered.* There isn't a doubt in my mind that Amon of Lavara feels the same way about his competition. Most likely Levi of Windale as well. Seavale's knight entices me to assume the same about them. As for the others, it's unlikely, but wise to act as though they do, too.

But we've only just begun—surely we're safe for the first few minutes, at least until we find this "artifact".

My armour and satchel deny me comfort in the position of sitting on my knees. At least my gloves protect my hands from the stinging cold. I swat away white specks from my hair. A sizable puff of air from my mouth betrays my every breath.

Despite the forest of spruce trees around us, an open, white field peacefully lies ahead. That peace is a lie. My mind tingles with every sense of it the longer I stare. Surely no death race is meant to be peaceful.

When I look over, Zenevieve and Ambrose have already stood. "Something wrong, Ember?" she asks, her words clouding in front of her mouth.

"Just fine." I grab her hand and hoist myself up. Even my best friend has to look down a little to meet my eyes. "Nothing we've never encountered before."

"Then let's race," she says with a confidence I almost envy. "What say you about this artifact we're meant to find?"

"I say"—I turn to Meredith behind me—"that the oldest usually knows where to find things."

She narrows her hazel-green eyes at me. "For an only child, you resemble the younger sibling quite well."

I internally roll my eyes. She does, however, have grounds to speak on that; she was a younger sibling before her brother was killed by an avalanche in the Arkan Mountains—just before his initiation to become my advisor. Meredith followed in his footsteps to honour his memory and aid me in taking measures to prevent similar disasters in the future. As tragic as her brother's fate was, I'm grateful for the gentle and even... motherly governess and advisor I received. She somehow believes that twenty-five is too *young* to have children, but she certainly plays the mother role well. From what I may assume, at least.

"I was going to say the same thing!" Ambrose chirps, gaining my attention. "That's why I always snagged Aiden and Abria whenever I lost my books back home. Or Anavieve's favourite banky—blanket. I mean 'blanket'."

Zenevieve's hands rest on her hips under her cloak. She raises a scolding brow at him. "You lost your *mage books?*"

"Adelaine lectured me *every* time, Zenevieve." It is probably the first time that I've ever seen Ginger's smile drop. "If I'm to hear it from you as well, I'll memorise them all cover to cover for the sake of never hearing it again."

I'm surprised he lost them at all with how many lectures he likely received. Evidently, the chaos of one Walsh wasn't sufficient for his parents: Ambrose is the middle of five.

Zenevieve sucks on her teeth and rolls her eyes.

There's one thing to be grateful for: the atmosphere only rivals Snowark's coldest springs, especially because I'm under my cloak. Still, I'm envious of Ginger: he has his clothes, mage robes, *and* a cloak to keep him toasty.

"I'd like to remind you all that we are in a *race*." Even with emphasis, Meredith's voice is tender. "We can't be distracted by conversation every time we meet a pressing matter. What of the artifact?"

"What of what I'm meant to do to find this artifact, Merry?" I ask. She narrows her eyes at me again. "I don't believe our rainbow friends back there provided a map. And unfortunately,"—I step towards the vast field of white, crystal-like snow—"the crown does not come with magical—"

The centre of my being is unexpectedly lulled forward. I stumble, my bow heavier on my back.

Meredith is quick to spot me with Zenevieve just behind. One of Meredith's hands is on my shoulder, the other on my back as she asks, "Are you all right, Your Highness?"

I straighten. I look up at her with dull eyes. She has an entire head on me. "Just fine."

Zenevieve's hand rests on my arm. "*You* tripped in the snow?"

"I didn't trip," I hiss, elbowing her in a dismal attempt with my thick layers. "There's... something pulling. Don't you feel it?"

Even Ambrose's brows furrow. Now I know I've made a mistake.

"What do you mean?" Zenny asks.

I bite the inside of my cheek. Surely I can't be the only one feelings something so... present.

"An invisible force of..."—my embarrassment threatens to consume my words the longer I speak—"some kind. Drawing me forward. You lot don't feel it?"

Ambrose comes to stand next to Zenevieve. "That sounds like magic," he muses. He rests a finger on his chin, rubbing it. "What exactly does it feel like?"

At least I'll never sound mad to him. For whatever foolish reason the boy's mind has concocted, he believes in me. I realised that when I was sixteen and Whiny Winston dragged me out of the council room after I screamed that the councilmen's plans to develop in the Dagger Woods were about as dense as they all were. Winston's grip dug into my arm as if he were *trying* to leave the bruises that appeared the day after.

The queen should have had you killed in the womb. A whisper has never been so loud.

Ambrose was passing on his way to the mage's tower for training when he spotted us. He pried Winston's grip off of me with his telekinesis. I had to pull the both of us away because the boy was terrified of Winston—and before I landed us in further trouble. The second we were alone and Ambrose turned to me...

They never give you the chance to be the princess they claim to need. One day, I ought to show them myself who you really are, not some clueless puppet.

I will never forget those words.

The white, open field in front of me radiates a stunning brightness. Snow has left no patch of the world uncovered. Something definitely wants me to take another step towards it.

I gather the courage to say, "It feels like I need to keep going forward."

"Perhaps that's it..." Meredith says on my other side. "Seeing as we've no map and no way to determine if we're travelling in the right direction, yet the artifact is meant to help us overcome the stage—I think this pull is meant to help you find it."

"Then why don't any of you feel it?" I ask sceptically.

"Likely for the same reason the Mages spoke to you seven and not us." Zenny slings a heavy arm around my shoulders. "Something about royalty, I don't know. Lead the way."

I can only hope that there does lie some part of a sensible ruler in me as I continue forward. My kingdom of three follows closely behind.

We travel across the snow for what feels like hours. Meredith later informs with her pocket watch that it's only been one. My knees instinctually buckle at the news, but I recover in time before I stumble. Constantly sinking into each step still drains me despite having spent years training with Zenevieve in the forest. The only good all the walking has done is maintain warmth to function. My fingers, toes, and even nose are numb enough for me to believe that my blood has begun to freeze under my skin.

My mind races with a thousand nagging doubts and fears that I can't banish. It's as if it's become so accustomed to Whiny Winston and his herd that it needs a substitute to function properly if I go too long without it. Why hasn't this pull drastically strengthened yet if it's the artifact? What if I've wasted the only resource we aren't steady on: time?

Those doubts reared a ghastly head as we approached the clearing of the forest we entered some time ago. Now all of our steps slow simultaneously as we exit and our sights meet our new obstacle: a frozen lake.

I was wrong. I knew it. Surely the artifact isn't on the other side of this death trap waiting to be broken!

"Emberly," Meredith begins beside me, holding out her arm in front of me, "we must rethink this."

"If the artifact is what's pulling her, then it's taking us in the right direction," Zenevieve says simply on my other side. "It wouldn't lead us to our deaths without ever giving us a chance to find it. It's meant to *help* us."

"Precisely." Meredith eyes her cautiously. I'm most surprised to see that dark-brown strands of her hair are finally sticking out from her bun. That only adds weight to her words as she tells us, "Perhaps my previous theory was wrong. We should consider the possibility that the pull is actually an obstacle of the stage. Something to test our ability to survive—our wit and mental clarity."

"Wouldn't it pull us all forward if that were the case?" Ambrose asks curiously. "I still think it's the artifact. We might not be able to pass the stage without Emberly, so it wouldn't try to... *off* her—"

"It's not a swear, Ginger." My eyes dull at him. "Are you lot following me onto the lake or not?"

His brown eyes widen. Zenevieve's black ones follow. "You're really going?" she asks.

Yes, before I can change my mind.

I shrug. "We only live once, after all."

Meredith eyes me for before passing them to Ambrose. "Then you will freeze over the lake to strengthen the ice. And you"—her stare lands on Zenevieve—"will go in front to ensure that the next step is secure."

Ambrose's freckled face lights up with his grin. "Easy!"

I wouldn't be so certain of that. If we can only see the faded silhouette of the other side, that is a *lot* of ice—but the last thing I'm going to give the boy is doubt.

He skitters past the clearing of the forest and to the edge of the lake. The three of us appear behind him as he kneels. A sheer, indigo wave that ripples like the ocean scatters across the lake. There is only one way to go: straight ahead.

I turn to Zenevieve. Her eyes are blinking too often again as she stares out.

Before I can ask if she's certain about going first, she takes her first step onto the ice. "Stay diligent and follow me."

We obey. The surface creaks under us with our first steps. Zenny stops for a moment in front of me, seems to remember her training, and then continues forward.

At least our sabatons have grips on the bottom so we don't slip.

"Do not stop for any circumstance," Zenevieve states in her naturally courageous tone. If not for Stupid Samson, I'd have made her captain of the Guard long ago. "Light steps and con-stant motion."

"And a few games while we're at it?" I ask cheekily.

"You're not funny right now."

I roll my eyes.

"Ambrose," Meredith says softly behind me, "add another

layer to the ice."

"Um..." he replies even quieter, "I'd need to stop and kneel."

"Is magic not possible while walking?"

"It... it is," he says diffidently. My focus homes in on Zenevieve's black coils to swat away my apprehension. "I, um... I—I—"

"Do not let your fear stop you now," Meredith replies quickly, realising her mistake. "The only thing that will help us now is doing as Zenevieve instructs, all right?"

The boy is seventeen, yet I often feel as if I'm talking to his six-year-old sister instead. Right now, though, I share his fears in full. I almost want to offer him my own encouragement if I had any. I'm still paranoid that my very voice will break the ice.

For his sake, perhaps I shouldn't have brought him, after all...

The icy air bites at the fuzz on my cheeks and nips at the tip of my nose. My very bones want to shiver under my cloak, armour, and everyday attire. Unfortunately, even shivering feels as though it will rattle the ice and encourage it to crack, too.

Also unfortunately—I'm now too afraid to distract myself with my own humour.

Zenevieve is all too quiet in front of me. I know she's calculating each step, every other one eliciting a creak. Going into her mind is dangerous for both her and me right now. That draws my attention to the world around me. Regrettably, that only includes the horizon that meets the muted-blue surface of the ice and white-and-grey sky. The forest can't be too far behind us; nonetheless, I cannot trust the ice.

What if we really die right here?

Don't. Find something else. Focus on something else.

I force my stare onto Zenny's curls again. The humidity of the cold makes them frizzier. At least, the winter cold does. Otherwise, I marvel at the dainty coils that her thick, black strands form.

What else, what else?

"Gently, now." Meredith instructs Ambrose softly from behind me.

Meredith—I think about how she only recently started leaving the dark dot under her left eye and the one above her upper lip uncovered. It took me two years to convince her that they were lovely accents to her narrow face, complementary contrasts to her golden-brown skin. She used to see them as flawed as a dirt stain on the marble floor. I told her that they were the arrows to her lips and eyes: the only form of flirtation she had, because the woman cannot flirt to save her life. I made her laugh that day. She took off the cosmetics the next day but applied it the one after. Eventually, her usage of them faded out completely.

It's a habit of that: desperately focusing on what I can find until I know that the forest behind us is too far away to run back to. I exhale shakily. The ice still creaks. The air still bites. Zenevieve's hair is still frizzy.

Ambrose is still releasing a whimper every few seconds. Meredith is still comforting him after almost every one.

"I—I don't think..." he starts after a record-breaking–long silence. "How much farther? Are we almost there?"

I press my lips together. "Keep walking, Ambrose," I say, refusing to look back. "I can see the bank."

A sigh of relief floods out of him. Unfortunately, that relief doesn't last long. He releases another whimper moments later.

"Can't we run, then?" he asks impatiently. "We'll make it!"

How I desire to do exactly that. It is all the more reason that I force my feet to stay in slow contact with the ice.

"It's at *least* thirty metres from here," Zenevieve states sternly. "If the ice breaks, we won't make it to the bank in time sprinting. Keep *walking*."

The trees on the other side have now gained colour even amidst the fog. My heart accelerates with every step closer we draw.

Ambrose's breath is set free in pants. "I can't do it!"

His red curls whiz past me.

"Ambrose!" the three of us call, maintaining our cautious walk as he sprints down the lake.

His cloak struggles to move with him. The matching indigo mage robes he has on underneath are heavy; I wonder how a stick like him is managing the speed that he is. Even if it's half the speed Zenevieve can manage in her armour.

"We can make it!" he calls, turning around and stopping. He furiously gestures for us to follow as a creak groans underneath him. "Come on!"

"Ambrose—!" I snap.

"Do NOT stop!" Zenevieve shouts, her walk tightening: she's restraining herself from sprinting after him. "Do not look back! *Walk* the rest of the way!"

His face falls in anxious disappointment after waiting for us to catch up. "I can't!" he cries, turning back around and pumping his legs. A crack sounds under his steps.

"Zen—"

She shushes me, holding out her hand. She doesn't call after him as he reaches halfway between us and the bank. Something crackles with his next step.

"It's going to break," Zenevieve whispers.

He'll fall through—

Zenevieve and I sprint down the ice as I shout, "Ambrose!"

He jumps, his feet tripping him when he lands. A final crack rattles ahead as his body slams onto the surface of the lake. The crack gives way to a crash below him. My heart drops with him as he falls through. His scream chills my bones more violently than any winter cold.

CHAPTER

"A BREATH OF FRESH AIR"

Leo

EZRA KICKS AND GRABS AT THE WATER SURROUNDING him. Despite spending practically his entire life in the water, it's as if he's lost control of his limbs, his icy eyes wide with stun. He's already lacking air with his bubble popping unexpectedly, and the surface is too far up: he won't reach it in time.

It doesn't matter: Sierra is already halfway between us. She's spent only the last four years in the water, but she glides down to Ezra like a dolphin. She brings him up just far enough to be clear of the crabs, which have covered half of the surface area of the reef's bed and coral.

As if she's willing to pop her own bubble if it means restoring Ezra's, Sierra grabs his face. Tiny bubbles furiously swarm and rise around them as Ezra furiously nods, and Sierra presses their lips together. Her bubble suit allows their lips to connect, and her cheeks expand before slightly deflating. Ezra slowly re-laxes in her hold and starts calmly kicking to stay upright with her.

A bubble begins to form between them.

"You're giving him a new one!" I call, bearing with the pierc-ing volume of my voice as it echoes back at me. "Don't stop!"

Sierra releases, keeping her hands on Ezra's cheeks. She doesn't waste a second to inhale and then press her lips against his again. With every breath she gives him, the bubble between them expands and slowly starts to wrap around Ezra, conforming to his body. It shrinks whenever Sierra releases for another breath, hence why she refuses to stay away for long.

At least, I know that that's part of the reason why.

She continues breathing a bubble around Ezra until his suit is restored. He exhales and pants in relief as she releases his face.

"Thank you," he says, a large hand on his heaving chest.

"Can you breathe easily?" she asks, panting lightly. "I know it's—well, secondhand breath, but—"

"I'm fine." He nods before his brows furrow together. "The air in here, it's... it's fresh somehow."

This is almost... too easy. Are the bubbles really that magical?

It strikes me then: no wonder we're able to continuously breathe in them without issue. We wouldn't be able to last more than a minute on this stage otherwise. Maybe we truly are meant to stay down here if the stage has provided everything we need to do so...

"Well, there we have it," Ithinor remarks flatly. "If we can restore the bubbles if they do pop, the stage wants us to remain underwater."

Exactly. At least Ithinor agrees with me. Something is keeping us here—

The artifact. Right: we're meant to be following and staying focused on that.

"That, and I can still feel the pull," I add. "It's gotten a little stronger the farther we swim down here. As long as it's safe to do so, let's continue following it."

"And may we also keep this as a lesson," Ithinor says, running an olive hand through his jet-black curls. "This race does not care if we lose our lives or not. *Now* do we understand why 'fun' isn't my favorite word?"

I hum doubtfully. "I don't think Ezra would be able to agree with you, no."

"Leo!" he snaps, reaching to smack my head; but I'm too far away. The muffling of his deep voice tames the harshness of the word, which makes me feel safer—and braver.

"Wouldn't you say the fun has been a *breath of fresh air*, Icky?"

"When we return," Sierra replies, "we're overthrowing you and making Ezra king."

"I must reiterate," Ithinor says firmly, leaning in to his words as he exchanges his eyes with us, "we must retain *alertness*. Staying here will cost more than we can afford."

My gaze falls with Sierra's to the vibrant reef a few feet below. The crabs are still viciously pinching their claws at us. "Then," Sierra begins, "as long as we can restore our bubbles if they pop, we should sacrifice a little of our caution about them and hurry."

Ezra takes turns glancing at each of us like one of us will

have the answer to his question: "How was that possible? Sierra isn't a mage, yet she was able to restore something magical."

Ithinor turns around and waves a hand out in front of him. A sheer, dark-cyan–blue wave ripples through the ocean, verifying whatever is in his head right now as he nods. He turns back around. "Magic has built this entire stage. The laws of reality have their own rules here."

"We're *swimming* in magic," I say, letting my body sway with the rhythm of the soft current. "Admit it. That is amazing."

"I wonder if a mage may somehow take control of a stage's magic to manipulate it," Ithinor muses. "I would test it, but I don't want any of you popping your bubbles for the sake of a magic experiment."

"Then let's not waste time testing and continue," Sierra announces, nodding at me.

I lead the three behind me farther down the reef. A beautiful and *real* ocean awaits us back in Seavale, and the only way to return is to go now; marveling at the rich vibrancies of color, even all the new breeds we've never seen before, may only serve as another trap. I can't imagine the curiosity begging Sierra to stop and examine each coral that catches her eye, because it almost begs me with the same intensity.

I do have to wonder if she and Ezra are holding hands behind me now.

Maybe bringing them both along wasn't the wisest idea.

Our pace has increased, even Ithinor's. The ocean's underwater currents are taking their toll on my arms again as I push through them, my legs enduring a burn that's invading them. The water pushes back against my hands and feet as I move, the iron scent of my chainmail potent.

For a portion of time, our bodies seem to demand that we all slow until the reefs eventually transition to rocks. Those transition to pebbles, which transition to plain, white sand the farther we swim. After the hidden crabs in the coral, I don't want to risk what may be hiding in the sands here.

The pull on my body soon grows strong enough to almost push me forward from behind. I look ahead: a dark crack stretches all across the width of the ocean floor. My stomach drops into the sea: a trench.

I know it. That's where the artifact is.

But I can't lead my team down there—if we couldn't even avoid danger from a bed of plants (though Sierra swears coral are animals somehow), how am I meant to bring them into an abyss of darkness and potentially life-threatening sea creatures?

We come to a stop at the edge of the trench. I peer down, about to scold myself because I have no source of light to see what lies down there—until something glows a light, pale green.

"What is that?" Sierra asks between tired breaths.

"That's it," I tell her. "The artifact."

"I'll grab it," Ezra says, but I hold out my arm to stop him.

"No. Let me." The words cause instinct to tighten in my chest. Regret threatens to consume it, but duty overpowers it all. "The monarchs are meant to grab it, I wouldn't be the only one feeling its pull otherwise. I'll go."

"You're proposing to go down into a *trench* of sharp rock and narrow space," Sierra says flatly, a brow arching incredulously over her green eyes. "What happens if you die?"

My eyes narrow at her. *Thanks.*

"Bring me with you," Ezra says, briefly glancing at Ithinor behind me. "Ithinor can bring us up if we find any threat."

I look back down at the trench. My heart shoves itself into my throat, blocking my swallow. "It's too narrow. Our bubbles will pop. I only want to worry about one person, and that artifact is pulling me. I can do it."

"Leo..." Sierra says, concern now coating her words. "It's really tight."

I know. I know, I know, I know. But I can't continue allowing this fear to rule such a significant part of me. If I came to prove myself to Seavale, to offer myself wholeheartedly, that means sacrificing my fears, starting with the three Seavalens in front of me first. If I can't even do it for them, I'm useless to a kingdom.

"I'll be right back." I exchange glances with my team as I swim backward. I'm directly above the trench now. "Maintain a close eye on me."

They each give a nod.

I look down, inhale, and swim down before I can change my mind. I won't let them see just how afraid I am.

Maybe it's the fact that my voice is trapped in this bubble, but my breath—let alone my heart—has never been so loud. Each inhale and exhale explodes in my ears. Every tremble is there. Everything is reminding me that I'm afraid.

As the seconds pass, the trench grows darker, save for what glows at the bottom. I almost can't see the texture of the walls. I close my mouth to force breath through my nose, but that only makes my teeth chatter. The ocean is miraculously a perfect temperature, but my body can't help but shake. Especially as I near the middle of the trench—and the black, stone walls close in even more.

I shake my head. I can't tell if that's the cruelty of my mind or not. That makes it worse.

I slow. The rock on either side of me is closer to my hands when I pull the water apart in front of me.

It isn't my mind. That's real. All right—

I realize that that *definitely* doesn't make it better.

Almost there, almost there, you're almost there.

My heart pounds against my ribcage, rattling the bones. Dark rock threatens to scrape my bubble open. I'm all the more aware of the bow and quiver on my back. Despite the bubble, the pressure as I swim lower and lower accumulates until my muscles are pulsing. At least I can finally see the sand at the bottom, illuminated in a soft, green glow as I near the artifact.

I reach the bottom. the walls on either side of me only a few feet away. I can't stand on the sand, but I can reach down and grab the green dot resting on it.

Leave, leave, leave, leave.

I grant myself one careful shove upward. The blue of the ocean beams above me, calling me. With a happy leap up, swimming up is twice as easy as down. I scarcely manage to avoid the middle area, where the walls grow even closer together.

The rip of blue above me opens wider until I finally break the surface of the trench. I exhale, maintaining a tight control on my breathing as my group swims up to me. Even Ithinor is grinning with pride.

"You got it!" Sierra chirps, her arms somehow finding the strength to move faster. "Let me see!"

I hold out my hand and open my fist.

"A seed?" Ezra asks, his dark brows furrowing.

I pull my hand back and show myself what I have: a green seed the size of Sierra's thumbnail. It's a muted leaf green once the glow fades. Actually—it reminds me of Princess Emberly's eye color. I remember her eyes because of how they complemented her auburn hair and even her freckles so well. This seed matches them almost exactly. Without the death glare.

"What are we meant to do with a seed?" Ezra asks, unamused. "Grow a forest of seaweed?"

"If we need something to hide in, yes," Ithinor says almost pensively, like he's truly considering the possibility of that. "This is magic, we know that; and it might grow something instantly to help us."

"Exactly, it's meant to help." Sierra's eyes linger on the seed in my palm. "But seaweed won't hide us for long if a threat comes along. What is this meant to help *with*? Showing us where to go next—?"

A low, reverberated wail echoes across the ocean. I wonder if our bubble suits have protected the noise from bursting our eardrums; the volume muted by them is still enough to encourage me to cover my ears. I refrain in fear of losing the seed.

"That sounded like..." Ezra says as he stares after his right. His right hand reaches for his sword, like the ocean is ready to test him itself. "...a whale."

My heart pounds like a hammer against a cloth. I gaze out over the ocean until my eyes snag on it: a large, dark-blue mass moves with impossible underwater speed in the distance, still too far to provide detail. It's a sea creature; but as the seconds pass, it begins to move toward the back of Ezra and Sierra in the distance.

Where we used to be.

Ezra looks behind him, Ithinor's eyes following. The mass is darker. Closer.

It wails again.

"It's a giant whale." Ezra turns back around to face me, his gaze firm. "Now would be a great time for a magical pull to tell us where to go!"

I look down at the seed in my hand. Planting is our only option, and I don't have time to waste.

"Let me plant this," I announce, lowering myself to the sand. "The whale appeared once we found the seed, so I have to assume that it's the main obstacle." I drop the artifact and bury it in the sand. It isn't dirt; but surely a glowing, magical seed can overlook that. "If this seed is meant to help, it should grow something to help us escape."

"Leo!" Sierra cries as Ezra instinctually reaches for his sword. "Grab it, there's no time!"

I look up: the animal fades from its silhouette into clear view. It's swimming straight for us.

Instinct overwhelms me; I grab the buried seed from the sand, never minding the granules I bring into my bubble. Not even with the help of magic could a human ever rival a whale— yet my team and I share the same idea to pump our legs and arms, despite the burning, pulsing ache I feel in mine, to escape.

A high-pitched wail reverberates all across the ocean as the head of a gargantuan, dark-blue whale draws closer. I whirl around with my team: we are mere specks in front of its jaw that stretches wide open. Water is suctioned inside, thrusting the four of us into its mouth.

CHAPTER 7

"JUST A SPARK"

Emberly

AMBROSE'S INDIGO CLOAK AND FIERY CURLS ARE ALL I see as he falls through the surface of the ice lake. His arms furiously flail before catching him on the edge of the break he's created.

The only reason Zenevieve and I reach him in time is because we began running after him before he fell. The ice grips on the bottom of our sabatons are all that is preventing us from slipping. Meredith calls after us both, but her voice loses to my will and initiative.

I drop to the ground on my belly despite the extra weight of my cloak and satchel; I don't have time to throw them off. I pray that the ice doesn't break under the extra weight. Amidst Ambrose's cries, I scarcely manage to grab his slipping hands before he dips under the surface. It's a miracle he managed for a couple of seconds with his gloves on. Zenevieve unclasps her cloak and throws it down next to me.

"Grab this, Ambrose!" she shouts.

His eyes widen in terror as he glances between my hands and the cloak.

"I've got you, Ginger," I tell him, "grab it!"

He takes Zenevieve's cloak with one trembling hand. Then his other releases mine and takes the fabric.

"Emberly, help me pull!" Zenevieve exclaims on the other end of the cloak. A surprising strain scratches her voice.

There isn't any way that Ambrose *is too heavy for her—*

"No, slowly slide away!" Meredith calls to me. She rushes past Ambrose and moves to where Zenevieve stands behind me. "You'll break the ice if you move too quickly!"

"Really, Merry?" I snap, using my hands to obey nonetheless. "Interesting, here I was about to enjoy a nap!"

By the time I slide away and stand, Meredith is gripping Zenevieve's waist. They fervently try to pull Ambrose out of the lake. His pale face is red with sobs as he pleads for us to save him.

"I've got you, Ambrose!" Strain still claws at Zenevieve's every word.

Something isn't right. "Zen—"

"Help us pull, he's too heavy!" she snaps, too focused on him to realise.

Too heavy. That's it.

"Don't let me go!" Ambrose exclaims. "Please, my family need me, please!"

I throw off my cloak and satchel and then lie down on my belly again, moving to his side. His cloak and mage robes are the issue. I grab my dagger from its sheath on my left side.

"What are you—?!" Ambrose cries.

I position Rowena's handle between my teeth before unclasping his cloak under his chin. It folds into the icy water below. That frees me space to work on his robes.

I straighten his right sleeve. Rowena's blade slices through the top of it from his wrist up to his collar. The right side of his robes sinks into the water.

Zenevieve and Meredith pull as I messily slide close enough to Ambrose's other side. Rowena cuts through the fabric of his left sleeve until it breaks the final seam at the collar. I shove the back of his robe off him. He is now light enough for Zenevieve and Meredith to pull him up onto the ice like he's an anchovy.

Those clothes doubled his weight. I could feel it in pushing off the back part of his robes alone. Their thick fabrics absorbed the water too quickly.

The remainder of the robes disappear beneath the dark-blue, murky water. When I look up, Zenevieve and Meredith are sitting on their behinds, breathless. Ambrose is stuck on his hands and knees in his taupe, long-sleeved shirt and brown pants. My first instinct is to grab him some dry clothes. At least his satchel survived; it's still closed with hopefully minimal supplies ruined.

Thank. The. Ancients.

"I'm sorry," Ambrose whispers frantically. Everything from his limbs to his breath is trapped in a furious, cold tremble. "I'm sorry, I'm so sorry—"

A terrible creak reverberates underneath us.

"Stop apologising and get to the bank, now!" Zenevieve

snaps. She scrambles to the boy and then pulls him up.

Meredith and I stand. I want to believe that we're close enough to the shore to sprint to it. Especially when a sizeable splash sounds behind us.

The ice under my feet is cracking.

I grab my cloak and satchel before I start sprinting. The ice we leave behind fractures off into the frigid water below. Scarcely in time, Meredith and I land on the sandy bank just as the rest of the surface breaks apart. I glance behind us. A large portion has disappeared. There is no going back now.

Zenevieve is close enough to throw Ambrose onto the bank of the shore. He lands with a muted, plush thud face-first into a pristine pile of snow.

Meredith's hands fall from straightening her dark-brown bun that's finally messy. "Zenevieve!" she snaps, panting.

"He's too cold to move fast enough," Zenny states breathlessly, marching up to the boy with me.

"And only getting colder in those wet clothes," I hiss, clasping my cloak back on. I take his sopping satchel off of him. My heart falls at the realisation that's only just arrived: "Your spare set of clothes is drenched!"

Zenevieve heaves him up. He leans heavily against her, quaking as he rises to his feet. He's a shivering, trembling stick of stun and pants.

"Ambrose," I snap, dropping his satchel. I grip his arms, looking up at him. "Listen to me! We need to get you dry!"

"He's in shock," Meredith says. Her footsteps approach behind me. "Not to mention freezing to death. I know there's a drying spell that extracts water; but if he's too stunned to respond to you, he's far too gone for magic."

My logic already knows what that means. I don't dare believe it, though, unless it comes from Meredith herself: "Meaning...?"

"We'll lose him if we don't warm him up immediately." She reaches into her satchel and digs out her spare clothes: a tunic and wool trousers. "I'll dress him. You two, gather sticks for a fire."

A fire? From what dry branches?

Nonetheless, Zenevieve and I rush off the bank and into the entrance of the spruce forest. I focus on the sticks on the floor while she reaches for the branches. Meredith and Ambrose have disappeared behind a few trees on the side of the bank. I hear her gentle voice comfort him and encourage him to follow her instructions.

"It's a miracle the boy hasn't set himself on fire all these years." I shake my head as I pick up another stick resting on the snow. The dark-brown colour tells me that it's damp.

"Hopefully he's learned his lesson." Zenny quickly breaks off a branch of the tree and then another. A harsh edge cuts her voice. "He'll realise that I know what I'm talking about and we need to take every threat here seriously."

It's as if she's angry at him for falling. Then again, I've never known her to be anything else other than protective of him.

I grab another stick from the ground. Other than Meredith's voice and Ambrose's whimpers, the forest is silent. My mind, on the other hand, is racked by doubt and scolding—and even regret.

"Did I do the right thing?" I whisper, rushing with Zenevieve to the next tree. "In bringing him? Was I being selfish in not choosing Zephyr instead?"

"Do not fall down this path again," she replies tiredly, hurrying to break off the next closest branch of the tree. "Zephyr is due to retire. He wouldn't have fared well here. Secondly, you are not responsible for everyone you know simply because you know them, Ember. Ambrose is his own person. He made a foolish decision despite warning, and thank the Ancients he lived to see the consequences of that... Perhaps he'll learn here what he never would have at the palace."

I know she's right. But how am I meant to convince myself that the boy's decisions aren't affected by my own? The crown spends its entire existence telling me that my decisions impact my people. Even my birth, something out of my control, reaped drastic consequences. Ambrose is part of my people. My decisions impact his life; does that not include what he decides?

"Ladies," Meredith urges. We turn around. She and Ambrose stand on the bank, her and Zenevieve's cloaks hanging from his body. Despite that, Meredith furiously rubs his arms as she speaks. "We need fire, bring what you have!"

Zenevieve and I run back to the bank and drop our collection into one pile. Ambrose's trembling pants send subtle shivers down my spine.

Meredith continues rubbing his shoulders and arms. "Can you conjure fire yet, Ambrose?"

A moment passes before he finally nods. I notice that his wet hair is no longer dripping; instead, ice is forming on it. When he slowly reaches his no-longer–gloved hand out from under the cloaks, his fingernails are already blue. Orange and yellow flicker from his tips. Sparks of fire inflate and then fall to nothing.

He sharply exhales, trembling. "I—I'm sor—ry."

"Don't be foolish," I tell him, unclasping my cloak. "We're only trying to save you, try again."

Even his lips are turning blue. His freckled face is a deathly white. "I'm t—too cold to—make a f—fire. I'm s—sorr—y."

Why is he apologizing for freezing to death?

The cold is already threatening to penetrate my armour as I come to stand in front of him. I reach up and bring my cloak around his shoulders. He's so skinny that despite all his layers already on, my cloak closes around him with ease. I hurriedly swat away the ice clinging to his hair.

"Th—thank you," he whispers, a soft smile touching his pale lips.

"Just a spark, Ambrose," Meredith urges softly. "That's all we need. We can build from there."

My limbs are already starting to shake. If the same is for Meredith, she's much better at hiding it; Zenevieve and I are both hugging ourselves. I almost miss Ginger's mage robes on his behalf, but he weighed about as much as Hungry Harrison with them on.

Shivering like a cat who's just seen Whiny Winston in a wig, Ambrose reaches out his hand over the pile. Closing his eyes, he lets it hover over the wood and then slowly exhales as it glows orange.

Steam arises from the pile, gently hissing as the sticks lighten in colour. Ginger exhales at what little heat I'm assuming the steam is giving off from his magic drying the wood. The sticks turn from a black brown to a simple spruce colour.

His quivering hand closes and then opens. Fire sparks from

his fingertips again. He reaches his hand into the wood, touching a single stick that takes the flame. His process repeats with as many sticks as he can manage. Then, he waves his hand again over the pile. A breeze gently passes through it, growing the fire. The flames finally latch onto the other branches.

Much to my disappointment, it's now time for me to step far away from the pile before the smoke reaches my nose. About half of me is content with sacrificing my lungs for warmth, but none of this lot would allow it.

I may end up freezing to death out here first.

At least Zenevieve is willing to stay with me metres away from the bank. I watch with envy as Ambrose's hands sprawl themselves out in front of the flames. My hands are warm enough in my velvet gloves, but that warmth isn't spreading to the rest of me.

Minutes later, what seems to be a brief disagreement passes between Meredith and Ambrose. Then, they approach us.

"I—I'm warm enough... to light my own fire," he says, holding out his hands with white palms facing the grey sky. A small fire ignites in them, allowing me to warm up, too.

"Bless you, Ginger." I exhale, scrunching and stretching my stiff fingers.

"Are you all right?" Zenevieve asks sceptically.

He nods. "I can—feel the heat—I create."

"He promises that he's all right," Meredith says. "I suppose his fire is evidence."

I shrug, revelling in the flames. "I may just have you immediately promoted to the royal mage after this. No ridiculous ceremony required."

His round, brown eyes widen in distaste. "And r—replace Zephyr s—sooner?"

"He's wanted to retire since I turned ten," I reply dully, glimpsing Zenevieve. "Why else do you think I agreed to letting him double your weekly training hours after your first month at the palace?"

"Emberly!" Meredith snaps, the tenderness in her tone somehow holding its ground.

"No, no," Ambrose says, scarcely managing a grin. "I ask—asked her to. I've l—learned so much since then—because of that."

I smile cheekily. "See? Ginger is fine."

Zephyr's age was only a part of that reasoning. The boy is a slow learner; he implored me so as to ensure that he would be able to replace Zephyr at all one day. Back then, it meant fewer hours I had to see him around the palace. As the years passed, it meant more opportunities to pester the councilmen together. Plus, he gave me a tray of lemon tarts in exchange, so it was a win-win-win situation.

Meredith scornfully scowls at me nonetheless.

I roll my eyes. "Think of it as the deal the Seven Mages set up when they first conjured the curse. See, Merry? I paid attention."

Ginger perks up. "Deal? What deal?"

I raise a brow. "You don't know how the curse and Last Kingdom came to be?"

"It manages to evade even most nobles, Emberly," Meredith answers. "Most have no purpose for knowing the story, other than the monarchs and governing staff." Then, a sight rarer than

Moody Myron's smile appears: Meredith's smirk. "Since you 'paid attention', why don't you explain?"

I scold myself for my own incompetence. "Surely Zenevieve isn't interested—"

"No." Zenny bites her full lip in her signature smirk. Her dark gloves turn orange above the fire's glow. "Storytime with Ember sounds like the perfect pastime right now."

My group's eyes are on me. I feel as if I'm sitting at the head seat in the council room. It's a similar-enough situation: everyone here is expecting something intelligent to come out of my mouth.

I stare at Ambrose's flames as I take in a breath. My mind slowly recalls the words of the book Meredith makes me study at the beginning of every year: "Long ago, the seven Ancient Rulers—the first kings and queens of the world, with their spouses—broke off into alliances, all with different plans for the world's future. War broke out among the kingdoms until the royal mages of each one gathered and conjured the curse that would kill the monarchs once they bore an heir. Your heir is what curses you, and all heirs are cursed with the same fate. And as we're well aware of, only winning this race will unlock the Last Kingdom and break the curse. Something about the true ruler proving themselves worthy or some rubbish."

Meredith rolls her eyes in the corner of my vision.

"But if that—that's the case..." Ambrose begins, mellower than I expected, "then why h—hasn't a monarch ever r—refused to bear—an heir? Or even adopt one—instead?"

I dare to meet his gaze. He's staring with an innocent fascination I almost wish I shared. "If we don't bear an heir of our bloodline, our kingdoms will fall once we die."

A familiar snake of guilt slithers around in my stomach as I speak the words. My mother chose me while knowing the consequences. The King of Snowark would never know me yet gave himself for my rule nonetheless. I was powerless in stopping either of them.

At least neither of them are alive to witness the disappointment that I am.

Ambrose's eyes widen. "As in—?"

"You'd all be homeless and have to flock to a kingdom that's competent enough to have a child, yes."

A sombre silence passes between us, even Ginger. At least his shivering has relaxed now. The fire in his hands seems to be diminishing.

Noticing, Zenevieve eyes him curiously and moves to stand next to him. A dangerous glint in her eyes ignites. "Are you feeling all right, Rosy?" she asks in her deceptively sweet tone.

He nods calmly, whispering, "Yes, I'm better. Thank you." Then, he closes his eyes.

Foolish boy. He's about to receive his—

Zenevieve shoves him without a second thought, almost knocking him over. His fire dissipates. "That's what you deserve for not listening to me! What did I tell you?"

"I'm... I'm sorry," he says dejectedly, having to try twice to reignite a smaller fire in his hands. He stumbles over to my side.

"Tired, are we?" I ask, arching a brow.

He doesn't reply, only exhaling fraily. "I was... scared," he says slowly. "I felt... the ice cracking—"

"It was *creaking*, not cracking," Zenevieve snaps through gritted teeth. "I know what I'm talking about—"

"He isn't dead, Zenny," I say dully, cursing the cold shudder that passes through my body. "We're on the other side."

Alive, I don't add. "Alive" would remind them that we just braved a life-threatening situation that *I* had led them into. "Alive" would remind them that I put them all in danger because I thought I felt some magical artifact pulling me in its direction.

Curse the stars. I can still feel it. It's stronger now that we're on the other side of the lake.

"Ambrose," Meredith says gently across from him. "Are you sure you're warm enough?"

Another slow exhale before the boy nods. The weakest smile I've ever seen from him passes his lips as he briefly glances at her. Then his eyes fall to the glowing flame in his hands. I can tell that he isn't looking at it; something in his mind has stolen his stare.

"I'm all right," he whispers, seemingly forcing his voice into a kinder tone. He jerks his hands, slightly growing the flame.

Of course he's not all right. I scold myself for questioning it. *The boy's been traumatised.*

I grind my teeth as I try to absorb the little heat his flame is providing. It angers me that we almost lost him, that he's been scarred, because of this blasted pull I feel. It angers me that I'm the only one who can feel it and my group must blindly trust me to take them to wherever it's leading us. I don't know if I want to believe that it's the artifact pulling me; why did Ambrose need to fall, why did Zenevieve and Meredith have to risk their own lives to save him, because we need an artifact meant to *help* us and I'm the only one who can lead them to it?

Because of me? Because I was "chosen"?

I exhale, grinding my teeth. It's just as Meredith said this morning: even though the council-herd aren't here to witness and chastise me for exploding, I don't want to give them even the subconscious satisfaction that they were right.

There's a minimal chance that I'll make it out of here. But there's also a chance that I *will* make it out of here—with Snowark still standing. Too big a part of me refuses to act on chance. I must act on what is real: Snowark has a chance of surviving, but only if I choose to take it on its behalf.

The flame in front of us disintegrates. When I look up, Ambrose's hands are falling to his sides. His eyes roll to the back of his head as his lids close.

"Ambrose?" Zenevieve urges as she and I grab his arms.

The three of us call his name as he sinks into our hold, unconscious.

CHAPTER 8

"IT MATTERS THIS TIME"

Leo

A PANICKED STUN FLOODS MY BODY AS THE WHALE swallows us whole. Immediately, a row of teeth enters the corner of my vision.

My survival instincts scream for me, "Grab a tooth!"

We force our way to the right side of the whale's mouth and wrap our arms around the nearest hard, yellow cone we can find. Sierra's arms rest on top of mine, and we grip each other for dear life. I can only hold on to her with one hand because the other holds the seed. I pray that Ezra and Ithinor are in the same position behind Sierra as we remain underwater and the current gushes past us.

These aren't like usual whale teeth... What breed is this?

We stand on the whale's gums in its cavernous mouth. Sea water pours in from its open jaw, threatening to take us with it.

"A whale's stomach acids are lethal," Ithinor calls. "It's safest up here until we figure out what to do next."

Save for the water gushing past us, quiet trails his words. My mind is left to run rampant amidst the chaos of the situation. Some part of me is blaming it entirely on me; but for the first time in my life, I'm struggling to pin down exactly how I led to it.

I only have one hope for us now, and it's resting in my clenched fist. *Do not let go.*

Sierra sighs in front of me. "I don't... I don't know about this—the race."

Ezra bounces his head up behind her to look at her. Ithinor is holding on to the tooth behind him. "What do you mean?" Ezra's deep voice asks.

She turns her head to match his eyes. "What were the Mages thinking? Is this secretly a plan to rid the world of its monarchs and anyone loyal to them?"

My eyes catch on a spot of the whale's brownish-red tongue, and I pause. *That... doesn't sound entirely implausible.* Practically each kingdom is ready for war against another. Even Vineah's "encouragement" toward a coalition against Lavara and Windale's allied forces has bordered on a threat, but accepting their proposal would make me partially responsible for Vineah's desired invasion of Snowark—a peaceful kingdom Vineah only wants for territory and power. I refuse to entangle Seavale's history in that; the court is still strategizing a rejection that won't end in another war.

Surely the Mages would allow us a chance to make things right, wouldn't they? I still haven't given in yet. That must be hope for something.

"We have a chance to survive, and we must take it," Ithinor tells Sierra calmly from behind Ezra. "We've already survived one challenge without the artifact. Now we *have* the artifact."

Sierra's cheeks redden. She must be thinking of how she saved Ezra with a kiss of life. Well, ten.

Finally, the whale's jaw shuts, submerging us in an ocean of pitch-black darkness. Water pours down the throat, draining until it's level with our waists, then knees, and then feet. Our bubble suits deflate the lower the water sinks.

"What do we do?" Ezra exclaims.

"I—I don't know," Sierra replies anxiously. "If they're deflating as the water sinks, they must be able to sense when we're in a dry space."

"And if that isn't the case and we somehow escape?" I ask.

Sierra's eyes fall onto me. "We pray the artifact helps us in time."

As the final drops of water fall down the whale's throat, we're left in silence—and air. The four of us immediately gag: the cavern of the warm mouth radiates a stench like vomit in the Seavale fish market's waste bucket. And the humidity gives no aid to the overwhelming reek of our new prison.

Prison. *Prison.*

We're locked in. The situation is all too familiar. And the whale's mouth reeks infinitely worse than even the most unkempt cell in Seavale's dungeon.

"I hope you're right, Sierra," Ezra exclaims between dry heaves, "because we *need*—to escape—now!"

With a hard swallow and one hand still clutching the seed, I feel Sierra tighten her grip on me. I'm fighting tooth and whale to suppress what is trying to rise into my throat from both the smell and my excruciating memories. The only way we may escape is by some unnatural miracle—

Magic. *That's right.*

"Ithinor?" I call, more shakily than I can help. "Surely your magic can do something!"

"I'll try," he replies. A glow of orange erupts from his fingertips: fire. He tosses the flames to the roof of the whale's mouth.

The animal violently shakes without so much as a hum. We're tossed around, my hold around the tooth weakening for the couple of seconds the animal is affected.

"You're tickling it!" I shout. At least I have the freedom to do so now without making myself deaf.

"Telekinesis?" Sierra asks, swallowing so hard that I can hear it.

"I..." Ithinor doubt is palpable. "I'm not sure that mine is strong enough to pry open the jaw of this large of an animal. I'll try, but I risk what we just experienced."

Silence echoes off of the wet, putrid walls for only a few seconds. It is only the fact that I can pace around the mouth if I absolutely need to that is preventing the wicked panic of my mind with the fact that I'm locked inside again.

"Hold on as tightly as you can," I force myself to say, swallowing another gag. "Ithinor, try it."

A white glow ignites in both of his hands. The two are folded together until he slowly tries to separate them with great strain. The whale's mouth remains shut, but its body tumbles as if defending itself. From the white glow that remains before it fades, Ithinor hardly manages to regain his balance and hold on to his tooth again.

So close...

"All right." I exhale, careful of my every breath. Disappointment drops heavily into my stomach, my insides sloshing. "No magic."

"The whale must come up for air eventually," Ezra says. "Surely—"

"We don't have that time." Sierra's words are tight, and it worries me. "There must be something we're meant to do, it can't end like this for us!"

A ringing silence trails her words. I know that we are all hoping that this won't be our first *and* last stage of the race. Part of me longs to say that I'm meant to get closer to the finish line than this. At least prove myself a little more worthy than being discarded on the first stage—the one that represents my own kingdom, at that.

I take another somewhat steady breath out, cursing the fact that I have to inhale the stench again. *What could our next step possibly be? Was this even meant to happen?*

"Leo," Sierra says in the dark. I can't see her; but I imagine her pointing at my fist as she says, "Look, the seed."

I carefully bring my right hand out from around the tooth. The green glow has returned, shining through the crevices of my fingers.

"A light source." I partially open my hand, unable to help my admiration of the green light the seed radiates. Some magic still manages to impress me. When I look up, only the shadows of Sierra's face are visible. "At least we have that."

"Leon," Ithinor adds, "I think it's time you think about what to do with that."

I suppress a scoff. *How?* What is a seed meant to do in a whale's mouth? Why would there be a seed at the bottom of the ocean? If it were meant to grow anything, it would have grown in the trench!

My breath is heavier in my lungs. *Pick anyone else to do this race. Please.*

"We can do this," Sierra says, like she's reading my mind. I'm thankful that I don't have to meet her eyes in full, just under limited light. "Take a second. Think."

With another tight breath, I turn my gaze back to the seed. All right. This is the artifact. This is meant to help us overcome the main obstacle... There's almost no doubt in my mind that the whale is exactly that, which means this seed has something to do with it—but there isn't anywhere to plant it here. And how does one tiny seed make a difference in a gargantuan whale?

I swallow to save myself from a sigh. "I don't know. Every plan I think of... doesn't have enough sense."

"That's certainly a first," Ithinor remarks. "You conducted hundreds of plans when you were younger."

"It's different this time," I tell him, fighting the impatience in my voice. "It matters this time."

"Good," he replies. "You acknowledge that. You have the right mind approaching this; now you know that you can trust yourself."

"How?" I ask dully.

"It was your strategy that enabled the success of all those plans, Leon," he says, unfazed. "Strategy is a part of you that has always existed. That instinct cannot be so easily erased. Now that you know how to control it, you can trust it."

I recall the day my water pump prank almost killed him in the courtyard. Part of my mind taunts that he's attempting to elicit my guilt with his speech, but I know him better than that. I have to believe him. After all, every plan *was* executed with complete thought.

Except for that one prank that almost exploded the royal treasury—but I was only eleven.

Right—we only have so much time. I need to figure this out.

I look back down at the artifact. A seed. There is one thing true about every seed: they need water and air to grow.

We're surrounded by ocean on the outside, but the seed would have no air. I'm not sure it was even close to growing anything just before we were eaten. There is no telling when the whale will open its jaw again. The tongue also hasn't reserved any water from the flood. Too much of it fell down the throat—

Wait...

No. No, this is mad. I must be mad for saying what I'm about to.

"I'm going to throw the seed down the whale's throat."

My team appropriately hisses a chorus of "*What?*"

"It won't grow in the ocean," I say, stepping away from the tooth. If there is anything I can do to communicate my surety to them, it's releasing the only thing keeping me physically steady. "There's no air. There *is* air in the whale. There's also a sufficient water source down below. Seeing as the seed is most likely magic, maybe this is all it needs to grow."

"Leon," Ithinor states, "I said it was your *strategy* that led you to success in the past. That seed is our only chance at overcoming this stage, and you want to throw it away?"

Something clicks in my head. "Yes—it is the only thing to help us, and that's by throwing it down."

"Wait," Ezra states. "Yes, water is down there—but so are stomach acids. The seed will disintegrate before it can do anything."

An urgent anxiety runs in my chest. Not only is time the one resource we aren't abundant in, but my body and mind are growing increasingly desperate to leave this rancid prison. But Ezra is right—and I know that. Still, throwing the seed is the only option we have right now. I can't persuade myself to wait this out, to continue standing here, because the longer we spend debating this, the less time we have to run—the more time we give the other teams.

I don't know what to do.

I shake my head, remembering what I do know: "Time is our most valuable resource right now. We need to try *something*."

"Then we must ensure that this is even a considerable option," Sierra says, still holding on to the tooth as she glances between us. "Leo, do you remember what the Mages said about the artifact?"

I swallow, carefully inhaling so as to minimize the reek my lungs take in. "We'll need the artifact to overcome the main obstacle—which must be the whale for this one. Maybe that's why the seed didn't grow out there. It needs to grow in here."

Silence lingers after my words for longer than I would like.

"I don't know what else we may do," Ithinor finally begins, sighing, "but if it's our only option—we must try it. The seed's magic may protect it. Otherwise, waiting for our next step could be detrimental."

I'm grateful that he's echoing my thought process now; I feel a little more rational.

I carefully inhale, preparing myself. "If for nothing else, then for the sake of time."

The unease in my bones swirls the current of nausea in my stomach as I await a response—from anyone.

Sierra nods. "I think this is our only logical option right now."

She's only a year older than me, but her approval means as much to me as Ithinor's.

"For the sake of time," Ezra adds, further solidifying my resolve.

I walk across the length of the spongy yet firm tongue, thankful that my feet are protected by my sabatons. The seed remains tightly held in my fist as I walk until I feel the smallest change in inclination. I steady myself, the eyes of my team heavy on me even in the dark. Part of me wishes I could take an arrow from my back and shoot the seed down.

I force in a deep breath and bring my right arm backward. With one step, I thrust the seed down the whale's throat.

CHAPTER 9

"THIS IS NOT SOMETHING FOR YOU TO PLAY WITH"

Emberly

ZENEVIEVE AND I CRY OUT TO AMBROSE AS HE FALLS into her arms. Sinking to her knees, she cradles his deathly pale figure.

"What's wrong?" I ask, kneeling to rub his arm.

Meredith arrives at my side and reaches her hand under his cloaks. She presses her hand against his chest—which, I realise, is scarcely moving.

Her face falls. "Exhaustion. His heart is weak, and his body is just scarcely warm enough to keep him alive. He needed to rest longer." She begins rummaging through her satchel. "Maintaining his fire spell stole his remaining energy."

Curse this boy, why didn't he say anything? Of all things, why did he *lie*?

"He's more likely to freeze to death while unconscious!"

Zenevieve exclaims, rubbing his other arm.

"It's all right," Meredith assures in a tone as motherly firm as ever. Taking out her flint and steel, she exchanges steady eyes with us. "Both of you, build an igloo as close to the bank as Emberly can manage. I'll keep him by the fire there. Hurry, go."

Zenevieve helps bring Ambrose back to the bank of the lake while I begin the igloo. A million curses run through my head as I flatten the plush snow. I just as quickly dust my hands together so that the snow doesn't saturate my gloves and freeze my hands. My steps are hindered as they fall into fresh batches; it's a heavy fight to hurry. My mind makes it all the more so.

Do not tell me he sacrificed his warmth and energy just for my sake...

I look up at the bank. Just as my eyes land on the fire, an icy breeze scrapes my cheeks. Though Meredith and Zenevieve are visibly worried about the wind, I watch as the dark-grey smoke is blown in the direction of the lake—away from me. That ensures my safety as I continue working. By the time Zenevieve returns to help, I've a big-enough patch of ground for us to build an igloo that will fit the four of us.

"What says Meredith?" I dare to ask.

Zenevieve follows me in gathering snow for a block. "She's firm in her theory that he's passed out from exhaustion."

I solidify the edges of my block. "Remind me to yell at the boy when he wakes up. How could he be so incompetent as to lie about how he was truly faring? We were trying to save him from exactly this!"

"I know you understand, Ember." Zenevieve's voice lowers to a register she only uses when she requires my full attention.

Like this morning—when the portal opened.

I look up to find her black eyes steady despite our hurry. She's already begun her second block. "He's just as we are," she tells me. "He can't help his instinct to protect those he cares about, even if it's at his own expense."

I close my mouth and resume my work. Zenny has had more practice with manual labour, but I still attempt to match her speed.

"The only difference between us and him is..." she says next, finishing her second block, "he hasn't learned where to draw the line."

I know the weight of that sentence: Zenevieve learned where to draw it when she was only five years old. Her twin siblings had to take care of her on the streets after their drunkard of a father tried to kill her; he blamed her for his late wife's death. The twins accidentally killed him in protecting her. They were only twelve at the time; it was either Snowark's alleys or being stuck in an orphanage to likely be separated.

It was when they ran out of food again that Zenevieve determined to step in. She tried to steal money and food from an alley marked by an infamous street gang. She knew it belonged to them; that didn't deter her sacrifice for family. When the gang caught her, the twins scarcely managed to save her in time. Zenevieve stepped in front of her sister to protect her from a stabbing. It was all for naught as her sister pushed her aside and received the blade nonetheless. Zenevieve hid and witnessed her brother fall to the same fate. That was her line.

I had no choice but to draw the line when I was five, too. That was when I learned about the curse. After all, if I sacrificed myself the way I'd like to for the people I care about, Snowark would fall with me.

I'm not even sure I want to know what would cause Ambrose to find his line.

My armour grows heavier with every breath as I move to gather snow and press it into a dense block. Each pant gathers in a thick fog in front of me that almost hinders my vision. My body heat combats the frigid cold reaching its icy branches into my limbs. When my curiosity wins, I look up at Meredith on the bank: she holds Ambrose close to the fire. Her hands furiously rub his arms and legs.

A couple of hours pass with no sign of awakening from Ambrose. Zenny eventually switches positions with Meredith when we're halfway done. It takes us until dusk to finish. When I place the last block, Zenevieve urgently calls from the bank that Ambrose is stirring.

At the same time, a wolf howls in the distance.

"I've got him," Zenevieve calls, picking up the boy. She rushes with him to our structure that sits past the entrance of the forest.

"I'm not the only one who heard a man-eating friend howl off in the distance, am I?" I ask, gesturing behind me.

Ambrose moans tiredly in Zenevieve's arms.

"I need to bring him inside," she states, moving past me and Meredith.

Meredith ignores me, too. Instead, she insists on climbing inside first to help bring Ambrose through the small entrance. We're trusting the snow to keep as much of his and Zenevieve's heat insulated as possible.

Ambrose fully comes to by the time I crawl inside. Zenny sits next to him, Meredith beside her. They're both taking off their armour. I realise with disappointment that that is wisest; we're about to be stationary and the iron will only draw away our warmth.

"Have a nice nap, Rosy?" Zenevieve asks. I take a cosy spot on his other side.

"Where are we?" he replies groggily. His soft, brown eyes gaze all around the minuscule space. "How did we get—?"

"We needed a shelter." I take off my gauntlets. "So we built one. You're welcome."

It seems as if the day replays in his mind; his gaze falls to the centre of the igloo. A frown pulls down his thin lips. "You're going to yell at me, aren't you?" he says in a melancholy voice I'm not used to hearing from him. Curse the stars: it melts the icy words I had planned to a puddle.

"No." I exhale, letting my shoulder armour fall off me. "But pull something like that again and I'll start *actually* calling you 'Strawberry'."

My insides cringe; I've never used a threat so weak.

All three group members smile at me. I roll my eyes and finish taking off my breastplate. The freeze immediately strikes my torso. My body succumbs to a shiver. Ambrose opens up his cloaks and wraps me in them, pulling me right up next to him.

"No, Ginger—"

"I've learned my lesson," he tells me. "It's your turn. Please?"

I curse the fact that he could be so kind to me after today. It's the fact that my body will help keep him warm that encourages me to obey. I hesitantly relax next to him, helping him pull the cloaks around me.

"It seems exhaustion really was the reason you passed out," Meredith says. "You slept for as long as your body needed to, which the fire helped with. How do you feel now?"

"Awake," Ginger says with confidence. "Really—well, a little sleepy, but I'm all right. Despite this cold. But Emberly's more hot headed than I remember, so it helps—"

I shove him into Zenevieve before pulling the cloaks tighter around myself. A wolf howls far off in the distance.

"Point proven." Zenny smirks, gathering herself into the fabrics on Ambrose's other side. The boy is skinny enough to provide just enough room for the three of us.

In blatant honesty, it is the first breath of relief I feel we've had all day.

Day. It has only been a day. I woke up in Snowark's palace this morning.

"Why weren't you honest earlier?" Zenevieve asks.

Ginger's face falls. Silence ensues.

"I—" He quickly cuts himself off with a foggy exhale. With another deep breath, a timid softness touches his features. "They told me not to."

"Who?" I ask. "The voices in your head?"

"The palace." He never raises his eyes from the ground. "When I first arrived. They told me my magic was the only reason I was there, I wasn't necessary for anything else. I had to remember that. I was meant to one day protect the princess with my magic and serve her and the kingdom's needs. If I caused trouble or couldn't prove my worth as a mage, they would send me home. But I needed—*need*—the salary. For my family... so I listened."

My swallow barely manages past my tight throat. The words set fire to my blood. The council used those same words against me growing up: I only existed for Snowark's sake. The kingdom's well-being was the only reason I was alive. Unfortunately for me, and unlike Ambrose's case, those words are true and I know it.

Still—he was only thirteen when he first arrived to start training. They knew mages have no choice but to start so young so that the palace will always have a trustworthy and strong mage. How could they say such a thing to a boy?

My heart skips a beat at the realisation: *There were two reasons he accepted the doubled training hours with Zephyr.*

Ambrose takes another deep breath. "Something small like illness was seen as putting myself before Snowark. Zephyr fights to keep me hired every time I fall ill... I suppose I thought—the same rules applied here. For the sake of survival."

An unfamiliar protective instinct awakens in me. Growing up in the palace, the staff were always protective of me; but they were relatively respectful enough. It was the council that wanted nothing to do with me. Snowark sees me as hope for the future; the council see me as a stain unworthy of bringing it forth. Then how could the same staff that believed in me have treated a young servant as beneath them? Snowark is proud, but prideful? Not according to its history, at least...

"The same rules don't apply here, you nutty nitwit." I nudge Ginger with my shoulder. "Speak up. You're a princess here, too."

Thankfully, smiles go all around. Ginger even expresses a chuckle.

"Thank..." he begins timidly. Zenevieve slides her arm

around him. "Thank you all. For saving my life twice today. I'll do my best not to be so foolish in the future."

He takes my right hand into his and raises it to his mouth. Shock mixes with stun in me by his impulsive courage; I don't find the words to deny him.

He presses a soft kiss to my knuckles. "Thank you, Emberly."

He even knows where to kiss? He really has grown in his time at the palace.

He turns to Zenevieve, takes her hand, and presses a kiss to her knuckles as well. Meredith receives her thanks from him last.

Zenevieve nudges him. "Lesson learned, indeed, Rosy—"

A howl echoes from outside. Closer this time.

"Right," Meredith says warily. "We're too far from the fire to keep any predators away from the igloo. We'll have to take turns keeping watch throughout the night. Two shifts per pair so that we can keep each other awake." She looks through her satchel before bringing out her silver pocket watch. "If we sleep now, we should each manage eight hours."

"And the fact that we're in a race?" I ask sceptically. Unease sloshes in my stomach; surely the other groups haven't needed the time we have to complete the first stage.

For all we know, a group is on Snowark's stage right now— if the rules deem it possible.

"We've no choice but to rest tonight," Meredith replies. "Ambrose has suffered intense exhaustion, and pacing ourselves properly is crucial. Considering this has already lasted a day, we don't know how long this stage will take, let alone the others. We'll need our energy for anything that may come next."

Exactly. In other words, wolves aren't the only thing we'll be keeping watch for.

Zenevieve and I won't allow anyone to hurt them. Hopefully, Ambrose's magic will be able to help defend us as well.

The night is frigid; thanks to me, the only fire we're allowed is from what Ambrose is able to provide during his watch shift with Meredith (after swearing on his life that he won't overdo himself again). Our "eight hours" of sleep turn into an hour and a half at most. I'm willing to bet Meredith's hair lacquer that I'm not the only one tossing and turning. I wake up what feels like every half hour. My watch shift with Zenevieve is hardly different from my abysmal attempts at sleep. Otherwise, my eyes are closed, and perhaps I even dream—but to label it as "sleep" is cruel.

Hours upon hours later, Meredith's groggy voice whispers, "Come, Emberly. We haven't much time."

I moan as I turn onto my back. Exhaustion deems my current position comfortable enough for sleep. I know it's lying to me.

Meredith helps me with my armour and then allows me out of the igloo. Zenevieve and Ambrose are standing around his ignited hands, warming themselves. He's returned her cloak but still wears Meredith's.

As if she's reading my mind, Meredith then offers me mine. I thank her, taking it. At least today is slightly warmer than yesterday.

"Ember," Zenevieve says, walking up to me, "do you still feel that pull?"

I exhale with a visible cloud of air. Unease crawls around in my chest. "Yes. If you lot still think it's worth following."

"I believe it's safe to say that it's the artifact," Meredith assures. "We've no other means of finding it."

I meet her upturned eyes. She's already redone her elegant bun for the day. There must be a mirror hidden in her satchel; I can't imagine such artwork being done without a reflection to help.

All she provides is an encouraging nod. She may trust me to a grave extent, but I trust her theories just as much.

Turning back to the forest, I exhale the memories of yesterday. "Onward, we go."

We stumble upon the entrance of a dark-indigo cave an hour later. The stinging, icy tendrils of the air slash my face just standing in the mouth of it. The pull is so strong now that I practically stumble over each step the closer we draw: this must be where we're meant to be.

"It's even colder in here," Zenevieve hisses, shivering as we walk farther into the tunnel. Her voice echoes off the rocky walls.

"Interesting, Zenny," I remark, "do you think it's due to the insulation of a *small, stone space?*"

She gently shoves me, almost pushing me into Meredith.

A small fire ignites in Ambrose's hands just as the darkness envelops us. Instantly, the air becomes a tad friendlier. "Meredith," he chimes, "you can have your cloak back—"

"Keep it, I insist." She straightens beside me, clutching her satchel's strap draped over her shoulder. "We're almost there.

Aren't we?"

Her eyes are heavier when illuminated in the firelight. I keep my gaze ahead. If this pull is the artifact, we're right on top of the cursed thing. That serves as my only motivation right now. The cold is the only thing keeping me awake after a night of non-existent sleep. We've been trapped in this frozen wasteland for almost a full day, and I'm ready to demand for our exit.

That exit is at the end with the artifact. It has to be. We can't be walking into a dead end. The pull is tugging me forward even stronger.

"I'm running for it."

Zenevieve's eyes widen at me. "What?" she and Meredith chime in unison.

"I'm running for it," I announce again, quickening my pace. "You'll discover the artifact either with me or after me!"

Their voices echo behind me as I dart down the tunnel. Ambrose's firelight dims the farther I travel. My group call after me, but I can't be bothered to obey. I must reach the end and leave this frigid death trap.

As if I don't receive enough of this weather on a daily basis!

Pounding metal steps resound from behind me. It's precisely what I want to hear. The tunnel remains dim but never completely darkens. My numb feet can't feel their steps, but my frozen legs continue. The satchel hanging beside me beats against my waist. My heart throbs, pumping a faint heat into my chest until I finally reach the end of the cave.

Thank the—!

I'm only met with another wall. On the ground and against it is a long block of ice. Something silver is trapped inside.

"Don't—don't do that!" Zenevieve pants with me as the three approach. "W—we don't have the energy—"

Collectively, their breaths slow as their stares fall to the ice on the ground.

"What is this?" Meredith muses, kneeling down.

"If I didn't know any better," I reply, kneeling with her, "I'd say this is the artifact you lot have been pestering me so fervently about."

The item trapped inside the block is long and skinny. Something silver for the first two thirds and black at the end.

Is this a sword...? Why would we need a sword when we have our own?

"Stand back," Zenny says. She grabs her mace. "No offense, Rosy, but I can't wait for your fire to melt it free."

We obey and watch as she raises her weapon high above her head. Then, she smashes it down onto the block of ice. It takes three tries before the block crumbles apart and frees its captive: a red-orange–veined sword.

An invisible force pulses in me. This *is* the artifact.

I pick up the blade by its black, leather handle. Instantly, my hand relaxes around it: even through my gloves, a satisfying warmth radiates from it. The sword seems to be infused with fire itself; a glowing, fiery veining travels all across it. Specks of what resemble embers are dotted across the blade.

How did this not melt the ice it was encapsulated in?

"Portia has competition," I remark at Zenny, glancing at the sword by her side. She shoves me again.

Ambrose's awe is exposed in a breathy laugh. "Whoa," he whispers with a grin. "Can I hold—?"

"No," I say, like he should have known the answer to that. He should have. "This is not something for you to play with."

He kisses his teeth. "I don't want to play with it! I just want to hold—"

Zenevieve shushes us with Meredith frozen beside me. Ambrose and I listen. A low growl rumbles on what must be behind the wall in front of us—if there's another side.

I dare to breathe. "Was that—?"

There is definitely another side: a roar echoes, boasting the evidence of a hidden creature.

Ambrose frantically glances around. "Where is that—?!"

The wall in front of us quakes. We step back, boulders and rocks tumbling down until a puff of freezing air bursts through the new opening. In front of us sits an ice cavern—and a scaly, sharp-fanged beast almost as tall as the ceiling.

CHAPTER

"WASN'T THAT A WHALE OF A TIME?"

Leo

LESS THAN A MINUTE HAS PASSED. I TIGHTEN MY GRIP ON Sierra's arms as we hug the whale's tooth, waiting. The seed has yet to grow—and I know the fact is lingering in everyone else's mind, too.

Please. Don't tell me we're stuck here until it grows. Don't tell me I threw away our only chance at escape.

"Anything?" Ezra asks softly in the dark.

No one replies.

My throat tightens as I swallow. *If only you could stop being a royal fool for longer than sixty seconds. Then you could actually manage to save everyone—*

"Wait," Sierra whispers. "Yes. Do you hear that?"

A subtle rumbling travels through the air. The sound grows, seeming to transfer into the whale's very being.

An earthquake rattles across the animal and intensifies with my quickening heartbeat. My survival instincts are set ablaze as a high-pitch wail pierces the air. I fight to keep my hands on Sierra's arms instead of covering my ears; if I release, I may find myself trapped here forever.

"Is this the artifact working?" Sierra exclaims over the growling chaos.

A forceful lunge jolts us toward the front of the whale's mouth, which is starting to open. My heart skips a beat, torn between stability and escaping.

When the whale jerks forward again, Ezra screams, "Go!"

I shove down the remainder of my fear and hold my breath, following my team as we rush to the front of the whale's mouth. Water floods past us, relief mimicking it in my chest as I realize that a bubble is inflating from my legs and up around me. It encases my head just before the water rises to my neck, protecting my satchel just in time. The whale's third jolt forward allows us the force we need to swim back out into the ocean.

My throbbing arms and legs burn, screaming at me to provide a longer rest. The only thing granting me enough adrenaline to overpower it is seeing my teammates work equally hard to bring ourselves a safe distance away.

When Ezra turns around, the rest of us follow. To my surprise, awe settles over me: the top half of the ginormous whale is colored in a dark blue, a lighter blue for its bottom. Matching dark speckles are scattered about. It's one of the more beautiful whales I've seen before. We float only about a hundred feet away, an easy distance for it to travel to swallow us again. But it can't: large, thick vines are rapidly growing from its throat and out of its mouth. Choking it.

One vine is skinnier and longer than the rest, reaching farther out from the whale. Amidst the sunlight reaching this depth, a bronze color shines in the rays, wrapped in the vine's tip.

The whale releases another cry and jolts forward, whipping the vine. The tip unravels, setting free the bronze item trapped: a key.

Adrenaline restores strength in my limbs, and I thrust myself toward it as it sinks to the sand.

"Leo!" Sierra shouts, but I can still safely see the proximity of the whale.

I swim for the key as it lands on the ocean floor. My fingers wrap around it, grazing the sand.

Got it!

I raise my head to turn around when another pull ignites in my chest. It guides me in the direction of a rocky reef off in the distance to my right.

That's where we need to go next. After my instinct with the trench and then the whale, I feel this answer in my bones.

I don't celebrate until I turn around and safely swim back to my team.

"You got it?" Sierra's eyes widen with awe as I hold up the key for them all to see. "You got it!"

Seven knobs ordain the shaft, the fifth one down elongated. At the key's ornate head are two sea waves, and then I find the small word engraved at the bottom of it: "bravery".

Interesting design... I wonder what the others will look like—or even say. I certainly *feel* brave after surviving almost being eaten by a whale.

"I know where to take this," I say. Behind me, the whale cries in its struggles against the vines. I turn around at yet another spine-numbing wail.

Sierra swims a little forward, sympathetic eyes on it. "I hate to see any animal suffering…"

For some reason, I can't help but feel for it, too. Despite being a breed I've never encountered before, this whale is too reminiscent of the ones back home.

Is this another test of the stage?

I take a deep breath in my bubble. I know why I am really here right now, what I am here for. I know what I have to do for the sake of myself and my team members: I close my eyes and turn away, in the direction of the rocky reef. "Over there—that's where we need to take the key."

I start my swim without objection from my team. Halfway there, a scream-like wail ruptures and stops us. I watch as the whale's body waves in the water, the vines finally stopping their growth. It continues bellowing with every movement, but we're able to cover our ears this time. I look away again.

Finally, it stops.

When I turn back, a large root of green vines is falling to the ocean floor. The whale is swimming away.

I catch myself sighing in relief.

"All right," Sierra says shakily, exhaling. "Now—let's keep going. Race. Last to the finish line."

I nod, ready to release myself from the trance of the ocean.

The bubble suits deflate as we rise from the water in the underwater cave, its dark walls radiating a calming ocean blue. The four of us gaze all around with amazement. Small pools of seawater rest in ponds scattered throughout the cave. At the end of it sits a cyan-blue–lined portal, which means we are exactly where we need to be.

"Has that been here the entire time?" Sierra asks. I turn to face her. "If we didn't need to use the key to open the portal, what could we need it for?"

My eyes fall to the key in my hand. I carefully stick it into my satchel. "I felt a pull leading us here only after I grabbed it. Maybe the keys are meant to lead us to the next stages. The Mages only said to collect them. So until then,"—I drop my bag onto a dry patch of stone—"wasn't that a whale of a time?"

Ezra smacks the back of my head. Even Ithinor joins Sierra in an eyeroll.

I rub my head. "I didn't miss that."

Ezra smirks. "I sure did."

"A toast to never being stuck underwater again," Sierra remarks, "so that he can always do that."

"So that I don't develop joint inflammation before I'm thirty-five," Ithinor adds dully, setting himself against the wall and on the ground with his satchel next to him. "I may never recover from that exertion. These robes are heavier than they appear."

Ezra exhales, setting down his supplies. "I'm grateful to finally rest safely. I don't think any of us are in the proper mental or physical state to continue if any of the other stages are like this." He gestures to the portal. "We didn't have a secure escape in the whale's mouth, but we do here. If we sleep for the night, we can move on at any time if we must."

"If we had magical bubbles providing us air underwater," Sierra begins, "perhaps the same rules apply to this cave and we won't run out of air. If we do start struggling to breathe, we advance to the next stage. All right?"

"Agreed," I reply, nodding in Ithinor's direction. "We wouldn't want Ithinor's bones shriveling up on us from the lack of rest."

"I'm *thirty*," he says flatly.

"Which means we must take extra care of you," Ezra adds, as though Ithinor should know that.

"You're only nine years behind, Sir Everguard." Even his sky-blue eyes are dull as he speaks. "Less than a decade away from following in my footsteps."

"Leave the poor man alone, you two." Sierra rolls her eyes. "It's time for supper. We need to replenish our energy."

She takes a grain bar, apple, and butterknife out of her bag, cutting the apple in half. "We'll split two apples between the four of us tonight. Rationing will be our biggest priority during meals—as long as the stages don't provide any food. Let's hope that that won't remain to be the case..."

You can't even call this a "meal", I'm tempted to say—but it's all we have. I don't want to steal the value of that from my teammates. Still, I more than miss the blueberry muffins from the castle.

My head bounces up in an idea, and I scramble for an apple from my bag before Sierra can offer me her other half. I cut it in sloppy halves with my own knife and then dart to Ithinor sitting against the wall. "Here, Icky! Split an apple with me."

His eyes narrow at me. "I won't be accepting any food from you as long as you keep attaching that name to me."

"Quite a shame," I tell him. I shove the apple half into his mouth.

"Leon!" He scolds me with his mouth full, but I'm already taking a seat next to him to witness Sierra approach Ezra with her other half.

"Here," she says softly, holding it down to him.

Ezra thanks her, gently reaching up as though his hands will break hers. They've known each other for almost four years, yet they're acting as though they're smitten upon first meeting.

I remember that day. My smile grows. *They couldn't say two comprehensible words to each other.*

Sierra takes the seat between me and Ezra, seeming to ignore what transparently saturates the air. "A coastal salad sounds wonderful right now." She sighs tiredly. "With crumble cheese and olives..."

"I miss Agatha's cheesy garlic eggs," Ezra says, leaning his head against the wall.

"Chocolate liquor cake," Ithinor adds dully, as though he's lost all hope of ever having another serving ever again.

I nod in understanding. "Blueberry muffins. Agatha has the best recipe."

Silence rests over us, save for the echoing dripping of the cave. The open portal continues radiating a blinding light from the back, but we're too exhausted to even think about jumping into the next stage. Right now, all I can think about is everything I miss from Seavale: sailing, swimming in safe waters, warming up under the sun along the coast, climbing the fruit trees... And yet, I can't help but remember everything I was finally able to leave behind.

"Do you think..." Sierra says as she turns her apple half in her hand, "teams can be on the same stage simultaneously?"

My apple half is midway to my mouth. I start to ponder the same thing.

"Well," Ezra muses in a deep voice, "do you remember what the Mages said about how the race functions, Leo?"

It was only this morning that we began, but I think my mind is still processing the day's events; it takes me a moment to recall their words. "We'll go through seven stages that represent the kingdoms. Each one has an artifact, like the seed, that will help us overcome the main obstacle. When we find the key, we move on to the next stage."

"Then it's a matter of if there are only seven stages the groups will pass through," Ithinor answers, "or if each team has their own set of seven stages. Forty-nine in total."

It has to be one set of seven, I think. *For only one ruler to win...*

Something doesn't settle well with me in that conclusion, but I can't place it. And I don't want to tell my team, either, because the conclusion is daunting if it's true. I don't need anything threatening their morale when morale is half the war. I learned that the day Lavara tried to invade.

My hand subconsciously travels to the long scar on my chest sitting beneath my armor. Ithinor says it was partly my furious determination that encouraged our army to continue fighting. A Lavaran soldier slashed his sword across my chest—Ithinor's healing magic saved my life after the battle. Still, I never stopped fighting, I couldn't. Supposedly, that allowed the Seavalen army the courage and inspiration to continue defending our kingdom. Fortunately for us, Lavara's pride told them that they only needed to deploy a small army to successfully invade an island. Despite the advantage we had, I gained the Guard's respect that day. Unfortunately, I've yet to gain anyone else's.

But that is what I must lend my team right now: courage. Inspiration. If I continue, so will they.

"If other teams can be on the same stage, wouldn't that change how accessible an artifact is?" Sierra asks. "Or how the main challenge is conquered? Or—do the stages reset every time someone new enters?"

After a moment of thought, she shrugs beside me, taking a bite of her apple. Her messy bun is smushed behind her as she leans her head back, green eyes locked straight ahead. I wonder if she meant to say her next words aloud after swallowing: "It'd certainly make it more difficult to protect everyone..."

The silence that falls on us is grim. I face in full the realizations that Ezra almost drowned and we were almost whale food. Our lives are anything but protected here.

That means that wherever you lead them, the outcome will be thanks to your doing. Their lives rest in your leadership.

I couldn't even protect myself from trouble growing up. How am I meant to protect these three now?

How am I meant to rule a brand-new kingdom I know nothing about if I win this?

I do not want to do this... but I have to. I need to.

I spend the night tossing and turning in my sleeping holder with the questions ringing in my head like a bell. Nobody seems to have a restful night on the uneven, rocky floor, as I find out when we awake. Especially as we gather our things and walk to the back of the cave to the portal, I can't prevent the fear that another team is going to arrive behind us. I can't prevent the fear that my teammates will suffer from my choices, both in the past and now.

The four of us stand at the mouth of the portal. Sierra rests a hand on my arm and looks up at me. Her chestnut bun is as messy as ever, and it's strangely comforting. Familiar.

"Where does the ship sail to next, captain?" she asks.

I wish I didn't have to answer that.

Ezra stands next to me on my other side, Ithinor on Sierra's. They're both patient with my response. All three pairs of eyes, though, remind me again what I'm racing for. I'm able to build a glimmer of confidence in my chest on that.

I look ahead of me and take a step into the light. "Let's find out."

CHAPTER

"STAY VIGILANT"

Emberly

WHAT IS THIS THING?! I THINK AS WE FACE THE FOR-
eign monster in the ice cavern. It's unlike any animal
I've ever seen or studied; I'm not even sure it *is* an animal. It's a blue-indigo beast. An ice beast.

We're going to die. This is how the race ends for us.

Sweat wraps around the warm, black handle of the sword I
wield. Meredith and Ambrose marvel at the monster that stands
on all fours. Zenevieve's eyes are hard on it despite her fearful
blinking—as if she's hoping every time she opens her eyes, the
beast will disappear. The misshapen, dark-blue scales tightly woven across its back reflect the glimmer of the ice walls: they're
hard. Zenevieve's mace might be able to shatter them, but not before the beast turns around and swallows her alive.

My eyes widen at its claws: they're the length of Ambrose's

forearm. Four ghastly fangs protrude from under the monster's lip. The only thing missing from its terror is a pair of wings.

I'm terrified out of my cursed mind.

"It—it isn't charging," Ambrose notes, reaching out a fair, quivering hand. He waves it over the entrance to the cavern. A sheer, indigo wave passes in front of us. Then, he reaches out. Nothing stops it. "Magic is barring it, like with the horses at the portal. Only we are allowed to pass through."

Defeating this monster is the only way to go.

I tighten my grip on the heated handle of the artifact. "If this world is so magical, surely you can—make it disappear or something!"

"If I *could* manipulate the magic here, don't you think I would have made the temperature warmer?" he exclaims.

I curse the fact that, for once, Ginger is right.

The monster stands on two legs as if demanding us to step inside. I immediately avert my eyes; Ice Beastie is definitely a he.

Meredith releases a curt breath beside me. "Emberly," she says, "that sword, it must be what you need—"

"Me?" My jaw drops. "You want me to fight *that*?"

My chest falls in realisation: the sword's glowing veining, the heat from the handle—what if there *is* fire infused in it?

That's why I need it instead of my regular one.

"We can't advance without fighting it either way," Meredith tells me. "We can distract it while—"

"No!" I exclaim, louder than I intended. "No," I say in recovery, "just... just give me—"

I can't think of anything else except going forward. But if my group fall in this battle, their blood will be on my hands, too.

Winston and Myron and Samson and all the -ons will have been right yet again.

My jaw tightens. *You blasted monster. You're about to know what fear is.*

I step inside the frigid cavern. Needing the least amount of weight on me, I drop my bow, quiver, and satchel. My group follow suit.

The temperature has dropped. Ice Beastie breathes everything but fire from his nose as he pants and bares his teeth. His misshapen, Rowena-sharp scales across his back stand on end. My mind is numb with the rest of me, trying to discern how to even begin an attack.

"Zenevieve," I whisper, "what do we do now?"

"Pardon?" she asks incredulously, blinking furiously.

"You're the knight and the only one who—!"

A ground-shaking roar bellows across the cavern, rattling my bones. Ice Beastie's maw drops, double the size of his head. A pale-blue cloud emerges from the back of his throat and billows into the space. Tiny ice shards scrape my hands and the sides of my face. I hold up my arms in a cross until the swirling cloud dissipates.

I look up with the rest of my group. Ice Beastie has disappeared.

"Where is he?" I ask in a voice so frantic that I have to verify it wasn't Ambrose who had spoken.

"Stay vigilant," Zenevieve commands, having already drawn Portia in her left hand. She stands next to me, facing the right side of the cavern. Ambrose stands on my other side, facing the left. Furious flames are ablaze atop his fingers. Meredith stands behind me, facing the entrance. My hand swims in my sweat trapped in my glove as I grip the fire sword.

I look forward. The wall is nothing but muted-indigo rock. It matches the monster's rough-looking, wrinkly skin, reaching one hole in the middle above us. We're practically standing in a short volcano.

Silence echoes across the room. Ice timidly crackles.

"There!" Ambrose shouts on my left. He throws a ball of fire at the wall. One round ball of yellow now glares at our group: the monster's eye.

The fireball explodes against the wall just as Ice Beastie's body fades from the colour of ice to his signature indigo. The fire scarcely singes his snout. His maw falls open again with a raging roar. He stands on his hind legs, drops, and then lunges forward. I throw myself towards the back wall of the cavern. The fire sword slips from my hand as I roll onto the ground and almost meet the ice wall.

Ow.

Hard and cold: the reason the councilmen's mothers never hugged them.

I prop myself up on my elbow, my hair falling into my face. When I look up, the yellow-eyed monster's glare is on me. He claws at the ground.

I almost challenge him by glowering back—and then I realise that his right eye doesn't glisten in the light.

Wait. That eye isn't yellow; it's bronze. The middle is bronze, the colour seeping throughout the eye. It also lacks the clear glassiness of an animal's eyeball.

It's fake. And the bronze is...

The Mages, what did the Mages say? Grab the artifact, overcome the main obstacle, and then grab—

"The key! The key is in the eye!" I shout. I glance at Zenevieve and Meredith lying on the left side of the cavern and then Ambrose on the right. "We have to get—!"

A fierce snarl rumbles across the space. Pounding throbs under me. I look up. Beastie is throttling himself towards me.

Just when I'm ready to close my eyes and accept death's semi-sweet embrace, a heavy body thrusts into me. Zenevieve and I skid across the harsh ground as Ice Beastie slams into the wall.

We fall onto our backs side by side. My breath is saturated with shock and adrenaline.

"Next time," Zenevieve hisses, sitting up and pulling me along by the shoulder, "*don't* stand in the way of a man-eating beast!"

I immediately take her advice and watch as orange sparks fall off of Ice Beastie's wrinkly head. He turns in Ambrose's direction. Meredith stands closer to the entrance. Her sword is drawn, but it will be a miracle if I live long enough to see her use it.

Ambrose thrusts his fireballs at Ice Beastie. Without wasting a second, he runs and then dives under the monster. His body slides to the middle of the cavern, and Beastie slams into the left wall.

Ambrose flips over onto his back, scooting backwards. "His—his skin!" he exclaims breathlessly. "It must be protected or something, my fireballs won't do anything!"

"Then don't use fireballs!" I shout, running to grab the fire sword from my original spot. "Use a fire *blast*!"

"Emberly, I think I—" Meredith begins from the entrance, but Ice Beastie's left eye dilates in fury. His maw opens again, unleashing another blinding cloud.

I shut my eyes and cross my arms in front of my face. The blasting cold and prickling ice shards scrape my skin. When it fades into the rest of the cavern, Ice Beastie has disappeared again. My cheeks sting with a thousand tiny scrapes.

The four of us gather in the middle of the cavern. I face the back wall again with Zenevieve on my right. Ambrose is on my other side. Meredith still faces the entrance.

"See it?" she whispers.

"No," Ambrose replies worriedly. He even glances skyward to look for our shy man-eater. Small, red scrapes now accompany his abundant freckles on his pale face. "I only caught him the first time because he opened his eyes!"

Despite her scared blinking, Zenevieve keeps her sword firmly held. Her stern gaze travels all across the space. My hand tightens around the fire sword. I briefly glance at the left wall— no shine this time.

When I look at the right wall, I'm almost offended by the ease: Beastie's now icy-blue foot sticks out amidst the dark ground like Nosy Nelson's nose.

The palace boys can play hide-and-seek better than that. Which is a bold statement: Ramses swears by the notion that if he can't see you from where he is, you can't see him.

"Emberly, listen," Meredith says. "On the beast's chest—"

It's as if Ice Beastie hears her; he opens his eyes from where he stands against the wall. Fading back to his indigo colour, he falls forward on all fours and starts his charge—straight for

Zenevieve on my right side.

Meredith and Ambrose dart back to the entrance, and I skitter backwards to the back wall. Zenevieve unsheathes her dagger and thrusts it at Ice Beastie's head. It only nicks him before bouncing off.

"Bring it here!" Meredith shouts, pushing Ambrose to the left side of the cavern.

"What?!" Zenevieve exclaims, walking the width of the room backwards. That allows me to move to Meredith and Ambrose.

Meredith tries again. "Have it stand, Zenevieve, I know where—!"

"Right! Forgive me for forgetting that I've *tamed* him!"

She holds out Portia in front of her with her right hand and then grabs her mace with her dominant one. When Beastie sets free another roar, Zenevieve hurls the mace into his throat.

A growly hiss abruptly cuts off the roar. Ice Beastie raises a foot and then slams it downwards towards Zenevieve. She barrels out of the way in time, in our direction. That turns the monster to us. He stands for only a second to thrust himself down onto the ground, hacking all the way. His misshapen scales bristle, his body mimicking a vomiting cat.

"Listen!" Meredith snaps, startling me. "I've been trying to explain that there's a lighter patch of skin on the monster's torso, where its heart should be. The artifact must be infused with the only fire that can defeat it! It needs to be thrown into its heart!"

My own skips a beat. I need to commit bloody murder. Literally.

I steady my voice as I exclaim, "Zenevieve, what if—?"

"Throw another fireball!" she shouts at Ambrose, darting to the middle again. "Don't stop, I'll fend him off!"

The worst part is that I can tell she really *didn't* hear me; she was already concocting a plan that involved me throwing this sword into Ice Beastie's heart.

I shouldn't have named him. I thought I learned that lesson when I was nine and found a fatally injured snow dove in the palace courtyard. Meredith warned me not to name her. I can only pray that Serena is in a better place than I am right now.

The monster hacks up Zenevieve's mace. It now lies on the ground, slathered in dripping drool. Not even Beastie has time to marvel at his creation as he focuses on Zenevieve.

Right. We need to escape this frozen death trap. Get to warmth. Safety.

I have to do this. There's no path around that. I regret it with everything I am as Ambrose's largest balls of fire yet fade into existence, accumulating more flames. Zenevieve furiously yet meticulously swipes her sword at the monster. There isn't visible damage on his snout, but he definitely doesn't appreciate her version of hospitality.

He huffs, stands on his hind legs, and shrieks an irritated cry. When he falls forward, another ice cloud billows over the cavern.

Instinct overwhelms my chest. I don't cover my eyes this time; that's the flaw in the beast's plan. As long as I squint, only a few ice shards catch in my lashes. I watch the monster's dark, crinkly form run up to the wall beside me and fade into the colour of the ice walls.

Don't tell me you're asking *for it.*

I tentatively step back as the cloud slows and then fades. My eyes fully open. I start strolling the length of the wall backwards. My stare stays on the monster's camouflaged form.

"I can see you, you overgrown, prissy cat!"

My group instinctively lower their arms, revealing the dozens of red scrapes across their faces. They instantly notice me walking away from them.

I continue before even Meredith can protest: "Fair's fair. I found you fair and square. Come out before I cut off your precious jewels with this thing!"

Perhaps the monster really does understand me; his yellow eye dilates again as he opens it. Fading back to indigo, he steps from the wall and stands on his back legs. The patch of light blue on the right side of his torso is exposed just as Meredith said. Before Ice Beastie can fall, I raise the sword.

"NO!" my group scream.

"You need to time—!" Zenevieve begins.

I throw the sword faster than she can speak.

The blade lunges into the bright-blue patch. The beast roars with every growl in his belly, falling into the wall behind him. An orange glow radiates from the sword. The veining unleashes a yellow-white light that bursts into a flame and crawls to the monster's torso. The rest of him is hungrily engulfed. A bonfire explodes to life before disintegrating into a million ashy specks. Ice Beastie's final cry echoes up to the top of the cavern and towards the sky.

Finally releasing my breath, I drop to my knees. My head is too light to keep me upright. I'm all the more grateful for my gloves as my hands meet the ground in a stun.

My name resonates across the chamber. It's accompanied by metal steps drawing closer to me.

Zenevieve and Meredith take one of my arms and wrap them around their shoulders, forcing me into a hug. Ambrose embraces me from behind.

"You did it, Your Highness!" he chirps.

Reality quickly jolts me awake.

"All right, that's enough," I say, raising my arms to break away from my group. They step back as something clinks against my knee.

I look down and take the fake eye—a ball of ice.

My breath clouds in front of me as I exhale. "I'll rather enjoy this."

I raise the ball, tacitly telling my group to step back more. With my remaining strength, I thrust the ice onto the ground. The sphere shatters like glass. Lying in the middle of its remains is a bronze key the length of my palm. Its elegant head bears a snowflake. One word is engraved at the bottom of it: "vigilance".

What? Is it saying snowflakes are vigilant? Snowark? The stage?

"We found the key!" Ambrose chirps. He gently wipes away the seeping blood from a few of the scrapes on his face.

I take it and stand. "Is that what you call it, Ginger?"

A bright light flashes in the corner of my vision. We turn to the middle of the cavern. Indigo lightning lines the portal that's opened. Another strong pull ignites in me towards it.

"We've unlocked the next stage," Zenevieve says breathlessly, grinning.

I exchange glances with my three groupmates. The open portal emphasises our reality; I'm reminded that we must hurry now more than ever. We've spent far too much time here.

Zenevieve gently wipes at her cheeks as she rushes to the en-trance of the cavern. "Let's hope this was worth it," she says, grabbing our satchels. She trots back to us and hands us our re-spective bags. We turn to the portal.

The same apprehension infects my chest, worsened by the stakes: we've no inkling as to how much progress the other groups have made in the time it took us to complete one stage. There very well could be someone waiting for us on the other side this time.

I turn to my group. "Stay vigilant," I state. "I don't trust any-one in this race for as far as I can throw Rowena."

One thing comforts me as I face the portal: warmth is guar-anteed to be on the other side. That is the only reason I'm first to leap in.

CHAPTER 12

"WE WILL ONLY WARN YOU ONCE"

Leo

REACHING MY FOOT THROUGH THE PORTAL, I MAKE contact with solid ground this time. Had it not been for the underwater cave, I would have forgotten what that felt like after Seavale's underwater stage.

As the rest of my team steps out of the portal, the ground uproots a pungent aroma of earth mixed with stone. Real land is a great relief after the ocean—until I realize that rock and stone surround us now in a narrow tunnel.

It stretches down to what looks like a small opening—but we're standing far back. Too far back.

Back under castle. The passageways—

"Leo?" Sierra asks, resting her hand on my arm. "Are you all right?"

I bite the inside of my lip, staring ahead. "I'm... I'm fine," I say, nodding. "Don't stop, let's—let's continue."

I can pace somewhat in the tunnel, but escape is infinitely better than simply trying to prevent my mind from a whirlwind of debilitating fear. And reminders. It's just like our mission yesterday morning: we have our exit in sight, and no time to waste.

We take our first steps—when voices resonate at the end of the tunnel.

The pounding in my chest intensifies. There is no safe way of predicting if the voices on the other end belong to potential allies or enemies, but anxiety is breeding like fungi throughout my being. My sabatons scrape the dirt along the ground at an excruciatingly slow rate, the stone walls carrying every step down the narrow space. I twinge with every echo, a prayer released from my mind that the people at the end don't prematurely detect us.

I want to race out more than anything. This is tighter than the passageways under the castle. At least, it feels that way. I may only go forward.

At a tortoise's speed.

I take deep breath after deep breath until Sierra and Ezra hold out their arms, barring us from continuing. One step farther and we'll be in the sunlit mouth of the cave—and exposed to the two people in wooden armor arguing on the vibrant grass outside. Wind blows so furiously that I can hear it, pushing back the girl's long, red hair behind her: Princess Cassandra of Soilera. The bottom of a cliff poses as their background, and my mind jumps with curiosity as to where we are now.

Wind. Cliffs. Definitely Windale's stage.

A vibrant, pink streamer stems from the princess's wooden helmet; and the tall young man across from her wears the same helmet with a yellow streamer. Princess Cassandra's cheeks have been stained red and with tears from her narrow, brown eyes. Conversely, anger carves her teammate's sharp features. He towers over her with a long, hooked nose. He's almost as tall as Ezra. Part of me is wary that he might be taller than me.

"This may be a trap," Sierra whispers next to me. "There are only two of them. They may have sent their other mates to hide and ambush us—"

"We have no hope in continuing!" the young man shouts at the princess, tightening his brown hands into fists. His posh accent leaves out many consonants in his speech, requiring me to listen harder over the wind. "I know you want to end it as terribly as I do! Soilera only cares about us if you become the new ruler, anyway!"

"No!" the princess cries firmly. I can't imagine that the wooden armor is comfortable. "They care about the *future*. Of course they care about us when I am the only one who can bring it, and now you're the only one who can help me."

"When will you give up?" he hisses, taking another step toward her. Despite their proximity, both of them have to shout over the wind. "When you watch me die in front of you as well? Because losing Wren and Cyprus on our own stage wasn't enough?"

"Stop!" Princess Cassandra exclaims, shoving her teammate away. "When did you become—?"

She begins to turn, but she turns in the wrong direction and catches the four of us in the mouth of the cave.

Truly, it was a brilliant idea to keep everyone standing here without a plan.

Regret stuns my chest as the princess's brown eyes widen, drawing the matching stare of her teammate.

I don't spare a second for a reaction and step into the sunlight. We stand in a small field no wider than fifty feet. Stone cliffs tower over us, the tallest of them so high that even Ezra is an ant in comparison.

At least a fear of heights won't be an issue.

I hold up my hands in surrender. "You've already lost two people?"

The princess and her teammate don't answer, but their scowls harden on me.

I tentatively step forward. "Your Highness, we're not here to hurt you, really," I say, adjusting my voice to the wind. "If your first stage was anything like ours, then it'll be easier to do this together. A group is safer than a duo. Right?"

The young man seems to forget his anger—at least, that it was directed at the princess—as he steps in front of her and reaches an arm out to protect her. In perfect honesty, every muscle in my body is fighting not to laugh at the wooden armor.

You're not lasting long in that. At least let us give you a chance at surviving this.

"We will only warn you once," he replies with a strong voice. "Let us continue in peace. Only then will we let you live."

Ezra steps up to my side, his right hand resting on the golden pommel of his sword. "His Highness has offered you a chance at survival," he says, matching his firmness. Unlike the rest of us, the wind carries his voice all across the terrain. "Prince Leon is above bluffing."

Well—now that's true.

Princess Cassandra snickers, lowering the young man's arm in front of her. "Really, now? The prince who spent his entire youth conducting childish pranks is above *bluffing?*"

I swallow hard, my fists instinctively clenching. How had Soilera heard about that? Why had that spread beyond Seavale's borders?

Ithinor steps into the daylight, wind blowing his black curls aside. "He is also the prince that led his army to victory against Lavara when they attempted to invade Seavale. You'll do well to respect a leader of his capability."

His words seem to take root: the two in front of us still, eyeing me with caution now as if they remember.

No, I don't want them to be afraid of me. I want them to believe me.

"I do not want to harm you," I repeat, taking another wary step with my hands still raised. "All I'm offering is to join together to create a stronger team. We can help each other and increase our chances of survival if—"

"You think us so foolish?" Cassandra exclaims, stepping past her teammate. The wind seems to increase with her voice. "I've lost *everything* to this blasted curse, and you think I'll throw away what crumbs I have left to a prince willing to sabotage his own kingdom? Dorian and I have sworn on our lives that we will either win this race or die trying—but I refuse to die by the hands of someone else, let alone a royal *jester* who thinks he's competent enough to fool me! My death will either be by my own hands or these *wretched* stages!"

She unsheathes her sword, and Dorian's hands bend into claws that he raises into the air. Roots shoot out from the dirt at his command. Cassandra's brown eyes lock on me. When she advances, Sierra grabs her own sword and charges for her.

Ezra and I lunge to the side as the two battle in the mouth of the cave. We refuse to fight a woman under any circumstances, but that rule starts to grow loose as I consider the rage Cassandra is swinging her sword with.

If you harm Sierra—!

An orange glow illuminates from where Ithinor stands, stealing my attention. He's conjured fire from his fingers and is streaming them at the thick roots Dorian is thrusting at him.

Ezra locks his icy-blue eyes with me as I slightly look up at him: His message is transparent: Ithinor may need help if the wind grows stronger and throws his fires askew.

Ezra unsheathes his sword faster than a lightning strike and storms toward Dorian in the middle of the field. The cliffs have us surrounded on all fronts, but the arena provides enough space for a fight.

Of course it does.

I grab my bow and an arrow from my quiver. My right eye aligns the arrowhead with Dorian's side as he continues growing root after root. Ithinor only disintegrates them with his fire, refusing harm toward him.

Dorian turns, noticing Ezra dashing to him like a gust of wind. The roots drop halfway to Ithinor, who immediately extinguishes his flames. Ezra more than knows how to cut through the wooden armor and run his sword straight through Dorian, but he doesn't. Instead, he uses the face of the blade to shove him back, pushing him to the ground. Ithinor conjures two fires and makes his way to Dorian. Ezra points the tip of his sword at his throat.

I can't fight the princess, and Ithinor and Ezra are managing Dorian on their own—but I can't do nothing!

The sound of clashing steel ceases, and I move my arrow to the mouth of the cave: Sierra is on her back and using her sword as a barrier between her and Cassandra.

I don't have to kill her—just protect Sierra.

"Careful, Princess!" I call, gaining her narrow eyes. They widen upon finding my drawn arrow. "I'd consider your next move *very* carefully."

Sierra kicks off Cassandra while she's distracted, jumping to her feet and holding her sword in front of her. Cassandra tries to bring herself up as Sierra maintains her distance.

Dirt and rock fly from where Ezra, Ithinor, and Dorian battle. My arrow instinctually moves back to them, a wave of hot panic flooding me. The ground has erupted from under Ezra and Ithinor, throwing them to the feet of the cliffs on either side.

My chest halts, my bow lowering as I start running to them. Dorian stands, and protective instinct surges through me: I launch my arrow. It strikes the ground at his feet, his eyes snapping to mine as I step toward the three of them.

"You don't have to do this," I call, nocking another arrow. "Stop fighting us and let us—!"

"Dorian!" Cassandra calls with strain, her blade deadlocked with Sierra's. "The boulders!"

Dorian ignores me and focuses on Ithinor. His hand glows with white magic, rises into the air, and then lunges in his direction. A small boulder next to Ezra flies toward Ithinor.

My fingers instinctually loosen around my arrow. "Ithinor—!"

The arrow launches itself into Dorian's arm as Ithinor sits up against the wall. Dorian shouts in pain. I don't know where to look as Ithinor throws his glowing-white hands forward. The boulder stops just in front of him.

My heart thrums louder in my head. I don't have the time to process that I've accidentally shot Cassandra's mage as he rips out the arrow from his arm and Ezra stands. Dorian tries again with another boulder, this time with one hand. Ithinor clenches his glowing-red fist, shattering the boulder to bits.

I sigh shakily, the thoughts barreling my mind. *Ithinor is safe. I only incapacitated Dorian, it's all right.*

I grab another arrow, but I won't be able to shoot it. One more arrow and I'll be his murderer.

If we can just convince them that we don't have to kill each other—

Ithinor raises green hands into the air. Grass explodes from the ground around Dorian, long blades wrapping around his hands in a tight hold. He forces one hand free, rage carving his sharp features. Then his hand, glowing white again, rises into the air.

Instinct swarms my chest, warning me. Something rumbles on the left side of my vision: a three-foot–tall boulder sitting on a high ledge next to the cave entrance. Dorian forces his other hand free of Ithinor's grass, raising it and the boulder into the air—

Ezra's sword slides straight through Dorian from behind before I can blink.

Dorian drops with another gust of wind. The bolder crashes straight through the ledge and into the ground. I lower my arrow.

Part of me can't resist the relief I feel.

Ezra, Ithinor, and I exchange each other's exhausted, staggered gazes. The other part of me can't resist the disappointment.

Why couldn't he have just—?

Two screams curdle the air. When I look over at the cave, Sierra is holding her side as Cassandra slams into the rock wall. The princess's eyes shut when her head impacts it. She falls to the ground on her stomach.

What knocks every sensation and thought out of me is when a boulder on a high ledge falls and lands on her back.

Holy mother of the Ancient Mages.

Reality around me feels distorted. I have to question if it is even real. The sounds. The scene. Even the people. I question if I am really standing on the dirt right now surrounded by cliffs and howling wind. If I'm having a nightmare. If my friends are really here or if my mind has put them here as a means of comfort.

But reality tightens its hold on me, and my gaze catches Sierra in time. Her hand, a crimson shadow underneath it, still presses her side. She falls to her knees.

I run. "Sierra!"

I kneel beside her and hold her head up, my heart throbbing in my throat. "Don't do this, don't you dare, I will never forgive you!"

Ithinor stumbles into the mouth of the cave as Ezra drops to her other side, placing an arm under her back and grabbing her hand. His usually deep, sonorous voice is filled with tears as he cries, "No, lily, you can't let this take you! Please!"

I glimpse him. It is the first time in the four years I've known him that I see his eyes glisten.

"Lily"?

"You—idiots," Sierra whispers with a strained smile. Her gasps are slow and shallow. "You have to—dress it—before I die."

The words leave a bitter, sour taste in my mouth. My brows contort in anger that she'd even think to speak them.

"We will," Ithinor assures as steadily as ever, kneeling beside Ezra. The solemnity in his usually vibrant eyes is all that tells me that even he feels the weight of the situation. "You don't need to worry, I promise—"

I don't think she hears him; her eyes silently roll to the back of her head, which grows heavy and limp in my hand.

CHAPTER 13

"THE SUN SEEKS MY LIFE"

Emberly

MY ONLY THOUGHT AS WE SPRING INTO THE PORTAL is that warmth is guaranteed to be on the other side of it.

"Warmth" is more than right.

I fall into another soft pile just as on Snowark's stage. This one, however, is made of coarse, hot granules. I can't decide which I despise more: both snow and sand burn the longer I stay in their clutches.

Sand. I definitely despise sand more. At least snow melts no matter where it wedges itself in your crevices. Sand is a prickly little irritant that's more stubborn than Stupid Samson. Unfortunately, when I stand, it is the only thing that surrounds us. The sun is positioned too closely to us in the boundless, blue sky. Rolling sandhills stretch for countless discouraging kilometres on all sides.

I don't know which is worse: Lavara's arrogant tool of a prince, or their stage.

The bitter cold of the ice cavern melts away into the searing-hot atmosphere. I dust off the granules from my hands, wobbling as I stand. The sun's rays burn into my back, straight through my cloak and armour.

"Who unsheathed the sun?" I exclaim, unclasping my cloak. I look at Ambrose, who is still in Meredith's spare set of clothes. He's already taken off his two cloaks. "Ginger, you cheeky little berry of luck. No armour to bake you alive. Here."

I ball up my cloak and throw it at him. The lanky stick is startled and yelps, throwing a fireball at it. His flames swallow the fabric whole and leave behind black ashes.

I shrug. "That works as well."

"Emberly," Meredith states. The shifting sand dunes are powerful enough to make even her stagger. "You don't know if you'll need that for another stage!"

I roll my eyes. "The stages are themed, and no kingdom is even *as* cold as Snowark." The heat elicits a sting from each of the scrapes on my face from Ice Beastie's breath. My mind reels at the fact that we were suffering the threat of freezing to death just seconds ago. Now I'm tempted to say that Ambrose's fire is colder than this stage.

I raise a hand to block the sun's scrutinizing beams. "Poor Ice Beastie. Now I know how he feels—felt."

"Right, let's not stay here for longer than we must," Zenny remarks, wiping the back of her forehead. "Spare us if you would, Your Highness; and tell us where the next artifact is."

Before I can shove her, I realise the pull. Sighing, I turn in its direction—whichever direction that is.

How are we meant to move quickly in this heat? Amidst our exhaustion from the excruciatingly little sleep we received last night, at that?

We move forward nonetheless. It's quickly proven that walking in sand is much more dismal than walking in fresh snow; there is no solid ground to meet our steps. Meredith and Zenevieve supervise our water intake. Meredith says that rationing in regular intervals is how our bodies will absorb the water instead of "processing it straight through". Complaining about the sun is one of two methods I have of coping: teasing Ambrose only provides so much entertainment before the heat draws out every last ounce of strength. Eventually, it takes our voices up to the sun to offer them as a sacrifice.

I don't know how much later, Ambrose yelps behind me. My knees buckle underneath me before I can turn around. Disappointment barrels into my chest upon feeling the weight of my waterskin and remembering that the warm water has already been sucked dry.

Zenevieve comes to my side and offers hers. "That's it—drink, now."

"No," I say, pushing it away, "you need that, too."

"Needless to say, Ember, you're a *lot* paler than I am," she replies dully, raising a black brow at me. "I have short hair, a greater adaptability to the sun, and the endurance training for unideal conditions. The least you should do for yourself is stay hydrated."

I roll my eyes and push away her water again. *You deserve it more, too*, is what I truly want to tell her.

"Let's rest," Meredith calls breathily. "We've no choice. They're both exhausted from the heat, Zenevieve. Pushing ourselves past our limits in these conditions is a death sentence."

"I agree." Zenny returns judgmental, black eyes to me. "Hence the necessity of *water*."

"Who needs real parents when I have you?" I exhale as I fall back in the sand. My bow and quiver on my back make my "rest" further uncomfortable. I'm already bereft of energy due to the lack of sleep last night and fighting a man-eating beast immediately after.

I raise my hand to shield my eyes from the sun. Zenevieve leaves my side to offer Ambrose her drink. "I'm swimming in my suit. Whose brilliant idea was it to establish a kingdom under these conditions?"

"Lavara's," Meredith answers simply, coming to sit by my head.

"I knew I should have punched His Royal Dunce-ness when I had the chance," I mutter.

She slaps my shoulder with the back of her hand. It retracts quickly upon making contact with the hot metal.

"That should teach you for next time," I tell her cheekily.

"Emberly," she whispers. She narrows her hazel eyes at me. "Don't be a brat."

I open my mouth before silencing myself. She reins me in yet again with that.

A foreign silence passes between us. Something feels lacking in our group. I finally remember that I'm not the only pale member.

"Zenny," I call, turning my head to avoid direct sunlight. "Give Ginger a nudge. I think he's dead."

"Would you at least pretend your grief if that were so?" Meredith asks, horrified.

"Rosy," Zenevieve asks behind me nonetheless, "are you doing all right?"

"The sun..." he answers in a scratchy voice. "The sun is evil, Zenevieve. The sun seeks my life."

"So dramatic," I whisper.

"You're one to talk, fire head!" he calls back breathlessly as Meredith slaps my shoulder again.

I scoff. "But *that*, you've strength for?"

Zenevieve groans. "Quit it. Ambrose, don't you have an ice spell of sorts?"

"Y—yes," he replies, panting. "But... I could destroy the waterskin..."

"Maybe that will be more helpful," she says, exhaling. "We'll find a way to put the ice to good use."

What happens next is a blur that my brain is too melted to process. Then, the soul-reviving crunch of ice reaches my ears.

I sit up and turn around. Ambrose is breaking off chunks of ice from his waterskin.

His thin lips are spread in a tooth grin. "Care for a snack?"

Excited adrenaline courses through me and grants me the strength to crawl messily through the sand. Zenevieve hands me the frozen waterskin. I bite off a piece. A cold so startling that it burns awakens the senses of my mouth and threatens to freeze my throat as it slides down. Cold stretches down the centre of my being, cutting my torso in half as it lands in my stomach.

I sigh with content and relief. "Bless you, Ginger. Have I ever told you that you're my favourite?"

"The heat must be causing you to hallucinate," Zenevieve remarks, arching a sceptical brow.

"We may be thankful that we've a source of cold water." Meredith smiles triumphantly. "As long as Ambrose can manage to only freeze the outside and not the waterskin itself."

The rest replenishes enough energy to start walking minutes later. Ginger continues sharing ice from his waterskin. Meredith must monitor him carefully: repeating the spell further threatens his stamina, and he's broken her trust in him after yesterday.

When the heat starts to alleviate, we finally stop again. The sun has moved to the other side of the sky.

Meredith allows us to set up camp shortly after. She permits Ambrose to turn his waterskin into the fuel necessary for a miniature ice storm that radiates a cold air. He can only maintain it if he stays in one place and his concentration is fixed solely on it. He must constantly feed it magic without over-exhausting himself again.

We each have a hearty meal of an orange and oat bar. Zenevieve has to handfeed Ambrose his supper. That's a source of laughter for her, and Ginger whines because he needs to concentrate. His narrowed, focused eyes and pursed lips as he takes each bite from her does provide quite the entertainment.

"I've yet to say anything," Meredith begins, taking her last bite of orange. Her sweat has overwhelmed her dark-brown bun. It binds the side strands to her face and causes it to droop. Still, she maintains her elegant authority. "But you've all done exceptionally well so far despite our mistakes. These have already been some of the most trying times we've faced in a while, but the teamwork you've shown is admirable. Truthfully, I see us crossing the finish line to the Last Kingdom."

This is a foreign side to her, physically and personality-wise: praise intertwined with encouragement without a suggestion for improvement. Her words almost feel like another test of the stage.

"I won't say anything of that yet," Zenevieve replies cautiously across from her, "but I'm glad to be stuck with you lot. And should Emberly cross the finish line, the Last Kingdom will have a great ruler."

"I'll be the greatest stable-girl of the land," I say in a heightened voice, reaching my hands out to the pile of ice. "You're too kind."

Meredith and Zenevieve roll their eyes. Ambrose remains quiet. It's a strange difference.

I turn my hands over. Cool relief coats my skin in an unfamiliar stinging sensation that startles me. I pull my hands away.

"What's the matter?" Zenevieve asks.

The top of my hands radiates a heat so intense that I can feel it even against the desert atmosphere. Most noticeably, though, they sting. They sting like a winter wasp. Even the dozens of scrapes across my face prick me even more.

"What's this?" I whisper in irritation. In what daylight remains, my hands are no longer white, but red. A tomato red.

Meredith gently takes my hand into hers, inspecting it. Her brows furrow in concern. "A sunburn," she notes. "We need palm seed oil."

"Rosy?" Zenevieve turns to him. She presses the back of her

hand against his startlingly red cheek.

"Ow!" he yelps, squirming away from her.

The winds of the ice in front of us instantly dissipate. Ambrose's eyes widen as he whispers, "No, no, no, no, no!" He scrambles back to the pile, his hands dancing in a melodic motion to revive the small storm.

"I'm sorry," Zenevieve says remorsefully, holding her hand that harmed him.

He only nods in acknowledgment, trapped again in his focus.

Meredith verifies that she's only mildly burned. Even Zenny has fallen victim to the devil sun, but she has the best case out of all of us. We all need palm seed oil—except we're in the desert. And palm plants don't grow in the sand.

Of course the only plant that can treat a sunburn doesn't grow where the sun shines the most. Cursed Lavara.

We draw even closer to the ice. According to Meredith, gently cooling where we're burned is the best treatment we have right now.

"They're certainly trying to weed out the runts," I say. "Don't you think that's a sign to go home?"

"I don't think it works that way," Zenevieve replies, as if she is genuinely considering my words. "Even if it did, no. You truly must be the ruler if that's the case."

I dully stare back at her.

She kisses her teeth and rolls her eyes. "*No one* has your persistence. What other ruler would tolerate Winston and his merrymen to the extent that you do solely for the sake of protecting her people, and with such resolve?"

I restrain a swallow. She doesn't understand why I have to. Yes, I willingly protect the people of Snowark—but enduring the councilmen is practically a clause in the contract of my curse. Zenevieve doesn't understand how tight their chains around me truly are.

Ambrose hums as though he's about to say something. Then, he seems to remember that his concentration must be kept on his storm.

"The councilmen do often speak of your tenacity," Meredith adds. "Of course, it's always meant negatively, but they find your refusal to adhere to their guidance... stubborn, to say the least."

"Guidance"—such as when they forced me three years ago to pass the increase of taxes to keep the royal treasury afloat so that the palace would be able to "rule properly in a time of hardship". I've fought an uphill war with them trying to alleviate the effects of that ever since.

"Interesting." I cock my brows. "A queen who won't follow the rules. Truly a strong foundation to build a kingdom off of."

Zenevieve groans, shoving me. "It means you don't let anyone push you around, prat. They only disagree with you because your solutions come from you and not any of their cult brothers."

"And what if they're right, Zenevieve? If my people are only following me because the law says they must?" I surprise myself with the sharpness of my voice—but that has always been one of my biggest fears no matter how patient the people have been with my rule. "What kind of a princess is harassed by her own royal council? What proof do you have that I'm anything more than a disobedient puppet in that palace?"

"Stop it, quit saying that!"

The three of us jump, our eyes pulled to Ambrose. He somehow maintains his ice storm—even as he scowls at me.

Did the little strawberry just snap? At me?

"I'm... I'm sorry, Emberly," he states, "but that's what the council says, and you know how much I disagree with it. I can't stand it all the more when you say them, too. You let those—rats win every time you do. I mean, yes, you're temperamental, you're cynical, sometimes you're outright rude—"

"Is this speech meant to *encourage* me?" I sneer, narrowing my eyes. "If that's what you so fervently believe, why does it bother you when I confess that about myself?"

"Because—" The boy struggles with his words, the ice briefly stealing his attention. Even when he finds his sentence, he refuses to match any of our eyes again. "Because then you let the council convince you that those things are weaknesses... but I think they're what make you a good ruler."

When I don't reply, he dares to look up. Despite the timidity in his gaze, somehow the boy has me sitting still in my spot like a child being reprimanded. Then I realise that that is exactly how I feel: like a child.

"What are you talking about?" I force myself to ask.

He shrugs smally. "I've always told you: you're an instinctual ruler. You know what to do because you know what you rule over, like when you wanted to prevent development in the Dagger Woods and they wouldn't listen."

My mind traces back to the memory. The first time Ambrose ever heard me lose my temper in front of the councilmen. The first time he ever told me that he thought I was a good princess.

"Not some clueless puppet."

"I think you don't like it when someone else is involved in Snowarkan matters because you sense that they don't know what's right for Snowark as you do," he says next. "That's why you're so disrespectful to the councilmen. You can read a situation and act on it properly. Just like with their ridiculous suggestions, and like when I fell into the lake and you cut off my robes. You know what to do, Emberly, no matter what they tell you. I think you could do with a lesson or ten in manners, but you've the grounds for a great ruler. I know we three think that. I'm tired of the council getting in the way of *you* thinking that."

The desert's silence echoes in my ears when he finishes. I question if I really have begun to hallucinate because of the heat.

"Where did that come from, Rosy?" Zenevieve whispers, eyes baffled.

I only catch the beginning of their conversation—Ambrose's denial to answer, which Zenevieve rejects—when Meredith speaks next to me.

"I believe," she whispers, "that that is the only scolding you've ever received that you *haven't* fought against."

I stare at the lanky boy in front of me as he engages with my best friend. Part of me wants to accept his words solely to satiate him. The other part refuses to accept that someone who killed her parents and will cause the death of her husband when she bears an heir can be a good ruler.

Fine. I don't allow myself to fully step into my role as a leader. But do I not even have control over that? Is Ambrose right in that governing is instinctual for me? Do I somehow *know* what to do?

If I do, it's Meredith's fault. Curse her hours of lessons and mentoring.

I sink in my spot. No. It's not her fault. Despite my opposition, she hasn't given up on me and left after realizing how intolerable I am. I suppose part of me still expects that she will. I don't want to suffer the same loss I did when I was eight by fully trusting in the promise of her presence...

She's already lasted longer with me than my parents' advisor. But I'm scared to make it easier for her to teach me if there's a chance she'll leave.

What if she doesn't?

The thought arrives before I can realise it was even forming. I've conditioned myself my entire time with her to believe otherwise; why have I begun doubting what I know now?

"*A lesson or ten in manners*". Meredith has given me her fair share of the same message over the years. And yet, I still allow myself instances like ignoring her wisdom or even snickering when she burned herself on my armour...

Pride and shame clash in my chest. I can't afford her eyes; mine remain on my hands as I whisper, "I'm sorry."

For a couple of seconds, Zenevieve's and Ambrose's whispers are all I can hear. Then, a gentle hand pushes my hair behind my ear. I look up. Meredith smiles at me with invitation.

"It's all right," she tells me. "You're learning."

My swallow is tight. She forgives me. I'm still surprised that she's accepted me again.

No—I can do this. Instead of being the reason she leaves, I can be the reason she stays. I'll show her that doing so isn't in vain; her efforts will bear at least some fruit.

Zenevieve gently shoves Ambrose, his focus hardening on the ice storm. "You're certainly getting braver," she whispers with a soft smile across her full lips.

"While we're sitting here," Meredith begins curiously, leaning towards me, "what of the artifact's pull, Emberly?"

Resistance pulls against it in my chest; this is the last discussion I'd like to have after our previous one about my leadership.

"Stronger than it was when we first entered." I move the tops of my hands closer to the cool winds in front of me. "Let's pray Ice Beastie doesn't have a long-distance relative."

"Are you able to compare—?"

"I don't want—" I state, harsher than I intended. Upon meeting Meredith's eyes, I humble myself under them and calm my tone. "I'd like to rest more before having this conversation."

First lesson in manners achieved: Meredith simply nods.

I chew on my cheek, wishing that I could tell her to stop asking about it—and so frequently, at that. And that makes me consider if Ambrose was right, after all: perhaps I hate Meredith constantly supervising me because I do know what to do. My instinct leads me just fine. I can lead us to the artifact if they trust me...

I swallow again. That is a terrifying thought—because I can also lead them to their demise.

We've yet to see any creatures or beasts, humans or otherwise; nonetheless, we take watch shifts again throughout the night because we're now out of our element. Literally. Any and all life-threatening surprises are on the table.

Sleeping on the sand is more abysmal than my greatest nightmare; I know because that blasted nightmare from that night in Vineah with Zenevieve visits me again. It must be this cursed race, the fact that I'm running against Vineah, that prompted it—it usually waits a few months. Thankfully, Meredith woke me up from it for my watch shift; I was awake enough to actually carry it out.

Today is no better than yesterday by any means except for the fact that we've Ambrose's ice for refreshment. Even worse, I have to put my gloves back on to protect my hands from further burning.

The sun is almost straight up in the sky when Zenevieve calls, "There!" Sweat drips from her face as she points at a grove of trees in the distance. "A... Oh, Meredith, what is that called?"

Meredith grins, following Zenny's finger. "An oasis! There should be good water—"

"Then hurry!" I shout. My eagerness lends me energy I know isn't really there. With sweat pouring down my body, I kick up the sand as I sprint up the sandhill regardless of my weapons and armour. The draw of the artifact strengthens. It rests in the oasis. I know that more and more as I reach the peak—

Two long, slender figures stick out of something black at the bottom of the hill. My group slow behind me as we walk down and approach: swords. Lavara's crest is branded on the pommels. Two black-armoured, rancid-smelling bodies are the sheaths.

"I know these men," I catch myself saying. I remember seeing them behind Amon on the platform. One of the bodies is long and buff. The other has only a thin chest plate; he was clearly undervalued as a teammate. Evidently, they both were.

I nod to myself. "Amon's knight and advisor."

"Emberly," Meredith begins warily, "if they've been killed by Lavara's swords—"

"Amon and his mage murdered their own teammates," I say.

Ambrose holds his—or, rather, Meredith's—shirt over his nose. His round, brown eyes widen. "Why would they kill their own teammates? Even their knight!"

"The prince is a prideful wart on the face of his kingdom." I try to keep my breath to a minimum as I speak. "He likely figured he didn't need his advisor and his mage can provide any protection he needs—and from a distance. Too many people on his team would slow him down and consume valuable resources."

Meredith and Zenevieve nod. Ambrose, on the other hand, stares with stun. "H—how do you know—?"

"I was graciously blessed with the privilege of meeting His Royal Idiocy at the beginning of this, remember?"

Not even Meredith scolds me this time. I take that as further encouragement, wiping the salty sweat from my upper lip. "I wouldn't put this past him for a single second."

Our eyes fall back onto the bodies. The sun's rays increase their heat and the stench the longer we stay still.

Zenevieve's words anchor my feet to the dunes: "Then it's possible for two teams to be on the same stage…"

I don't turn my head to meet her eyes. The words are loud before she even speaks them: "These men could have been us last night."

My body stiffens. I put the oasis in my line of sight. *This truly is a* race.

A race to ultimate sovereignty. No—I cannot allow anyone

who possesses this capability to become the ruler of the Last Kingdom. Not with Snowark on the line. I despise to admit it, but even I would be a greater choice than Amon. And Luciana. That means I only have two options: the fate of Amon's men, or finishing this race.

If only the decision weren't so easy.

The searing sun threatens to overwhelm us if we stay for any longer than necessary; we quickly proceed to the oasis.

I cannot end up that way. I can't allow any of them to end up that way. We need to hurry.

Arriving at the bank, the water compels me forward almost as strongly as the artifact. It's so clear that I can see something resting in the middle of the oasis: an arrow.

My heart skips a triumphant beat. Impulse courses through me as I go to step into the water.

Meredith shouts my name in a scold. "Don't adulterate the water!" she calls breathlessly. "Fill your waterskin first, give yourself as much as you can carry."

"And then we really ought to bathe." Zenevieve's voice follows in pants as she arrives at my side. "We haven't had the opportunity since the morning we left. We're on the third day—"

"It's been *three* days?" I exclaim. "No wonder I'm sticking like Ambrose to a bucket of flat cake syrup."

"Drink, fill your waterskins," Meredith urges gently again, ignoring me, "and then bathe. Quickly."

At least Zenevieve doesn't say she told me so after I criticised her for bringing soap.

The water is impossibly cold for its atmosphere. That makes it all the more of an excruciating wait for Meredith's approval for me to grab the artifact. After all, we've no intimation as to if another group will sneak up on us as we take turns in the oasis. I wonder if this is the same water Lavara bathed in or stepped into, or if the stage somehow managed to reset for us.

I deny myself any further thought on it; I'll throw up more than just the water I've already drunk. Surely the water wouldn't be so crystal clear if that were the case...

I'm last to change into my spare set of clothes. Only then does Meredith allow me to go after the artifact. I cringe with each step in the water, all too mindful of the dirt and sweat mixed into it now. All the more reason to pump my legs harder to reach the middle of the pool faster.

I hold my breath as I bend down and grab the arrow. The cold water comes up to my shoulders as I wrap my fingers around the white, wooden shaft.

I bring up the arrow and instantly notice the stone head that gleams in the sunlight: it's covered in ice. White wisps of air swirl around the fletching. It's as though ice itself is infused into the arrow; even the wood is cold to the touch.

I turn around to face my group. "I've got it—"

Waves slosh all around me, the trees of the oasis shaking. I lose my balance and fall back into the filthy water. I don't have the capacity to worry about that: with one glance at my groupmates at the bank, I'm not the only one feeling the world rattle. Ambrose has fallen onto his bottom in the sand, and Zenevieve scarcely keeps her balance as she helps him stand.

"Emberly!" Meredith calls, refusing another step forward.

I dart out of the water, running with her as the ground rumbles. The sound of gushing water soon follows. I turn around as we fumble through the sand: water and sand fall into an expanding hole in the middle of the oasis. The round top of what looks like a dark-grey volcano starts to emerge.

I freeze. The artifact—the volcano was only unlocked once I grabbed it. If Ice Beastie came after I took the fire sword, then this arrow must have something to do with the volcano. It has to: the main obstacle of the stage has been unlocked.

But a volcano is only accessible through the top...

My mind runs faster than a rabbit's heartbeat: *I can either suffer the entire climb up, or close my eyes and be brought up.* I won't be able to get around the main obstacle, and I'll have to stand at the top either way. I need to make this decision now.

My stomach churns, heart rising into my throat. Before I can change my mind, I run towards the emerging volcano.

My group shout my name. I don't hear anyone following me as I sprint; that makes it all the more difficult to disobey their pleas to stop. My stamina and balance ignore the resistance of the sand that crumbles under my steps. I grab onto the first ledge I see and secure my feet as the volcano continues to rise.

I don't look behind me or beneath me. I can only pray that my group grabbed on after me and joined me in the ascent to the sky.

CHAPTER 14

"COME ON UP"

Leo

SIERRA LIES MOTIONLESS IN MY LAP IN THE ENTRANCE of the cave. Regret and fear rack my chest, and even Ezra is furiously holding back tears in front of me. Desperate prayer after desperate prayer is sent from my mind as Ithinor streams a green flow of magic into Sierra's exposed gash on the side of her stomach. With every passing second, less and less blood pours from her wound. Soon, it dries around her skin; and there only remains a dark-crimson line. I try to resist my distress as she stays asleep; I know she wouldn't wake up immediately. I must give her time, but every second is one that she could cross the line between life and death and leave us—leave me alone— here.

"All right..." Ithinor says breathlessly, exhaling from effort as he slouches. "I accelerated her healing to help the blood clot and protect the wound. It isn't quite as deep as I feared. As long as my magic reached her in time... she should be all right."

My relief is tentative. "When will she wake up?" I ask.

"At least a few minutes," Ithinor replies flatly. "I focused on preventing her from losing more blood. How long she stays unconscious depends on if she passed out from blood loss or shock—or even both."

I look back down at Sierra. Stray chestnut strands from her bun stick to the sides of her pale face. My memory replays the battle Soilera started with us, the gruesome deaths the princess and her mage suffered... how close my best friend was to the same fate.

"I should continue healing her," Ithinor says, his breath heavy. "Once I rest."

"Thank you, Ithinor," Ezra replies with a raspy voice. "Really."

His startlingly blue eyes are dedicated to Sierra's peaceful face. A shiny stream runs all the way down his dark cheek. Each passing minute reminds me of how little time we really have in this race...

Morale is half the war, and Ezra and Sierra bring each other a happiness only the other can. And if they permanently lose the chance to tell each other that... they may regret it to a perilous extent.

"Tell her," I tell Ezra minutes of silence later. "You need to be honest with her before you lose her for good and never have the chance to."

What I can only hope is regret flashes across his face as he licks his lips. "You don't understand, Leo," he whispers. Ithinor listens intently beside him as he continues resting. "I value what we already have. I'd protect it with everything I have. If I tell her, it will permanently alter how she perceives me. I never want her to look at me and think that she can't talk to me because I'll allow my feelings for her to blind my judgment. I want her to always see me as safe. I want to keep her in my life for as long as I can."

"She won't trust you if she can tell you're hiding something from her," Ithinor says between slowing breaths.

Even he notices what's between them.

"Or if she reciprocates," I add, "which she does, and you only ever dance around it. Did you not see the look on her face after she gave you a new bubble?"

Ezra's eyes waver from mine briefly as though he's too ashamed to recall the memory.

I rest my hand on Sierra's shoulder, sighing. "I don't want either of you regretting what you never have the chance to—"

Sierra stirs underneath me, a grunt rumbling from her throat. My eyes dart down to hers, which are squeezed shut as she awakens. A moan of pain erupts from her lips; and she winces, bringing her hand to her side.

Ithinor gently moves it away. "No, no, your wound still needs to heal."

"Wow, this hurts." She hisses in a breath, her voice groggy. "Is... is that wench—really dead?"

A tense silence falls over us. We three glimpse each other, the memory swarming my mind again.

"Both of them," I reply, rubbing Sierra's shoulder. Reality barrels into me as I say, "And now we know that teams can be on one stage simultaneously..."

She receives my unspoken message of needing to hurry, and nods solemnly. Her green eyes move to Ithinor. "Thank you for healing me."

He exhales. "Of course."

"Are you all right?" I ask him carefully, noting the heaviness in his eyes.

He nods. "Just about. Healing is the most demanding magic—still, I'd like to give Sierra one more treatment before we continue."

She nods, verifying that she needs it; and he ignites his magic again.

"Leo," she Ezra goes to stand guard at the entrance, ever the surveyor. I refuse to leave Sierra or Ithinor; I won't deprive them of the rest they need, but that doesn't prevent the protective instinct protesting sitting here after what just happened. As though the two bodies lying dead on the field are ready to rise up again. But we can't have half of our team incapacitated by exhaustion in case another does arrive—that is why I wait.

The minutes are long and tense, but eventually Sierra and Ithinor agree that they're ready to continue. The four of us finally step back onto the windy field.

Cassandra lies under the boulder that crushed her on our right. To our left is Dorian, face-up in the grass. The blades furiously blow over him in the wind. I can't see the blood on his chest nor on his arm, where I accidentally struck him with my arrow. I'm thankful for that. My mind may fall with them if I focus on them.

We've eliminated an entire kingdom from the race.

The realization drops onto my chest like an anchor. Does

that mean that we've eliminated an entire kingdom from the face of the world...?

This is worse than the royal treasury. Even worse than when I almost killed Ithinor. This is—

I force my thoughts away from the princess and her mage, from the entire kingdom of Soilera. If I think about any of it, I will take myself out of the race, too.

Focus on Seavale. The people with you.

"Do you feel another pull, Leo?" Ezra asks as Ithinor begins treating Sierra again. He needs to raise his strong voice over the howling wind, his gaze landing on the towering cliffs on all fronts. As if he's trying to block out the reality on either side of us, too. I think we all realize what acknowledging it will do to our minds. We will not have defended ourselves in vain.

I completely forgot about that. Amidst the battle and then Sierra's injury, the artifact blatantly slipped my mind. But now...

I turn around to face the cliffs behind me, looking up. I take a tight breath in. It's up. Sierra can't climb the cliffs in her condition, even with Ithinor healing her right now—but staying longer than we must is not an option.

I point up, shouting, "It's somewhere up there—I think on that middle ledge..."

My chest tightens at the fact: someone has to climb up to grab it. As much as I regret it, I am our least risky option; Sierra and Ithinor are out of the question. Ezra may be stronger, but he doesn't have over a decade of ship-shroud climbing experience as I do. I'm familiar with the right technique. I may not have as much strength, but I have enough...

"Leo?" Sierra calls warily, arching a brow at me. "What are

you thinking?"

We don't have another choice.

I turn to Ithinor. "Icky—will you catch me if I fall?"

His eyes widen with the rest of my teammates', his green magic disintegrating.

"You're not climbing that," Sierra shouts, almost in a matter that I think my mother would have. "Ezra is the strongest—"

I explain my thought process to them. By the end of it, the three glimpse each other in what looks like an even mixture of defeat—and doubt.

Ithinor takes a deep breath, continuing his healing magic on Sierra. "I don't like the idea, Leon. The risks are—"

"It's our only option," I tell him. "Just like with the whale."

Not even the wind is louder than the quiet that follows.

His face remains stolid, despite Ezra's and Sierra's skeptical gazes, as he tells me, "All right. I'll do my best to catch you if it comes to that—but you will listen to Ezra in case he *is* able to provide wisdom."

I nod. I know better than to allow my pride right now; I weigh more than the boulder Ithinor had to protect himself from earlier, especially with my chainmail. The wind will also threaten his hold on me. He *did* once save me when I fell from a ship shroud a few years ago; but I've grown since then, I was wearing only linen, and the breeze was mild that day. Ezra might be able to catch me with the help of Ithinor's telekinesis—but that's if they're fast enough and the wind is low. The likeliness of a fall without stunning damage...

I have to do this. It's like a shroud... Enough like one, at least. I hope.

I reach behind me to take off my bow and quiver. I keep only my dagger sheathed around my waist in case there's an immediate threat defending the artifact.

My chest shakes with unease as I step up to the foot of the cliffs. The wind harshly pushes against my left side. I try to repeat that the cliff is like the shroud ropes—except none of my grips or steps are guaranteed.

Similar enough. Similar enough. Pull yourself up and rest when you can.

The nervous burn in my torso intensifies as I find my first hold on the wall. The rough texture doesn't dig into my palms as harshly because of my calluses. I try to hold on to that glimmer of optimism as my right foot steps onto a small ledge.

As I push myself up, a terrible, dull ache grips my arms and legs; Seavale's stage inflicted more damage than I wanted to admit. That means slow steps—the longer I feel the burning. The wind may be cooling me down against the exercise, but it's also causing me to work harder to stay upright against the wall.

Sierra offers encouragement. Ezra provides what aid he can when I reach for what looks like a safe grip and try to find my next secure step. Strong gusts push against me, threatening my ascent and demanding more strength that I feel fading. The minutes pass too slowly, especially because I need to rest every minute or so. I'm quite a ways away from the ground; I'm tempted to ask how long it's been, but I focus.

Every rest I take, I shake out my arms for minimal relief. Pacing myself is critical, but I can only wait out the minutes because the throbbing burn in my limbs is forcing me to. I inch closer to the halfway point at a snail's pace, where a ledge the width of the entire cliff resides. The pull in my chest reaches for it—for the artifact that has to be somewhere up there.

My thoughts are trapped in anything that will steal my mind away from how my muscles feel as though they're about to tear. Away from how the cold rock *is* digging into my palms now. Away from the sweat making each hold more slippery. Away from how hard the wind is pushing against—

"Leo, NO!" Ezra's voice booms far below me.

My right foot tries to land on a ledge too short for the tip of my sabaton. I press down before my brain can realize it, and my foot slides off. A gust pushes me far to the right, my foot flailing as my body leans.

My jaw opens for a scream just as a firm force grips my body, stabilizing me. I find a safe-enough ledge a little higher, my breath flooding out of me as I secure my grip on the rock.

Ithinor—you saved me again.

"You—you're almost—out of range!" he shouts from the ground. His voice sounds distant, which offers me a flicker of hope. "The wind—hurry!"

I swallow hard and force myself to look up: it has to be only a few more steps. I must do this, I have to do this.

The artifact's pull grows stronger with every inch. Despite the stultifying ache in my limbs, I climb until I'm only a head away from the ledge. The pull intensifies as if it's excited that I'm here. It's even stronger than the wind.

I'm here, I'm here.

My sore palm makes contact with the cold, flat surface of the ledge as I pull myself up one last time. I go to stand until the wind pushes me back, my head almost colliding with the wall in front of me. I slump against it, exhaustion and sweat saturating my body. My throat sears me with every breath, but the powerful breezes are cool against my face and hands.

My team offers praise down at the bottom. I'm grateful that they don't ask questions; I don't have the energy to answer them.

My breathing eases as the minutes pass. The artifact's pull is all that remains. I turn my head to the left. Somewhere over there.

"Sierra," I shout, recuperating my strength. "Time?"

Her Vinean accent always seeps through the most when she shouts. "Almost half an hour for you to climb. You've been up there for almost ten minutes."

Too long. Stand up.

My legs wobble underneath me as I do. I steady myself against the wall, pressing my back against it.

"Leo?" Ezra calls.

I can't see my team, but that doesn't mean that they can't see me. "I'm fine," I shout, sliding against the rock inch by inch. My armor protects me from its jagged edges—and the relieving cold of the stone. The wind against my sweat is my only respite from my body heat. "Wait there!"

The ledge is about five feet wide, but I can only note that for a split second before I press myself harder against the wall. I can't focus on how I only have five feet separating me from life and death.

Every inch closer to the artifact, wherever it's hidden, my hands press against the rock as though a switch is hidden somewhere. As my eyes travel along, they finally snag on a dark crevice a couple of feet away.

There. There, there, there.

I reach my hand inside, my fingers wrapping around something thick, cool, and smooth. I pull out a bundle of... a vine.

This is it.

Only because the vine's purpose is to help us, I know what to do: it reminds me of a prank I pulled when I was twelve and used a rope to climb down the castle to tap on the maidservants' window. Three of the older castle boys held the other end of the rope in my bedchamber so that they could quickly pull me up after each tap. The third time, I dropped a bag of a water-and-flour mixture on top of the maidservant who furiously opened the window.

My lips purse. I force the memory away; it isn't like that this time. I'm not doing this for a prank—I'm doing this to save my friends.

I tie the vine around my waist. Seeing as it's meant to help us overcome the stage, it should be strong enough to carry us all.

I carefully slide myself against the wall roughly to where I first landed, the rest of the vine wrapped around my hand. With my legs still trembling with exhaustion, I kneel and then lie on my belly to safely look over the ledge. Ithinor is healing Sierra again. When they all see me, he stops and they take a few steps to the side to align with me.

"Ezra!" I call. "Do you trust me?"

"Always, captain," he yells back.

Please *be magical like the seed.*

Still on my stomach, I throw them the rest of the vine. To my amazement and relief, it stretches all the way down, never pulling on me. Even more miraculous—it isn't affected by the wind.

Impossible, I think with a cautious relief.

"Wrap that around yourself," I shout. "I have a good feeling."

"Leon," Ithinor calls back dubiously, "do you truly think it's wise that we risk our lives because of a 'good feeling'?"

Moments like these lessen the guilt of leaving my princely decisions to him when I was a child: it was likely best for Seavale at the time.

"It's... the same instinct that spoke to me in the whale," I reply. "Just—trust me."

Ezra takes the vine and secures it around his waist. The vine lengthens as he pulls on it to fasten it around himself—as though it grows according to our need. The process repeats with Sierra, whom Ezra helps to fasten it higher up around her torso because of her wound. Ithinor is last, but there's enough vine for all of them.

Do these artifacts have some kind of limit...? I think a little too late. *It wouldn't break because they're all coming up at the same time, would it? How else would we use the vine if not for that?*

"Are you all right, Sierra?" I ask.

"Stable," she shouts. "Only sore. Ithinor has been healing me, it's all right. Let's hope this vine does what we need it to."

I nod. "Then come on up."

Ezra turns to her. I'm too far up to hear anything, but he points behind him and seems to ask her something. She timidly reacts, glancing at Ithinor as if he has what she needs.

Did Ezra just offer to carry her? Can he really endure that?

He nods, turning his back to her and kneeling. She wraps her arms around his neck and legs around his torso. Giddiness is trumped by unease in my stomach for them as they begin the climb.

Instantly, Ezra's round features contort in confusion—almost hesitance. "I can't feel my own weight," he calls. "Or even Sierra's. The wind isn't even pushing me."

My brows furrow, my heart beating faster with what I'm hesitant to call hope. "Do you feel anything, Icky?" I shout.

"Only the desire for Ezra to slap you, Your Highness."

I grin. The vine immunizes us to weight and wind!

I won't have to help them up, then. Magic is truly miraculous.

Ezra's head pops up in less than half the time it took me to climb up here. I step back to allow him room, and he pushes himself and Sierra up and onto the surface. Sierra carefully slides off of his back when she has enough room.

Ithinor arrives seconds after. Remarkably, he isn't even out of breath as he slides onto the ledge. "If only all climbs could be like that," he mutters, standing with my help for balance.

I chuckle. "This is amazing. I know that even you are impressed."

I face the wall again, take my first step, and pull myself up for the second half of the climb. Incredibly enough, my muscles don't scream in protest this time; I can't feel my own weight. If anything, I'm heavier against any direction the wind blows in. It's as if I'm climbing in place—yet I'm moving upward.

This feels so much better.

The relief relaxes me to the extent that it almost immunizes my hands to the jagged edges of the rock. My foot almost slips again, and Sierra warns me to stay focused because we're still susceptible to falling—an all-too-grim reminder. That's when my hold tightens and my feet secure themselves more firmly.

When I grip the edge of the top of the cliff, my fingers dig into dirt. My chest relaxes in triumph as I pull myself up and then slide onto the grassy surface. Grass has never felt so soft as I move away from the edge and watch my teammates follow suit.

"My wound didn't even stretch open!" Sierra exclaims as we stand. Her delicate features then contort in a wince as she moans, her hand hovering over her side. "If only the artifact could have rid me of this soreness..."

"Allow me to help with that," Ithinor replies, his olive hands aglow with bright-green magic again.

I grin, untying the vine from my waist. The wind provides a glorious cooling sensation on my face. "Thank the Ancients for this thing."

"And what about you?" Ezra says, arching a brow. "You managed *half* the climb without the vine so that we would have it."

I roll my eyes. "What else was I meant to—?"

He holds up his hand. "Accept credit when it's due."

"And you trusted your instinct," Ithinor says, his healing magic fading from his hands as he nods at me. "Of which has been right and led us to the key twice now."

He gestures behind me, and I turn around. A bronze key sits on a pillar—of *cloud*.

I exhale. "Wow..."

My team follows me to it, and my fingers graze the top of the pillar. The cloud feels cooler than the air, droplets of moisture licking at my skin. The pillar is somehow unaffected by the breeze.

I chuckle. "Look at that: I've my hand in the clouds."

Ezra smacks the back of my head, but a grin is stuck to his face this time. "That was your worst attempt yet. Move."

The three of them follow suit, reaching for the pillar. "Moisture!" Sierra exclaims, excited, green eyes wide as she looks up at me. "Leo, do you know what this means for the scientific research facility? Now we know that clouds *aren't* solids!"

Ezra and I smile at her passion and insatiable wonder. His eyes themselves seem to glimmer every time he looks at her.

I hope you find the right time to tell her eventually.

I note the gusts of wind designed in the key's ornate head. It almost replicates Seavale's exactly, save for the winds instead of waves. This time, the third knob down the shaft is elongated. A word is engraved at the bottom of this key's head, too: "tenacity".

"Bravery" on Seavale's, and now "tenacity" on Windale's... Do these words have to do with the stages themselves? The kingdoms? Telling us the greatest traits of each one?

"Bravery" is more than accurate for Seavale. And I imagine the same for Windale, given that their entire kingdom is founded on terrain like this stage.

I take the key and put it into my satchel. The cloud pillar swirls upward, taking the shape of a tall oval. Its center brightens into the blinding mouth of another cyan-lined portal.

The next stage. Wow—we're already on the third one.

The rim of the portal crackles and dances like a perpetual lightning. While I'm tempted to rest a little more, Soilera gave us too big of a reason to continue for as long as we can. I pray that the next stage will offer respite as I look back at my three team members. They remind me again what I'm running for—and for the first time since the portal in Seavale opened, I no longer only feel as though I have to do this, but that I *can* do this.

I step inside, my teammates close behind.

CHAPTER

"THERE'S THAT LOVELY SMILE"

Emberly

"**W**E'RE COMING, EMBERLY!" ZENEVIEVE SHOUTS below me. I grip the volcano for dear life. "Hold on!"

Sincerely—what do you think I'm doing?!

When the volcano finally stops rising, I open my eyes. I've a couple of steps to climb before reaching the top. My sunburned hands ache for the cold oasis water that disappeared beneath this colossal cone of death.

"We're almost there, Ember!" Zenevieve calls. Closer this time.

Right. My group came after me. They followed me despite my madness, after all. That's somewhat comforting.

I don't dare look down: I know we're up high. Very high. Much higher than that night when Zenevieve and I were little and she saved us from Vineah's guards after I fell from the tree—

"Come *faster*, Zenevieve!" I exclaim, succumbing to my cursed fear. I squeeze my eyes shut tighter. "My muscles aren't scared of you and will not hesitate to drop me if they see fit!"

My voice shakes against my better judgment reminding me that Meredith and Ambrose are here, too; I don't want me tumbling down an eighty-metre drop to be their last memory of me. *Actually, that isn't the most embarrassing death. Rather understandable, if anything*—especially for someone who has no climbing experience. Despite wanting to, I never had the chance to climb Snowark's mountains. Stupid Samson said that the boulders weren't strong enough to carry human weight and would crumble under me. Zenevieve had to tell him that those rules only applied to his mother. I had to restrain myself so hard from—

It's not working. It's not working. My very thoughts are trembling in fear no matter how fervently I try to distract myself.

"It's all right," Meredith says breathily, appearing at my side. Her slim face shines under the sun, beads rolling down her brown skin. I've never seen her so unkempt in the time she's served me. Even so, care coats her hazel-green irises. "Zenevieve will hoist herself up and then pull you up. Ambrose can use a spell to freeze—"

"I really don't care, Merry," I tell her. My breath still shakes as I exhale. "If you'd be so kind as to *carry on* with it, my limbs are about to drop me."

Curse their eyes. They were never meant to see this.

My mind teases me with the probability that Meredith knows exactly how afraid I am. It's all right for Zenevieve to know, and Ambrose can barely tell his left from his right, but

Meredith? I need to impress Meredith. I still need to provide her a reason to stay. She knows exactly how unworthy I am to rule; that means I have all the more to prove to her. Meredith is meant to feel honoured to serve me. She can't feel honoured if I give her nothing to feel honoured about. If I don't help her stay.

Zenevieve pushes herself with a grunt to the mouth of the volcano. After gaining her balance and assessing the width of the edge, she reaches down for me. Now I know why Ambrose was so terrified to grab her cloak when he fell into the lake: I don't trust the fading strength in my muscles. Even with Zenny's help, climbing those last steps is nothing short of petrifying.

I'm surprised the boy made it up at all... and Meredith.

"Careful," Zenevieve says, my torso coming to rest on the lip. She cautiously sets down my hands to bring Ambrose up next. "We don't have a lot of edge before you roll down the crater and into the vent."

Hot air blasts up into my face from the volcano's vent. It's as if it's breathing.

Ginger is, of course, easiest to pull up. He then uses his magic to freeze us in place in case we're tempted to fall off.

Finally. I'm safe. Terrified, but safe.

We stand at the edge of the crater, able to overlook the world around us. The desert beyond is almost beautiful. I'm tempted to marvel at the plush appearance of the beige dunes. Wind licks at the peaks, swirling granules of sand into the air and blue sky.

"How did you lot climb up here?" I bring myself to ask.

"It wasn't too terrible," Zenny replies simply. She'd likely shrug if she could. "There were rather distinct footrests and grips. Almost as if the stage wanted us to climb this."

So I'm not mad. We're where we need to be.

"Well, we aren't quite immune to molten lava, are we?" I let my eyes fall down the volcano. "Unless this is a mission of sacrifice: the one with the purest heart and all. Ambrose, jump in."

Zenevieve snorts, but Meredith doesn't allow even a freezing spell to stop her from scolding me. "That's terrible." She locks eyes with Ginger standing next to Zenevieve. "Don't listen to her, Ambrose."

"What if she's right?" he asks worriedly. "I'm the greatest hope we have if that's the case!"

I would purse my lips if I could. Part of me is a little proud of him for his expanding wit; another part is ashamed because no part of that wit is false. I certainly haven't the proper heart for that kind of sacrifice.

"You're both unbelievable." Meredith sighs. "The artifact, Emberly—is that arrow... magic?"

My eyes fall down to the cold artifact in my hand. "Certainly feels like it. Like ice."

"If the sword on the previous stage was infused with fire, perhaps this is infused with ice—which means it likely has the power to freeze whatever it strikes."

The entire reason I grabbed onto the volcano was because I knew that the arrow was connected to it. It's the only rational conclusion. Standing up here now, though, doubt whirls in my mind: a tiny arrow to an entire chasm of lava?

But Zenny said that it was as if we were meant *to climb the volcano.*

"Doesn't even magic have limits?" I ask incredulously.

"It does," Ambrose chimes, "but it depends on purpose. If that's what the arrow can do, it will freeze just about anything."

Then that's it: shoot it into the volcano. That seems to be our only option.

But Ambrose would have to unfreeze me...

"I'll shoot it," Zenevieve says. I can bet Rowena that she's reading my mind. "Give me—"

"No," I state, "I'll do it. Unfreeze me, Ginger."

Fear will not weaken me any further.

White waves of magic glow and swirl around the boy's unmoving hands. The paralysis begins to fade from my arms, gradually crawling to the centre of my body.

I don't rush lest I jolt into the volcano because of my sudden mobility. Once my arms are free, I take my bow hanging on my back. My legs are steady thanks to Ambrose's magic having yet to reach them. I take advantage of it and nock the artifact.

I home my vision on the middle of the volcano. My fingers release my bowstring. The arrow shoots forward, disappearing down the vent.

Silence ensues for only a couple of seconds. A large crackling resonates throughout the chamber below. The sound boils up to us, trails of ice spreading with it. A spiral grows along the walls of the volcano, twirling down and into the belly of the beast.

"Ice, however," I remark as my legs are set free, "we're rather familiar with."

"I'll go first," Zenevieve says. "Stay close behind."

She takes the lead after Ginger unfreezes the three of them. I take the position behind Zenny, Meredith behind me. The cold all around us is hardly enough to compare to that of Snowark's frozen wasteland; the desert radiates such stultifying heat that the cold combats it directly. It almost evens out the temperature. The severe sunburn on my cheeks is partially satiated.

Thick ice wraps all along the inner walls of the volcano. Zenevieve carefully scoots farther down the path to make room for the rest of us, her armour audibly scraping it. I shakily settle myself in, realising that the middle of the spiral dips. It's as if a path has been carved into it to ensure that we don't fall off as we slide down.

Good, because Ambrose would slip straight off.

The little strawberry takes deep breaths behind Meredith. I dig the tip of Rowena as far into the ice as I feel safe so as to not start sliding forward. Still, Ginger's fear-fest doesn't have much time left.

"You won't fall off, Ambrose," Meredith assures gently. "I promise."

His lack of an immediate response prompts me to close my eyes; it's a long way down, and we're still no closer to the ground. We're still up high. I try to deter those thoughts. I try to focus on the cold of the ice and enjoy how it works against the sun. We're so close to the sun. We're high up. It's a long way down.

"You only fell last time because you didn't listen to me, Rosy," Zenevieve calls from in front of me. "We are quite literally meant to take this path. You can trust me, remember?"

I hear a few deep breaths in rhythm with my own. My heart palpitates alone in my chest. Thankfully, Meredith's soft praise sounds behind me for Ambrose getting on. With her instructions, he secures himself behind her.

Finally.

"Proud of you, Rosy," Zenevieve calls. With a gentle push, she starts sliding down the ice path. I've no choice but to take Rowena out. I squeeze my eyes shut the entire slide down. My body skates across the surface, my stomach soaring as we curve. I refuse to worsen it by opening my eyes and watching the blur whizzing past us.

Agonizing seconds later, my body slams into Zenevieve. My feet land on solid ground—ice. I praise the Ancients in my head as Meredith's body pushes me forward. Then again as Ambrose comes in—and then rolls off the path.

I knew it.

"Earned yourself another faceplant of ice, Ginger?" I ask, discreetly exhaling the rest of my nausea. "There's a world outside of the cold, you know."

I stand as Zenevieve rushes to him. I've never been so grateful for solid ground.

"You did well, Ember," she assures, pulling up a shivering Ambrose by his arm. "The worst is over. At least, from what I may assume—this stage has been relatively easy. Compared to the last one."

Easy for you lot, perhaps—the ones who aren't deathly terrified of heights.

"Suspicious, isn't it?" I say, letting my gaze travel all around the iced-over chamber. "First we need to battle a monster, and then we only need to shoot an arrow into a bowl of lava?"

An eerie silence settles over the space. Were we only meant to prove ourselves on the stage that represented our kingdom? Surely a race in which only one may rule the Last Kingdom would offer a more challenging and—well—lethal course to the throne.

Meredith's gaze is pensive as she walks along the black walls. "I don't see why every stage has to present a monumental challenge," she muses. "Each one tests a different part of us whether big or small."

I arch a sceptical brow. "I doubt the Mages would have thought to be so meticulous for a death race."

"Considering Ambrose almost froze to death and then we *were* almost eaten by a monster," Zenevieve begins as she dusts off his shoulder, "forgive my doubt of the idea, Meredith."

"Or maybe we're cursed to endure the same thing over and over again," Ginger remarks a tad bitterly, furiously rubbing his arm. "Look: we traded one frozen lake for another! Clearly, no other world exists for us except the cold. Can we please hurry and find the key?"

He's right: we've not only landed on top of another ice lake, but also another cavern. Still, the freeze is a relief against my burned face and the scrapes across it.

"Ice Beastie?" I call out, carefully stepping forward.

No response. The room doesn't fade into a cloud of blinding fog. No yellow eyes open on the walls.

"All right..." Meredith says softly. "Let's focus on the key. The arrow seems to have dissipated like the sword. It's fulfilled its purpose. I think we've overcome the main obstacle. The key should be here somewhere."

The Ancients are good for something, at least.

"Let's hurry," Zenevieve says, walking to the other side of the chamber. "We never know if or when another team will arrive."

Her words fade to the top of the volcano, carrying me towards the centre. My gaze stays upwards, marvelling at the rock and then finding the mouth. Blue sky blares above me, a cylinder of heat spiralling down it. With the ice around me, the temperature is almost perfect. I feel safe. I almost want to stay here until the race is over.

I look down, adjusting my neck. Then I see it.

"Zenny," I call, the word echoing across the space. I kneel to the bronze key stuck in the ice. "Your mace."

My group arrive to the middle, bending down with me.

"Perfect." Meredith smiles at me, placing a hand on my shoulder. She quickly retracts it, hissing. Evidently, the metal is still too hot.

"Are you all right?" I whisper.

She dismisses it, nodding.

"Stand back," Zenevieve announces, grabbing her mace in her left hand. "As our friend in the last stage demonstrated, ice can cut."

"No!" Ambrose exclaims, reaching out to her. "Please, let me melt the ice this time. It's only a small portion, I can do it."

The three of us glimpse each other with knowing eyes. The lake left a far more indelible mark on the boy's mind than we thought.

Zenny sheathes her mace, nodding. "Go for it."

"Thank you," he replies, igniting orange magic in his sunburned hands. His brows contort in concentration as he scrutinises where the key lies. The surface of the ice bubbles before giving way to water. Mere seconds later, the key sits at the bottom of a small pool.

Zenevieve grins at him before kneeling down. "Nice work, Rosy." She takes the key and shakes off the water. Standing, she turns to me and holds it out. "I believe this is yours."

"Unfortunately," I reply. "Evidently, I've yet to master disownment like the rest of the world."

"Emberly." Meredith's scold is dull this time.

I turn around, maintaining an innocent smile. "What? I've you three now, don't I?"

She challenges me with her own. "There's that lovely smile. It's been a while."

I immediately drop it. "What a shame: now you've scared it away for life."

The smirk in her eyes is amusing. "I was starting to think you forgot how to—"

Zenevieve snickers as I grab the key, ignoring Meredith. "Zenny, do you hear something—?"

Ambrose yelps before I can look down, Meredith shouting, "Ladies, the portal—!"

A blindingly bright, indigo-lined portal opens underneath me. I cry out, shutting my eyes against the light as it swallows me and my group whole.

CHAPTER 16

"YOU SURE KNOW HOW TO BREAK THE ICE"

Leo

A MISERABLE FEW DAYS PASS AFTER COMPLETING Windale's stage. The cliffs transition us to Snowark's frigid wilderness, and defeating the monster in the ice cavern "rewards" us with Lavara's desert wasteland. We're accustomed to humid warmth in Seavale, but Lavara's stage shatters my previous boundaries of tolerance. The dry air is negligible compensation against the heat. We apply a regular coating of palm seed cream every half hour to avoid a sunburn. On the absolute dimmest bright side, my tan improves under the sun.

The cold oasis allows us to refill our waterskins and then bathe before we grab the ice arrow and freeze the volcano. Now the key sits in the middle of the ice floor in the volcano's chamber, and I'm ready to bring our team one step closer to the end of this death race. Lavara's weapons standing in the sand—what had to be symbolizing graves—were too great a reminder of what we are really running for.

"Leon," Ithinor says warily, taking my arm as I step to the middle of the chamber. "Are you sure we should progress so quickly? We haven't rested since—"

"We're on the fifth day," I tell him hopefully, our voices echoing across the cold cavern, "and we're about to unlock the *fifth* stage. We need to keep going as fast as we can."

"This may be as fast as you can go," he replies, slightly looking up at me with his blue eyes, "but consider your teammates."

"We must pace ourselves." Sierra places her hands on her waist and meanders to me, the ice creaking under her. Ithinor has managed to progressively heal her sword wound over the last few days, so it's only a terrible scar now. She's faring just as well as the rest of us; but after such a heavy wound, I can't fault her for insisting this so heavily. "Don't push yourself just to wind up needing all of your strength for the next stage."

"I understand that," I state, "but we don't know if we're ahead or behind. It's been almost a week, the other teams could have—"

"Leo." Her sweet voice remains firm yet soft.

My words catch themselves in my throat, and I force myself to swallow them. Sierra is not the same girl who came to replace her uncle as my advisor when he passed four years ago. If anything, I learned how to start growing into my own role partially by witnessing her grow into hers; she used to encourage a few small pranks before we became close enough for me to tell her how one of my pranks almost killed Ithinor. After that... it was as if she had decided to grow with me. The older sister I never had.

Especially since because I went "sober", she was the only one close to my age who would talk to me, besides Ezra.

Ithinor steps up and rests a hand on my shoulder. His eyes soften. "At a certain point, rest becomes the most productive thing you can do."

I purse my lips in impatience and reluctant agreement. Despite the last thirteen years of his wisdom, it manages to take root in me as if for the first time every time he speaks it.

I take a deep breath. "Even Lavara has lost two members. And I don't..." Visions of Princess Cassandra and Dorian flash across my memory. "I don't want to be caught in another fight."

Ezra's broad shoulders fall in a sigh. His large hand tightens around his sword.

Ithinor stares at the key stuck in the ice below us. "Sierra?"

She turns around. "Grab the key. But we rest on the next stage no matter *what*."

Ithinor nods, quietly exhaling. Orange magic glows in his olive hands, and he concentrates it on the ice in the center. It melts into a small, growing pool of water, leaving the key resting at the bottom. Ezra bends down, takes it, and reaches it out to me.

I smile at Ithinor. "You sure know how to break the ice," I remark, taking the key.

Ezra smacks the back of my head, scowling. "I need to teach you—"

The ground opens up underneath us in a bright light before he can finish. I scream, instinctually gripping the key tightly as the familiar mouth of a portal sucks me in with Ezra.

Sierra shouts after us. I can only hope that she and Ithinor are safely close behind as my eyes shut against the blinding light.

Though I'm falling, an invisible force shoves me backward. I almost open my eyes, but the light overwhelms my vision and forces me to shut them again.

What is happening?

My body remains weightless and suspended in magic, pulled in all directions outward and yet inward simultaneously. Another force jolts me back and forth too quickly for me to count how many times.

In a blink, my body is spat out of the portal.

A rough, textured surface catches me as I roll out. I mount on my hands and knees the second I stop. Dense, tightly knit-together tree branches and leaves rest under my fingers. A... platform of some kind.

I look up. We're surrounded on all fronts with thick, dark tree trunks and vines. A dense canopy hangs over us, allowing only sunlight to peek through and cast a thousand shadows. The humidity rivals Seavale's—almost doubles it, if anything.

Through squinted eyes trying to recover, I see that my team has landed in front of me. Sierra lies on her back, Ezra is on all fours like me, and Ithinor lies on his stomach.

What... what happened in the—?

My stare freezes on the four people lying behind my team.

"Stand up!" I exclaim, scrambling to my feet and rushing to Ithinor. My eyes never leave the people only yards away and sitting up as I pull Ithinor. "Stand up, look!"

Sierra, Ezra, and Ithinor are quick to obey. We back away as the other team takes notice of us and does the same—except for one.

"Emberly," I hear the tallest and seemingly eldest of them

whisper to the Princess of Snowark. Her accent is noticeably prim and proper. "Come here."

The princess hasn't taken a few steps back like her team. I'm somewhat relieved: beyond the four of them is a never-ending, yellow sky. The platform has an edge, and I'm unsure if they've noticed. Unease sloshes in my stomach for them.

I force myself to look back at the Snowark team. The princess and I lock eyes.

Wow.

The death glare I received at the beginning of the race upon first seeing each other has disappeared. Instead, it's faded into recognition—and caution. Neither, though, restricts the enchantment of her sharp eyes that match the shade of muted-green leaves. Her wavy, dark-auburn hair contrasts with her light skin, complemented by freckles across her narrow nose and her cheeks—which have been severely sunburned. A scar marks the right side of her forehead. She's the shortest one of the group—the shortest one out of all of us.

I definitely don't want to provoke her... unless she earned her scar from a foolish accident like how I earned mine.

Next to the princess stands a young woman who is no doubt her knight, her black eyes that match her curls and skin sharp. Her full lips are locked in a glare. The tall woman, who warned Princess Emberly to come closer, radiates maturity in her silver armor, especially with her elegant bun. A lanky, pale boy stands beside them, as tall as the woman. He's the only one not wearing armor and has also been burned by the sun.

I almost want to be the first to speak—but intuition is warning me of what Princess Emberly and her knight are capable of.

After Princess Cassandra and Dorian...

I'm tempted to take my bow and quiver off my back to show amicability, but the princess also has one on her back. Instinct advises me to keep mine on—which means my goodwill must be all the more convincing.

I take in a deep breath. I need to try. Joining together is the only thing that will keep us all alive rather than murdering each other, and someone needs to announce that.

"Snowark," I begin, daring a step forward and holding up my hands. "We don't want—"

Everyone instantly engages their weapons except for the lanky boy. Even Ithinor's hands are held out in front of him in swirls of red magic.

"No, wait!" I exclaim, turning between my team and the princess's. "Please, allow me a moment to explain—"

"Everyone is quite aware of the rules here," Snowark's knight snaps in a smooth voice, her left hand gripping her steel sword. A speck of sunlight from the canopy shines in her black eyes, exposing the depth of their darkness. "I just don't see why you lot are so quick to fight to the death!"

What?

"Apologies," Sierra says mockingly, stepping up to my side. Her sword is firmly raised in front of her, her free hand hovering over where Cassandra struck her. "It's custom in Seavale to defend yourself when someone raises a weapon against you."

"Oh, *forgive* me," the knight replies, sarcasm dripping off her smile. "I thought this was a death race where the last standing monarch inherits the Last Kingdom!"

"Zenevieve," the tall woman hisses, placing a hand on her

shoulder. She eyes my group with authoritative, hazel eyes, lowering her own sword. By how slowly she moves, I can tell she isn't used to wielding a weapon. "We don't wish to harm anyone. We only raised our weapons on instinct, but it isn't easy to lower them when our opponent stays ready to fight."

"Respectfully, madam," Ithinor replies lowly, the red magic in his hands intensifying, "we've every reason to be wary."

His eyes move to Sierra, who seems to just now realize that her hand hovers over her side. She takes her sword into both hands, adjusting her stance.

The woman's eyes soften. "I see. You were already harmed by another team—"

"And we won't hesitate to defend ourselves," Ezra states, striding to stand in front of us.

Princess Emberly snickers. "I didn't realize the power of love was all we needed to survive," she says, looking at her knight—Zenevieve, the woman said. "Do you know where I can find a soulmate around here, Zenny?"

"All right, all right." I step in front of Ezra with my hands still up. Both groups raise their weapons again. "It's evident that *neither* of us want to harm each other. We should stay firm in that."

"Yes!" the tall, redheaded boy chimes, running to meet me in the middle. Zenevieve reaches for him but immediately retracts. "We saw what killing did to Lavara, and then we saw it again on Windale's stage when two more had already been killed—the *Princess* of Soilera, at that!"

A chill crawls down my spine. *If Snowark finds out that we were the ones who killed them...*

The boy grants equal attention to both sides. "It's done no good for anyone. Death isn't the answer to every solution—"

"Ginger," Emberly says dully with crossed arms, blatantly interrupting him. "You just said 'to every solution'."

Ginger—a strange name, but I don't want to offend their culture—pensively looks up at the canopy overhead with round, brown eyes. He then shakes his head furiously. "See? Death ruins the mind! It's bad, terrible, we shouldn't give in to it. We need to be at our strongest at every possible moment now."

"We don't *want* to kill each other," I say again. I turn around and lock firm eyes with my team, prompting them to lower their weapons. I turn back around to Snowark. Ginger still hasn't tried to attack me, which is somewhat of a relief. "Seavale swears that—"

Emberly snickers, brows remaining skeptical as Zenevieve lowers her sword somewhat. The princess, however, narrows her sharp eyes. "You truly expect us to trust the infamous Prince Leon Wales of Seavale, do you?"

A protective instinct rises in my chest. The words are sinisterly familiar. "What does Her Highness mean to say?"

A grin plays on her lips as she bites it. She's... amused. "Forgive me if I find it reckless to place my faith in the prince who spent his years of youth sabotaging his own kingdom."

I drop my eyes to the ground, swallowing my anger. *All* the kingdoms know of my past, and I only know the other monarchs' names and portraits?

Emberly scoffs. "And let's not forget the obvious as well, shall we? Why would I ally with the kingdom ready to aid our enemies in a selfish, unwarranted invasion?"

"Seavale was never about to accept Vineah's proposal," I state, tightening my jaw. "We haven't found a secure way to deny them without potentially inciting—"

"You're a master of convenience as well," she sneers.

I steady my angry breath. My gaze hardens on her. "You speak on things you don't fully understand."

A challenging brow arches high into the air. "Really? Let's see." She steps forward, unwavering in her resolve. Her eyes seem to see straight through me and everything I've ever done the last nineteen years. "Given that you spent so many years in a perpetual cycle of foolishness, I'm left to assume that you avoided repercussions for such. That requires a skillset of charisma and persuasion of basic aptitude. Your kingdom would have had you endure disciplinary action of some degree—unless your pranks were too harmless to raise serious discussion. Judging by your reputation exceeding the boundaries of Seavale, I must dismiss that." Her next step is careful and slow. "Therefore, you possess a quality that earns you either mindless redemption or hopeful faith in your character—or both. And I know better than to allow my group to fall into that trap during a *death* race, of all things."

Anger bubbles into rage. Mindless redemption? Disciplinary action? I've spent the last five years all but selling my soul to earn my redemption, and I still haven't received it. And I've *more* than received my dose of disciplinary action, even if it wasn't for my pranks directly. The princess is ignorant in her entire speech.

I fight every muscle to stay where I stand—and keep my mouth firmly shut. No matter any of that, I cannot allow my anger to threaten my team's safety.

Emberly has commanded the entire platform's attention—

like she's activated a magical ability. Even the trees and vines seem to listen to her stern voice, the breeze carrying it beyond us.

She stops only a few feet away from me and Ginger. "You're a dangerous opponent and impossible ally to trust." Her tone hardens as she drops her arms. "Soften our resolve now, encourage us towards your protection, only to slaughter us and take the key for yourself so you can get to the Last Kingdom first—expand your playground, just as Vineah is offering you,"—she leans forward, her gaze penetrating mine—"no matter who is lost during construction."

"I'm more worried about your fatal ignorance, *Princess*," I hiss, meeting her where she stands. She doesn't even falter as I glare down at her. "Are we meant to believe that you're so innocent and perfect? You never did anything foolish in your youth or were as much of a royal brat as I was? Spare your breath. At least I grew out of my foolishness, but I can't even tell if that redness on your face is a sunburn or your temper flaring."

She unsheathes her dagger when the tall woman pulls her back, Ezra grabbing me. Not an ounce of regret flickers in my chest.

"That's *enough!*" the woman barks. Her group flinches, telling me that they're not accustomed to this sharp tone or volume from her. "Like it or not, Emberly, the prince is right and you know it: neither of us want to kill to advance."

"It seems we—both disagree with what we've seen the last week," Sierra states. Her sword remains in her hand but at her side. "There is no purpose in fighting right here. If we can join together, or even formally agree not to—"

"Why not ask the other kingdoms to ally with us while we're

at it?" Emberly asks chipperly, irony drowning her words. "Right, I remember: they're dropping like the arctic foxes in the Dagger Woods!"

I despise the silence that ensues afterward, furious that nobody knows how to argue that. Furious that, as much as I fight it and curse it and scold it, her words can better repeat and echo against the chamber of my mind in that silence:

Just a playground. Expand your territory. Be as imprudent as you desire.

That is your past and nothing more. You've worked too hard to become who you are now!

Then why does it bother you so much unless part of you is still that foolish, selfish little boy?

My fists tighten, my gaze focused on Emberly's—and hers on mine. That death glare has returned in full force. The essence of fire itself burns in her eyes, like she is the author of flame; and part of me wants nothing more than to extinguish it with the waters of Seavale.

"So *your* solution, Princess, is to eliminate more of us?" I say. "That's how we proceed? You'll risk your teammates so easily, and you doubt *my*—?"

"Do you need the world spelled out for you?" she exclaims, brows pinching together. "At least I've the *basic* maturity to know—!"

Something shoots behind me. Ithinor cries out in pain, grabbing my and Emberly's attention. He stumbles to the ground, holding his shoulder. An arrow has pierced straight through his robes and sheathed itself into his shoulder.

"*Ithi*—!"

Something whizzes behind Emberly. I identify it as a dagger when it sinks into the left side of the woman's chest.

CHAPTER 17

"LET ALL THAT YOU DO BE DONE IN LOVE"

Emberly

MEREDITH FALLS TO THE GROUND OF DENSE branches and leaves. That blood-freezing scream is the most I've ever heard from her, leaving my body paralyzed—and hers with a dagger next to her heart.

Zenevieve and Seavale's knight and advisor unsheathe their swords. Ambrose activates his magic in red swarms of waves and glimmers.

"Fall back!" Zenevieve and the knight shout.

The prince runs to his mage and I to Meredith. We loop our arms underneath theirs and drag them to the nearest tree trunk. It's thick enough to hide them both, and we lean them against it. Meredith's brown skin has already lost its glow, and the mage's breaths are uncomfortably shallow.

"They attacked somewhere far off and hidden," Leon states

next to me, throwing off his bow and quiver from his back. "Which means our teams likely won't be able to..." Still kneeling, he faces me. "Quick, give me your dagger!"

"Excuse you?" I hiss. "Who do you—?"

He reaches for Rowena nonetheless and grabs her too quickly for me to stop him. "Ask Ithinor!" he shouts. He darts out from the tree's protection to behind one metres away.

Who does he think he is?! My fists ball up beside me, but I can't stay angry for long—not when I look back at his mage. At least I know his name; I can comfort him after his keen ruler left him for dead. I doubt killing me is on his agenda right now.

"Ith... Ithinor?" I ask, kneeling between the two of them. I rest a careful hand on Meredith's shoulder, which is hauntingly still. "What is he doing?"

"G—give me your—hand," he whispers.

I obey for his sake.

His eyes glow white as his grip tightens. "He's—fighting back. The element—of surprise."

His hand loosens around mine as he closes his eyes. I can't tell if it's because he's dying or if he's finished with his magic—whatever he cast to know of Leon's doing.

I turn to Meredith—whose chest has nearly stilled.

Sensation drains from my arm as I shake her shoulder. "Meredith! No, Meredith!"

Ithinor grabs her hand, wincing. Green waves of magic swirl around their connected hands. Seconds later, Meredith gasps lightly. My breath is unlocked, my being falling light with relief. Her chest rises and falls more prominently—enough for me to know that she's alive.

"I'm... here," she whispers. I curse the geniality of the scrapes on her face from the ice monster's breath—compared to the dagger in her chest. "Em... Emberly."

"Yes, I'm here."

Green magic continues flowing into her from Ithinor's hand. Yet still, her breaths are slow and shallow.

I'm not ready to accept the fact that she should be dead right now.

"Listen. Listen to me," she says airily. "I—I need you—to know something—"

"Don't speak as though I'm about to lose you!" I cry. I don't think I'm trying to give her hope; I think I'm asking her to comfort me. Just as she's always done. Just as she is always meant to do. I cannot lose that yet. I cannot lose her.

"Listen." Her breath is too thin for my liking. "Going forward... stop letting—your mind judge you. And control you. Your mind—lies. But your actions—surpass it."

I swallow. I refuse to waste time arguing with her on that.

"And so," she whispers next, "you must let—all that you do—be done in love."

"'Love'?" I repeat softly. "H—how am I meant to—?"

"Promise me—Ember. Promise."

My lip quivers beyond my control; I don't want her to see me like this—especially now. I force myself to nod. A war wages in my head against the tears pricking the back of my eyes.

"I promise."

"Thank you." Somehow, she manages to take my hand.

"But I'm not—I'm not losing you," I tell her in a whisper as weak as her own. "I'm not losing you, I can't, not you. I can't,

Meredith, please. Please, you're the only one who..."

Her eyes soften to their motherly quality. She slightly lifts the corners of her mouth. "You... are no... less."

I can't cry. I can't be weak right now. I have to be better for her right now. She must stay, she needs to stay with me.

Ithinor's controlled breath is steady as he keeps his eyes closed. Sheer, faded green still flows from his hand. I've not the slightest inkling as to how he's managing healing magic in his state. I wonder how he could possibly be all right with cutting his own life short for the sake of a stranger. Meredith is worth it, but he doesn't know that.

I turn my head. Leon has disappeared from the tree he was hiding behind.

He's fighting back. I truly hope his plan isn't as foolish as all of those childish pranks he conducted in his youth. Curse after curse rings in my head; my being shakes with the anger that I am not the one fighting back. I am not fighting for Meredith when she's spent over half my life fighting for me.

"Ithinor," I say, never releasing her hand. Thank the Ancients it's still warm. "Tell me the prince knows what he is doing."

He nods feebly. I want to demand for more information, but the magic still streaming into Meredith holds my mouth shut.

I squeeze my eyes closed and Meredith's hand tighter. Amidst the shot arrows, Ambrose's protection magic igniting, and swords deflecting arrows, I pray all the more fervently. It's all I can do when Meredith can't speak.

Two distant screams rupture the air. I freeze. My eyes refuse to open. As if they're too scared to accept that the world is still moving.

Another scream tears through the air.

"Leo!" comes moments later from the rest of Seavale's team. Crunchy footsteps sound from the other side of the tree.

That same instant, Meredith's hand grows limp in mine. Everything in me drops.

No. No, no, no. She isn't dead. She's right in front of me, she can't be dead. Ithinor is still healing her!

I open my eyes. Her hazel green doesn't greet me this time. Ithinor still holds her other hand—but the green magic has faded.

There's nothing left to give.

"Meredith," I whisper. The corners of my blurring vision catch my groupmates and Seavale coming around the tree to meet us. I don't hear what they're saying, shaking her hand with a jolt. "Meredith. Meredith!"

She doesn't stir.

"*Meredith!*" I cry, grabbing her shoulders.

You can't abandon me, too! I continue shaking, desperate for a response. Desperate to convince myself that she can hear me. *I can be better! I'll do better, I promise! Please don't leave! You were supposed to stay!*

For the first time in my life, she does not respond to me.

I rip out the dagger from her chest and pull her towards me. I curse the armour that didn't protect her from the blade as I wrap my arms around her. My fingers dig into her back, covered by wretched iron that should have protected her. That dagger shouldn't have penetrated through. That dagger shouldn't have killed her.

Meredith's blood is ready to stain my own breastplate. I

want it to. I want any permanent mark of her. I'm not ready for her to leave me. I'm not ready to release her as another memory. I'm not ready for her to break her promise, to let her go in my mind—yet all I'm able to do now is hold her in silent agony. My tears scream for release. And I want to obey them. I want to sob as if the world only includes me and Meredith.

But I can't. The world only includes me. Meredith is gone.

CHAPTER 18

"YOU DON'T NEED ME ANYMORE"

Leo

"ITHINOR!" I EXCLAIM, KNEELING DOWN TO HIM AND cradling him. My hands don't know what else to do, I don't know what to do as his olive skin starts paling. The blood gushing from his shoulder is so abundant that it's already soaked through his cyan robes—and the stain is growing.

I won't let you die here, you're finishing this race with me!

"It's all right," I assure, his body growing heavier against me. The sun pokes through the canopy of branches and vines above us, illuminating his half-open, sky-blue eyes—and just how pale his skin is quickly becoming. "You'll be fine, just give us time to—!"

"No," he whispers. "No, Leon. I won't be. But that's—all right."

"You will!" I exclaim, restraining myself from holding him tighter. "Sierra will—!"

214

He raises his good arm, touching my hand. "It's all right," he whispers slowly—with a finality I curse in my head with every swear I know. "Because—you're ready. You're ready to begin your life—with your own conscience. Not—not led by mine."

The rest of the world fades away as I press my forehead against his black curls. "No, no, don't say that. I still need you, I can't continue this without you, please!"

With an urge of strength, he presses his hand against my arm as if to reassure me. "You've led us—during every stage. Not me." The remnant of a smile touches his lips. "I saw... your leadership. The man you've become. You don't need me—anymore."

I do. I do, I do. He is the only father I've ever had, the only one who's stuck with me since I was a child. I can't be alone. I can't.

Please don't give up on me, too, not you. You said you wouldn't.

"Please," I whisper, fighting the tears with every muscle in my body. "Please—"

He exhales. His whispers is nothing but air. "Stop doubting. Your heart is—your greatest strength. It... will guide you. Your head will—protect you. Act... in one accord."

His eyes gaze into mine. That faint smile subtly traces his lips in a wicked goodbye. "I'm proud of you, Leo. I am."

"No, no, stop," I tell him, watching his eyes fully close. "No, you can't—!"

He stops breathing in my arms.

"Ithinor." I shake him. His head of black curls lolls to the side. "Ithinor. No, you can't do this, don't give up on me! You promised! Ithinor!"

My body tightens to stone as anguish racks every part of me. Regret, despair, fury, impotence. I squeeze Ithinor and hold him as tightly as I need to. I can do that now. I can bury my face into his neck and silently beg him to come back. I can fight against my tears with every ounce of strength in my body, pushing against them mentally and physically. I can bury my ragged breaths as I clutch him against me, cursing the fact that his heart is still faintly beating under me. It taunts me—that his life is so close yet has already departed.

Curse the stars. Curse the arrow, curse this race—!

Sierra's airy sobs are muffled as I keep my head buried in Ithinor's neck. I raise my damp eyes just enough to wipe them. Sierra and Ezra stand in a tight embrace next to the wide trunk of the tree. Even he has allowed a couple of tears to fall: they've left behind shiny trails against his black skin. His icy, dull eyes stare dead ahead of him as Sierra stays safely wrapped in his embrace.

"I know, lily..." he whispers, choked by his cries.

In front of me sits the Snowark team—mourning as well. Zenevieve stands with her back against the trunk, her face buried in her dark hands. If she's crying behind them, she must have practiced hiding it a thousand times. Ginger kneels beside Meredith, bowing his head of red curls. His shoulders move up with every sob.

Emberly releases Meredith from her embrace. Not a tear has slipped down her cheek. Her eyes are swollen with red, but she keeps her jaw firm. She takes Meredith's hands into hers and presses a kiss to them.

My gaze starts to blur on them to where I don't realize Ezra coming to kneel behind me. He holds my shoulders as Sierra kneels next to Ithinor. We silently embrace. I close my eyes. For some reason, I was convinced the that the rules of life and death didn't apply to us here. Maybe to the other teams—they're our opponents. But to us... To us? To Ithinor?

He isn't dead. He was just here with us, he can't...

We aren't exempt from anything. Which means we must move forward as soon as possible. I'm not even allowed to mourn Ithinor in full, if at all.

Somehow, Ezra manages the courage to speak first. "I regret saying this," he begins in an unstable voice I've never heard from him, standing, "because these two—deserve more time with us. But if anything, this only shows how much danger we're really in. We... we need to continue."

My hands tighten around the man in my arms. *No. I can't.* That means running this race without him.

Please, Ithinor. What do I do? What am I supposed to do?

To my surprise—and disappointment—Snowark doesn't argue. Emberly tightens her hold on Meredith's hands as if she's about to burst, but then her grip relaxes. She gently places Meredith's hands back in her lap.

The six of us stand without a word. Based on the edge of the dense foliage platform, there isn't any ground to bury Ithinor and Meredith in. Ginger seems to realize this at the same time I do; he grabs a few loose leaves from the ground and then brings it to Sierra. "For him," he whispers. "You can throw it off the edge."

Ithinor deserves so much better. I can't help the anger that bubbles in me at the thought. But it's the best option we have.

Sierra humbly accepts the offer. Ginger turns around to collect leaves for Meredith.

Ezra and Zenevieve drag Ithinor and Meredith to the edge of the platform. The jungle ambiance is fuzzy all around me. No one

offers a few words, but that's just as well: I still can't trust anything to come out of my mouth lest it end in tears. Snowark
thanks Meredith, and we apologize to Ithinor.

A dreadful pull in me reaches for Ithinor when Ezra throws
him down. I feel a hundred lashes against my chest as he falls farther and farther down in the void with Meredith. The two of
them soon become black dots that ultimately fade from existence.

Walking through the jungle in silence for a couple of minutes
brings us to a clearing. We find the bodies of Prince Levi of Windale and his mage at the edge of it. Emberly's dagger is stuck in
the dead center of the prince's chest, and mine has sheathed itself
in the mage's neck.

That's how the dagger penetrated straight through Meredith's armor: magic was what threw it. For all I know, magic was
involved in Ithinor's death, too.

Deserved, I think bitterly. *Thank the Ancients I struck you both.
You deserved that and a thousand fires from the lake of hell.*

Emberly and I extract our daggers from Windale's bodies.
Somehow, we have the same idea: to wipe our blades clean on the
corpses.

"Windale is out of the race," Sierra says behind us.

I still in the humid air. Soilera, Windale... How many kingdoms are still in?

"Look." Sierra's firm voice shakes. I turn around. I've never
seen her green eyes so hard. "We have an obvious choice: either

continue losing our friends and face this same fate, or band to-gether for the sake of survival, if nothing else!"

I swallow. The grief in my best friend's voice threatens to overwhelm me. Apparently, that's true for everyone: no one dares to object.

I know what Ithinor would say right now. No part of me wants to believe it unless I can hear the words from him himself. But the most I can do for him now is honor his memory—no mat-ter how angry this makes me.

I take the chance before I can change my mind: "Fine." I turn to Emberly and stride up to her. She immediately points her dag-ger at me.

"Relax, Princess," I hiss, staring down at her. I have an entire head on her in height, and I have to restrain my pettiness from taking full advantage of that. "Believe it or not, I'm not the heart-less brute you take me for. And I don't want to lose anyone else. Are you in or not?"

Her eyes ablaze, her grip on her dagger tightening. I can al-most see her mind calculating her response.

"For Meredith, Emberly," Zenevieve states behind me. Even her voice is trapped by a rigid grief. "Come on."

Emberly's jaw is so tight that I almost worry she's about to shatter her teeth. Finally, a new resolve hardens her glare. "Never mention the scar or a word about my temper again," she sneers, almost too quietly for even me to hear. "Then I'll give you my hand, and we will formally agree."

I reluctantly swallow my pride. "Fine. As long as you never mention my history ever again."

Then—and only then—is when she falters. Her brows

straighten as her eyes dart between mine before she seems to realize that she's softening. She sharpens her scowl again. "Deal."

We shake our hands once firmly. Hers is delicate and soft, save for her callused fingertips.

Bow on her back, protective of her dagger, calluses—she must be startlingly familiar with weapons. You do not want to create an enemy with her.

I think I already have.

"All right," Zenevieve says lowly behind me. I turn to face the rest of my expanded group, Emberly stepping back and away from me. "I know I'm not the only one asking why three groups were put onto the same stage. Something isn't right. Which have you three come through already?"

"Seavale," Sierra replies, hands on her waist, "Windale, Snowark, and Lavara. In that order."

"We've come through all of those, too," Ginger says, brown eyes curious as his gaze wanders to every member of my team. It's as if we're a new species and he wants to savor every moment with us that he can. "Snowark, Lavara, Windale, and then Seavale."

"Then there doesn't seem to be a specific order like I initially suspected," Sierra muses, gaze falling to the platform. "But... would the Mages be so disorderly in designing something so convoluted—?"

"Why does it matter?" Emberly interjects with a harsh edge in her voice. "We're stuck together now, and we need to survive. That's all there is to it."

Zenevieve exhales, nodding. "Right. Then we should—introduce ourselves. I'm Zenevieve. That"—she points at Ginger—

"is Ambrose."

"*Ambrose*". *That makes much more sense for a name.*

Zenevieve loosely gestures to the princess behind me. "Of course, you know Emberly."

"How could we not?" I mutter.

"What's that, prat?" Emberly spits, stepping up to me.

"Nothing," I reply, turning to face her. "Just that you like to make your presence *quite* known—"

She holds the tip of her dagger dangerously close to my throat. "I can make good on that on your cheek right now—"

"Stop it!" Ambrose snaps, stepping between us with Sierra. Emberly steps back, stunned eyes on him. "You two are worse than my siblings! Anavieve is six and *still* has more sense than you! How can you possibly think to bicker so childishly like this amidst what just happened?"

Sierra's scolding eyes dig into me as she leans in close. "I thought this side of you disappeared. You worked far too hard to become better than this, do not tell me that you're willing to throw it away for the sake of an argument!"

I swallow, my throat still tightened by my anger. "Better than this". Ithinor's supposed pride in me rings in my ears.

"Surely we can last until the end of the stage," she says. "We don't need to lose anyone else—from our team or otherwise."

My indignation submits to her, but my words still fall short. Emberly and I catch a glare from each other one last time.

"Then let's focus on what matters," Ezra begins, the timidest I've ever heard him. His large hand rests on the golden pommel of his sword. "Soilera is dead. Now Windale. We don't know about Magery. That leaves—"

"—the arrogant dunce from Lavara and insidious brat from Vineah," Emberly hisses, aggressively sheathing her dagger. "Windale got what they deserved."

My eyes fall onto the bodies of the prince and his mage. Rage flourishes through my veins, and my hand tightens around my dagger. I still can't bring myself to sheathe it.

"Then if we're banding together," Sierra says, gaining my attention, "I'm Sierra, and that's Ezra. All together, we now face up to three kingdoms, one of which is infamously ruthless and another—seemingly so. We managed to protect each other just now despite being separate teams, so we're bound to stand at least a chance against the others. As long as we all force ourselves to work together."

"Protect each other". I'm tempted to scoff. But Ithinor and Meredith were attacked before we even knew we were being watched...

Why did Windale wait so long to attack? Or... did they hear us arguing and went back to eliminate us?

I exhale. Ithinor's dying words echo in my head. *Your heart will guide you. Your head will protect you. Act in one accord.*

Then that confirms the decision to join with Snowark—and never let down our guards.

After looting Windale's satchels for food and supplies, we don't know what to do other than throw their bodies off the edge. It's then that I remember Sierra's words about resting on the next stage—no matter what. Every fiber in my body wants to, but my mind is running rampant with any harrowing thought it can find.

My heart tells me to rest because it's too heavy. It can't continue. But a deeper part of me wants to force me to keep going. It tells me that I don't deserve rest. I don't deserve to take a moment for myself. I'll get someone killed.

At a certain point, rest becomes the most productive thing you can do.

I almost shiver away the thought. Ithinor is still here. I want to believe it. I want to believe that resting would be productive right now. But how do I know it won't lead to anyone else's death?

We were on Lavara's stage for longer than I cared to admit: the sky is a little more orange than yellow now. The sun must be starting its descent. That means only enough time to set up camp and have supper before sleeping for the night.

Sierra sighs in defeat as though her mind is running with the same thoughts. "We swore to rest on the next stage no matter what,"—she holds up a hand at Ezra, who begins to protest—"and I know that staying in one place isn't wise. But seeing as this is definitely Vineah's stage, we know that they won't be attacking. Magery is running without armor, and Lavara only has two members. In the worst outcome, it will be six against four. So I insist that we set up camp for the night. Especially for the sake of our mentalities."

Nobody replies. I can't help my gratitude for her justifications.

We can't start a fire directly on the ground without burning off the entire platform we stand on. Reluctantly, we wet a patch of it with some of the water in our waterskins and then gather a dry pile on top of the patch. Emberly goes to stand against a faraway tree when Ambrose ignites the pile with his magic. He and Zenevieve bring out two halves of bread and spread a meager amount of jelly from a short jar. I don't admit that I'm envious; dinner consists of oat cakes and another apple half for us.

I turn my head, watching Emberly sit against the faraway tree. She holds a piece of bread in her hand, her bow and quiver sitting beside her. Not a single bite has been taken.

Why is she sitting all the way over there? Zenevieve and Ambrose didn't even question it.

I press my lips together. Everything in my mind tells me not to do this...

You worked too hard to become better.

Ithinor would have told me to do the same thing. I have to try for him.

Against my mind, I stand up and approach the Princess of Snowark.

"I don't—" she snaps, then swallowing her words. She sets down her bread on top of her satchel, taming her tone. "I'm in no mood to endure conversation with you right now."

"I'm in no mood to ally with a team that I'm still mostly convinced wants to kill me and my friends, yet here I stand," I tell her, dropping my hands to my side. "This race is all about the things we hate, in case you haven't noticed."

"Is that why you're here?" she asks mockingly, narrowing her eyes. She's so small under me that I'm tempted to kneel down to her level. I would still be taller than her if I did. "You've come to accuse me of murderous intent and being a—what was it you said—a 'royal brat'?"

My muscles tighten. The words almost sound foreign on her lips, but I know they're all too familiar from a boy I've tried so hard to bury over the last five years.

"I know—how you feel right now." I kneel nonetheless. "We both... we both lost someone dear to us. Ith..."

I can't bring myself to say his name without my vision blurring. Then my eyes match the angry ones of the princess. Fighting the tears becomes that much easier; I refuse to let her see me be anything less than she is. "Ithinor was the only father I ever had. He raised me. He was the only one who didn't leave after I gave him every reason to."

"And Meredith was that to me." Emberly reflects my steady tone. "Congratulations, you have my backstory. Now, consider the fact that our groups are suffering from the same loss and have no one to relate to them. You and I are already on the same page, you prissy lion cub; yet you chose to waste your time on me instead of consoling someone who actually wants it."

Did she just call me a—?

I mentally shake it away. "You're the only one sitting away from—"

"I don't need to explain myself to you," she snaps.

I bite my lip, restraining my temper. Realizing I have no hope of reaching her, I shake my head. "Fine. I don't know why I bothered trying."

"Neither do I."

"You're right about just one thing." I stand. "We're enemies in this race, and nothing will change that. I hope you know what you've asked for."

Two of us stand guard for a couple of hours at a time throughout the night to ensure safety: one from Seavale and one from Snowark. Understandably, Emberly and Zenevieve don't trust Ezra to be left alone with Ambrose, but Emberly and I refuse to partner; I take my shift with Ambrose and Emberly takes hers with Sierra. During our shift, I'm not surprised when I learn that Ambrose isn't even eighteen yet. He definitely enjoys conversation no matter who it's with. I'm not sure how close he was with Meredith because he ensures that the conversation never veers in that direction. Maybe that's how he distracts himself from the grief; after all, his soft smile and friendly words temporarily take my own mind away from the day...

Something is immediately amiss the next morning as I open my eyes. The realization strikes me like a venomous snake: Ithinor isn't waking up with us.

Every vital part of me sinks. The anger has subsided somewhat and left a severe aching in its wake. My very initiative is trapped under an anchor.

No, you must keep running. For him. None of this can be in vain.

Just looking around the jungle, it stretches on and on with scattered, thick tree trunks; a dense foliage ground; and hanging vines from the branches overhead. The width of the platform is generous, but falling off is still a threat.

Amidst Ithinor's and Meredith's passings, something is absent in my chest. Everyone is under the weight of their own loss as Ambrose extinguishes the fire and Sierra, Ezra, and Zenevieve pack up camp.

I look over at Emberly, who stays against her faraway tree with her things already packed. She keeps a finger against her chin as her brows furrow in concentration.

Her body straightens.

Glancing at my group, I dare to walk over to her. The sunburn across her lightly freckled cheeks and nose is as bright as ever, and I wonder how long ago she earned it.

"Is something wrong?" I ask cautiously.

When her eyes meet mine, they don't hold the contempt I've already come to know. It's as if she's too busy in her thoughts to realize who is actually standing in front of her. "The artifact."

"What?"

"It was so easy," she says, her eyes narrowing, but in thought this time. "The pull, it brought us to every step of the stage. But now—"

I realize the other reason my chest feels so empty. Something *physical* is missing, too. And apparently Emberly has felt that emptiness as much as I have, in more ways than one, as our gazes lock.

"What's the matter?" Zenevieve calls, hands on her hips as she walks from camp to us. The rest of our group gives us their attention.

"The artifact," Emberly answers. Her eyes dart between the people in front of her. Our group seems to finally unlock in their own minds what we've been missing.

"Perfect," Sierra says, walking to us next, "we'll follow you two with the pull."

"That's just it." I drop my hands to my side. "We don't feel the pull. At all."

CHAPTER 19

"YOU CAN'T TAKE ME OUT JUST YET"

Emberly

ONLY ONE THING PROVIDES SLIGHT COMFORT AMIDST the revelation: the pull on every other stage eventually grew so strong that it threatened my steps when I drew too close. That means that Windale didn't have the artifact before we threw them over the edge. Even if that were the case, we would likely still feel something gnawing at us to follow it.

I relentlessly curse the past; I relentlessly curse the fact that the one time Meredith wasn't here to incessantly ask about the artifact's pull was the one time I needed her to.

I curse that she wasn't the one to wake me up this morning. She was supposed to wake up with us.

This race wasn't meant to kill her. She was part of my group. They were all meant to stay safe.

I swallow down the thoughts, forcing them far away from my rationality. The last thing any of us are now is safe; I cannot allow my weaknesses to hinder my survival any further.

Sierra suggests moving farther into the jungle; there must lie something ahead eventually, she reasons. The other stages had us travel great distances before we arrived at our final destination.

She sounds like Meredith when she reasons through a matter. I suppose that's why she's the prat's advisor. When Sierra announces that we should continue walking... I almost hear Meredith tell me to as well. It feels as if she's watching me from somewhere. I want to believe that more than anything—that she can see me right now. That she wants me to know what to do. That is what prompts me to follow the group deeper into the jungle.

Dusk threatens its presence long hours later. If Snowark and Seavale ever talk to each other, whether during mealtimes or breaks or walking, it never delves past superficial conversation. Even Ambrose struggles to find a topic for us all to engage with. I still don't feel the artifact, but I won't be the first to admit it. The prat can be the first; I refuse to look like an incompetent fool. He fits the bill more precisely, anyway.

I've been keeping track of the days since we began the race: the next morning makes eight as we continue our venture into the jungle. Our water supply is low. Zenevieve and Sierra order that we stop walking every once in a while to rest because of it; that is less water we're using to replenish our strength.

The prat stays silent, keeping his place between Sierra and Ezra. I'm unaware of how arrogant and pompous a single man can be. He tried *consoling* me two nights ago about Meredith. Why was I on his mind? Is he still futilely trying to earn my trust?

Do you truly think I'm that much of a fool? I wish he could hear my thoughts. *You're just like the councilmen—and I swore to prove them all wrong.*

It's just past noon when the trees' leaves grow wider and darker. The air is moister here—and smells dustier.

"Rain," Sierra notes, looking up and holding out her hands. Strands of her messy bun stick to the sides of her pink face in the humidity. "Rain is coming, we should collect the water." She turns to Ambrose. We stop with her. "Ambrose, are you able to control the direction of the downpour? Concentrate a portion of it so it lands where we need it to?"

His burned cheeks blush behind his abundant freckles. "I... I might. As long as there's no wind. I've never—"

"The boy isn't used to *liquid* downpour," I say, crossing my arms. "We don't receive much in Snowark, save for summer. It's rare even then. Hence the name: *Snowark*."

Sierra presses her lips together. "I understand that, Emberly," she replies calmly.

I shut my mouth. Even her patience reminds me of Meredith. It may be an advisor's duty to bear with their monarch—but I'm not Sierra's monarch. Yet she still has patience with me. Now I hear Meredith telling me, "Don't be a brat."

Sierra's features soften on me as if she sees my thoughts. Then, she takes her green eyes back to Ambrose. They look Vinean despite how Sierra is supposedly from Seavale. "Do your best, Ambrose," she says. "Anything will be better than what we have now."

The skinny strawberry smiles down at her, nodding. "At your service."

After setting up the waterskins, Ezra alerts the rest of Seavale that their food supply is low as well. Zenevieve walks up to me and relays the same information: we've only one night's worth and then the little that Windale had.

There's a smirk missing from Zenny's lips as she quietly asks, "Care for a hunt? Before the rain begins and the game's driven away?"

That question used to instil excitement. It used to be an invitation to play games in the forest and challenge each other's abilities. Now it's an excuse to escape—a temporary escort out of reality rather than an enhancement of it. Right now, I need her and she needs me. For distraction if nothing else.

I nod before turning to the group. "Zenevieve and I will hunt for dinner before the rain chases it away."

"Are you sure it's safe to separate?" Sierra asks warily, furrowing her brows. I still swear that I can hear traces of the distinct, horizontal Vinean accent in her voice. "We don't know where the other kingdoms—"

"You'll find my and Zenevieve's expertise with a weapon sufficient," I tell her. "We're more than capable of defending ourselves."

She exhales, turning back to camp. While the rest of the group pays no mind, the royal prat keeps his eyes on me for longer than I can allow. He stands from setting down his satchel beside the pile meant to start a fire.

It's as if my glares are your favourite slice of pie, I think. I feed him another one.

Zenevieve and I travel forward and towards the left side of the platform. From edge to edge, we have at least a couple hundred metres of space; we've the hunting space we need.

My knees instinctually wobble as I glance at the left edge.

Zenevieve willingly follows me farther away from it. The tree trunks are thinner in this area. A greater abundance of their branches sit overhead, as well as vines. Creatures scatter across their playground in the trees amidst the dusty humidity. Every rustle is a tantalizing sound for my stomach: a meal makes each movement we hear.

"Don't lose Rowena over the edge by throwing her," Zenevieve tells me, standing with her back against mine.

"Do you take me for a fool?" I scoff. "No meal is worth losing her over."

Within those few sentence, quiet begins settling over the warm jungle. We slowly turn. Zenevieve's dagger is firm in her left hand and Rowena in mine.

"I truly hope we didn't make a mistake by leaving Ambrose alone with them..." she whispers. "At least he's got his magic to protect him."

"Against the mountain of a man Seavale have for a knight?" Unease rocks in my chest the longer the idea sits in my mind. "Perhaps one of us should have stayed behind."

"I have to believe that they're not so terrible," Zenny says. "For the sake of everything we argued when we first met. After all, Sierra's proven rather resourceful; and Ezra seems gentler than his build suggests. As for the prince... well, what say you about him?"

"What say I?" I ask dully. "We'll be here all night, but let's start with his arrogance. His stupidity! His pride and audacious belief that we're mad enough to believe that he isn't another prat who wants an all-powerful throne to himself."

"Tell me how you really feel," Zenny mutters. The animals

may be quiet, but I can hear her smirk. "Forget 'handsome', did you?"

I pause, now facing the direction we're meant to eventually continue in. Zenevieve stops with me. I turn around. She raises a brow at me.

I smack her shoulder with the face of my dagger.

"Ah, I see." She scoffs playfully. Her weapon drops to her side. "You simply don't want to admit it. It's all right, no one faults you for thinking—"

"Is this how you hunt nowadays?" I snap, turning back around. "Focus."

She kisses her teeth. "I'm only trying to ease your nerves. Animals can sense when a tense presence is nearby."

"You wish to ease me by confessing your crush on the Royal Prat of Seavale?"

She elbows me from behind. "Merely an observation. I've never seen anyone with eyes so blue."

"Or a head so big," I hiss. "Or smirk so cocky or cheekbones as high as his ego or—"

Zenevieve frivolously chuckles. "Never mind, you've said enough! It's worse than I thought."

"Is this your sick way of distracting yourself from Meredith?"

The words fly out of my mouth before even my mind knows that they're there.

Zenevieve stills behind me again. I only dare to turn back around to face her when she does. Her full lips are parted as if I've slapped her across the face. In a way, that is exactly what I've done.

"Pardon me?" she whispers.

"How could you say such things in light of her death? It was two days ago!"

"You think me so careless?" she hisses. Her upturned eyes narrow, hardening on me. "How could you ever bring yourself to say something like that?"

"Why else would you be so crude?"

"You've no reason to be so defensive or insensitive!" She takes the last step she can towards me—taking advantage of the inches she has on me and blatantly looking down at me.

She knows better. She knows how that makes me feel. I truly have crossed a line.

Let all that you do be done in love.

Meredith's dying words send ringing echoes through my head. They grip my temper by its throat. I remember how I felt just before apologizing to her on Lavara's stage. I remember her leash she would use on me to remind me of my place. She isn't here to remind me anymore. And while I don't want to admit my mistakes, Zenevieve is now the only person in this world worthy of my humility. Especially because I'm being a brat right now.

"I'm sorry." My gaze falls from her scolding eyes. "I... I wanted to be better. For her. But it seems my decency went with her. It's as if—I'm unsure how to even function without—"—a sudden breath interrupts me—"without her always..."

"You can always be better, Ember." Zenny's voice softens to melted butter. She rests a hand on my arm. "As long as you've the will to be."

Then why haven't I learned after ten years with her? Even after she's...?

234

Gone. In an instant.

I swallow hard. "She's not dead, Zenevieve. She can't be."

Silence blares from my best friend. She won't even look at me. Her armour looks heavier on her right now.

I was supposed to be better for her. I finally convinced myself that she would stay, and...

A hundred curses run through my head. Against every warning to myself—against every lie I told myself—I had grown attached to Meredith. More than that: I had *adopted* her into my life. I warned myself for years that she wouldn't stay, to not attach to her, all to no avail. She arrived too early in my life. What child wouldn't attach to the gentle, loving mentor that tolerates them, encourages them—even unrightfully believes in them? Each day was bearable with her. I was heard and cared about and, dare I say, content with her. I loved her. And despite how much I've supposedly grown since I was eight years old, not once did Meredith ever hear those words from me. I always thought I couldn't allow myself to love her because she would abandon me, too. She would leave me with a broken heart.

And she did. The second I allowed myself to love her, to accept her place in my life—no matter how often I feared it—I lost my advisor nonetheless.

It is the first time I've ever lost someone I cared about—and I can't even afford to grieve her here in a death race. Am I truly meant to continue as though her loss means nothing?

"How do I do this if she's gone?" I dare to whisper. "How do I pretend I didn't lose the only mother I ever had?"

"You don't." Zenny raises her hand to my shoulder. "You honour her memory so that nothing was in vain."

I shake my head. Every breath is shaky beyond my control. "I don't—"

My sight snags on a small creature running up the bark of a tree behind her. It stops in the dead centre of the trunk.

Shushing Zenevieve, I sheathe Rowena. I slowly reach for my bow behind me and then an arrow. The humidity minimises the sounds of the branches and leaves I step on. They're too soggy to create much sound; that makes each step easier. When I'm a few metres away, I relax my arms, keeping them firm. My fingers release the arrow.

The squirrel scampers up the tree the second my bowstring snaps back. Unfortunately, that doesn't even matter: my arrow misses. A yelp erupts from behind the tree.

Zenevieve raises her dagger. I nock another arrow.

After a moment of rustling, the Seavalen prat emerges from around the tree. He holds up my arrow. "I think your aim was off, Princess," he says in that strange, lazy accent with the hideous "r" pronunciation. Just like cursed Windale's. "You can't take me out just yet."

"You scared the squirrel away!" I exclaim, lowering my bow.

"And you didn't even hit the tree." He wiggles the arrow in his hand. "Which means you would have missed anyway."

"I'm about to make sure this next one meets its target, you royal dunce—"

Wait. If he was nearby...

...he had to have heard everything Zenevieve and I said about him.

She presses her lips together beside me as though she's been caught. I swat her shoulder with the back of my hand. My inside wince at the sting of my sunburn. Zenevieve kisses her teeth and rolls her eyes at me.

"Well, evidently, nothing is going to bite here except you lot." She exhales and runs a hand through her frizzy curls. "I'm going farther into the jungle to try alone. I think we're scaring away everything nearby. Gather some firewood for anything I nab."

"Zenevieve," I whisper as she turns around.

Even the prat chimes, "I only came to survey—"

"Or hunt here, I don't care," she says, facing me. "I just need to try on my own, all right?"

"We'll tell the prat to leave, we were just—"

"Emberly—" Zenevieve raises her hands. Just as quickly, she clenches them into fists—pulling the reins on herself. "Let me go alone for a bit. Please."

I don't understand it at first. She wanted to go together for the sake of distracting each other. Why is she suddenly unable to focus with me around like we were doing just moments ago, before—?

Because distraction will prevent her from grieving—and, therefore, weakening. That was why I needed her, too. Together, though, we landed at the feet of our mourning nonetheless. Zenevieve wasn't as close to Meredith as I was—but I realise that she still has a loss to grieve. And any "distraction" I provide her will only lead straight back to her loss.

Without another word, she turns around. I grip my bow tighter and watch her walk deeper into the jungle.

Muted, crunchy footsteps approach behind me. I reluctantly turn around. The prince has stepped closer to me but still keeps his distance. He sighs and bends down to pick up a stray branch. One sentence echoes in my mind: *Don't be a brat.*

Fine. At the very least, Seavale hasn't tried to slaughter us yet. Admittedly, they have that in their favour. I won't gather somewhere else out of spite and fan the flames—but I also certainly won't waste my words on the prince.

Mounting my bow on my back, I walk to the trees on the left side of the area. My stare scours the ground for the driest sticks. Of course, they're all closer to the edge: less humidity. My mind repeatedly instructs me to avert my gaze from it.

"Why don't you grab your bow and I'll help you hunt?"

I freeze halfway up from picking up another stick. Only the councilmen have *that* much audacity.

My teeth grind together as I straighten. I turn around. The prat already has more sticks than I do.

This prideful wart of a—

"Excuse me?" I ask lowly.

He nods curtly at the bow hanging on my back. "Archery. I've been handy with a bow for half my life. I could help you practice."

My lips uncontrollably stretch into a disbelieving grin. Before I can process my actions, I drop the sticks. This dolt is serious.

"I've been shooting since I was a girl, *Your Highness*," I spit. My hands beg to ball up into fists. "If you're going to judge my skillset based on a single shot, I'd re-evaluate your 'expertise', you arrogant prat!"

He blinks. I've stunned him for only a moment. All too soon, he recovers. "Well, I definitely wouldn't have missed—"

"Zenevieve distracted me!" I exclaim, marching up to him. "I had that arrow perfectly in line, I simply didn't shoot when I was clear headed!"

"Is that what you say every time you miss?" he says, running his tan hand through his dark hair. He stares back at me with deep-set eyes that I wish weren't so blue—eyes that make me hesitate to curse him.

I open my mouth to try nonetheless. My glare snags again on the slit in his left eyebrow: the scar. How I desire to use it as ammunition, but I must assume that it's just as bringing up my own. I despise that he has that, too. I despise that we have such similar markings. Such similar losses. Such similar people who have left us.

Worst of all, Leon's smirk isn't teasing right now. It's victorious. Like he knows every thought going through my head.

I doubt it. It's his arrogance.

His broad, chainmail-protected chest *is* intimidating—especially because I'm an entire head shorter than he is. I have to remember that he's taking advantage of his build. I, on the other hand, have one better: a mind. The mind may always be stronger than the body.

"You haven't the slightest idea what you're talking about, prat," I snap. "Perhaps you didn't hear the conversation just before I took my shot. If you had, I can't imagine even the Prince of Lavara being so heartless."

In truth, I can. But it delivers the message: something softens in Leon's resolve now. His cocky smirk drops, and his eyes relax.

Then, he steps back. "I'm sorry," he says.

"I'm sorry"?

I scoff, amused as I turn away. "Right."

"I mean it." His words are no longer harsh. A softness coats them now, as if they're seeking my approval. "You're right. Really, I want to know—if I may—how you're doing after... that."

I stop walking. It's the first time he's spoken so sincerely to me.

Let all that you do be done in love.

My jaw tightens. I almost regret ever hearing those words. Surely they don't apply to him. Surely...

Don't be a brat.

I grind my teeth. *Fine. I'll play along.* But that absolutely doesn't mean that I have to invite him to a seat at my table.

"I'm fine if I don't think about it," I state. That more than includes when I'm in the presence of someone who is likely collecting my weaknesses.

The prince is silent. That moment doesn't last long enough. "Yes, that's how I feel. I won't be able to move forward otherwise."

Then don't raise the matter next time. I scarcely manage to bar the words in time.

I bend down and pick up the sticks I dropped. Just ahead, closer to the edge, sticks litter the ground around another tree. They appear fully dry.

I exhale. *Don't look at the edge.*

I walk to the foot of the tree. The trunk, I know, grows infinitely downwards beyond the platform. I wonder where the tree's roots are, if it has any, as my fingers scrape the sticks. The area in front of me is barren now. In my arms is half of what

Zenevieve would need to cook a mouse.

The edge has more. But...

A light chuckle ripples behind me. "You seem a little—on edge."

Don't tell me he thinks himself a jester as well!

I turn my head and glare at the royal idiot. "I'd be more worried about what will happen to you if you don't shut it, prat."

"I'm only concerned about having enough wood, Princess." He nods to the meagre pile in my arms.

It's as if he knows that that title boils my blood. I grind my teeth, my hands clenching the wood tighter. Fine—to the edge, I go. I will not allow this lump of horse manure the advantage of knowing my greatest weakness. Not even Meredith was allowed to know by my tongue, only by my pathetic example during Lavara's and Windale's stage; I never wanted her to have yet another reason to pity me. I certainly will not relinquish anything to this dolt.

I'm not stepping over the edge, I repeat to myself. *The ground is dense enough to hold me. We're meant to stand on it. It's all right. I'm safe, I'm fine. I'm safe.*

Crouching, I inch a step around the tree despite my instincts. My torso tries to lean as far back as possible. The next stick is a little farther out. I reach forward when my balance overcompensates, straying right. Panic urges me to stand, but my body leans over. I scream as the edge pulls me backwards and towards the void.

"*Emberly!*"

I squeeze my eyes shut. Wood clatters in the distance. Someone grabs my hand as my body falls, pulling me into a strong, metal figure. We step away from the edge, my frame firmly locked in an embrace. My eyes refuse to open. I'm shaking. My face stays pressed against the cool sensation of chainmail.

I'm not falling.

My hot breaths are trapped in front of me. They inflame the stinging sunburn on my cheeks. I can't stop trembling. Paralysis has stunned my being. My every motion is mindless, my mind rendered blank in my terror's wake.

I desperately try to control my pants of fear. Someone pants above me—with relief.

My heart still beats like a rabbit's moments later. I only realise how much time has passed when the arms around me loosen. I remember that I'm being held safely away from the edge. I instinctually look up. A pair of deep-set eyes that match the sky back in our world meet my gaze.

Leon is holding me.

I urgently step away, stumbling. He grabs my wrist again, this time swinging me around so that we swap positions. He is closer to the edge now.

Why—why would he do that? Why would he be willing to take the risk of falling?

I don't... I don't want to shove him off the edge anymore.

How dare he?

"I didn't—" he urges, holding up his hands, "I didn't mean anything by that, I promise—"

"I know," I state. I unclench my sweaty fists. "I know."

Why would you save me? Why would he save me? How did he get to me in time?

Instincts. That's how. He has good instincts. Even worse, he has good intentions; there isn't any way he would have saved me—of all people—in time otherwise.

He shouldn't have done that. He shouldn't have done that and he knows it.

Why did he?

I open my mouth. My thank-you catches in my throat like a fly in honey. I have to force it through against everything my mind is telling me: "Thank you."

I turn and walk back the direction Zenevieve and I came from. My hands are still trembling. My knees are still shaking. There are no sticks in my arms.

Zenevieve takes another bite of squirrel thigh next to me. "Thank you for the wood." She nudges my shoulder with hers as we sit a good distance away from the fire.

I look up at Leon sitting with his friends and Ambrose at camp. They feast on two colourful birds Zenevieve caught and swap jokes with each other, jokes native to Snowark and Seavale. I heard Sierra reveal a moment ago that only her father is from Seavale; her mother is from Vineah. That was where she was raised. Nonetheless, she has always felt more at home at Seavale. That's why she chooses to speak with Seavale's accent.

I can't fault her for that. I know what it feels like to not belong in your own kingdom. After today, I struggle more than ever to fight that narrative. After all, I'm petrified of something as small as heights (which certainly don't feel small when you're up there). I couldn't even conquer it during Windale's stage;

Zenevieve had to climb and find the vine with my instruction. Today, when I finally tried to conquer that fear for the sake of helping my group, I almost had myself killed.

Had it not been for...

"Ember?" Zenny offers me a piece of meat. I shake my head. "What happened when I left you two? Were you really arguing like he said when I heard him shout your name?"

I press my lips together. This race has elicited enough of my weaknesses. Zenevieve knows most of them already, but constantly being so open with them will only develop a dangerous habit. I can't confess what truly happened.

"He proved himself competent enough in gathering sticks," I finally say, folding my hands in my lap. "That's about all he's good for. He's a royal, infuriating, insufferable prat no matter how—handsome anyone may think he is."

She nudges me again, chuckling. "Don't let him hear that last bit, or he may just—"

"Your Highness, Zenevieve!" Ezra exclaims from the fire. His sword is unsheathed, his startlingly light eyes fixated above us. "Come to the fire, now!"

Zenevieve and I sit up from the tree and follow his urgent gaze upward: gargantuan snakes with the legs of a centipede are crawling down the trunk, baring their fangs and ready to strike.

CHAPTER 20

"ICE CAN BURN JUST AS MUCH AS FIRE"

Leo

ZENEVIEVE UNSHEATHES HER SWORD, AND I ALMOST expect Emberly to fall back. Instead, she grabs her bow sitting beside her, throws her quiver around her shoulders, and shoots an arrow. It strikes one of the creatures in the middle of its head before I can blink.

That's what she was talking about. She was right: I assumed that she was only familiar with melee combat, and I judged her based on one shot.

Sierra runs from my side, sliding her sword out and running to Emberly and Zenevieve. She slices one of the snake monsters' heads clean off with a swipe as Zenevieve thrusts her weapon through another's.

I turn around and grab my dagger. A centipede-snake's hundred legs crawls toward me. I run up to it and leap to land one foot on its neck. Bending down, I run my dagger straight through its head.

No skull—all right, that will make this easier.

The firelight exposes another approaching beside the one I killed. I grab my sword from its sheath as it opens its mouth to strike, and plunge it straight through its throat. I continue switching between dagger and sword, either stabbing or beheading the centi-snakes crawling toward me on all fronts. Emberly's bow flings arrow after arrow behind me.

I really hope she isn't missing with all those arrows! I don't have the time to verify as I thrust my dagger into the thick, tough skin of another monster.

Ambrose throws fire at every head that moves to strike him. Ezra defends him from behind, and I cover Ezra. The bitter, dusty stench of monster blood and sweat begins to swirl with the humidity, but I can't afford to cover my mouth; I'm hardly able to defend myself *and* Ezra. There are only three of us—

If only we had Ithinor to help. My rapid, tired breaths threaten to choke me as I slice off another head. *He would protect me again, he...*

Something is stuck in my throat. I run a hand through my hair as I try to swallow it, closing my eyes. The memories flash beyond my control, regret pressing down on my chest. *He always covered me. Saved me. And I couldn't even save him—*

"Leo!"

Ezra jumps in front of me, his sword jabbing the head of a centi-snake lunging for me. The creature lifelessly drops to the ground, and Ezra whirls around. His stern face is saturated in sweat, furious eyes demanding an explanation.

"Thank—thank you!" I tell him, shaking my head. "I'm sorry, I'm here, don't stop!"

Before he can reply, I move past him. I cannot think about it. I can't. I can only afford one thought right now: the years of training I spent with the Royal Guard. Protecting the people still with me.

I urge the adrenaline through my veins as another centi-snake poses to strike. I drive my dagger into its flesh, my sword slicing another before I turn and thrust my dagger into its head, too. I look up in time to see Sierra behead a centi-snake advancing toward Emberly. As Emberly turns around to face her, she opens her mouth but then raises her bow. Her arrow strikes a monster lowering itself from the branches above Sierra. It falls limp from the tree and behind Sierra's feet.

She just saved my best friend. Evidently, their watch shifts together have served them well. My chest swells in gratitude.

They exchange a friendly glance before turning back to the remaining creatures. I follow suit, deflecting an incoming strike targeting Ambrose. Fatigue claws at my limbs, but I can't afford to falter for a second.

I unsheathe my blade from my last centi-snake, ready for rest—until another, twice the size of its clan members, encroaches on Ezra as he cuts off a head aiming for Ambrose. The giant's gaping maw poses to strike. I lunge forward, intercepting its attack with my body and slashing at it with my sword. The monster, its head even bigger than mine, hisses and screeches in retaliation. Its jaw drops again, and my next slash fumbles. I brace myself for its strike until a blast of fire pushes it away. I look behind me: Ambrose's pale, sweat-drenched face is carved by brave determination. I grin a thank-you at him as Ezra's sword decapitates the giant. It slumps to the ground in a lifeless heap.

Our exhausted panting is the only thing I hear in our area by the fire. The air is thick with an eerie silence as we reserve a moment, gaping at the bloodied grave of centi-snake corpses.

"Well," I begin breathlessly, "they didn't need to throw such a hissy fit."

Ezra isn't too tired to smack me on the back of the head. "Do you really think now is—?"

A scream ruptures the air, cutting him clean off.

We turn. Sierra is slicing the head off of a snake monster whose jaw is clamped around Zenevieve's calf. Its fangs have penetrated her armor as though it's jelly.

"Zenevieve!" Ambrose cries, running to her as Ezra and I hurriedly sheathe our weapons. We follow him to where the ladies stand by the tree, far from the fire. Ambrose and Ezra drape Zenevieve's arms over their shoulders. Sierra urges them to drag her to the fire and Zenevieve to keep her right leg raised.

Emberly stays behind, clutching herself. I watch her as Zenevieve chimes, "Ha, interesting—the more it tingles, the more I can't feel it."

I'm not the only one with terrible comedic timing.

At the fire behind me, with Zenevieve's permission, Ezra takes off her right leg armor for Sierra to address the bite. I turn around and watch Sierra slow, her hands hovering over Zenevieve's calf.

"Red and swollen," she announces. "A little discolored. And you said it tingles and you can't feel it?"

Anxiety bubbles in my chest as Zenevieve confirms. My

mind finishes the diagnosis: *Venom.*

Ambrose quickly proposes to extract it with his healing magic, and Sierra promptly agrees. I turn back around and meet Emberly's observant stare. Her wavy hair sticks to her pale face with sweat, eyes locked on Zenevieve as she continues holding herself. She still won't approach the fire even when her best friend is being tended to there.

My curiosity fizzes. "Venom isn't contagious—"

"I'm aware," she snaps.

Silence trails her words, and I can't be bothered to even try to understand her.

I walk back to the fire. The flames are almost too hot amidst my remaining adrenaline as I kneel beside Ezra. "How is the wound, Sierra?"

She sits across from me, applying pressure to the bite with a cloth. "Ambrose extracted at least most of the venom. Enough for her to survive. I only need to dress it now and ensure she stops bleeding. These are—terrible bite marks. Almost like being stabbed with a letter opener."

I internally wince, pursing my lips. When I risk a glance at Emberly, she has yet to steal her gaze away from us; yet her eyes aren't even red. I'm not sure that the woman knows how to cry.

Minutes pass, and the sweat along Zenevieve's brow intensifies. She's asked a couple of times if we can move closer to Emberly, but Sierra needs the firelight. Zenevieve finally closes her eyes, her head lying in Ambrose's lap. The firelight further reddens the burn across his face. He rubs her black coils back with a gentle hand as he asks, "How are you feeling, Zenny?"

"Don't call me that, Rosy," she replies dully with faint

breaths. "You have to earn that first."

"You get to call me 'Rosy'," he says incredulously, dropping his hand to his side.

She smiles with full lips, eyes still closed like she can see him through her eyelids. "I do. I've earned it: you used Portia as target practice, remember?"

Ambrose exhales dejectedly, and I wonder who Portia is. I exchange a confused glance with Ezra, who sits on his knees next to me.

"Zenevieve," Sierra begins, resting a gentle hand on her shoulder, "he has the right idea: how do you feel? I'm concerned by how much you're sweating."

"Oh, fine." She exhales. "Just fine. Don't you lot love summer? It's a lovely day, isn't it?" She opens her eyes, curiosity settling in her round, full features. "Say, when did we arrive in Seavale?"

Sierra presses a hand to the back of her forehead. "She's feverish."

Zenevieve scoffs, closing her eyes. "I'm *kidding*. Feverish, yes, but not hallucinating."

"That isn't funny." Ambrose scolds her, scrunching his brows together.

"Calm down, Rosy," she replies, turning her head slightly in his lap. "If I can take care of you, I can certainly take care of myself."

"Then I'm grateful to say that you'll be fine," Sierra says. "Hopefully, this won't transfigure into an infection. For now, your body is trying to naturally expel the remaining venom."

I look up at Emberly again as if to verify that she heard the news. She simply sits with her back against the same tree fifty feet away, her knees close to her chest. A litter of dead centi-snakes lies around her, but she doesn't appear as worried anymore. She seems to be... observing.

Why does she absolutely refuse to sit by the fire?

"Are you done dressing the bite?" Zenevieve asks, peering at Sierra through one open eye.

"Yes," she replies cautiously.

"Then take me to Ember." Zenevieve closes her eyes again. "She needs me."

Sierra exhales, letting her body slouch. "All right. Ezra, can—?"

"No," Zenevieve says like a child, pointing at me. "I want him to do it."

The three of us gawk, but nobody protests. I'm unsure how to interpret her request; it's as if even she has a spiteful vendetta against me, knowing how Emberly and I regard each other.

Only for her sake, I carefully pick her up with one arm supporting her back and the other under her knees. Sierra, Ezra, and Ambrose are quiet behind me as I carry her to Emberly. Her green eyes light up, and she stands from the tree.

"Zenny." She sighs in relief as I set her down. "Are you all right? Did they hurt you?"

"Not this time, Ember," she replies. "They're safe for tonight."

"You're sweating," Emberly notes. "Are you feverish?"

Zenevieve shrugs. "A more peaceful state of mind to pretend what is not there than confront what is."

Emberly briefly meets my eyes, seems to remember that she

despises me, and then looks back down at her knight. "Have you gone mad?"

Zenevieve sucks on her teeth, scoffing. "Can a woman not *pretend* all is fine? Is that a crime now?"

Something like realization seems to pass over Emberly. Her shoulders slouch as she exhales. All I can do is watch them exchange a dynamic I'm not fluent in.

"Why isn't the handsome one talking?" Zenevieve asks skeptically, opening one eye. She directs it at me. "You're not *that* scared of her, are you?"

"Scared?" My throat borders on a scoff. "Of—?"

"Are you certain that would be so hard to believe?" Emberly asks, raising a challenging brow.

I cock one of my own, rubbing my mouth. "I do. Me, my high cheekbones, and I."

Her hand grips her dagger. "Are you ready to find out *how* curiosity killed the cub, prat—?"

"Children, children!" Zenevieve chimes below us, resting her hands on our knees. "We just fought a clan of life-sized snake bugs together, surely you can make peace by now! Or if you two don't shut up, I'll haunt you both from the grave."

"You're not dying," Emberly snaps. "Never joke like that again."

Silence trails loudly after. The weight of those words presses heavily on my chest.

Right. Those snakes could have killed us. Any of us. And I almost cost the battle for myself *and* Ezra.

He shouldn't have had to save me. I should have been focused, I should have been maintaining the fight for my group at the front of my mind. And yet, my mind has become my greatest threat. Grief almost cost me my life tonight. Ithinor's dying words were grounded in me finishing this race without his guidance and wisdom, and I almost immediately proved them all to be in vain.

I can't allow myself to be so easily consumed, I cannot drown myself in the unchangeable past. Ithinor gave his life in the hope that I would have mine. At the very least, I need to survive—if for nobody else's sake, then for his. Surviving... that is all I can do for him now.

"Then stop bickering," Zenevieve tells us. "If not because you realize in full what happened tonight, then for my sake right now."

Emberly and I lock eyes again. I press my lips together. Silence passes between us, but I think I feel an understanding with it: she and Sierra saved each other tonight, and Ambrose saved me. Seavale saved Snowark, and Snowark saved Seavale. That is what Zenevieve means—and that's why I sense a tacit agreement pass between me and Emberly.

"Do you insist on staying in the dark?" Sierra calls from behind us at the campfire. I turn my head and find that the other half of our team is staring after us.

"I don't know," Emberly replies, "do you plan on washing off the blood and guts from yourselves? Because otherwise, the darkness makes it rather easier to talk to each other without vomiting."

I'm uncertain whether she's being blatantly un-ironic—because part of me is inclined to agree with her. Evidently, the three of them agree and walk over to the tree, kneeling all around

Zenevieve.

"Miss us, did you?" she chimes, keeping a hand over her eyes.

"I miss home," Sierra replies between me and Ezra, "which is why, with Zenevieve stable, we must discuss these stages. We know that each one represents their respective kingdom, and each has an artifact that pulls the monarchs to it. But three days have passed now with no pull. There must be a pattern with all the others and when the pulls began—maybe we're meant to solve a riddle of sorts to unlock the next artifact."

"The pull was immediate for every stage except this one," I say. "As for the artifacts themselves... the only thing I can think of... It's almost like they're—"

"Patterned," Emberly muses, eyes mindlessly fixed on the ground.

"What's that?" Sierra asks, leaning forward.

"Patterned," Emberly repeats, but she retracts upon meeting Sierra's eyes. "They're... Well, they're all the opposite of their respective stage in some way: Snowark's ice with a fire sword, Lavara's lava with an ice arrow, Windale's wind with a rooted plant, and Seavale's water with—I suppose a representation of land."

"I thought so as well!" Ambrose chirps, his brows furrowed curiously next to her. "So I'm *not* mad."

"I wouldn't go that far, Ginger," Emberly says, but Zenevieve is close enough to smack her for it.

"I think..." I begin in realization, unsure of where the words are coming from, "that's exactly what it is, they're patterned."

"Then if so," Ezra begins, on Sierra's other side, "then what

254

is the opposite of Vineah's jungle? Or vines? Or... trees?"

We exchange glances with one another as though we're hoping the other will have the answer. It is definitely my hope right now.

"Solving that may be our only hope at finding the next artifact." Sierra exhales and kneels to stand. "Until then, we'll keep surviving and be on our guard. Before we experience something worse than a bite."

"Speaking of..."—Ezra glances all around at the centi-snake corpses—"do you suppose these are edible?"

"Anything that breathes and has flesh is edible," Zenevieve remarks, a hand still over her eyes.

An eerie silence smothers the air—because it's true.

"Is that the fever speaking?" I ask.

"No, that's Zenevieve." Ambrose shrugs. "The rain when you're too sunny and the sun when your storm is brewing. She's very talented."

A few centi-snakes approach as we prepare for bed; but when they happen upon their clan's bodies, they immediately retreat. We devote that observation to memory in case, the Ancients forbid, we run into more.

Zenevieve is well enough to walk the next afternoon, though she's now hindered with a small limp. Thanks to Ambrose drying the centi-snake meat, we have a lifetime supply of jerky for food. The rain this morning also refilled our waterskins. Morale is as steady as it was when we first began the race...

I bite my lip as my group takes another rest. The warm climate provides a humidity so intense that my shirt and pants under my armor is sticking to me. But pacing ourselves with rest truly is vital.

The most productive thing you can do.

My jaw locks. We're on the fourth day of traveling in Vineah's stage, but Ithinor has only been gone for three. The realization twists the blade deeper in my chest. I've woken up three mornings in a row expecting him to greet me for the day—and three mornings now, I've had to overcome a debilitating wave of mourning and regret. To force myself to be better for my group.

It's easy to be reminded of him. It's even easier to remember him when nothing else occupies my focus. His memory burns in my mind all the more in the calm—in the rest. There's nothing else to think about except him when we're left to the silence of traveling. I promised myself last night that I wouldn't allow the past to affect my survival—but grief is no respecter of persons or initiative. At the end of it all remains my regret that he isn't here when he should be.

He would be so disappointed in me if he were. I've done nothing to solve our escape, Sierra is doing all the work. And my treatment toward Emberly ever since...

I can't do this without him, I told him. How do I become someone worthy of his pride if he isn't here to guide me anymore? How am I meant to honor his memory like this? His death—

I swallow, hardly managing to suppress my shaky breath out. The wound is reopening. Why now? Why is it spiraling out of my control now?

We're safe. We trust each other enough now and nobody's life is in danger. I've run out of distractions.

I'm trying to continue without the weight of the unchangeable past, but I feel just as trapped in my grief and this reality as I did in those cells under the castle when I was a boy. If I can't find a distraction, I need to endure this alone before my team suffers the consequences—like how Ezra almost did last night.

"I'll be back," I whisper to Sierra next me.

"Where are you going?" she asks, brows furrowed in caution.

"I'll only be a few minutes." I don't have a way of revealing that this is about Ithinor without ripping open the wound completely. "I'll—forage while you rest."

I'm grateful that she knows how to hear the unspoken messages in my voice. "Don't wander too far," she tells me.

I walk deeper into the dense foliage of the tree branches and bushes, never minding the eyes I feel on me. The vegetation grows thicker the farther into the jungle we travel, but I'm glad for the extra covering just in case.

"Leon."

I stop. "Leon"? Is that really—?

"I'd like to come along. If I may."

Emberly Whitaker just asked, "May I?" To me.

I turn around. She stands with a calm stature, stray strands of dark-auburn hair sticking to her lightly freckled face. Her bow on her back is missing... as though she's trying to display amicability. For once. The first time ever, as far as I'm aware.

This must be an important matter. But...

Part of me wants to turn her away. Another part is dangerously curious about what she could possibly want with me that doesn't involve threatening or insulting me—possibly. And the biggest part warns to not burn a bridge in construction. It's as though her presence in front of me right now is... another chance. As though Ithinor can hear my thoughts, wherever he is, and is watching over me.

Distraction, I realize.

On top of all that... Emberly understands. With Meredith. She understands in a way not even Sierra can.

All I manage is a nod. I wait until she arrives at my side before continuing my walk into the jungle.

"Congratulations," she begins with downcast eyes. "You are the third person ever who has genuinely earned these words from me, besides Zenevieve and..."

I glimpse her in time to watch her swallow.

Her gaze stays low. "I'm sorry."

I freeze, but she rolls her eyes as she stops with me. Half of me is convinced that I hallucinated the words. My mouth falls agape until I regain the ability to speak: "Did you say—?"

"Before you make me regret those words, I'm going to tell you that I regret being so harsh in my initial judgment towards you. I won't apologize for being wary, but—there was perhaps a... politer way to approach it."

I restrain a smile; she'll likely only interpret that as a challenge, and I've already received far more from her than I ever expected to. "Thank you. Admittedly, I wasn't entirely right, either... and I potentially crossed borders that I maybe shouldn't have approached."

She hums. "That apology was so terrible that I'm starting to think it wasn't one."

I roll my eyes. "I'm sorry. Better?"

She nods, and we continue walking. "Losing…" Her eyes have never evaded mine for so long. "Losing Meredith—and then almost losing Zenevieve—held up a mirror, if you can believe it. And…"

I nod. "Don't. You can stop there. I… I know."

"You do, don't you?" Only now is she brave enough to meet our eyes.

I almost stop walking again, letting my stare fall into hers. "I do."

She turns hers back down to the platform. "But do not misunderstand: I won't forget the last four days just like that. I've learned a few things—but letting my guard down isn't one."

I take a tight, deep breath. "Four days…"

"Yes, four. Shooting an arrow isn't the only thing I can calculate."

I shrug. "You'll understand my surprise in how you were actually accurate this time."

She shoves my arm, which actually manages to make me stumble. "Drop that, prat."

How is she so strong?

She stops walking, turning to face me and crossing her arms. Neither her petite, short build nor how I have an entire head on her steal from her intimidating nature, forget the scar on her forehead. She peers up at me. "As I said, and before you forget—I do not suggest you cross me again, Prince Leon."

Something has shifted this time. There is no trace of resentment anymore. She isn't challenging me; she's daring me—almost tempting me to engage this time.

The dappled sunlight shines through the dense canopy of tree branches above us, casting shifting shadows on her delicate features. I look down into her sharp, calculating eyes. Her challenge has lent me the courage on its own.

"Why?" I ask, cocking a brow. "Would your blade actually touch me this time?"

Her eyes stay with mine like her dare is growing in intensity. Those muted-green irises become a stormy sea of power, and her resistance slices through the humid air. It's her turn.

"Your mistake, prat," she whispers.

Her callused fingers grip my wrists and pull my hands behind my back. She shoves my back into a tree I didn't even realize was there. The impact knocks out my breath, my bow and quiver unable to soften it. My stun leaves her time to retract her left hand, unsheathe her dagger, and press the icy blade to my throat.

It's as if the blade wants me to remember the kingdom it was forged in.

"You're playing with fire, cub," she whispers, her breath tickling my chin. Her grip on her dagger is too steady for a woman who supposedly doesn't want to kill me. "And I'm from the kingdom of ice. Let me warn you now:"—she leans forward, pressing the blade harder against my skin—"ice can burn just as much as fire."

My heart pounds like a hammer against cloth. She can definitely sense it through my armor. Why is my heart beating straight through my chest? Why can I scarcely feel my breath?

"Your move," she says.

A surge of adrenaline courses through me. My right hand jerks free from her hold. I grip her wrist, holding the dagger against my own throat. Her eyes widen ever so slightly, betraying a hint of shock.

"Are you ready to see how far I'm willing to cross, Princess?"

The impossible happens: her eyes fail, breaking away from mine. Her hold on the dagger weakens. I release her wrist like I've broken her. I almost think I have.

"Princess?"

The word shatters whatever trance she was under: the tip of the blade pokes the bottom of my chin. "For your sake, I hope you're a fast learner," she states. "Quit calling me anything related to the crown, or Rowena *will* taste your blood."

I can't laugh; I know that she will make good on that promise.

I hold up my hands in surrender. "Understood, firefly."

Maybe my mind has been playing with the word without my knowledge, because it falls from my lips without thought. Emberly's eyes narrow at me, but she doesn't question it. It's almost as though she's too afraid to push herself past where she's already gone, but something tells me that this border is far from where she's usually willing to stop at.

She finally lowers her dagger. "Then I'm done with you for now," she says. "Finish finding your berries or whatever you're scavenging for."

My mouth falls agape as she turns and begins walking back in the direction of our team. "I never said—"

"Shake the dirt off your fur, cub," she calls, pushing aside a low-hanging branch in her way. "You're easy enough for the illiterate palace boys to read."

CHAPTER 21

"IF YOU NEED TO FALL,
FALL INTO ME"

Emberly

A FEW SNAKE MONSTERS JOIN US JUST BEFORE BED THAT night. Throwing their corpses around our camp deter any that try to approach. Being far from the fire, I have to keep an extra corpse by me as I sit against my tree.

I'm grateful that Zenevieve and Ambrose aren't foolish enough to expose why I must ostracise myself from the others. Nonetheless, it's a surprise—a pleasant one, I'm unsure of— when the five of them walk over to sit with me. Even stranger, conversation is effortless now. Snowark learns that Seavale adores gold because it resembles the sun: something they treasure. Seavale learns that silver is sacred in Snowark and we consider gold a "dirty" colour; I reveal how ridiculous I've always found the entire notion. It is also when Leon confesses how he first thought Ambrose's name was "Ginger" when we all first met; he never questioned it because he thought it was a Snowarkan name. His story, though I'm slightly envious of the fact, wins the most laughter. Admittedly, it's an interesting exchange of culture until we fall asleep. We forget to take watch shifts that night.

I almost wake up in a panic because of it. Thank the Ancients that when I open my eyes, my group are still alive by the fire. They must have migrated to it sometime during the night.

With a bitter-tasting monster meat breakfast, we're on our way even farther into the jungle. We aren't allowed much walking time before the rain picks up again. The droplets are warm and dense enough to bathe under—and the density of some parts of the jungle graciously provides the opportunity. It somewhat alleviates the exhaustion of walking mindlessly afterwards. My hair is still dripping wet over an hour later. The humidity has not once paused for rest, unlike us.

"Five days," Sierra announces after swallowing a gulp from her waterskin. I'm certain that she knows her hair won't dry if she keeps it in that dishevelled bun she adores. Still, she maintains the style. "We've been trapped here for five days now with no pull of the artifact. Now I *know* it's time that we take initiative, surely!"

"Those words have usually ended in trouble in the past," Leon muses, narrowing his eyes.

"It's a simple solution," she replies. She tucks her waterskin into her satchel and then places her hand on the bark of the tree beside her. "I'll climb up and see if I can find anything in the distance."

"That's rather high up," Ezra—the giant—notes unsteadily.

"An astounding observation," I remark. "Do you suppose that's why she chose to climb it for a bird's-eye view?"

The brightness of Ezra's eyes dull when he looks at me. He chuckles when Zenevieve shoves me.

To his credit, though, even he needs to tilt his head almost completely upwards to surmise the height of the jungle trees. And the dense awning of branches, leaves, and vines conceals the top.

"Don't worry," Sierra assures, taking off her satchel. A faint smile touches her lips. "How do you suppose I entertained myself growing up in Vineah when I wasn't studying?"

The boys each advise her to be careful. Sierra reassures them as she steps away from the tree. After a brief breath, she runs towards the trunk. Her right foot lands on the bark, and she jumps with her other foot. Grabbing the second-lowest-hanging branch, she pushes herself up with ease, even in her chainmail. Moments later, she disappears beyond the canopy.

I nod in approval. "I don't think I'm worried about her."

"I am," Ezra whispers beside me. His gaze is hopelessly glued to the small break Sierra has made in the awning.

"What do you see?" Leon shouts.

Sierra's Vinean accent seeps through as she calls back, "I think..."

Seconds pass, leaving us in the ambiance of jungle birds and insects.

"All right, I'm coming down a step. There's only covering for miles."

"Be careful, lily," Ezra calls. "Please."

His plea stirs a bout of impatient confusion in me. He knows

Sierra better than I do; even I've no reason to doubt her ability after all she's already shown. Where is his confidence in her?

Unless his care runs deeper than casual friendship—as the pet name suggests.

The tree in front of us rustles as Sierra takes a step down. Then I hear another. Her shadow is soon cast the closer to the break in the canopy she draws.

She reaches her foot down without a branch to catch her step.

I instinctually step forward with my group, our voices crying out against it. With a jolt down, Sierra's body breaks through the awning. A scream tears from her throat. No matter how fast we run, she hurdles down faster and crashes through the platform.

I've never heard so many voices scream one name at once. Most surreal to me, I never thought I'd be one of those voices.

I freeze behind Zenevieve at the hole Sierra's body made in the ground. A hot panic floods into my face. I can't stand too close to the edge. I can't look. Mostly because I know that there isn't anything to see—only hear as Sierra's scream curdles the air. It grows distant. I can almost feel it vibrate in my bones as a pull ignites in my chest. Towards the hole. As if I need to jump in after her. As if I can save her.

No. Not like that. She was right here. Not just like that, she was right here, she was just here—!

Leon yanks Zenevieve and a hysterical Ezra far from the edge, pushing me and Ambrose back with them. Deep, ragged breaths rack Leon's throat. My mind is trapped in the memory of watching a woman fall to her death. I don't know what to think. Leon and Ezra can't endure—

A sonorous chirp echoes throughout the abyss underneath us. Far down, a woman grunts.

Was... was that...?

Fear stuns my being, anchoring me down. Zenevieve and Ambrose carefully lean forward. Ezra almost breaks past Leon's arm barricading him. In a blink, that familiar pull in my chest glides upwards... towards the edge of the platform behind us.

Leon and I turn around: a gargantuan, graceful bird of orange and yellow feathers flies up from under the edge. Green tips its wings, whose grand feathers are spread far out and soaring through the air. Sierra is gripping its back.

My breath falls into my stomach. *She's alive!*

Wait. That pull—it's following Sierra's precise path.

The bird. Is the bird the artifact?

It approaches the landing of the platform, rapidly flapping its wings. Lowering one to the ground, Sierra safely slides down. Our group dash to her, but Ezra is fastest. His embrace seems all too instinctual as he picks her up, burying his head into her neck. His arms wrap all the way around her. Most amusing, he stands almost a head and a half taller.

Sierra exposes a grunt. Ezra pulls away, asking, "Are you all right?"

"Stiff," she airily answers, her words tight. "A little sore. Those were—quite some falls, but I think the... the armour protected me from severe damage. I need to stretch for a while."

But she made it, I whisper in my mind. The heat in my cheeks is evaporating. *She's all right.*

"That bird just saved her," Zenevieve whispers next to me. "How did...?"

Despite the triumph undoubtedly beaming in him, I can scarcely detect a faint smile on Ezra's full lips. Determination carves his irises now. "All the more reason I'm not waiting until I lose you for good and never have the chance to tell you this." He glimpses Leon. "I've said this to you as a friend, but allow me to say it in a new light: I love you, Sierra. I've been absolutely in love with you for the last two years. I've never met a woman more determined, more persistent and passionate and strong—all while firmly upholding the kindness, generosity, and care that you do. That is why I love you; and now that I've said it, I never want to stop saying it."

"Ezra—" Sierra whispers breathlessly with a grin.

He holds up his hand. It's as big as her face. "You don't need to reciprocate, that isn't what I want from you. My only desire is for you to know that no matter where you are from, whether you feel like you belong in Vineah or Seavale—you'll always belong in my life for as long as you desire."

All right, the confession adds up. But have they blatantly forgotten about the titanic bird standing behind him that's likely listening to every word of this?

Ezra takes Sierra's hand and presses it against the left side of his chest. "My heart has been beating for you for a long time now, lily. And it will only continue to do so if it may."

Sierra stands on her toes and stiffly reaches her arms around his neck. He eagerly bends down to meet their lips, his hands falling to the small of her back.

I tightly purse my lips. "Thank you for reminding me what I'm *not* missing out on," I mutter to no one but myself.

Zenevieve smacks my shoulder. I glare at her. She rolls her

eyes and kisses her teeth.

"This is *adorable*." Ambrose wipes a tear from his eye. "This is how Abria's fiancé *should* have done it! I'm telling her the second we come home."

"Rosy, shhh," Zenevieve whispers, bopping his nose.

"I love you, too," Sierra replies, regaining my attention. Her light hands rest on Ezra's dark cheeks. Her eyes reflect the awe and splendour in Ezra's right now. She presses another kiss to his lips. "But now you're officially stuck with me until the end of the race."

"Only until then?" He grins. "I was hoping we'd have at least a few more years after that."

Don't tell me that this is what love does to you. I truly am cursed if this is my fate.

Only then do Sierra's eyes land on the enormous bird still perched at the edge of the platform. They turn to face it in full.

"Did they completely forget about that?" Zenevieve asks, as if she's fascinated by the mere possibility.

"Love is blind," the prat and I say in unison. Our gazes race to each other's, reciprocating mutual shock. I shove him when he starts to crack a smile.

We approach the yellow-and-orange bird—which stands twice Ezra's height. I feel it in every bone now: this animal is the artifact. Or... it's holding it somewhere.

I step closer. My eyes fall to the thin, brown rope wrapped around its neck. Hanging from the rope is a wooden boomerang.

I reach out to pet the animal's neck. My hand effortlessly glides down its velvety feathers. "So it's *you* who's prolonged our stay here, is it? Withholding the artifact from us?"

As if it understands me, it chirps in reply.

"I can forgive that," the prat remarks, running his hand down the bird's wing. "You're quite beautiful. And wonderfully soft."

"How many of your feathers can I bring home for a pillow?" Zenevieve asks in front, hands on her waist.

The bird squawks. Perhaps I've been in this race for too long; I'm almost fully confident that it truly can understand us.

"Zenevieve!" Ambrose scolds her, crossing his arms.

"What?" she asks defensively, shrugging. "I'm kidding!"

"No, you're not," he replies dully with my thoughts.

She smiles at him. "You're getting closer to earning that 'Zenny' nickname, Rosy."

Evidently, the air here is driving us all mad.

I walk around to meet the bird at the front with her, testing its fluency: "May I?"

It bows its head.

"You're too kind." I take the brown cord and bring it over the plush feathers. "Much more gentlemanly than Ice Beastie... 'Gentlemanly', correct?"

He chirps as if to verify.

It *is* strange that I can trust the colossal bird in front of me; the beast certainly wasn't kind enough to hand us his false eye for the key. He was too preoccupied trying to devour me, Zenevieve, Ambrose, and—

My hand freezes. The face in my memory cuts me like an ice shard.

I exhale. I gently scrunch my fingers in the bird's orange feathers. Orange was Meredith's favourite colour. It reminded her of sunrises and sunsets. She loved animals, too. I wonder how much she would have loved such a beautiful—

"Ember?" ripples Zenevieve's voice behind me.

I shake my head, blinking it away. *No. Don't think about it. Move forward.*

I look up into the bird's white-lined, brown eyes. "Actually, I doubt you know Beastie. Unless you can travel across the stages—"

"Emberly," Zenevieve says flatly. "You're trying to make conversation with a bird."

"Zenevieve Lathrop," I snap, feigning offence as I glare at her. I pet my new friend's neck as if out of spite. "You'll address *Tart* appropriately."

Her eyes dull at me, her hands on her hips. "Remember what happened to the last creature in this race you assigned a name to? And the time before that?"

Bubbles actually *succeeded* in eating us; Beastie merely tried to. That's why Meredith always warned me against naming things... The second something has a name, its humanity is born. The second it becomes easier to attach to.

Then I suppose she should have never told me her name, either, I think bitterly. *And if that's truly the case about names, she should have never stayed at all. Not if she was going to break her promise as soon as—*

I tighten my jaw, cursing my mind. I already swore to banish my thoughts of her lest I'm rendered unable to move forward. I cannot be so weak as to break that because of a simple reminder. If I fall behind, my group will suffer the consequences with me— and I will not lead anyone else to their downfall just for my sake.

Move forward. Move forward.

I look back up at the bird. "Why have you arrived only now? We were just as lost in this jungle five days ago."

Tart chirps again, nodding towards his back. His yellow-and-orange–feathered, green-tipped wing falls in front of us.

"He wants us to climb on?" Sierra asks, stiffly stepping away from Ezra's embrace.

"Flying through humid air is certainly better than walking through it," I say, stepping forward. My gaze freezes on my foot.

On the bird. Flying. Over the never-ending abyss.

High in the air. After I almost fell into it a few days ago.

No. I can't do it. I can't do it.

"I've got you, Emberly," Zenevieve whispers, appearing beside me. Her dark hand rests on my arm as she slightly looks down at me. "I won't let you fall."

"No." I firmly meet her eyes. "You're still experiencing dizziness from your fever, be sensible."

She shakes her head dismissively. "I've got you."

"We almost lost Sierra to the abyss minutes ago," I state with an acidic sternness. "If you fall, the bird won't be able to save you. No."

She scoffs with a gentle smile. "Let down your pride, I think I know how to—"

"I won't lose you like we lost Meredith!" I snap.

I've done the impossible: startled Zenevieve.

I don't dare to catch the five other pairs of eyes on me. Including Tart's. Not when the sting of my nose is so intense. When I need to pour my focus into suppressing every last reaction pooling into my chest and head right now.

I swallow everything back down. "I won't let you, end of discussion. Someone needs to stabilise you—and Ambrose."

Sierra stiffly walks forward with Ezra. "I'll keep you steady, Zenevieve," she assures. "Ezra can stabilise Ambrose."

"Ezra could *carry* Ambrose," I mutter, crossing my arms.

Ginger mimics me, sneering and looking down at me. "I don't see anyone struggling with you, either."

Zenevieve holds out her arm in front of me, stopping me from plucking the little strawberry. Still, she beams with pride at him. "She only means you're travel size and convenient, Rosy." Directing her attention to Sierra next, she doesn't drop her arm held out in front of me. "I accept. Thank you. Please do be careful with Ambrose, though, he's fragile."

"The boy broke his arm rolling down a hill last summer," I add, pushing down Zenevieve's.

He opens his mouth to argue. Ezra picks him up first. One arm supports Ginger's back, the other under his knees. He gives up and sighs.

"You are terrible to him," Zenny tells me, turning to face me in full. She bites her bottom lip in a grin.

"We established a special agreement years ago." I wave my hand in dismissal. "Limitless banter in exchange for fresh cheese."

She gawks as if the pieces are finally coming together. "The kitchen thinks you're a masochist! You can't have milk, yet you ask for cheese every other morning. It was all for him?"

"You can't have milk?" Sierra asks, green eyes wide with fascination. "What do you drink with your cookies? What about chocolate? Or—?"

"It's my burden to bear," I tell her dreamily. I motion to Tart with the hand holding the boomerang. "Let's—get on with it."

Sierra helps Zenevieve mount. Thankfully, she stabilises her just in time when she has a dizzy spell. Gratitude blooms in my chest for them both.

"Are you sure you're all right to do this, lily?" Ezra asks, turning his head to look at her.

"As long as I keep my movements to a minimum, it's all right," Sierra replies.

I take in a deep breath as I observe the four straddling Tart's back. Someone is missing.

Where is the—?

Leon clears his throat. I turn my attention to him meandering towards me.

"Don't plunge Rowena through me for asking," he begins, holding up his hands in surrender, "but if you're worried about falling off—I'm willing to help. If you'd like it."

My eyes dull. "Shoving me off the edge so that I don't have to ride the bird isn't 'helping', prat."

He bites his bottom lip, grinning as he glances sideways.

Don't do that. Stop doing that. Quit—

"Would keeping you steady on Tart's back work, then?"

I despise that he's actually adhering to the names I've given to certain things. I despise that he's offered to keep me steady. I despise that I don't feel the overwhelming urge to carve a scar along his sharp, triangle-shaped jawline.

"Rowena knows your name," I state. I rest my free hand on her silver pommel. "Take this as your warning."

He nods once. "You have my word, firefly."

"And—"

My words catch in my throat. For some reason, I can't bring myself to tell him to stop that right now.

I loop the cord around my neck to keep the boomerang secure. After mounting Tart, Leon allows me to guide his hands to where I'm comfortable with him steadying me from. He rests them firmly on the middle of my waist.

I pray that he can't feel my heart hammering under my breastplate.

Tart turns to overlook the endless, yellow sky. A storm of nausea roars in my stomach. Nerves of hot steel burn and pop inside me like sparks at a fire. I can almost feel my body rattling my armour. It's Windale's stage all over again.

I feel Leon lean closer to me. My heart skips a hard beat. "Close your eyes," he whispers into my ear. "If you need to fall, fall into me. You won't knock us off."

His breath tickles my skin, sending pulses of lightning down my spine. My teeth chatter in fear. Each breath is stifled by a reason my mind tries to bury. It doesn't want to admit that I'm afraid. I'm still afraid.

I can't be. Stop it. Vineah's stage—of all stages—will not conquer me.

And I certainly refuse to let the prat know that I'm afraid.

I close my eyes and anchor my thoughts to the ground. Tart's wings spread and flap down once. With one jolt, we're off the platform.

I bind my thoughts to dirt, to the palace grounds of Snowark. I think of the courtyard, of the hard marble floor of my bedchambers. I remind myself of its cold that my bare feet darted across the morning Zenevieve told me the portal was open. That was ten days ago.

A week and a half ago?

I make the mistake of picturing the portal open at the edge of the kingdom. The view I saw from my bedchamber window. How high we were.

How high we are.

My head swarms with dizziness. I start to fall back, suppressing a yelp that threatens to erupt from my throat. Leon's grip on my waist tightens. He pushes against my leaning. I'm upright whether I like it or not.

"You're all right," he assures softly.

"Keep praying," I hiss. "It's not working yet."

The seconds all too slowly fade into an eternity as the wind whips back my hair. I'm grateful that Sierra keeps hers in a bun; her hair isn't slashing across my face right now.

Is my hair whipping Leon?

I almost make the mistake of opening my eyes and turning my head.

I'm too short for my hair to whip his face. His upper chest and neck, most likely.

He's still pushing back against me. He's staying close. My breaths grow shallower.

Sweat and heat radiate all across my face. *I need to vomit.* I need to vomit and there is absolutely nowhere for me to do so privately.

I try to focus on the temperature next: the air gliding past us is at least some relief against the warmth. I anchor my thoughts to that: comfort. In some ways, I'm physically doing better than I was on the ground. Despite the milk-curdling nausea churning in my stomach.

No, don't think about milk!

Just as I'm ready to throw straight up on Sierra, Tart's wings start flapping more rapidly. I feel us descend, which is more than enough prompt for vomit. Tart lands a second later.

I open my eyes and jolt forward, sliding down his wing the second he lowers it. My mind ruthlessly fights the sickness, forcing my stomach to keep breakfast inside. I can replenish the lost food thanks to the jerky; still, I *refuse* to vomit in front of everyone here.

I take a few more swallows and deep breaths. My head swirls, but the nausea is settling.

"Ember," Zenevieve calls behind me. Her hand soon finds my shoulder. "Are you all right?"

With another swallow, the sickness dies down. I straighten, nodding. "Finally. Yes."

I turn around just as Ezra, the last person off of Tart, slides down. The group's gazes are snagged on the stone temple standing beside them. It's nestled in the vines and overgrown tree leaves and branches. Moss encroaches on the fading, crumbling stone. Similar markings of the boomerang around my neck are carved into the rock.

I look up: the temple's top is covered by the canopy. No wonder Sierra couldn't spot it from her bird's-eye view.

"Tart knew where to go," Ezra notes, turning to face the temple. "I think we're finally at the main obstacle."

"Thank you, Tart," Leon says, facing him. "You made the trip *fly* by."

Thankfully, Ezra smacks him on the back of the head. The cub rolls his eyes, nudging him. Still, Tart doesn't leave, only observing us.

The six of us gather in front of the wide entry arch. A world of darkness awaits us inside. Dust, damp trees, and humidity combine in a whirlwind of scents in the entrance.

Leon's hand rests on the stone of the archway. He curiously hums. "It's moist in here."

"Shall we give the man a prize?" I ask, crossing my arms. Zenevieve slaps my shoulder.

The prat only glances at me. "It's especially warm in here, I mean, Emberly," he replies dully. He looks back into the temple, moving to step forward. "It's as though there's an entire—"

"Leo, allow me," Ezra says. He holds out his arm, barring him. "You don't know what's in there."

"Neither do you." Leon gently pushes his arm down. He steps forward nonetheless. "It is my duty to—"

A click echoes in the temple as he trips. Ezra grabs him and steadies him as a whoosh darts through the air.

"*Leon!*" Sierra and I cry.

An arrow has shattered his chainmail and pierced the right side of his torso.

CHAPTER 22

"THIS IS WHY LEMON TARTS ARE MY FAVORITE"

Leo

THERE IS AN ARROW IN MY CHEST. AN ARROW IS IN MY chest.

Emberly's cry echoes louder in my head than Sierra's as Ezra catches me, holding me up. Sierra rushes over. The arrowhead sears through my skin, having gone straight past my chainmail. I can't determine how deep it is because I can't bring myself to look at it; all I know is that it burns. And it's cutting. And the stun infecting my chest isn't enough to numb me to it.

"You're all right, Leo," Ezra assures, dragging me away from the temple entrance. His voice is almost muffled in my ears like it was in the bubble suits during Seavale's stage. "You'll be fine, I promise!"

The words are wickedly familiar, my heart throbbing in my head. Sierra grips the shaft as Ezra undoes my belt to take off the top part of my armor. I gasp, the corner of my vision catching Snowark coming to stand by. I'm not sure she realizes it, but Emberly's features are contorted in a similar fear she had when Zenevieve was bitten by the centi-snake.

I hiss in a breath, yelping as Sierra draws out the arrow. A pained moan curdles in my throat. She tautly exhales as she drops the arrow, the wound radiating a sharp, hot sting.

"Hold on, Leo," she says as Ezra releases me. She struggles to raise my chainmail with Ezra. I remember her fall, how stiff I know she is; and I can't help but worry about the pain she must be causing herself in her haste. "I'm only able to take out the arrow because we can address the wound immediately and Ambrose can close it. Just a moment longer."

Thankfully, her calm maintains my own.

She takes off my gambeson next, leaving my linen shirt. The edge of my vision catches it then: a pool of blood soaking through it. It's the size of Emberly's palm.

Ezra quickly lays me down onto the platform, and Sierra and Snowark kneel beside me. My breathing starts to steady as Sierra pulls my shirt up, grunting with every movement. I fight the grimace at every one on her behalf—or maybe that's due to how the cut in my chest seems to tear open a little more with every breath.

The bottom of my vision notes the forearm-length scar I earned during Lavara's invasion attempt, now exposed in full down my chest. I'm all too aware of it as Snowark stares. The shock is fading; my rationality is seeping into my mind now.

That was... far too close for comfort.

"Right," I say, my breath tight as I glimpse the jungle temple in front of me. "I wouldn't walk in there."

"You truly are full of remarkable revelations today," Emberly snaps, arms crossed firmly over her chest.

Is she... angry at me? For being shot?

Now you know you're going mad.

Sierra takes a cloth from her bag as Zenevieve slaps Emberly's arm. She closes her mouth. Ambrose stares with a hard swallow at my wound—one of them, at least.

"I don't think the arrow was poisoned," Sierra announces with relief, gently dabbing around the wound. "No discoloration, we only need to treat this quickly before he loses too much blood."

"What is that?" Ambrose asks shakily, pointing at my chest.

I grunt at the sharp sting as Sierra continues dabbing and gently wiping with the tonic-doused cloth. "You're..." I begin tightly, "most likely aware of Lavara's invasion attempt on Seavale a few years ago. "I—earned this during the battle."

Emberly's eyes remain stuck on the scar, Zenevieve nodding in approval and Ambrose covering his eyes.

"Are you both all right?" Zenevieve asks, glancing between me and Sierra.

"I'm much better than he is," Sierra replies with strain, focused as she drips more of the mending tonic into my chest.

I hiss again as she dabs with the cloth. "I'm fine," I say. "It's just—a cut."

"Roughly half an inch deep," Sierra adds. "Thank the Ancients that this was stone: it still has the potential to be lethal, but with your proximity to the temple, if this were obsidian... What matters is that we can save you. Ambrose, can you heal him?"

Ambrose? What about—?

My throat tautens. I manage a hard swallow as I briefly close my eyes. I can't believe I keep forgetting.

"Of course." Ambrose scoots closer despite the transparent queasiness knitting his face together.

As his light hands ignite with green, I have to pull my eyes away to distract myself from the memories. I've spent over half of my life with only one mage in front of me, and the discrepancy now is a horrendously cruel reminder that that mage will never stand in front of me again. I'll never have the same treatment. I struggle to stomach how the curls next to me are red instead of black.

No. I said I wouldn't let this affect me anymore.

It isn't as though I can simply forget him altogether. Nor would I ever want to. But how do I remember him without the suffocating heartache?

I try my gaze on Emberly. The second I do, I catch her eyes already connected with mine. She instantly moves them away.

It's as though she's too afraid to show care.

Did I really hear her call out for me...?

A sheer, graceful wave of green continues streaming into my wound. A cooling sensation flows under my skin, and I feel minuscule sensations stitch themselves together slowly but surely underneath the surface. It's a gradual process, but the sting is alleviating.

"Thank you, Ambrose," I say, but he remains quiet. His brows stay knitted in concentration, a hard bulb passing in his throat as his eyes stay fixed on my wound. The sunburn on his freckled cheeks has lightened, the red only adding a false blush now. Either he isn't trying to suppress his true feelings or he doesn't know how to, because I'm well aware of his discomfort. I appreciate that he's healing me nevertheless.

He exhales with a grunt as Zenevieve scoots up next to him, resting a hand on his shoulder. Nodding, he seems to ease in her hold as he takes deep breaths. "It's—my pleasure, Your Highness."

Emberly finally scoots closer with the rest of them. She still eyes the scar on my chest, but then she blinks and looks at Zenevieve. Sierra finishes dabbing my chest as Ezra grabs my shirt.

"Are you sure that you're all right, Your Highness?" Ambrose asks.

"Almost perfect," I say, sitting up and pulling my shirt over my head. Another hiss of pain betrays me. "My thanks to you and Sierra."

Zenevieve nods, the entrance of the temple then gaining her eyes. "How are we meant to grab the key if this entire place is rigged?"

Ambrose shrugs, still breathy. He runs a pale hand through his curls. "Throw the boomerang into the dark and hope for the best?"

"Try a genuine suggestion for once, Ginger," Emberly tells him flatly. "You may find them rather helpful."

"That is genuine."

Upon our quizzical stares, Ambrose's words grow cautious. He takes turns glancing at each of us. "Only since... well, it's the artifact. Surely a boomerang is meant to be thrown, and the key is definitely in that temple. For all we know, it's trapped inside a giant plant that needs to be cut through or something; but the only way we're managing that is from a distance with all the traps likely inside."

He holds even Tart's stare when he finishes. Ambrose retracts under our eyes and clears his throat, rubbing his neck. "My youngest sister, Anavieve, has this book where the little prince's crown is stuck in a giant rosebud—never mind."

I open my mouth, but then it settles in my mind. I look down at the boomerang hanging from Emberly's neck. *A boomerang flies a specific path. And if it's magical like the other artifacts... maybe it* knows *the path it's meant to fly. The edges aren't sharp, but...*

Flying. Wind. If our theories are correct on the other artifacts, then this one must be Windale's. What if it can fly fast enough to cut through something?

"I think he's right," I say, carefully picking up my gambeson.

Emberly's eyes widen at me. "How many stories did the strawberry tell you during your watch shifts?" she asks, sarcasm hardening her words. "He hides things in those stories, you know—"

"It's called 'imagination', Emberly," Ambrose remarks, smirking. "You're simply jealous that you don't have any."

Her eyes dull as they land on him. "I have plenty, Ginger. I happen to know it doesn't work because I imagine you disappearing all the time, yet here you are."

Zenevieve rolls her eyes and scolds her, but Ambrose only grins triumphantly.

Ezra and Sierra help me with my gambeson. I clear my throat above Snowark bickering to regain their attentions. "In any case, based on the heavy vegetation growing out the windows and around the temple, there are too many obstacles in there for us to navigate inside without setting off more traps."

We stand, Sierra and Ezra aiding me with my armor as I continue. "We know that this boomerang is magical because it's the artifact. There's no telling if it has the ability to cut once we throw it *unless* we throw it. And the key being trapped in a giant plant may not be too far of a stretch—just as Seavale's key was trapped in the whale, Snowark's was trapped in the beast's eye, and Lavara's was trapped in the ice of the volcano. Almost every key so far has been stuck inside our final obstacle. And we know that this temple is the last one for Vineah."

I'm surprised that Emberly managed to stay quiet during all of that. Instead, she gently shoves Ambrose's shoulder. "When we get back, you're being demoted from palace mage to librarian in the children's section."

"I *love* children," he replies. "We can plot to invade the palace on the weekends."

Zenevieve grins, hands on her waist. "This new you is certainly one to be noticed, Rosy."

His grin melts into a smirk. "I suppose Emberly taught me more than she meant to."

"See? My imagination still isn't working." Emberly rolls her eyes, running her hands through her dark-auburn waves that have grown frizzy in the humidity. She then faces me, taking off the boomerang around her neck. "Are you absolutely certain about this? We throw this, it spins around the temple, and we find the key?"

It made much more sense when I said it.

That's a first.

I turn around. Tart still sits perched on the platform. Now I *know* that he hasn't left yet for a reason.

Your heart will guide you. Your head will protect you. Act in one accord.

"You were the only one mad enough to throw the seeds down the whale's through," Sierra says, looking up at me and nudging me. "Not to mention Windale's stage."

To my surprise, the words offer ease. My heart is anxious to bring my friends to the next stage—to protect them on the journey there. And right now, my mind insists on what is brewing in it. They're of one accord, and that is how I know to act on it.

I face my team again, nodding. "Let's mount Tart again."

"You have a plan?" Ezra asks.

"No." I nod at Ambrose. "Ginger has a plan. But I say we follow it."

Equal exchanges are passed until they obey—except for Emberly, who exhales, closing her eyes. I'm convinced that she's silently cursing me in her head.

"We won't travel," I assure her. "Tart will stay in one place and keep us a safe distance from the temple so that none of the traps strike us."

She shakes her head at me before walking up and shoving the boomerang into my hand. "You'll pay for this later, cub," she hisses, continuing to walk by me to mount the giant yellow-and-orange bird. That leaves me standing in front of him.

"Tart," I say, "I'll need you to catch me when I jump."

He chirps as if in reply.

"I hope you really do understand me."

"Give him time," Emberly remarks from behind Sierra on his back. "It's a skill that requires years to master."

She never takes a break.

I exhale. Tart's round, brown eyes blink before he turns to face the vast, open sky. Sierra tells Emberly to hold on tightly to her, and Tart flaps his wings before leaping from the ground. He flies off the platform and lowers himself, granting me the easiest position to jump onto his back when I must.

I approach the entry arch of the temple. The dark almost compels me forward, my curiosity at an all-time high. But especially with this tight arrow wound in my chest to remind me of its dangers, I don't want to take the hand of death and have him escort me inside.

I bring the boomerang to my side, toss it forward, and then run to the edge of the platform.

Emberly yelps as I land behind her, and I grimace at the stretching of my fresh wound. "Go!" I call to Tart, restraining my hands from placing themselves on Emberly's waist again. "A little farther!"

Tart obeys, Emberly scolds me, and I hold her shoulders instead to keep her secure as we fly away from the platform. Tart circles around and comes to face the temple again. A hundred sputters, clicks, and snaps echo below. Seconds later, a gush of water surges past the entrance of the temple. The stone blocks burst out from their place, crumbling into bits as the temple collapses. The rushing water floods through the ground of dense foliage, flattening the branches and leaves in its way.

Whoa... We would have been swept away in the current.

As the water seeps into the ground, Tart flies back to the edge and lands. We each descend his wing, where Emberly immediately turns around to shove me.

"You said we wouldn't travel, you insufferable prat!" she hisses just between us.

I open my mouth to reply with my instinct—but I remember where those words stem from and humble mine. "I'm sorry. But I'd rather you be nauseous than a victim of whatever traps were waiting for us in there."

I almost expect her to reach for Rowena, but she only exhales with a glare. Then, she turns to Tart.

Suppressing a smile, I follow her to his yellow-feathered head. I stroke the velvety texture of the orange feathers on his neck. The rest of our team approaches on either side, petting him in thanks with me. His feathers are cool despite the warm air, and I can almost feel a resounding heartbeat as my hand glides down them.

"Birds are my favorite animal for a reason," Sierra chimes beside me, a warm smile beaming on her face. "Their intelligence is remarkable. I've even befriended a few in both Vineah and Seavale." She leans toward Tart's front. "Thank you for saving my life."

He cheeps in response.

Emberly reaches up her hands and cups his head—as best she can for such a massive animal at her height. He bows it as if he knows exactly what she wants to do. "Thank you," she says. "This is why lemon tarts are *my* favorite."

Tart coos happily in her hold. When she releases him, he holds his head high, allowing the six of us to step away. We face the temple ruins and approach as if another trap is waiting to activate. Arrows and blades as tall as Emberly sit scattered about the fallen stone and crumbling walls. I step over the debris with my team, noting the string, rope, and vines lying pathetically across the stone. Each one tells of its mission to catapult a death sentence toward us.

Not anymore.

Ambrose gasps beside Zenevieve, pointing at the middle of the temple. "I was right!"

We follow his finger: a large, green plant bud, wide enough to trap four of us inside, has been cut in half. In the middle of it stands a short, thin pillar of vines, intricately woven to create a secure hold on the key that's wrapped atop.

"There's only one," Emberly notes. "But we're still technically two different groups."

"It may have something to do with us being on the stage simultaneously," Sierra says, needing Ezra's help to step over another large chunk of stone. She stiffly arrives at my side. "The stages must reset somehow and in some way that allows different teams to face the same challenge for themselves. That's my greatest theory based on what we've witnessed. But when two teams merge…"

Awkward glances are exchanged all around. The unspoken question of trust lingers in the air almost too heavily for me to breathe—but it's the only option we have.

"I don't know about you lot," Emberly says, climbing over the stones and boulders that sit in her way, "but I've hated Vineah since the beginning—no offense, Sierra—and I want out of this cursed place."

She approaches the broken plant vessel but then pauses. Then, she turns and faces me. "Are you coming, cub?"

She wants me to grab the key?

I walk past the stares of our team and lunge over the boulders. Coming upon the plant vessel, a pool of water sits in the bottom.

This must have been where all of that water came from, setting off the traps when the boomerang cut through.

Speaking of, the boomerang is nowhere in sight; it must have dissolved like the other artifacts. It's finally time to escape.

"You take it," Emberly says. "In case it sets off another trap."

I knew there was a catch. But after her reaction to my arrow wound, which still stings enough to repeat the memory in my mind, I'm not sure I believe her reasoning entirely.

"Suit yourself." I reach forward. "I want out of here just as much as you do."

My fingers wrap around the small, bronze key, pulling it free from the vine tendrils. Behind us, a white light flashes into existence. We turn around to find the opening of a cyan-lined portal.

"Thank the Ancients, let's leave!" Ambrose exclaims, taking Zenevieve's hand and pulling her through the rubble. Sierra and Ezra gradually make their way behind them, as he must be mindful of her stiff frame.

She turns her head to me and Emberly after Ambrose and Zenevieve enter the portal. "I'm surprised she allowed him to escort her just like that."

Ezra snickers, taking her hand. "We'll pray he's still in one piece by the time we arrive."

They step over the boulders and walk into the portal.

Emberly scoffs next to me. When I look over, she's shaking her head. "They're right. How isn't the strawberry afraid of the woman who once threatened to shave his head for touching her sword?"

I blink. "What?"

She looks up at me, arching a brow. "You think I'm so terrifying, cub? Never give Zenevieve a reason to write your name in red. It's not ink she'll write it in."

My mouth isn't left open for long; she nods to the key in my hand. "Does that key say something, too?"

Curiosity revives in me, and I hold up the key. Small vines stand in the middle of the head. I read aloud the word at the bottom of it: "'Patience'."

Emberly's brows furrow curiously. She leans forward to meet Tart's stare, who is still perched in the same spot he landed in. "Does that have to do with why you took so long?"

He tweets. I'm almost completely convinced that she truly can understand him, because I have no inkling as to whether that was a yes or a no.

"What do these words mean?" I ask, recalling the keys I've studied over the last few days. "'Bravery' on Seavale's, 'tenacity' on Windale's, 'endurance' on Lavara's..."

I look away in thought. The keys must be relaying each kingdom's greatest strength. Seavalens are brave enough to embark across the seas in search of history, treasure, and discovery. Windalens must be tenacious enough to survive and thrive in their kingdom's challenging geography. Lavarans have a strong endurance against their climate, and so on. But why would the keys reiterate this to us? In a death race, of all things?

"Don't stay for too long lest you fall behind," Emberly chimes, climbing over to the entrance of the temple and then the portal. I follow her path when her gaze catches on Tart again, and she stops. I step up to her side, our bows on our backs making the perfect pair.

Tart tilts his head. Then, he releases an eager chirp, like he approves of our destination.

He positions himself to face the sky again. His green-tipped wings flap downward before he takes off.

"It's difficult to find even a Seavalen parrot who is *that* friendly," I muse.

"The palace boys are only ever that friendly when you bribe them with cakes and biscuits," Emberly says flatly, her eyes following Tart's path until he disappears behind the trees.

She looks up at me again. Her lips part as though to speak, but her words seem to catch in her throat first. It's a moment before she asks, "Is your wound all right?"

My next heartbeat is a little harder. Emberly Whitaker is concerned about the "Seavalen prat"—me.

"It is," I reply, as if she truly needs the reassurance. "And your sunburn?"

It mimics Ambrose's: a mere blush across her lightly freckled cheeks and nose. Her forehead and chin have almost returned to normal.

"No longer as annoying as you are," she replies. A foreign, almost undetectable smile grazes her lips this time.

She nods toward the portal. With one look into the white light, we step inside.

CHAPTER

"SIMPLY SOMEONE TO BE PROUD OF"

Emberly

I F NOT FOR ZENEVIEVE CATCHING ME THE SECOND I STEP out of the portal, I would have instantly received a face full of dirt. Upon looking up at her, her cheeks, nose, and forehead reveal that she's paid that price so I didn't have to.

We're trapped in a tunnel of solid dirt. The moisture in the air is half of what it was in Vineah, but dew still saturates it. The scent of soil envelops us. Small holes have been poked all across the ceiling for daylight to stream in; we're at least a few metres down.

Soilera. Couldn't it have been a field of flowers or something?

"Thank you," I tell Zenny, stabilizing my footing on the ground. The portal closes behind me as the prat comes in. "Are you still feeling all right? With the bite, the limp—?"

She kisses her teeth and rolls her eyes. "Leave it be, it

scarcely stings anymore. One more healing session from Rosy and the limp should fade completely."

I look at Sierra, who stands between Ezra and Ambrose. Straightening after a stretch, she shrugs as if to say that Zenny's theory is plausible.

"At least we've light," I say, exhaling. "Only the Ancients could have predicted it: your idea worked, Ambrose. I may have to stop calling you 'Ginger' as your graduation present."

His brown eyes hopefully widen. "Really?"

"No."

Zenevieve scolds me, but I've no time to listen: this time, the pull of the artifact is immediately drawing me forward. We have nowhere to go but deeper in the tunnel.

I turn to verify with the cub, but he's closing his eyes and swallowing.

I thought *he was abnormally less irritating.*

"And what has your mind?" I ask him.

He doesn't reply—only shakes his head slightly.

"Leo?" Sierra says before I can. She steps up to us and gently takes his arm. I already notice a little more motion in her after stretching. "Come here, come with me."

She guides him a few steps down the tunnel. There, she starts speaking to him in delicate whispers. His eyes remain closed all the while.

"Is he all right?" I ask sceptically.

"He doesn't fare well in small spaces," Ezra replies. His head is almost touching the ceiling. I need to stifle my laughter. "Sierra is the only one who can calm him down."

"What happened?" Ambrose asks curiously.

Ezra's full lips press together in a tight wince. When he speaks, his deep voice rests into a new softness. "Just before his sixth birthday, his tutor threw him into the smallest cell in the back of the dungeon after he refused lessons. The castle forgot that he was down there amidst trying to prepare his birthday celebrations."

My jaw drops before I realise it. *No. Impossible!* Surely his staff couldn't have been so resentful as to—

Zenevieve gasps in horror beside me with a wide-eyed Ambrose. "They didn't!" she whispers.

Ezra nods gravely. "He was trapped down there for almost a full day."

I'm unsure of how to reply or even react. The councilmen would purposely do that to me if they could evade the consequences. But Leon's sixth birthday, based on all that we learned about Seavale during Vineah, was before he met Sierra and Ezra—even Ithinor. To have lost your parents, not even have a friend, and then be forgotten by your own castle...?

They cared enough about him to celebrate his birthday but not enough to remember that he was locked up? Is the monarch's birthday celebration voluntary as it is in Snowark? Or are they required to celebrate it?

"My brother is the same way with small spaces," Ambrose says beside Zenevieve. His voice is strangely dejected. "He was simply born that way... The last time I tried getting him to hide in the broom closet with me to sneak up on our sister Abria, he accidentally punched me in the mouth and fell out of the closet."

I sigh, shaking my head.

"Will this be an issue throughout this stage?" Zenevieve

asks Ezra with a concern I almost envy.

"As I said, only Sierra is able to reach him right now."

I roll my lips together. The cub is to small spaces as I am to heights. Now I understand. That is how I patiently wait out the next minute.

Upon Leon and Sierra's return, his stare stays with the ground as he takes deep breaths.

"We're fine," Sierra assures. "No need to worry."

"Can I speak to him?" I ask, pointing at Leon. "Will he break if I do?"

She sends me a glare of disapproval, putting her hands on her waist.

I hold up my hands. "He isn't broken, understood. You could have simply said no." I direct my attention to him. "Leon?"

"Yes?" he states, refusing my eyes.

This is how he copes, I suppose. I can't ruin that.

"Do you feel it?" I ask, daring a step forward. "The artifact?" He nods. "Yes. Ahead."

Zenevieve holds out a protective arm. "Wait. It's almost midday, and we're still gathering our energy. Not to mention the fact that Sierra has yet to rest after her fall. If Leo is able, we should eat and reserve a few moments before continuing."

"I'm fine." His head snaps up to meet her eyes. Sierra raises a sceptical brow before he turns to her. "Really. Let's eat."

She understands him better than anyone here; I trust her judgment when she sighs and says, "Only so we'll have the strength if another team is dropped here."

After ten days, I'm more anxious than ever to cross the finish line. It doesn't matter if we're in first place or last anymore.

But I also know that as long as Leon feels well enough for a break, we must take advantage of it.

It's Ambrose's idea to eat in a circle so that we can face each other during our meal of bread, jerky, and fruit. Why he finds pleasure in looking at other people eat is beyond me.

Leon steals my attention as he takes a spot beside Sierra. I exhale. Then, I walk to his other side and plop myself down.

He blinks upon realizing and then opens his mouth.

"No need for that." I hold up my hand. "I only have a question for you, cub."

That, and the others are too engaged in conversation to care that the only spot left is next to this prat.

He hangs his head and briefly closes his eyes. It's as if he's calculating his every move for this conversation. Or perhaps he's still coping. It's likely the latter.

"Ask away," he says.

I open my satchel. My food rests at the bottom, which is becoming more visible with each day. "What *does* Seavale think of you?" I ask. "I certainly know what I think of you, but what of your kingdom?"

"I'm pretty sure I know what you think of me, too," he replies, chuckling lightly.

With my glare, his smirk drops.

He clears his throat. "It's as you most likely suspect." He grabs a piece of broken-off bread from his satchel. "My past behaviour didn't leave the most reputable impression among the staff, least of all my subjects. So I..."

"You...?"

He presses his lips together. Curse the holes in the ceiling;

they intensify his eyes' sky blue twofold as they focus on Zenevieve and Ambrose's direction. Zenny is shoving Ginger's shoulder. When he tries to shove her back, she unsheathes her dagger. Ginger surrenders.

Leon's gaze never returns to me. "I had to run from the castle staff when the portals first opened. I knew they were going to subject me to... reminders. Why I wasn't fit to run. Why I was the wrong choice, how foolish I was going to prove myself to be. Their version of encouragement. This race was my last chance to prove myself to them, all of Seavale. I wanted to show that I was willing to fight for our future wholeheartedly. Prove that I could be the leader they needed when no one else was able to fulfil the role."

For the first time in my life, my mouth is glued shut. My words don't find their usual reaction time. Horrifyingly enough, the story about five-year-old Leon being locked in the dungeon is that much more believable now.

If they still don't accept him after he almost laid down his life for them all, they never will. They don't deserve him as their ruler.

"Then," I say, "I suppose you find great pride in ruling now. Inheriting the throne one day is the ultimate feat to prove yourself."

He snickers, covering his mouth. "Not in the slightest."

My head pushes itself back, touching the dirt wall behind me. I was wrong?

"I spent the first fourteen years of my life watching people fall into my traps. The castle boys started following in my footsteps—and that filled me with pride. I was proud of being a 'leader' to others, children who looked up to me. I definitely wasn't receiving that from anyone else around me."

I'm quite familiar with the feeling.

He takes a bite of his bread. Silence takes him again until he swallows. "I was eleven when... Ithinor made his first grave attempt with me. A few of the castle boys and I almost burned down the royal treasury—"

"You did *what?*" I ask, my mouth falling agape. How had all but *that* tale managed to evade global attention? "You said you were eleven!"

"Eleven and adept at stupid pranks." He shakes his head. "Ithinor—convinced the castle to stay silent about it. In fear of Seavale conveying weakness. Lavara happened to invade three years later, so it was wise..."

He was only fourteen when he earned that scar...

The image is all too vivid in my memory. The pale, taut skin slashing his chest. My cheeks warm as if the sunburn is still pulsating.

Leon exhales, swallowing. "That was when Ithinor finally told me the real reason my parents were dead: that a death curse killed them when I was born. Before then, my advisor—before Sierra—told me that they had passed from disease."

"You were *eleven* when you were informed of the curse?" I can only hope that my furrowed, shocked brows aren't offensive to him.

"My advisor encouraged the castle to withhold it from me for the sake of"—he scoffs—"preserving my innocence or childhood or something ridiculous of the sorts. Wonderful decision that was. So I accepted the curse as my fate. I was destined to die the same way every other monarch of Seavale had. I might as well have made the most of every day since nobody could take my crown from me."

Why wasn't I brilliant enough to do that?

"Fourteen grounded me to reality," he says next. He takes another brief rest to bite his bread. It reminds me to take out a persimmon and eat as he speaks. "Not long after Lavara's invasion attempt... Ithinor became the greatest victim of my pranks. I tampered with the waterpipe in the castle courtyard thinking it would only give him a spray. And it did—with more force than I was anticipating. The water knocked him back, and he banged his head on the ground."

My jaw is frozen open before I can take my next bite. The cub's reputation goes further than I thought.

"The physicians suspected that he had a skull fracture. And when I was finally allowed to see him, he tried yet again to reason with me. He told me stories about the monarchs that had come before me, how they ruled with such care and equity that they were *leaders*, not simply monarchs. And despite everything, he saw me on that path if I would just have the willingness to walk it. But what I remember most from that day..."—he swallows, like the memory is too excruciating to recall with his own lips—"is when he told me that he believed in me. He would never give up on me. On helping me achieve that."

Meredith. Meredith promised me the same thing eight years ago in the library during lessons.

Leon and I really did lose the same thing our first day in Vineah.

My chewing slows. I have to remind myself to unclench my jaw. This is a foreign experience: someone who understands me in a way that not even Zenevieve does. And I think I understand Leo, too, because the more he talks about Ithinor, the more I remember Meredith. The more I'm able to relate his experiences to my own because they parallel each other so exactly.

He takes a deep breath, recollecting himself. "After that, I finally realised the person I wanted to become: simply someone to be proud of. The man Ithinor could already see in me."

I bite the inside of my lip. I know it isn't officially my turn to share—I didn't even have a turn—but I want to take it nonetheless: "My parents were the quintessence of majestic but humble—what Snowark is meant to represent."

Leon snickers, bringing out an apple half. "What happened with you, firefly?"

I shove the apple into his mouth.

"It was a joke!" he says, chewing.

"Yet I'm not laughing," I tell him curiously. "Interesting."

His words do elicit a train of thought from me. A quiet yet heavy breath escapes me as I lean against the wall. I take my last bite of the persimmon before continuing. "Believe me. That's what I would be willing to wager that the people of Snowark really think of me. I can't understand it otherwise—they've always maintained their hope for my rule even after my revered parents passed... despite my minimal voice thanks to the cursed councilmen. I think my own people pity me."

"Why?"

I firmly match our eyes. "I learned about the curse when I was five. That is what happened with me—because once I learned that some hidden high authority stole generations of monarchs from their children with a death curse once those children were born—stole parents from innocent children—I never took it well, you could say.

"Then I had my first official meeting with the councilmen when I was fourteen." I exhale tiredly, shaking my head. "Our economy was receding and I knew what to do with it after... everything I was taught and advised on. But Whiny Winston and the lot shut me up. I—admittedly—lost my temper and said something along the lines of how we shouldn't trust anyone with the face of a horse's bottom to be the head of the council—"

Leon bursts out laughing, which only briefly grabs the attention of our group. He apologises between guffaws. I catch a communicative look flash across Zenevieve's face, who is now undergoing Ambrose's healing magic again for her leg: nobody is asking what's just transpired because they don't want to ruin the conversation between me and the prat. She shakes her head before turning back to Ambrose.

I will *punish you one day, Zenny.*

"Please, continue," the prat tells me, passing a hand over his grin.

I roll my eyes, taking out my own bread. When I open my mouth, the words fall short. My mind recalls the memory in full. The remnants of its shame steal back my solemn attention. "The nobles were there that day. Many of them."

Instantly, I regain Leon's solemnity as well.

"They watched the council make a fool of me—and me give in to every trap they laid for me. I was promptly escorted out of the room. Winston came into the hallway moments later and said that my temper would never allow me to rule successfully. Called me as vile as the Princess of Vineah herself. And now the nobles knew it as well. As you can imagine, authority and I aren't on the most agreeable terms."

That was the day I swore to never lose my temper again. Not in front of the council, at least. Not in front of anyone in the palace.

Leon shakes his head. I want to believe that it's in disbelief.

"What?" I dare to ask.

"It's disconcerting to know that someone like him exists." He gestures to me. "And I suppose part of me is conflicted because—you're an authority figure."

And I shouldn't be.

"And I despise it," I tell him instead. My throat tightens on me. "It's all because of this blasted curse, but I follow the laws nonetheless because Snowark is doomed to fall if I don't. Anything I do to defy it—refuse to bear an heir, run away, end my life—Snowark will fall because of the curse. Some cruel ultimatum. And I want—"

I cut myself short, turning my eyes away. My thumb rubs the chunk of bread in my hand. Leon sits in silence, expecting me to continue. But I won't.

"What do you want?" he asks, softly.

"Nothing." I shake my head, dismissing it. I put the bread into my mouth. "I want nothing."

I want children of my own someday. I want Snowark to have a ruler descended from its regal royals. I'm the one who broke the generational blessing of perfect rulers, but the Ancients know how much I desire for my own heir to resume it. I don't have it in me. But I know that they will.

They would have.

"It sounds like the curse stole both of our childhoods in the same way."

I raise my head. Leon is back to staring at the centre of our circle. Almost as if he didn't mean for me to hear that.

"Robbed us of being children," he says next. "If we wanted to be children, it came at a cost. And it was too heavy for either of us to bear at that age. So we were eventually forced into submission, to be the people our kingdoms needed—or wanted—us to be. It all rested on us. It still does."

Our eyes find each other. In that single gaze, he transfers the words directly to my mouth.

"We need to finish this race," I whisper, "before our people fall with us."

His startlingly blue eyes soften. I wonder if mine are as much of a map as his are to me. I dot the landmarks, the curves and lines drawing his irises that make me miss the sky back home. I catch myself holding my breath. The scar slitting his left brow boasts his fierce abilities despite the tenderness he has for his kingdom—those he cares about. My scar feels accompanied by his. Understood. Perhaps that is why I don't feel alone when I look at him. I don't feel alone; that is why I can't tear my eyes away from his. But I don't know why he can't look away. And for a fraction of a second—the Ancients as my witnesses—his eyes dart to my lips before bouncing back up.

We're inches away from each other.

I spring back, my head banging against the dirt wall. The bow and quiver on my back do nothing to cushion the impact.

"Dare I ask if that hurt?" the prat asks. He reaches out a tan hand that I smack away.

"It's dirt," I reply flatly, narrowing my eyes. I rub the tingly spot on the back of my head. "I would expect you of all people to be familiar with it."

He cocks a brow. "After spending so much time with you, yes."

I shove his apple into his mouth again. He drops his hands, his eyes dulling at me.

"There we are." I gesture to his face. "Your true form: a dead pig."

The prat takes the apple out of his mouth. "Has anyone ever told you"—he shoves it in my face—"that you're sour to your core?"

I thwack away his hand again. "I hope that apple tastes as dismal as your ridiculous attempts at humour."

"You'd know all about dismal attempts at humour, wouldn't you?"

"It's only natural after learning from the best for so long—!"

"All right, children," Zenevieve announces from the other side of the circle. A knowing, sly smirk rests on her full lips. "Make nice before we continue."

I send her a glare despite her immunity to them. *How long have this nosy lot been listening in?*

"I wanted to spread preserves on my bread." Ginger pouts, shifting to sit on his knees. "But I've run out."

Zenny nudges him. "Don't worry, Rosy. We'll take Ember's jam when she isn't looking."

"Only if you lot want to finish the race without your hands," I say, grabbing Rowena's pommel.

Sierra ignores us all, resting her hand on Leo's shoulder.

"Are you sure you're all right?"

For the briefest second, he turns to look at me—but he never reaches me. Instead, he locks eyes with Sierra. "The sooner we finish this stage, the better."

For whatever foolish reason my mind can't conjure, I wish that he *had* reached my eyes. Just to tell me what he was thinking. To tell me if his thoughts were anywhere near as ludicrous as mine are right now.

"One moment, you're threatening the man with your dagger," Zenevieve whispers, just about walking normally again as we travel down the passageway. It's then that I realise why she requested to chat in the far back of the group. "The next, you're inches away from him and gazing into his eyes. You've never been so transparent."

I narrow my eyes. They send her another death glare. I curse her immunity to them. "You determine now the best time to discuss these things?"

"They're all the way up there for a reason." She nods at the four, who are metres ahead of us. Her whispers are absorbed by the soil around us. Still, an urgency ignites in my chest at the thought of Leon at the very front—or even Sierra, walking alongside Ambrose ahead of us—overhearing us.

I grit my teeth; at the same time, there's an urgency to put Zenevieve's madness to rest. "I was looking at him because he was looking at me. We were mourning the sheer ridiculousness of the race and the curse... It hasn't affected you the way it's affected me. He knows the sacrifices I've had to make since my very birth. He is first-hand validation of the burden I've carried my entire life."

"Do you know what that's called, Ember?" Zenny asks, arching a brow.

"I've no doubt you'll tell me regardless of my answer."

The daylight illuminates the sheer depth of her black eyes as we pass the holes' lights in the ceiling. "Finding solace in someone who understands you," she says. "And when that someone is as attractive as he is, that typically leads to at least one of you feeling for the other."

I bite my tongue. *Someone who understands you.* My mind cruelly adds "someone who knows your sufferings" to that. I swallow down the memories again.

"That's partly why Ambrose and I have the friendship we do." Zenevieve's whispers lower. "We both know what it means to miss a sibling. And he helps me heal from what happened with mine... That allows me to feel as if I don't have to carry the weight of the world anymore. He helps me realise that not having all the answers, fumbling at times, taking a break and laughing every once in a while—being scared... it's all right. It is all right. I'm not the 'weak and small orphan girl that was taken in by the palace' in his eyes as I am in everyone else's. You are the only other person who has seen me for me. And Ambrose has given me that respect since the day we met."

"He had to, or you would have run Portia through him."

Her gaze maintains a gentle authority over me. "That's simply it: *his* respect isn't the palace boys' fear."

A petty resentment bubbles in me; her words make all the

more sense now. But I don't *want* to have that with the prince. I don't want anything with Seavale when I'll likely lose them all in the end. It isn't safe to find solace with them, least of all with Leon.

"Ember?" Zenevieve whispers.

My thoughts are invading again. My mind speaks for me before I can realise what is prowling in it: "What are we to do if we reach the end and must kill them to win?"

She pauses beside me. Our group travel farther down the passageway. Their steps are cushioned by the dirt. I don't blame them for not realising that we've stopped.

"Well... we do what we've been doing," Zenevieve replies, "and stand together instead of letting each other fall."

I don't know if I believe that. If I can believe that that is even an option. I don't want to allow myself to believe that. To believe another self-fed lie. I know better, just as I always do.

Just not enough to learn—because the smallest part of me, even now, is still hoping.

CHAPTER

"WHAT OTHER OPTION WILL WE HAVE?"

Leo

EZRA AND I HAVE TAKEN THE LEAD WITHOUT INTEND-ing to. The tunnel is too narrow to fit three people side by side, but I suppose it works in my favor: having only one person beside me offers me a little more space—no matter how suffocatingly trapped I feel. There is hardly any excess space between the walls and our shoulders. Emberly and Zenevieve are in the far back, and Ambrose is talking Sierra's ear off. Still, I think she enjoys his conversation; she definitely enjoys indulging his curiosity.

"Are you all right?" Ezra whispers to me.

I exhale, rubbing my sweaty palms together and keeping in synchronization with his steps. "The sooner we escape, the better. I definitely didn't mind the openness of Vineah's stage."

"And your wound?"

My hand instinctually rises to the right side of my chest. Ambrose gave me another brief healing session before we started walking; it's closed, that's more than certain, but it still stings just enough to irritate me.

"Fine. I'll live."

Ezra chuckles. "Good. I mean no offense, but I'm surprised you're handling this as well as you are. Having to stay in one place while Ambrose healed you, and especially when we sat down and ate."

At his words, the first memory my mind flashes is how close I found myself to Emberly. How ensnared the sea of her muted, leaf-green eyes had me, every detail of her irises shining amidst the small streams of daylight. How her company and conversation somehow felt as comforting and safe as Sierra's or Ezra's.

How stupid I was to allow my eyes to trail down to her lips.

I've never even allowed that to happen with Sierra; I've never been *confused* about where I stand with Sierra. I always thought she was pretty, but something about our friendship barred me from wandering too far with the idea of anything beyond it. Emberly... She's beautiful. Anyone with sense and without a grudge will admit that. She's witty and strong and willing to travel great lengths to protect her loved ones—no matter how hard she tries to hide the fact. But she is also written by fate to be my enemy. The person I'm most likely meant to kill should I win the race and become the ruler of the Last Kingdom. There may be only one ruler, yet I find myself effortlessly drawn to her as though the condition doesn't exist. It feels as though we were never *meant* to be enemies... as though the world tried to make us into that first before we even had the chance to exchange hellos.

"I was all right because I was distracted," I tell Ezra. I can almost feel the sun's warmth from the small holes poked above me as I walk in and out of their light. It carves a deep ache in my chest for the sunny days in Seavale while aboard a ship. "As long as you distract me well enough, I'm fine."

Ezra chortles, stifling his laughter. "I had a clear view of your 'distraction', captain," he says, grinning. "I knew she herself was just as distracted when she, of all people, didn't catch me staring at her after a solid minute."

If the woman catches me *glimpsing* her, she's ready to draw her—

I shake my head, interrupting the thoughts that trail after. "It's been a terrible few days. We need much more rest than we can afford."

"Right... I suppose that I shouldn't encourage those thoughts. The end of this will be all the more difficult."

My steps almost pause with my mind—but the last thing I want is everyone overhearing this conversation. The only thing telling me that they don't hear us is the fact that Emberly is now bickering with Ambrose about a cheese wager, and Sierra and Zenevieve are trying to establish peace.

"You don't mean... killing them, do you?" I ask.

"What other option will we have?" Ezra whispers sadly.

A familiar resistance flickers in my chest. It's just as when we were resting in the underwater cave on Seavale's stage and Sierra theorized about the functionality of the race; I came to the conclusion that there can only be one set of seven stages for there to be one ruler. Since then, I'm fairly certain it's been proven that there is only one set of seven. But something still doesn't sit right with me at the theory in its entirety...

If only one ruler is meant to emerge from all this, why would the race send three teams to the same stage simultaneously? To slaughter them all? To faster see who would be the last one standing?

Strictly speaking, we've broken the rules of that for the last five days. Uniting with Snowark instead of killing them immediately—

Uniting. That's it.

"*They who unlock the Last Kingdom prove that they possess what a uniter requires—that you are the sovereign the United should hold at its helm.*"

What if the Mages hadn't meant uniting the sovereign's kingdom with the Last Kingdom, after all? It disobeys every legend I've ever heard about the prophecy and winning the race—but my instinct can't help but rebel.

I recite the Mages' words to Ezra. "Was eliminating our competition ever strictly established?" I whisper at the risk of my words being misinterpreted by the people behind us. "We've survived well without killing Snowark. We've protected them and they've protected us. Emberly even saved Sierra from one of the snake monsters in Vineah our second night there. The only true conflict we've encountered was in Windale and the beginning of Vineah—when another team sought our lives."

Ezra remains as solid as stone as he walks. His head almost skims the ceiling. I can't help but worry about the thoughts running rampant in it. The front door of my mind opens to doubt, and I swallow. I know why he's hesitant: I'm not sure I'm ready to fully believe it, either. I don't know if I can allow my mind to run freely with the chance that I can keep the friends I've made. The chance that I may not have to relinquish what my efforts have produced. I don't have to relinquish Snowark... right?

"What if 'uniter' actually means uniting us?" I whisper. "Our world is falling apart: Seavale against Lavara, Vineah unjustifiably seeking our help against Snowark, Magery dividing into two because of the war between—"

"I think you have that part right," Ezra replies, more gravely this time, "where the ruler of the Last Kingdom is meant to unite all seven kingdoms. That's why it will be the *Last* Kingdom: it's one of ultimate power and reign. But that's why there may only be one ruler. Absolute power cannot be split by seven—it's not absolute, then."

I don't want to believe that. I can't bring myself to believe that I will have to kill to rule. That I will have to kill Snowark. I don't want to believe that they're temporary.

Ezra continues nevertheless. "It is my sworn duty to protect you, Leo. That's why I must be wary about this. If you *and* Emberly become the rulers of the Last Kingdom—"

"—the curse will be broken, and we'll both live to see an heir inherit the throne."

I don't know where the words came from, but I know that they're true. Whether it be my heir or hers, we'll both live. That must be possible; why can't it be possible?

What if this idea is just mad enough to be the answer?

"You truly don't believe in killing to win this?" Ezra eventually asks.

"I cannot see how it's necessary. And I don't believe that Snowark is willing to do so, either. If we all stand against it—who will stop us from winning?"

I look ahead, relief blanketing my chest: the tunnel is about to lead into a room. Now Ezra can't argue.

Finally, I think, fighting an urgency in my steps. *We're*—

I restrain myself from running just in time: a low growl rumbles just before we approach the entryway. My vision pieces together the segments that the small streams of light provide: two large, brown paws with black claws the length of Ezra's hand.

The room's ceiling is higher than the tunnel's, accommodating the brown bear standing a foot taller than Ezra on its hind legs. It falls on all fours with a heavy thud, unleashing a bone-shaking growl with dilating black eyes.

CHAPTER

"MY BITE IS A LOT WORSE THAN MY ROAR"

Emberly

ZENEVIEVE RUNS INTO THE ROOM WITH AMBROSE AND Ezra. Ambrose's hands are already aglow with furious fire. My steps, though, grow wary as the bear comes more and more into view.

Ezra unsheathes his sword with an immortal speed. All too late, he realises Ambrose's fire. He reaches for him as the flames gain the bear's attention. "Ambrose, no!"

Teddy snarls before Ambrose can attack, its gargantuan paw swiping across his face. Ambrose tumbles to the floor, holding his cheek.

Zenevieve calls out to him, unsheathing her sword with the speed of lightning. Leon is stuck in the entryway for a reason unbeknownst to me as Sierra runs into the room. I watch her rush to the right side and kneel with strain by Ambrose.

I stop at Leon's side. An invisible force causes me to stumble. Now I know why Leon is still: the artifact. It's in this room; but unless Teddy is here to hug us until the portal opens, it certainly isn't it.

Teddy knocks Ezra's sword clean out of his hand. It turns upon Zenevieve raising her own weapon. Its beady, black eyes harden as another growl reverberates across the room. A large paw swats away Zenevieve's sword, which lands beside Ezra on the left side of the room. Zenevieve reaches for her dagger—but the bear swats her in the opposite direction.

My senses finally revive. "*Big* mistake, Teddy," I hiss, reaching for Rowena—until my hand stops above her pommel.

I can't grab it. What is this? My fingers are frozen in their position. My hand only hovers above my pommel. Why can't I move? Why can't I unsheathe the dagger? Grab an arrow behind me—?

Fury ignites in Ambrose's brown eyes in the time that I hesitate. Sierra reaches to press a cloth doused in light-blue liquid against his cheek. Despite the crimson staining his skin in numerous trails, he leans away, igniting his hands again.

It isn't fire this time. Furious, white light crackles with the thunders of Snowark's most violent storms. Worry swirls like a blizzard in my stomach.

"Big mistake, you oversized plush toy!" Ambrose shouts. He throws his arms out in front of him, shooting a beacon of lightning at Teddy. "I'll turn you into a new stuffy for Anavieve for that!"

Wait! I shout in my head. The lightning zaps the bear. He releases a terrible growl at the same time I find myself reaching for him. Leon bars me from entering the room.

Teddy wobbles on his hind legs as Zenevieve props herself up. She grabs her mace from her side. Ezra holds her sword and his own. Keeping low, Zenevieve swings her mace under Teddy's feet, tripping him. His body falls straight back. Ambrose shoots another blast of lightning at him.

Dirt sprinkles down upon the bear's impact with the floor. I furiously wipe it from my hot face. My heart accelerates in my chest as I watch Ezra run up to the animal. He plunges his sword into Teddy's heart.

Something twinges in mine.

A heart-wrenching, guttural cry rattles the air. Zenevieve grunts as she forces herself to stand with her sword in hand. With a final thrust, the blade pierces straight through the bear's throat. His scream is cut off just as Ambrose zaps him one last time.

I can see the picture only too clearly because of the small holes in the ceiling: drops of a crimson that matches Ambrose's bleed into Teddy's brown coat. His breathing doesn't heave for long. It fades into soft pants that breathe guilt into my soul.

Images of Meredith's laboured breathing as she squeezes my hand flash across my memory.

Teddy's chest slows. The life in his eyes fades to dullness. Just like Meredith's did.

The bear stops breathing.

Just like Meredith did.

My team sharply exhale. Panting is all that fills the room. Everyone but me for a reason I can't place. My breath is shallow and has been for the last few moments.

I don't want to cause any more death.

I blink, startled by the thought's arrival. This bear is different from the snake monsters. Different from the giant whale. Different from the ice beast. Teddy is different.

"What in this world is a bear," Ezra begins breathlessly, wiping his upper lip, "doing underground?"

"Bears are abundant in Soilera," Sierra answers, faithfully tending to Ambrose's gash in his cheek. "They usually teeter along the forest border between Soilera and Snowark."

That's true. It's why we saw a bear while traveling to the portal. When Meredith...

Sierra's tone grows more curious with each word. "But I can't imagine why the Mages would have us kill a monster, spare a whale, and then kill a bear..."

Because this race is cruel. It steals. It's unfair.

"It was either us or it," Zenevieve states. She sheathes her bloodied sword, her round features firm. "That's all that matters. In life or death, I'll always sacrifice my empathy for life."

Some kind of cruelty drips off of the words. And I curse the fact that they also possess some kind of truth.

"Emberly," Leon says beside me. He reaches out a hand but then retracts. "Do you feel that?"

I blink away the stinging of my eyes. I need to keep them on the ground, away from the bear, to stop whatever is flooding through me. That allows me to focus on the pull, on the—

The artifact. The artifact is *inside*—

"No," I immediately say. I dart across the room and through the opening on the other side. "No, no, I hereby concede my artifact privileges to anyone ghastly enough to grab it this time."

"We'll get it, Ember," Zenevieve assures in breathless pants behind me.

I walk into the passageway. I don't even want to *hear* flesh being ripped apart and intestines sloshing around amidst the—

I pull up a hand to my mouth. My body heaves forward at the stench, or perhaps my mind is already taunting me. I swallow once it's safe. Unfortunately, footsteps accompany that.

Somehow, I've come to recognise those pesky, nosy footsteps by now.

"In your defence," the prat begins, emerging from the room's exit, "it's a rather disgusting place to hide the artifact."

"I'm so grateful to have the prince's approval," I reply flatly, leaning against the wall. A hole in the ceiling is streaming light directly into my eye, but I don't move. I try to restrict my breaths; I can't determine if I really do smell Teddy's intestines because he lies so close or because my mind adores playing cruel games with me.

"Maybe you've influenced me with your astute ability for observation," the cub begins, meandering to the other side of the passageway, "but I can't help but notice your... turmoil."

"'Turmoil'?" I laugh and then gag. The wet earth is definitely absorbing the odour of the bear's guts. I swallow, crossing my arms. "Big word for the little cub. Especially considering how inaccurate it is."

He eyes me pensively, his gaze furrowing. "You hesitated when you reached for Rowena. That hasn't happened before. Did... having to kill the bear upset you?"

"Not as much as you do, if it makes you feel better."

He doesn't flinch. The arrogant prat is confident that he knows me right now. And to my abysmal disappointment, he does.

I lower my head, swallowing again. I only realise the answer when the words find me: "Meredith's favourite animal was the bear."

Standing by as the animal was killed... it felt like witnessing her death as a result of me all over again.

If not for the race. If not for me running the race. If not for my shameful existence. I hate that I can never escape it no matter where I am.

Sloshing curdles from the room. I squirm, anxious to drown it out: "And what might be your valiant excuse for not acting, cub?"

He mimics my position against the wall. "You learn when not to interfere when it comes to battle. Even when your friends are the ones fighting."

He hesitated because of strategy. I hesitated because I fell into my Ancients-forsaken emotions.

If my glares had the ability, a hole would be burned into the wall in front of me right now. I think my final straw has been pulled. I cannot keep falling victim to this wretched heart, allowing my memories and losses to affect my survival. My teammates' survival. There is nothing I may do to recover my loss; that is my burden to bear, not theirs. I must throw in Meredith's sacrifice and run. She already made it; there is nothing I can do to retrieve it.

But that means letting her go.

No... I can't. If I let her go, I lose her again.

But they need me. They need me to be better. If I keep remembering her—

"Firefly?"

Curse this prat. I'm even showing him more than he was ever supposed to see because of this.

Do not be weak. Do not be weak.

I exhale my remaining thoughts. I force my mind forward, back into who I must be. "You can admit it if you were scared."

He cocks his brow. "You would never allow me to forget it if I had been."

"Nonsense," I reply. It's as if he knows to distract me right now. "Of course the little cub would be scared of a big, bad bear."

He chuckles—or perhaps it's a scoff. I can't determine if the curvature of his lips is a smile or a smirk. He shakes his head. "What have I done to earn you calling me a cub?"

That certainly isn't the initial reaction I was anticipating. It's as if... *Is* he trying to distract me?

"Quite the opposite," I say. "It's what you've *yet* to do that's earned it. 'Leon' means 'lion'—but you, Your Highness, are a cub."

He glances to the side as if he doesn't want me to see the smile on his face. His finger mindlessly taps his thigh. Then, his eyes as blue as the sky I wish I could see right now return to me. "You'd be surprised. My bite is a lot worse than my roar."

I narrow my eyes. "Are you threatening to bite me?"

His head catches back and he blinks, straightening. "No— no, that's not what—"

"That was abysmal, I *felt* my internal organs shrivel up and die."

His tan face is aflame with red, mouth snapping shut. He presses his lips together. "I see why you love lemons: they're sour and bitter like you."

The prat *is* doing it on purpose: I'll gladly take advantage of my insult privileges, and he knows that. "How did the little cub ever put it together?"

He rolls his eyes. "I *wonder* how I could have possibly—"

"You certainly weren't so keen on that conclusion a few—"

"Forgive me, the lack of air has done terrible things to my brain, you see."

"Oh, I guarantee that that has *little* to do with what's wrong with your brain—"

"*You two!*"

The prat and I jump, standing from the walls. Ezra stands in the archway of the room. A clear vial of water hangs from his fingertips. It's as tall as his pinkie finger.

His scowl is equally exchanged between us. "Put aside the childish I-like-you banter and focus!"

I gag again. This time, I don't think it's because of Teddy's guts that are definitely sprawled across the floor right now.

Leon glowers. He meets Ezra in the middle of the narrow passageway. Zenevieve, Ambrose, and Sierra pile up behind him, exiting the room.

"What is this?" the prat asks. "Seawater?"

"It almost looks like it," Sierra muses. "But I wouldn't drink it to find out."

Leon holds up the vial in a stream of daylight. Though the sample is small, I catch minute particles dancing about in the water. Tiny bubbles cling to the surface.

He pops open the tiny cork and brings the vial to his nose. A smile stretches across his lips. "It *is* seawater."

My curiosity almost begs me to smell it, too; I've never been allowed anywhere near the coast on either side of Snowark. That's just as well: I'd rather avoid any space that aquatic life regularly uses as its lavatory.

"*Are* we meant to drink it?" Ambrose asks. Now he holds Sierra's cloth—grimly painted with crimson—to his cheek. From what I can see, his gash is no longer pouring blood. He must have healed himself somewhat.

Leon presses his lips together as if he's considering the notion. Then, he turns to me. "What do you think?"

What? What do *I* think? Why would he trust me with the answer—even care about my input? This is clearly Seavale's artifact. He should be the one to figure out what to do with it.

Especially because I've only one mad idea for it: "If not drink it, pour it."

I receive the appropriate looks of scorn and disbelief from all but Leon. Instead, he raises an inquisitive brow. "Dare I ask what's inspired the idea?"

I glimpse Zenevieve beside me, who challenges me to answer competently. "Well, what else are we meant to do with a tiny bottle of water? Roll it on the ground?"

"Maybe!" Ambrose chimes. "We play that game all the time at—"

I hold up my hand. "Fascinating, Ginger, truly, but we'd only need the bottle itself if that were the case." I match my eyes with Leon again. "The water itself is the artifact, should it follow the pattern of all the others: dirt to water this time. The bottle is merely the vessel. The only way to utilise water is to release it. No?"

I'm not sure if I'm grateful for the fuzzy silence afterwards; my group are either harshly scolding my incompetency or have had their doubts silenced. Despite how I can't fault my own logic, I also can't prevent the fear that I've overlooked something blatant.

Leon, however, doesn't have that infectious mien of doubt on his sharp features. If anything, I can almost hear the gears turning in his head. Why doesn't he think the idea mad—?

"Aye aye, captain," he says, pouring the water.

"Leo!" Sierra exclaims, breaking past Zenevieve and Ambrose. "What if—?"

The water bubbles upon contact with the dirt. Immediately, it erodes the ground, travelling farther down the passageway—as if it's flowing from an infinite source. Our attentions are snagged as the water seeps forward until turning left, around the corner.

We don't speak, rushing after it. Well, as well as we can with a rigid Sierra.

Weaving around turns according to the water trail, multiple tunnels offer themselves to us on the way. I don't allow my curiosity the energy to wonder about them. The water continues down one path. That is the only guidance we follow until we enter our next room. Then, the water evaporates.

Brilliant. Absolutely brilliant.

Two dark tunnels continue straight. The artifact, however, doesn't show us which way to take.

CHAPTER

"LILIE𝕾"

Leo

MY MIND RACES WITH MY HEART AT THE SIGHT OF the two short tunnels before us. These are half the size of the passageways we've been walking through. I don't know if I can manage it. Nothing will allow me to feel safe if I'm trapped in there.

"Leo," Sierra begins, stepping up to me, "it's all right—"

"I'm fine," I whisper, trying desperately to steel my resolve. It's one of the few times that I've ever lied to her. "Don't focus on me, let's—let's figure out what to do."

The room's eyes are glued to me, all the more worsening the anxiety. As if he's reading my mind, Ambrose steps up to me, still holding the bloodied cloth to his cheek. "It's not too terrible, Leo!" he chirps. "My siblings and I play this game all the time at home—well, except the worst punishment one of us ever has is landing in the cows' waste pen instead of the stables to ride to a picnic."

Admittedly, he elicits a small smile, especially as Ezra and Sierra burst out chuckling. I glance at Emberly and Zenevieve: I'm not sure the humor has reached them.

Instead, Zenevieve furrows her brows, her black eyes glinting in a small stream of daylight from the ceiling. "How did one of you ever come up with that? Actually, no, how do you even arrange something like—?"

"I do believe there are more important questions to be asked, Zenny," Emberly tells her. My heart thrums a little harder. "For example, how are we meant to pick which tunnel to take?"

The room settles at the question. I can feel everyone's thoughts whirling around in it, and I run my hand through my hair as though to stimulate some of my own against the taunting fear. Part of me doesn't want to pick a tunnel to go down; the other part is haunted by the fact that I have no other choice *but* to go down one of them.

"Why wouldn't the water lead us down the right path?" Ezra asks, his hand resting on the golden pommel of his sword. Sierra stands beside him, lightly nodding in agreement. "The artifact is meant to help us overcome the main obstacle. Surely this isn't..."

I heavily sigh, defeat infecting me as I shake my head. "The tunnels aren't the main obstacle. I think it was the maze we traveled through on our way here. Pouring out the water wasn't exactly the most obvious solution, but it showed us the path to take. I have to hope that this is the last part of the stage."

Sierra steps forward and turns around, facing us. "The plan is obvious: split in half. Three in one tunnel and three in the other. We only need to determine which three are going where."

"Then first we should establish where Leo and Emberly will be." Ezra glances between us. "There is no other way to say it: if one tunnel proves to be the... *wrong* tunnel, we can't risk losing both of you at once."

"Meaning we'll have the privilege of separating?" Emberly asks hopefully, glimpsing me. "I've just received my second wind."

"So Leo in one tunnel," Zenevieve says, emphasizing the words and gently shoving her, "and Ember in another. As for where to put Rosy and the knights...?"

I press my lips together in thought, my eyes bouncing from each member as I move them around in my head. Something doesn't sit wholly right about the arrangement no matter how I order it. There are too many variables, especially considering I don't think I'll be able to survive this next step unless Sierra is with me.

"I'm concerned about a few things," I announce, gesturing to Ezra. "For one, it will be a miracle if Ezra can move with ease in there, given the small entrances. If there is any immediate threat, he won't be able to fight—or even allow his group to escape easily."

Sierra furrows her brows together, hands on her hips. "Are you suggesting leaving him behind?"

I open my mouth to argue—although, the more the words settle, the more I realize that that is true—but Ezra holds up his hand. "Perhaps that's wise, lily," he says. "Just because we defeated the bear doesn't mean another threat isn't imminent. Especially if that other threat is another team."

"You can't fight a team on your own—"

"No, but I can call for help. I can also fend for myself long enough for the rest of you to return and help me. And if one group is the wrong tunnel, they can escape more easily and come back to me so that we can alert the others and take the right one."

Sierra's green eyes radiate the unease I feel with the idea, but I also can't help but see the rest of the pieces falling into place: the power balance is more equal now between one knight for one tunnel and a mage for the other.

"Then I'll stay with—" Sierra begins, but her mouth closes the second she meets my anxious gaze. Thank the Ancients for that, because the wave of nausea that flooded me at those words was almost enough to knock me over.

"—Leo," she says, nodding. "It's better if I stay with Leo for this part." She faces Ambrose and Zenevieve. "What about you two?"

"I should go first in my tunnel," Ambrose says, lowering the bloodied cloth from his cheek. A clotted, dark-red gash is all that remains. Emberly's eyes slightly widen at him as if she's surprised by his initiative. "I can stun an enemy in case we do run into trouble, and give us time to crawl out."

Sierra nods. "Then you'll need more time and space to escape—a stun may not last as long as you need it to. Zenevieve, are you willing to go before me and Leo?"

Zenevieve's glance at Emberly requires no translation; I more than understand the hesitance to leave a best friend behind. It seems unfair that I'll have mine but neither of them will have theirs.

"Oh, just go," Emberly says dully, nudging her. "If they give

327

you trouble, it's nothing Portia can't resolve. And it isn't as if I'll beat up the little strawberry." She gestures to the left tunnel. "There isn't enough room. He'll be fine."

I can't help but follow her hand. *Not enough room. That's more than true.*

Ambrose narrows his round eyes, peering down at her. "I'm beginning to question protecting you."

"You'll grow used to it," she replies.

I can't help but wonder how she can possibly maintain such a casual demeanor about this. One of these paths could lead to one of our demises. Potentially even both. And yet we've no choice but to take the next step forward. She *must* be as unwilling to do this as—

She takes Ambrose's cloth from a clean corner and drops it to the ground. "Give yourself another healing session before you trip and tear open that nasty gash."

"You do care!" he chimes, vibrant, green magic igniting in his hands. Emberly slaps his arm as he holds out his hands in front of him, directing the stream to his cheek. Sierra reminds him to spare his energy where he can. Moments later, the beginning of a scab is left behind.

"Good." Emberly pulls him to the left tunnel entrance. He bends down and crawls inside. "Don't forget to poke His Royal Prat-ness with Portia for me, Zenny," she calls, following Ambrose inside. "Time is wasting away, if I may remind you lot."

Morbid curiosity begs the question of what they can see— of what they'll find. If their path looks different than what ours will. All the while, part of me regrets having to leave them behind on one route while we try another. I know how this could end. I know that we all do. It strikes me then that maybe that is what maintains Emberly's lack of solemnity: distracting herself before the possibilities affect her performance, such as how I distracted her from her grief over Meredith. It's just like me with small spaces, and it's just like me right now.

She has that mastered much better than I do. It's almost concerning.

All Zenevieve manages in response is an eyeroll. The dust in the air must be irritating her eyes, because she blinks rapidly now as she faces us. She nods to the right tunnel, meandering to the entrance. It cuts her height exactly in half. "Shall we?"

Sierra verifies with Ezra again that he will be all right alone. Then, she needs to spend another minute with me ensuring that I'll be able to endure such a tight space for we don't know how long. It's a difficult, perhaps even impossible, promise to make that I'll be all right or feel safe—if there's a difference.

Zenevieve moves to her hands and knees and then crawls inside. Sierra gives me a squeeze on my arm before following after. I glance behind me at Ezra.

"Distraction," he mouths. "You'll be fine."

I nod my thanks. I'm only allowed a couple of deep breaths, my mind rapidly trying to convince itself again that this tunnel is not the same thing as the dungeon. Finally, I lower myself to my hands and knees and crawl inside.

There is much to distract myself from.

Damp soil cakes on my skin with every slow crawl forward. I've no trouble with taking our time for the sake of our safety—except for the fact that this is the smallest space we've been forced into since this race began. Still—it's rather wider than I anticipated, more than enough to accommodate me without brushing my shoulders. I suspect that even Ezra would be able to fit in here with excess space. My bow on my back has enough room, too, meaning I may turn around relatively easily if I must.

I hope.

Breathe. As Sierra said—focus on what you know. Remember where you are, still breathing, under the protection of your friends and yourself. You overcame this in the trench. In the cave in Windale's stage and Snowark's. The walls are not closing in.

I'm not locked inside. I'm not locked inside. I won't starve this time.

"Are you all right, Leo?" Sierra asks in front of me.

"Fine," I reply, keeping my gaze on my hands.

Too many moments pass before Zenevieve says, "It must be lovely to always have access to the sea. I've always wanted to try sailing. And by the way Leo swung from those vines in Vineah, surely he's an expert."

I know exactly what she is attempting, and I gladly accept the effort with a chuckle. "Years of sailing since I was eight, in fact."

"It's not the only reason we call him 'captain'." Sierra chuckles.

"You've certainly racked up a list of nicknames for yourself, Your Highness," Zenevieve says curiously. "And you're fortunate to be at the back—I'd otherwise obey Ember and poke you with my sword."

Ah—Portia is her sword.

"Ember is something, isn't she?" I ask with a feigned curiosity. "It's easy to fire her up."

Sierra stops crawling, lightly thrusting her foot into my

chest.

"Sierra!"

"That didn't hurt," she says dully. "And Ezra isn't here to thwack you."

Zenevieve ignores Sierra completely, a sly mischievousness creeping into her voice. "You seem to have noticed a lot about Ember, Leo."

"And you don't even know him that well yet," Sierra adds. "His favorite thing in the world is the sun on a calm day of sailing out in the sea. The look on his face when he embraces the warmth is the same look he has when he looks—"

"As if I'm staring at her for all hours of the day!"

"No, Leo, just more often than you realize." Sierra's chuckle is sinisterly sweet. Four years ago, I would have tripped her for this conversation.

"You think Ember isn't as stubborn?" Zenevieve scoffs. "She swears up and down that she was only looking at His Royal Prat-ness because they were having a conversation. Sheer ridiculousness."

I sincerely cannot place whether the words are meant to be sarcastic.

Is this really their way of distracting me? I'm not even sure if it's working or not; I suppose embarrassment is just as distracting as *enjoying* a conversation.

"I've never heard such affectionate insults," Sierra says. "Even Emberly seems to have—"

"So where *did* 'lily' come from?" I ask, anxious to change subjects even if it means she kicks me again. "I've never heard Ezra call you that until the race."

She stops crawling, turning her head to scowl at me. Now my curiosity refuses to release her.

"This must be an interesting story, indeed," Zenevieve simpers.

Sierra has to scamper to catch up with her. She then clears her throat. "What ever do you mean, Leon?"

"Now, now," Zenevieve chirps, "if the boy wants a story, tell the boy a story."

Sierra sighs, briefly hanging her head. "Ezra and I were walking through a market last summer for my birthday, and the wind blew apart a flower display at one of the merchants' booths. A swirl of lilies attacked me. One was caught in my hair and hanging out from behind my ear when they all blew away. The merchant apologized and offered a free bouquet. Ezra went to accept, but I insisted on paying since it was only fair..."

"And?" I say, hearing her unfinished sentence.

She exhales again, which seems to provide her the courage she needs. "The merchant told me that I was just as beautiful as his lilies, and Ezra—accidentally—agreed out loud. We had a laugh about it, but the name stuck. For one reason or another."

Not quite the dramatic tale I was expecting—but it is definitely alleviating the pressure of the walls better.

"That was last year, you said?" Zenevieve asks. "And the man only confessed to you *today!*"

"I can't speak for him," Sierra replies incredulously, "but on my own behalf... it was a matter of fear that confessing would sabotage our friendship. Surely he can compliment me from a motive other than romantic—I didn't want to misconstrue his intentions."

Zenevieve starts to speak again, but she quickly cuts herself off. "Yes, I suppose so."

Like her friendship with Ambrose. I can't imagine Ambrose remarking anything romantic to Zenevieve—and living.

"And what is more beautiful than being thwacked in the face with a hundred lilies?" I say, maintaining my gaze on Sierra's sabatons.

"That aligns with our regular adventures," she says. "So I suppose the nickname became rather appropriate in most circumstances."

"Including in the face of death?" I ask before I can realize the words in time.

Zenevieve stops at the front. She turns her head, her eyes gleaming. "What? Death? When?"

I didn't want Snowark to know that we practically murdered Soilera.

Another point for your reckless impulsivity.

"Soilera," Sierra eventually replies. Her tone is indiscernible as though in an attempt to keep the story impartial. "We met them on Windale's stage. The princess struck me with her sword. Ith..." She takes in a small breath, exhaling almost silently. "Ithinor healed me. Saved my life."

"That was when I heard 'lily' for the first time," I timidly add. My hands sink deeper in the dirt. A circle of daylight shines on them in a different spot every time I crawl forward. "Before we knew that she would survive."

A stuffy silence overwhelms us. Anxiety convinces me that I can hear the mechanics of Zenevieve's mind turning, that I can hear her piecing together the puzzle for herself.

Perhaps I really did hear it, because then she says, "Soilera attacked you. That's why you were so wary of us when we first met, isn't it?"

Nobody answers, but confirmation saturates the air.

"Then we've no time to waste." She crawls more fervently now; and Sierra and I gladly, quickly follow. "Soilera didn't defeat you on Windale's stage, and they certainly won't defeat us now on theirs."

I can happily concur with that.

My palms begin to sweat as we slowly make our way farther down. Dirt clings to my skin and between my fingers, but at least it's still cool. I wonder when my next opportunity will be to clean my hands—let alone myself.

"I can't wait to return to the Guard after this," Zenevieve mumbles. I almost don't catch the words. "Nothing, and I mean *nothing*, will scare me. They certainly ought to promote me to captain after this."

Sierra snickers. "Poor Ezra will be stuck with 'Captain Everguard'."

A smile beams across my lips as Zenevieve laughs. "You must be kidding!" she exclaims. "He's a *knight* and his name—"

"Leo!"

I stop crawling. Sierra and Zenevieve follow suit. Both of them turn their heads to look at me—as if I know why Ezra's voice is bellowing from down the tunnel.

Instinct is alive in me, and it's frozen me in my place. For a reason unbeknownst to me, my mind is screaming at me to turn around and leave the tunnel. My heart skips a beat as I look behind me: we've made terrific progress, but Ezra is bent down at the entrance.

"Leon!" he screams. "It's Emberly!"

CHAPTER 27

"IT'S NOT YOUR FAULT"

Emberly

DENSE SOIL STICKS TO MY HANDS AS GINGER AND I crawl through the noticeably narrow space. The walls almost skim my shoulders. My bow on my back is even scraping the top of the tunnel. After a few seconds, I leave behind my care of dirt climbing under my fingernails. I'll let it dry on my hands once we escape before dusting it off; our water source is still too scarce to risk wasting on frivolous comfort.

"We're on the *sixth* stage, Emberly," Ambrose remarks in front of me. He chuckles to himself. "Incredible. I'm actually surprised at how much I've learned in this race. Ask me anything, I'll likely know the answer this time."

Needless to say, his rear end isn't the scenic view I was hoping for; I keep my gaze on his feet that inch forward almost too quickly for my liking. His lankiness is providing him an unfair advantage.

"How about this one: how in this *world* have you managed to wrap Zenevieve around your skinny little finger?"

The stick laughs at me. "Is that what you think? It's quite the opposite."

"Kissing her hand on Snowark's stage, pulling her straight into this one, daring to shove her back while we were eating— you've managed to escape it all without so much as a scolding."

"She threatened to use her dagger on me after that last one," he states, as if he truly has to prove himself correct.

I roll my eyes. "Ginger."

"I don't know," he says. A second passes. It almost sounds as if he's weighing the words in his mind first. "I suppose it's— just as with you and her. She isn't merely my friend. She's more like... my big sister."

Incredible: the strawberry has managed to put it into terms that I not only comprehend—but understand with my entire be- ing. He truly has grown during his time here.

"I had to leave behind four siblings that were my entire world when I was thirteen," he says next. "I may only ever visit my family five times a year. I think Zenevieve felt for me because of that—seeing as how she lost her siblings when she was much younger. I felt for her because I had to say goodbye to two older siblings of my own. I suppose we compensated for each other be- cause of that... After all, her teases reminded me of back home— she could be mean, but it always had the sense that she was trying to have fun with me."

"You know mine were only ever fun teases, too."

"For *you*, perhaps," Ginger replies. I roll my eyes. "After we made our deal, I think that's when that started being completely true. I don't mind it at all, I have fun *with* you now. But Zenevieve, she was my friend from the start. One time, Ramses ambushed me in the palace stables; and she ambushed him right back. Her dagger gave him that scar on his arm."

Zenevieve did that? To protect Ambrose?

I wonder if her influence was why he had the courage to stand up to Winston that day in the hallway...

"Who knew it would take one freckled stick to soften her?" I sigh. A small rock grazes my right hand. "You truly are a man of talent, Ginger."

He snickers. "I think she only feels for me for the same reason I do her. She always makes me feel bigger than my abilities. She believes that I can grow stronger, just like Aiden and Abria do. Just like my real older siblings. She's also taught me a lot during this race. So have you, actually."

I scoff, a pebble sinking into my left palm. I restrain a hiss, pausing to brush it away. "What could I have possibly taught you, Ginger?"

"How to be brave. Because the more scared you are, the braver you are when you act despite it."

I run to the first excuse in my head: "I'm following Zenevieve's lead as you are."

"Maybe that's part of it," he replies, "but I think you're also feeding off of her bravery to forge your own. Remember when you saved me from the lake?"

"Zenevieve and—"

"I told you: *you* knew to cut off my robes."

The moisture in the air intensifies. Heat radiates from my

cheeks. The holes in the ceiling don't provide enough fresh air.

"You threw the fire sword into the ice monster's heart despite us telling you not to. You were scared to shoot the arrow into the volcano yet did it because you had to. You threw the seed down the whale's throat because you reckoned plants grow in water 'no matter what kind'."

I don't understand. This is the same boy who demanded that I believe in myself during Lavara's stage, yet my ears are burning at the same words now; why is it all the more difficult to hear these things from him?

"You have admirable instincts, Emberly," he tells me next. "I've always said that about you. Please believe me when I say—"

"I won't hear this again." My palms feel heavier on the soil. "Focus."

"You did the same thing in Lavara," he says, as if he doesn't appreciate the fact. A blurred memory curdles in my mind at the mention of it. Something my mind is desperately trying to suppress. "Why don't you ever want to hear about your own—?"

"I said to leave it be, Ambrose!"

The soil all around us absorbs the resonation of my voice—not the volume. If anything, it's all the sharper. I cringe with regret and shame.

Ambrose stops in front of me. "I'm... I'm sorry."

Even this situation is familiar. It is too familiar. My memory can't stay buried.

"I only mean to say that I still believe that you are a good princess, and it hurts me that you don't believe—"

"Because the supposedly 'wonderful' princess that committed all those things is the same princess who had Meredith killed!"

That's why. That is why this conversation is all the more difficult now: all those things happened when Meredith was alive. Ever since she left—I haven't been good for anything.

Curse this man: my jaw is quivering no matter how hard I lock it. My fingers are digging into the soil as if they can clench into fists straight through it.

"That wasn't your fault," Ambrose says.

"How could you possibly say—?"

"Because that isn't who you are," he states. "How you were so protective over us when we first met Seavale, how you were ready to tend to her and do what was in your power to keep her alive—that is who you are, you *protect* the ones you love the best you can. There was little to do about her, Emberly, I know you would have if you could. That wasn't your fault. It was Windale that prompted violence. They are at fault, not you."

"It isn't just Meredith," I whisper. I only realise that the words are true when I speak them. My memory isn't the only thing ripping open. It's guilt. It's anger. It's helplessness. "It isn't—just Meredith..."

"What do you mean?"

"I killed my parents."

My heart drops into my stomach. It's as if I'm hearing the words for the first time.

I am. I've never confessed that aloud before.

Ambrose hangs his head of red curls. "The death curse killed your parents."

"If I hadn't been born—!"

"But you were," he tells me, "to keep your kingdom alive.

Had it not been for you, Snowark wouldn't exist. Your parents knew that."

"How much crueller should it be to know that they loved me enough to keep me nonetheless!" I long to control my voice, to speak gentler to him; but my resentment of the past, of its immutability, has already stolen my authority. "Lovely, Ambrose: they wanted me knowing they would never have me. Where does that leave me? No better than where I was."

My teeth ruthlessly grind together. I don't know how much longer the marble wall behind my eyes will last. He doesn't know. He doesn't understand. I don't want to believe that my parents loved me. I can't bring myself to believe it despite how my mother chose to die for me, the king gave his life for my sake. That makes every taunt, every wicked reminder, all the truer.

"Whether they loved me or not..." I say with a shakiness I can't control, "I am the one that brought forth my parents' deaths."

"They died because of the curse brought about by your birth," he dares to whisper. "Not by *your* hand. You never committed anything against them."

You never committed anything against them.

I swallow a hard lump the size of a boulder. Every step in this race has been taken with that guilt, that pressure to make their sacrifice right somehow. Now, though... I remember a large reason I'm running this race despite having no choice: not only to protect Snowark, but also to avenge my parents and every other monarch stolen by this curse. My rule may have brought forth my parents' deaths, but that doesn't steal my initiative. If I run, if I allow a worthy ruler on the throne of the Last Kingdom, even if it's not me, they will be avenged.

"Emberly?" Ambrose turns his head to look at me.

I nod. "Let's go, Ambrose," I say, gaining control of my voice. "We need to prepare your induction as Snowark's royal mage—and tell Whiny Winston and the herd that we did it."

"Yes!" he exclaims, excitedly crawling forward. I think I'm able to keep up with him this time. "Finally, you're just as eager as I am to win this. It only took ten days."

"Stick around you long enough and not even Moody Myron could avoid such a contagion."

He focuses his round, brown eyes on me again, smirking. "You secretly like it, don't you?"

Somehow, the boy pushes the corners of my lips upward. How dare he?

He has the audacity to return it, too. "You *can* smile! How lovely."

I drop it. This situation, those words, feel familiar, too. "Tell anyone and I'll let Zenny shave your head, after all."

"I know you wouldn't. And we could all do with some kind of relief from time to time. How do you think I've put up with you all these years?"

I roll my eyes. "I *have* taught you too well, Ginger."

He shakes his head, continuing his eager crawl. "I've always liked it when you smile." His arms stumble when he reaches a certain patch. "I can imagine why you don't do it often. But it's very pretty. And you can see how it lights up the rest of you."

Now I remember why it feels so familiar: Meredith said something similar to me on Lavara's stage. She knew why I didn't smile often, too. That reason became all the more transparent only days later—when we arrived on Vineah's stage. And yet, hearing it from Ambrose now feels... somewhat comforting.

"Are sappy speeches your next method of emotional relief," I tease, "or do I have to—?"

"Wait." Ginger's voice is unfamiliarly deep.

I stop. "We don't have time—"

"Stay there," he commands, his next crawl slow. Suddenly, he furiously turns around. Fear carves out his irises as he shouts, "Go back! Go back, now!"

His hands briefly sink into the ground before he jerks them back out. That puts more pressure on his feet and knees. The bottom half of his legs sink into the soil—mud.

Quickmud.

"Ambrose—?"

He pushes back on my shoulders when I approach. My fingertips touch something softer than the normal soil.

"No, stop!" he exclaims, pressing against me. His thighs sink faster. "Emberly, don't—!"

I crawl backwards. My eyes furiously dart around the tiny tunnel, looking for anything to pull the man free. Instead, they snag on what lies ahead: a wall of dirt.

We picked the wrong tunnel.

Ambrose's arms hover above the dark-brown mud. He is still shouting at me to go back.

No. No, this isn't it—I'm not meant to give up here!

Your mind lies, but your actions surpass it.

I grab Ambrose's hands, squeeze my eyes shut, and pull against his every command. My hands grip his wrists and then his forearms for more leverage. We pulled him out once, I can do it again. I can save him—!

"Emberly, *stop!*" he cries.

I open my eyes. I've made him sink past his hips. His satchel is halfway swallowed.

No. No, no, no...

"You're encouraging it," he tells me shakily. I've never heard him sound brave. And even right now, it's broken. The gash on his cheek taunts me all the more viciously.

"Your magic," I command, falling back on my hands and ignoring the puncture of another pebble. "There must be something you can use! Your telekinesis!"

His hands flicker with sheer, glowing waves of white. He shuts his eyes in concentration. Strenuous effort knits his brows together, and his freckled cheeks flush with red. Then, he exhales, panting as the magic fades from his hands.

"It's too heavy," he tells me with a cracked voice. "I can't move it—"

"They try again!" I cry. "Now!"

White magic flashes in his pale, shaking hands. They tremble all the more furiously with his effort as he tries to separate them. The mud around him bubbles and gurgles against his force—sucking his satchel under as the mud rises to his waist.

"Wait, stop!" I exclaim the moment his arms fall.

Ambrose pants with exhaustion, his hands hovering over the mud. "I can't—I can't do it, it doesn't matter, Emberly, *you* need to survive this! I don't matter—"

"Do not say that!" I shout, grabbing his hands. I use every ounce of strength in my muscles to refrain from pulling him. "How dare you give up, you said it yourself! Your sisters need you, Zenevieve needs you! Curse it, Ambrose, if you need to hear it, I need you! All right? You matter, act like it, *please!*"

"My sisters..." In the space of seconds, his terrified frown twitches into a tearful smile. "Promise—promise me that you will protect them under your rule. And—and take care of Zenny for me, too, please. They'll need you." His brown eyes are too gentle on me. Half of his torso has disappeared under the surface of the quickmud. "But you—you don't need me. You'll be fine without me."

"I've only been fine *because* of you!" I exclaim. The tears have demolished that marble wall. They overwhelm my vision in a merciless flood. "Why do you think I picked you instead of Zephyr? Do you know how often I need to remember why I'm still running in this death trap, how often I need help to endure it for another day? *You* are that help! You remind me why I still have a reason to fight! Every morning in that forsaken palace, every morning in this cursed race, I can't, I can't lose you, too!"

A tear trickles down his red cheek. Yet he smiles at me. "No. You've fought your way through for all of us throughout this, and I don't even think you know it. You don't understand how strong you are, Emberly; but I hope you realise it soon, I really do, because Snowark needs you. The Kingdom *needs* you."

"Stop talking like it's the last time we'll ever meet!" I cry, my grip on his hands trembling.

He releases a breathy chuckle. His chest has sunk beneath the surface. He pulls his hands from mine and into the mud. It swallows his arms whole.

No. No, why are you giving up, why aren't you fighting this?! Don't you dare give up, you can't—!

"Thank you—for your honesty," he tells me. "I'm—I'm glad you're not running away from your heart anymore. It's why you've so much potential. And you've started growing into it. So—so please don't run away from it anymore. Please, you're better with it. It's why I'm—so proud that you are Snowark's princess."

"Stop," I whisper, hanging my head and squeezing my eyes shut. Tears drown my lashes. "Stop it, don't. Don't, don't, don't leave me, too, please...!"

I am not worth their sacrifices! Why do they give themselves to an unworthy rule?!

"Emberly," Ambrose whispers.

I look up. My heart drops out of my chest: Ambrose's chin hovers above the mud now.

"It's not your fault."

I reach out; but he shakes his head, pursing his quivering lips. He turns it up as his neck is fully submerged.

"No, no, no—!"

His happy, round, brown eyes smile at me one last time. "It was a proud honour to serve you, My Queen."

"*Ambrose!*"

He closes his eyes as the back of his head sinks into the mud. It swallows his light, freckled face in one fell swoop.

CHAPTER 28

"TO MAKE THIS RIGHT"

Leo

"EMBERLY!" I SHOUT, THE OPENING OF THE TUNNEL growing closer. Ezra has left the entrance to tend to her. I push harder against the ground in powerful strokes like the soil is water and I'm swimming. A sharp ache pulses harder and harder under my arrow wound on my chest, but no part of me has the ability to care. "Emberly!"

My heart throbs in my chest and my head swims, but right now I know I need to leave the tunnel. I don't care how much progress through the tunnel I've already made. I know that we went farther than I thought I'd be able to endure. And I also know that I'm willing to undo it all as long as Emberly is on the other side and I can help her when she needs it. My heart and mind are in perfect accord.

I grunt at the sharp pang under my wound when I hear it:

her sobs. A beat skips in my chest. They exponentially grow the closer I draw until I claw at the ground, pulling myself out of the entrance.

Ezra stands in the middle of the dirt room. He doesn't dare to approach a trembling Emberly on her hands and knees at the left tunnel entrance. Sierra is next out of our tunnel and then Zenevieve. Emberly's head hangs low, her body arching with sobs. Her bow on her back is tarnished by dirt staining its limb and wedged between it and the string.

Something isn't right. What happened to—?

"Ember!" Zenevieve shouts, running to her and kneeling beside her. "What's wrong? What happened? You need to talk to me, where is—?"

We all notice it at the same time: Ambrose never follows Emberly out.

No. No, no, no, this...

I wait. I wait and I keep waiting, I keep hoping, I keep expecting a head of red curls to leave the left tunnel entrance. It stays dark. Emberly stays alone.

Not him. He couldn't—he can't—he was just—

My stare gravitates to Zenevieve when her shoulders slump. Her black eyes, a new darkness consuming them, rise to somewhere in front of her. Tears break the barriers of her eyes.

"Ambrose," she whispers airily. It's a far cry from the woman I've come to know. I swallow a hard lump in my throat. "No, Ambrose..."

It isn't possible. How could—in there, he couldn't have—

Tell me this isn't real. Tell me I'm trapped in my head again. A nightmare, anything, please.

Zenevieve's hand shakily draws to her mouth, one hand resting on Emberly's shoulder. She drops her head. Emberly never stirs from her hands and knees. The dirt beneath her soaks up her tears as they fall.

I lock my jaw. Something has numbed in my chest. I keep expecting to see a grinning, freckled face emerge from that tunnel next. My jaw grows tighter for every second that I don't. The stinging pressure behind my eyes worsens the longer I stare at the empty dark.

Zenevieve wraps her arms around Emberly, unleashing a fierce scream that rivals all of her previous battle cries I've heard. Emberly rises to her knees, embracing her. A bone-shattering sob erupts from her throat, as though she's releasing everything she's ever felt since childhood.

I squeeze my eyes shut. It steals my very ability and desire to breathe.

Something moves in the corner of my eye. Sierra walks to their side, embracing them. Her shoulders heave as she breathes, silent tears of her own falling. My best friend is hurting for them, and that makes me hurt all the more. Seeing Zenevieve hurt makes me hurt all the more. Seeing Emberly hurt threatens to push me over an emotional edge I haven't encountered since Ithinor stopped breathing in my arms.

Amidst my devastation, it is suffocating to imagine her own. I want to embrace her. I want to hold her. Be the strength she's run out of to the extent that she doesn't care who sees her cry anymore.

Ambrose was good at that. It was practically his calling. Now I keep anticipating him to come and wrap his arms around his friends. Tell a story. Give us a reason to smile in a vicious cycle of traps and death. Comfort us. And every time, he never appears. I realize. I remember. We're now permanently stuck in that vicious cycle.

A heavy hand rests on my shoulder. I look next to me and up into Ezra's eyes, dull even under the stream of light shining down on them. A silent message passes between us, but I can't translate it under the weight of my grief. When he looks back at the girls, I follow. Maybe that message was that it's all right to comfort them—feel with them—because my feet move without thought. I kneel in front of Sierra and Zenevieve and wrap my arms around them as far as they can reach. Zenevieve trembles harder at my touch, wailing. I rest my head on Sierra's. Her deep and ragged breaths slash at my chest with every one. She's always had a deeply empathetic heart. Right now, though, that empathy must be consuming her—because it's consuming me. Empathy has become sympathy. This is our loss now, too.

I watch as Ezra approaches behind Emberly. He falls to his knees, reaching his arms around her. His fingers stretch to even Sierra and Zenevieve. We can't ask for the story. We can't ask that of Emberly right now. We only know one thing, and it is all that matters: the result of that story. It's the only thing we're allowed to focus on right now.

The battle I faced on Vineah's stage upon Ithinor's death has sounded its next war horn. I can't squeeze my eyes shut unless I release the tears pushing against them. My nose burns like fire. I hold on tighter to my friends to fight it, to fight the overwhelming, forceful urge to cry out.

Seventeen. He was only seventeen. He didn't deserve this. He didn't deserve this, not Ambrose, not Ithinor, not Meredith...

I grind my teeth together in another desperate attempt to cage my vengeful cries. I've yet to turn it into anger, but I'm quickly approaching that. They were stolen from us. All of them, all of them needed, all of them stolen by what they gave themselves for.

But I can't cry. I must be stronger. Stronger for all of them, for Emberly. I won't worsen things by weakening and reminding her what just happened by releasing my own grief. I must be stronger.

Wiping away her tears, Zenevieve raises her head with deep, ravaging breaths. She carefully releases Emberly, who buries her face into her hands as she sits on her knees. Ezra releases them as Sierra stands, helping a wobbly Zenevieve up. Emberly was the first and is now the last one on the ground.

She tries to stand, bringing one knee up; but she falters in strength and falls forward on her hands again. Her body arches in another round of powerful heaves and harsh sobs.

None of this should have happened. She should have never had to endure this.

Or maybe *that* was the message Ezra tried to give me: I need to be the one to approach her. She needs to see that she really *isn't* alone right now; her friends will always comfort her, but the one person written by fate itself to be her enemy? Even he longs to be there for her.

I kneel down in front of her. My hand carefully reaches out for her shoulder, my other following. I slowly lean her toward me, inching my arms around her.

She throws her arms around me, unleashing another bloodcurdling cry.

I press my lips together, my hold instinctually tightening around her small frame. There's a soft pulsing where my arrow wound should be; but the longer I hold Emberly, the more it fades into nothing. No wound is greater than the agony I feel right now. But I lock my jaw again. I cannot weaken in front of her. And not even my mind can tell me that this is wrong, that I shouldn't be comforting her right now. I know that holding her is right. She is pulling strength from me, and I'm pouring it out wholeheartedly.

Have it. Take as much as you need. I'm so sorry.

My heart rampages in my chest, regret and vengeance throbbing in my veins. Too little of it is alleviated when Emberly's cries begin to fade into fierce breaths. But at least she's breathing. At least the initial sting is cooling. At least I can be there for her right now.

At least I can be what she needs.

It's never been more difficult to fall asleep despite the pitch blackness we're submerged in once day turns to night; we know we can't proceed with the mindset we're under right now. The other teams are far from our minds, it seems, seeing as not even Sierra objects to sleeping in that dirt room. She doesn't even hesitate to.

The most excruciating part of the night is having to hear Emberly quietly cry herself to sleep for I don't know how long. Zenevieve's cries are much quieter—as though she's had more practice concealing her tears. But with Sierra being the only thing between me and Emberly, Emberly's whispered sobs may as well be blaring into my ear. Lacerating me with each one. I only fall asleep after she does. That sleep is heavy—deeper than any I've had in longer than I can remember. Grief is at fault for that. We all sleep longer than we intended to because of it.

It's strange to wake up with only four other people. Heavy. Stunning. Debilitating.

I miss taking night shifts with him.

We wordlessly crawl all the way through the right tunnel. My wound provides enough pain to distract me, especially after I abused it yesterday. Soon, though, that becomes more and more of a burden—given the mage who helped heal it to begin with. I need to anchor my thoughts to Emberly the rest of the way, watching her feet as she crawls forward. It deters the sensation of the closing-in walls if I can focus on someone else, if I can focus on her.

Don't think about it, I repeat to myself. *Emberly is in front of you. Breathe. Focus on her. Breathe.*

We finally crawl into one last dirt room, able to stand and stretch. There is nowhere to go except back the way we came. A dirt pillar stands in the middle of the room with a bronze key sitting on top of it.

Sierra, Ezra, and Zenevieve exchange glances. Then, each stare lands on me. All I know is that the last stage lies beyond the portal that this key will open. The thought should thrill me, send my heart to kingdom come—but I'm furious. I'm too angry, too bitter and resentful, to continue satisfying the sick, cruel will of this death game.

Now the potential is too great: the potential of loss in whatever lies ahead in the final stage of this race. If we lose even one more...

"It's not fair."

None of us expect the fragile voice in the entryway. When we look over at her, Emberly has her arms crossed and eyes stuck on the key.

My breaths are trapped in the cage of grief. I tap my thigh to restrain my anger. We wait for her to continue.

"It is not fair," she states slowly. She doesn't shift. As though she's daring one of us to move. I catch my friends hanging their heads in what can only be agreement.

"It isn't FAIR!" Emberly screams, slamming her fist into the corner of the dirt wall. A chunk flies off and skitters to the pillar in the middle of the room. Emberly's usually muted, leaf-green eyes are ablaze in a new shade of the morning light from above. She gestures her every word. "We lose everyone we love, innocent participants are sacrificed and thrown to the slaughter, we fight for our lives in a race, and for what? Ultimate sovereignty? Is that what we're doing this for? Control over other people?"

My mind runs with her speech. Zenevieve licks her lips, Sierra exhaling.

Emberly unsheathes her dagger, whirls around, and slashes at another part of the corner. Her dark-auburn waves fly with every swing. She hacks at the dirt again and again before turning again, facing us. "You dare to tell me that simply because *one* chosen ruler was born, their mere existence sentences all others to death? We're only here to fill the gaps? Why are the rest of us even participating if all we're destined for is death? Formalities?

Protocol? I'm *sick* of protocol! Why does my existence sentence EVERYONE I love to their deaths? What are we doing this for, *tell me!*"

I stride up to her. Sierra calls to me, failing at pulling me back; and Ezra and Zenevieve warn me to not interfere.

Emberly's eyes harden as she stares up at me. Her breaths are fierce like a lion's.

"I know why I'm doing it now," I state. "Vengeance and revenge. To honor the lives unnecessarily lost during this, to avenge the people we should have kept, and to take revenge against the ones that orchestrated all of this—because it's not fair, and may the Ancients banish me to hell if I die before I finish this forsaken hellhole of a race."

The anger Emberly initially stared at me with hardens into determination.

"We're going to make this right," I tell her. "We'll either win this race or die trying, but we are going to make it right. Ithinor, Meredith, and Ambrose will not have died in vain."

I turn around, facing our team. They each nod in approval as Emberly steps out from behind me and walks to Zenevieve.

Fresh tears glisten in Zenevieve's black eyes. "For the ones we lost," she whispers.

"To make this right," Emberly tells her. With one last glance back at me, she grabs the key.

A blinding light opens in the entry of the room. This time, indigo lightning crackles around its rim. The smallest whisper in my mind wonders about the word likely engraved on the key's head, but the rest of me refuses to indulge any further in this. I curse the Ancients' every last riddle of this race as we step inside the portal one by one.

CHAPTER 29

"YOU ARE NOT MY ENEMY"

Emberly

MAGERY IS THE LAST STAGE WE'RE TAKEN TO. HOW fantastically brilliant—to be surrounded by a land of magic when my mage was just killed by this blasted race.

Killed because you brought him here.

The fact doesn't even cause a tremor of rage in me any-more—that the councilmen were right again. I think I've stopped fighting it. I think I've lost my last shred of evidence and hope to prove them wrong; that's made it inevitable to accept. Perhaps that's why I can't feel the sting anymore. They resent me because I killed their rulers; I resent myself because I killed my subjects. I can never outrun that.

Our feet smash the grass. Before us is a wide, beige path that cuts the plush forest in half and stretches down to a large, violet light in the distance. A cool-toned haze surrounds us. There is no sun. No daylight, yet it isn't night.

I bend down and run my fingers through the grass. The blades are so soft and cool that it almost feels as if dew rests on them. This time, however, the air is dry. The humidity has dissolved completely.

Thank the stars.

The world is illuminated by the twinkling of fireflies. They decorate the forest of dark cherry trees on either side of us, as well as the bushes growing along the beige path. Bird coos echo gently throughout the air. The forest is alive with magic.

Ambrose would have adored this. This would have been his favourite stage. He was one tunnel away.

I shouldn't have brought him. I never should have brought him. He would still be training at the palace, still playing with his sisters at home, if I'd never brought him.

No matter what crown I wear, there is nothing I can do to change that.

No... No. You will not have died in vain, Ambrose. I will make this right, even if it is the last thing I will ever do.

A vengeful anger racks my mind. My will against the Ancient Mages, against this race, is threatening to blind my initiative. It is impossible to do anything out of "love". Part of me is tempted to believe that it always has been. My every motivation is fuelled by an insatiable, blazing fury now.

The five of us walk deeper in on the wide path cutting the forest in half. The ambiance and inherent tranquillity of nature is tauntingly soothing.

"Wait." Sierra takes her place in front of us. We stop. "Are we truly ready to continue just because it's morning? After we've been rattled in—more ways than one?"

"I don't think we're any better now than we were last night," Ezra says, stepping up beside her. "If this really is the last stage, we need to be in as strong of a condition as we were during the first."

"Particularly because this is Magery's stage," Sierra adds solemnly. "I never conducted much study on the kingdom, but I do know that there are vicious creatures there called 'pixies'. Despite how small they are, they'll rip you limb from limb before eating you. If this stage at all reflects—"

"Who cares about some insects we can swat away with a sword?" I sneer. My anger boils, rising to my lips as I cross my arms. "How about the terrain itself? It was *just* proven that we don't need another living thing to *kill*—!"

"Emberly!" Zenevieve snaps, coming to stand in front of me. Her dark eyes peer down at me. "We don't need the reminder! Just agree that we need to replenish ourselves, and move on!"

I can't remember the last time Zenevieve shouted at me out of anger. It was likely when the guards took her in from the icy streets of Snowark—fourteen years ago. She was defensive and traumatised, and had me pinned as the spoiled-rotten royal brat who couldn't possibly understand what being an orphan was like. Neither of us knew of the death curse yet; I'd learn about it next year. Otherwise, she has never expressed such severe anger towards me—*at* me—before.

She is crumbling in front of me, and my heart is decaying at the thought. It feels as if my rule is slowly killing her, too. I don't know if my heart is physically strong enough to beat with that blood of guilt coursing through it. My tears on the Soilera stage already shattered the eighteen-year-old wall in me that was once there. Now I feel them threatening my eyes again in burning pricks.

I turn away from Zenevieve, walking to the nearest tree along the main path. I press my back against it, never minding my bow and quiver. My hands firmly rub my face. As vividly as I can feel each piece crumbling off of me, I'm determined to keep my tears inside this time. I'm determined to rebuild the wall. This race, the Mages, will not break me.

Padded footsteps whisper in front of me. I remove my hands. Zenevieve ambles towards me.

"I'm sorry." She stares down at the seemingly teal grass. "I— I didn't mean... I only—" A lump passes in her throat before she looks at me with reddened eyes. "I'd like a minute while the others gather—if you'll allow me."

"I don't want to talk about it—"

"Neither do I," she snaps, startling me. Contempt and anger knit her brows together and harden her glare. "But I need to know. I *need* to know, Emberly, because you were there in his final moments! I wasn't!"

"I was also the one who *caused* his final moments!" I cry, pointing at myself. "I don't want to talk about yet another death that stains my hands! *I* brought him to the race! *I* let him fight in a war between me and the death curse! *I* let him go ahead of me in that tunnel! He was barely two weeks away from his eighteenth birthday, and he'll never see that day because of *me*!"

The second I allowed myself a moment of enjoyment in his presence—found myself happy with him, allowed myself to smile as if all were all right—I lost him. As soon as I allowed myself to attach, I was punished for it again. But Zenevieve won't understand that. She can't. We lost the same persons, but not the same people.

Tears soak her cheeks as they stroll down. "Please. Just tell me what happened. He was... Please."

I sniff, raising my head. Fireflies glint above me. Gazing into their lights somehow helps shield my own tears.

"He told me to go back because he felt something wrong with the ground. Quickmud."

Zenevieve squeezes her eyes shut.

"The harder I tried to pull him out—the faster he sank... And then he had the nerve—to give up—on himself, on his life, on...!"

I swallow, looking back up at the fireflies. They float above Zenevieve's head. How much I'm willing to kill to be as blissfully unaware as they are right now.

"I should have told him," she whispers, hanging her head. "I could have... I would have kissed him goodbye, I could have... I should have at least told him—exactly what he meant to me. He was my little brother. I lost another brother."

Her face contorts in a grief I've never seen plague her before. Silent sobs shake her shoulders as she squeezes her eyes shut. I rack my brain for the right words. I've never had to console her to this degree. We've never endured worse than the night we sneaked out of the palace and the Vinean soldiers ambushed us. Beyond that, Zenevieve knows that the last thing I know how to comfort are the emotions I suppress.

"You showed it better," I say, "than words ever could have

done."

Her shoulders still, but her eyes tighten themselves all the more.

I do what she's taught me almost always achieves comfort: "Come here, Zenny."

She steps into my arms, resting her head on my shoulder. My body shakes in another round of sobs. I breathe out any last tears threatening me. She mirrors me almost exactly—except she releases her tears. It is now the second time she's expressed her grief in full openly, in front of others.

I say "almost always"—because despite how I have my best friend in my arms, my heart is still too heavy to beat properly.

"Thank you," Zenny whispers, pulling away. She wipes her eye dry with her knuckle. "All right... I—I need to hunt."

I nod her off. I want to come with her for the distraction—but we will only remind each other that we've lost half of our team. It is only us now.

Half of our team.

Zenevieve turns around. I close my eyes. This is precisely why I built that wall: so that I'd never have the need to experience my cursed emotions. I discovered during this race that my heart is one that desires to feel. Meanwhile, I live in a world that punishes that indulgence. If you dare attach to anyone, you'll weaken after you lose them or even almost lose them. That has run its course twice. I cannot afford it after everything else I've spent the last eighteen years building—for myself and Snowark.

I open my eyes. Sierra sits on Ezra's shoulders as they pick cherries on the other side of the wide path. Only a couple of trees down, Leon leans against a tree. When Zenevieve reaches his side of the path, he stands from it. She walks deeper into the forest as he begins his way to me.

For the first time since we've met, my mind is rendered silent at the sight.

He holds up his hands in surrender. "I know," he says softly, "you don't need my condolences or comfort. But"—he drops his hands, fully approaching—"that doesn't change the fact that you have it. Especially because..."

The prince retracts into silence. He holds his forehead and sniffs with a heavy sigh. Yet when his eyes rise to meet mine, I can't find any glisten or redness.

"We're... we're a team, all right?" he whispers. "I don't care who it is you find comfort in. Just don't do this alone. Please."

My grip on myself falters. The grass pulls my gaze back down.

"I can't..." Leo mutters. "I can't lose you, too."

I look up at him—but that doesn't verify that I heard him correctly. Despite his previous attempt, red has now stolen his eyes and nose. After Soilera, I know Seavale shares my and Zenevieve's grief about Ambrose. But I don't know to what extent. After all, Leo didn't know him as long as I did—but here he stands mourning him. Just as I do.

"How close were you to him?" my morbid curiosity whispers.

He takes a deep breath. "Not as close as you. Of course. But taking watch shifts in Vineah together allowed us to become friends..." His shoulders move up in a helpless shrug. "He was everyone's friend."

Even mine.

"I hate him," I catch myself whispering. My heart despises me for uttering such despicable words. It knows that I don't mean it, but every bone in me feels like I do. "I hate him for sinking, for sacrificing himself for me when he knows what I did, what I've done!"

Leon furrows his brows. "What did you—?"

"I killed my parents." My body tightens. I curse how my voice is ravaged by my own desperation and impotence. "He knew I killed my parents, he knew Meredith wouldn't have been killed if not for me bringing her to this race. And yet he—he told me that I didn't kill them, that Meredith's fate was out of my hands. And then he sank. Right in front of me."

Leo turns to face me. I don't know how, but he must sense that I've more to say. Part of me wants to despise him, too, for knowing me past a superficial degree. The other part of me wants to fall into anyone who will give my imprisoned mind the key to escape. And I think Leon Wales holds that key right now.

"He told me that it wasn't my fault. He referred to me as his queen. His *queen*, yet I couldn't save him. Not even when I tried. I really tried, Leon, and the man still—sank! I couldn't save Meredith, my birth killed my parents, and he *knew* all of that yet had the nerve—!"

"Stop."

The blue of Leon's eyes is all the more intense in the cool-toned atmosphere of the forest. I can't decide which iris to focus on. Especially as the whites of his eyes gloss over.

"Ithinor told me..." he begins softly, "that my parents willingly gave up their lives to bring me into the world. Knowing exactly what would happen to them—knowing they'd never meet me. Or see what a fool I'd become. In that way, I was almost grateful that they died when I was born. On the other hand—I never realised what it meant, what it felt like, to... attach to other people. To feel something beyond superficiality. Not until Sierra. And then the portals opened, and that was all turned around... This team turned all of that around. And now I know exactly what my parents felt when they decided it was time to bring me into the world. To ensure Seavale's prosperity."

He leans against the tree next to me, cautious of the bow on his back. "If I die while fighting for my kingdom or any of you, it will be my sacrifice. My decision. And I'll want you to enjoy whatever it unlocks. Knowing Ambrose—I know that that is exactly how he felt about the matter, too."

Was that why he didn't fight...? Why he was seemingly so all right with—dying? He begged for his life when he fell into the ice lake, yet when he sank—

"Because that isn't who you are."

"They'll need you. The Kingdom needs you."

"It's not your fault."

He... knew. Not only was he willing to make the sacrifice, but he knew that my mind would bear the weight of his death as my own fault. That was why he maintained his smile. He was likely petrified to the last second—silently screaming for his life, for a miracle—and for my sake, the most conversational person I'd ever known remained silent.

I shut my gaze. The thoughts are suffocating me from the inside out.

"Don't do that," I whisper. I force volume into my voice. "Don't you dare speak of your sacrifice as though you're next."

"Not as long as my team needs me." Leon's voice is steadier than mine. I'm envious yet can't help my gratitude. "Enemies in this race or not, we're a team."

My jaw locks again, and I uncross my arms. "Who should determine that we're enemies? Will you so easily accept it if that is what this race decides? Do you still consider me as such? Why should the Last Kingdom decide whom I should and shouldn't kill, who does and doesn't earn my trust?"

"I agree," he says too simply, nodding once. "That's why you are not my enemy. I know who the real one is after losing everyone we have. The enemy of my enemy is my friend. That's why I implore you not to do this alone. The grief, the weight, the responsibility—not anymore."

Friends...? He would go so far as to consider us friends?

"For once... you have one thing right," I reply. Because I know who the real enemy is now, too: the puppeteers of this race. Leo is my enemy's enemy as well, and he is stronger as my friend than as my rival.

"Thank you." I've already spoken the words by the time I'm aware of them. My voice is too quiet to be my own. "For trying."

He crosses his arms, a soft smile touching his lips. "It's simply an honour to have finally earned your trust."

I shake my head. "Not on your life, cub. I'm only appreciating the offer to... lighten the load."

I don't think Leon wants to harm me. I don't think anyone on the Seavale team does. But if I bridge the gap completely, I risk enduring something like yesterday three more times. I cannot afford that. Now more than ever.

"I'll take it," he says. Then, he extends his left hand.

I pause. People usually offer the right hand. Has he really taken note of which one I use?

I hesitantly take it. His skin is calloused and tough. I wonder just how many ship shrouds he's climbed in his lifetime.

"To never being alone," he tells me.

I don't know if I can agree with him entirely on that. I don't know if I can trust it. And yet... I want to satiate him for his effort. Agree on it as a thank-you and nothing more.

I raise our hands to shake on it—but it feels incomplete after everything he displayed in Soilera. Especially with the sincere gentleness in his eyes trying to wrap around me in an attempt at comfort.

"How about..." I begin tentatively, "a truce?"

The eyebrow with a scar slitting it rises high into the air. "To what?" Then, the corners of his lips turn slightly upward. "Insulting me, perchance?"

"I'll more than enjoy my insult privileges, prat," I say, tightening my grip on his rough yet warm hand. My heart beats harder at the mere thought that mine rests in his right now. "I only propose that... amidst everything, we restrain ourselves from being so—irritating towards each other. Do you accept?"

After a moment of hesitance, he firmly shakes our hands. "I do and propose the clause that if I earn the name of 'Lion', you drop 'prat' indefinitely."

"All clauses added are meant to be realistic, *cub*."

"You're already breaking our truce, firefly."

A smile threatens my lips—and I immediately lock it.

No. Don't you dare.

I drop his hand, taking advantage of the first topic that

comes to mind: "Where did that ridiculous name come from?"

"'Firefly'?" He shrugs. "You told me not to mention your temper."

I bite down on my lip. *Firefly*. How original.

"And the 'fly' part?"

"Oh, simple." He grins, running a hand through the grown part of his dark-brown hair. "At the time, it was because you were a little pest."

I narrow my eyes. "Rowena is in dire need of target practice—"

"But now"—he gazes and points up at the twinkling bugs floating above us—"it's because under the right circumstances... you light up the world around you. And you leave everyone marvelling."

My heart beats faster than it did when we ate at the beginning of Soilera's stage. I bring my gaze back down. When Leo smiles at me, the swirling anxiety in my chest grows into a blizzard. My nerves are ablaze, sweat lining my palms. I find myself grateful that I don't need to shake his hand again. And for the breeze that blows by, helping my palms' case.

Of all people, why is he the one able to distract me?

The adrenaline of it all swirls in my head. I fall forward, holding my forehead. Leo is quick to catch me, firmly holding me up as I rest my hands on his arms.

"Are you all right?" he asks. "Will being friendly require *that* much adjustment?"

My nose is aflame with the woody, charred air. Smoke. Smoke, there is smoke nearby—

I dart my gaze to my right: Sierra has set up a campfire on the path.

Run, I need to leave, run—

My vision blackens, and I blink it away. Another spout of dizziness pushes me to the side. I lean harder against Leo's arm. The air thins in my lungs. My throat sears me with every inhale.

Zenevieve is gone. She's the only one who—

"What's the matter?" Leon urges, trying to hold me straight. "You need to talk to me, are you all right?"

I open my mouth, but air is scarce. I almost don't have the strength to stand, certainly none to walk. He is the only one keeping me up straight.

I point with a trembling finger at Sierra and the campfire on the path. "Sen—"—I wheeze again, my throat swelling—"—si—tive."

"What?" he asks, glancing at where I'm pointing. "The smoke? Is it—?"

I nod feebly. My head falls forward, my senses swarmed by the spinning world. My knees buckle underneath me. Now Leo is the only thing holding me up at all. I can feel my full weight leaning on his arms.

"Sensitivity?" he whispers with an edge of realisation. "You're sensitive to smoke—?"

My body forces a dry heave, officially desperate for air.

Within a second, he tears off my bow and quiver from my back. Nausea swirls in my stomach as he swoops me up. Cool air blows past my face, my body jostling in his hold. My head screams for stillness, but my lungs work overtime to suck in the clean air the farther from the smoke we draw.

"I'm so sorry," Leon says as he weaves between the dense

trees and bushes of the forest. "You'll be all right, don't worry!"

I swallow, choking on my own saliva that has no room to go down. My chest is shrivelling up, suffocating on the lack of air. My eyes shut against the moving world above me.

"No, stay with me, Emberly!" Leo exclaims. "Just a moment longer, please!"

It's—almost too late. I cling tighter to his chainmail with every ounce of strength that remains in me. *He'll think I'm dead.*

Maybe I will be this time.

I can't leave him like this.

But it would all go away... It would save my loved ones. I'll never have to lose because of joy again.

The abyss encroaches on my mind. It's alluring. No need to think. To breathe. To feel. It will be only me and a final end to my curse.

"Emberly!"

I force myself to open my eyes. The world has stopped moving. Leo is kneeling on the ground, holding me close to his chest. The pressure in my head is explosive—tingly. I can almost feel his beating heart—or that's my own beating in my head. His grip is still firm around my shoulders.

The name is nothing but air as it narrowly escapes my lips: "Leo—"

My head dips back as my awareness finally dissipates.

CHAPTER

"THERE'S NOTHING MORE TO DO"

Leo

"E MBERLY!" I CRY AS SHE FALLS LIMP IN MY HOLD. I use my arm to support her hanging head, pushing it up and letting it lean against my chest. She's even smaller in my arms. I gently shake her. "Don't do this, wake up! Talk to me!"

This is why she always sat far away from the campfire. Wonderful: I've finally made amends with her, and her life is slipping through my fingers.

"Please, wake up!" I tell her, shaking her again. I push a piece of her hair out of her lightly freckled face, my finger brushing against the scar on her forehead.

I can't lose you, too. I will not lose you, too, please!

"Zenevieve!" I call. Emberly won't awaken in my grasp soon enough, and Zenevieve is her greatest chance at survival. I look over my shoulder. An empty, dense forest of trees deprives me of hope. "Zenevieve, please!"

I look back down. Emberly's face is—almost blue.

She can't breathe!

I lay her onto the cool, soft grass, grateful that I know what to do: Seavale sailors are trained in resuscitations in the event a fellow sailor almost drowns. I know that this situation isn't identical, but it's the greatest option I have.

I take a deep breath. Our lips will have to touch. I'm all too aware of how Emberly would slaughter me with Rowena in a blink if she were conscious.

But I will not let you die.

I press two fingers against the side of her neck. A faint beat pulses slowly under them. She doesn't have much time.

I tilt up her head to straighten her neck. With another deep breath, I pinch her nose closed, bend down, and press my mouth to hers. The touch of her lips is a soft surprise, but I force my mind away from it. I exhale every second of my breath into her, her body remaining still as I release.

I won't give up on you. Please, don't let me lose you now!

I give her another breath before coming up. "Zenevieve!" I shout again. Emberly's chest is still unmoving under her armor. I fold my hands on top of each other and place them on the middle of her chest. There isn't time to remove her armor, so I press down and start counting in my mind.

My hands tremble as they come to rest on the top of her head and the bottom of her chin, repeating the process. Her lips are still warm; and that encourages me to keep exhaling, even when she doesn't stir as I come back up.

"Come on, firefly," I whisper, desperation choking me. I call for Zenevieve one more time before giving Emberly another breath, the weight of each one growing heavier as her body stays limp. Sweat beads on my forehead as I come up again, a sense of lightness swirling in my head. I hold my head, every second urging me to continue. I start again on compressing her chest, restraining my urgency from affecting how fast I press. She still doesn't stir.

"Leo?!"

"Thank the stars," I whisper, scrambling to stand. I run to meet Zenevieve, Ezra, and Sierra weaving through the trees and bushes. "Zenevieve, you're the only one—"

"Smoke?" she demands to know, holding up a hand to stop me.

"Yes, she was exposed—"

She darts past me, Ezra and Sierra following with the same urgency to Emberly's frozen form in the grass.

"What's wrong?" Sierra urges. "What does—?"

"We need to take her farther away from the fire," Zenevieve states. A subtle cry shakes her voice, and she sniffs as she wipes her nose with the back of her hand.

"I'll carry her," Ezra says, already scooping up Emberly. She resembles a child in his arms. "Show me where to go."

"Away from the smoke!" Zenevieve snaps, dashing deeper into the forest.

Ezra is as fast as Sierra and I are even with Emberly cradled in his arms. My heart beats all too harshly as Zenevieve leads us down, finding a clearing amidst the trees and bushes.

"Here!" She points at the ground. "Set her down, keep her

breathing!"

Ezra obeys as Zenevieve digs furiously in her satchel. I kneel down by Emberly's head and continue resuscitations.

I only manage to give one breath when Zenevieve exclaims, "I've got it!"

I look up as she kneels at Emberly's other side and grabs her arm. She fumbles as she slides off the metal armor, turns Emberly's pale arm over, and grabs a minuscule injection needle sitting on her satchel. Next to it is a rolled-up tobacco leaf, whose end is smoking.

"What are—?" I begin, but Sierra holds out her arm in front of me. With one look at her gravely shaking her head, I shut my mouth. She's telling me as a physician, not a friend.

Zenevieve injects the green fluid into Emberly's vein and then takes the tobacco leaf. She holds it up to Emberly's nose, swaying it back and forth. All the while, she furiously blinks back what must be her tears.

I gawk. "Isn't smoke what caused this?"

"*Wood* smoke, you arrogant dunce!" she snaps, glowering at me with sharp eyes. "Do you think I'd be such a fool as to knowingly give my best friend a treatment that would kill her?" She gestures to my hand. "It's not as if holding her hand will revive her!"

I look down: my hand has unknowingly wrapped itself around Emberly's.

I release it, literally biting my tongue with a side-scowl from Sierra.

"Tobacco smoke and a nettle serum injection is the only treatment that's ever worked for her," Zenevieve says. She sniffs, maintaining her rapidly blinking eyes on Emberly. "We... we can't do anything else other than wait."

Wait? When Emberly is still unconscious?

"How do we know she isn't still suffocating?" I ask, fighting a bite in my voice.

"There's nothing more to do even if she were!" she snaps. "You think this isn't torture for me every time this happens? Why do you think we try so hard to avoid it?"

I can't help but wonder how many times it *has* happened as Sierra brings a hand to Emberly's nose, under the tobacco leaf. "She's breathing," she announces, joining us in a relieving sigh.

"Our physician's court is still determining exactly why tobacco smoke opens the throat," Zenevieve tells us. Her eyes never leave the leaf in her hand, as if it is the only comfort she has now. "All we know is that it does. I hope it still does."

Ezra rests a large hand on Sierra's shoulder, glancing between them. "Is this why she never sat with us by the fire?"

Zenevieve only manages a nod. My mind is no more satiated. Emberly has yet to stir, and there isn't anything we may do.

"How long before she wakes up?" I dare to ask.

The tip of Zenevieve's nose quivers. "It can't be long. It can't take this long if she's breathing, she..."

It can't take this long. The words echo with a frightening uncertainty in my mind.

I furiously shake my head. "No, there must be—"

My words are cut off as Emberly shifts with a moan below us.

CHAPTER 31

"DO YOU NOT HAVE THE POWER?"

Emberly

A BURNING PAIN SEARS MY THROAT EVERY TIME I IN-hale. My lungs feel as if they're unfolding after being crumpled for a hundred years. Something soft holds my head, cradling my body.

I'm... alive. Zenevieve reached me. Leon retrieved her in time.

My eyes flutter open to a sky of dark branches and teal-green leaves. Zenevieve's eyes are eager on me as she sits beside me. Leo, Sierra, and Ezra reflect her on my other side.

Something is wrong about this scene.

"It's all right, Ember," Zenevieve whispers, "you're all right."

I'm all right. The words don't settle well in my stomach; if anything, they curdle as I stare back at the four faces looking down at me right now.

There are only four. That's it. We're missing one face, a smile that made it a little easier to wake up. And that reminds me that I'm actually missing two.

"Can you hear us?" Leo asks. He and Zenevieve place a hand on my back to help bring me up. "Do you need anything? How do you feel?"

"Confused"—I blink groggily, holding my swimming head—"as to why you think asking a disoriented patient one hundred questions is the proper way to greet them. If you aren't careful, I'll start to think you care about me."

A dizzy spin whirls in my head upon sitting up straight. All four pairs of hands reach out to keep me steady, but I reject them.

"Terribly sorry to say," Sierra begins, "but we do care. Why did you never say anything? We could have—"

"Back when it was relevant with all the campfires in Vineah, we weren't exactly the best of friends that we are now," I reply. The dizziness stirs a sea of nausea in my stomach. "Forgive me for thinking that my supposed rivals would use my greatest physical weakness against me in a—"

—*death race.* I can't say those words ironically anymore. Discredit the severity of my loved ones' fates.

"Has this always happened?" Sierra asks.

I feel like a patient in the physician's wing. "Since I was nine. Nothing I haven't experienced before."

"Are there any lasting consequences?" Leo asks.

"I'm fine, prat. What are we all doing staying in one place during a race?"

"You need to recover," Zenevieve commands. An acidic resolve coats each word. "We aren't leaving until you do."

"Rather foolish if you ask me," I mutter.

"I don't care," she snaps. "We're staying here until you're well enough to travel."

I don't know if I'm the only one who can read her anymore. In this moment, at least. It is all too apparent who is at the front of her mind right now. It is not me.

With a painful swallow that I fail to conceal, I look up at the four faces in front of me. I regret that there aren't five. Six, even seven.

I press a hand to the soft blades of grass. They almost feel like feathers. The dirt under my palms warms at my touch. The silence is quickly becoming as suffocating as smoke. In the quiet, there isn't anything to deter my mind from the truths of the present.

Sierra straightens. "Emberly raises a critical point. The race won't stop for the sake of recovery. While we're dormant, we should do what we can and plan our next steps. Can you two feel the artifact's pull?"

That cursed artifact. I've only one thing to look forward to: this is the last time I will ever have to find one.

Leo glances at me. "I do. It's pulling..."—he points deeper into the forest—"that way. Down that path that cuts the forest in half."

I nod my verification—for which my head is quick to punish me.

Zenevieve exhales, falling next to me to sit on her bottom. "Then we'll leave as soon as we can. Especially if there are pixies hiding here."

"The main path is there for a reason," Sierra says, "so it's likely best to travel it until we find the artifact."

"Only if you're feeling well enough," Leo tells me. "If we run into trouble with you still unwell..."

He doesn't need to finish. My jaw tightens, locking my words inside. I hate when the prat is right. Especially since it means that I have to hold my team back right now.

Even the forest falls to silence with us. I don't think anyone knows what to say. It is impossible to know. Still—I wish that someone knew.

Sierra exhales, mimicking my and Zenevieve's sitting position on her bottom. Ezra decides to stand guard a few metres in front of us. Perhaps that gives Zenny the right distraction; she follows suit and discusses something with him before guarding the territory behind him.

"At least we can rest safely with them," Leo whispers. "Ever the protectors..."

Sierra nods gently next to me. The sight almost makes me dizzy. "That's why they're in the knighthood. I wish I could have been there the day Ezra was knighted."

I fight the incredulity in my voice. "You weren't?"

"No." She runs her fingers through the grass. "I arrived in Seavale shortly afterward. I didn't even know him yet."

With a brief glance at our knights, my curiosity claws for the distraction. Anything to relieve my mind of the smothering quiet right now. "Then why do you wish you had been there?"

"No particular reason," she replies. "Only to have supported him during an important event of his life. He had already missed the actual ceremony and was knighted the day after."

"That's allowed?"

"No." Leo lightly chuckles. "I stopped at nothing until Captain Lancaster made an exception. Ezra had already completed training as everyone else, and as one of our greatest trainees, at that. I caught him rushing out of the castle at the beginning of the ceremony and followed him all the way to his house. It turned out that his mother was in labour with his twin sisters. With... well, his father having passed a few months prior, Ezra was the only family available for her."

I close my mouth the second I realise it's open. The man was ready to sacrifice knighthood for the sake of his mother. His dedication and loyalty rival even my resentment's towards the councilmen; it's no wonder Leo insisted that he be knighted nonetheless.

I look back at Ezra. He stands as diligent as ever, still yet observant with a hawk's eyes. A strange comfort seeps into my chest. I feel doubly protected under his and Zenevieve's watch.

"I remember when Zenevieve was knighted," I say. "My only regret is that I wasn't inducted with her."

"You certainly have the talent for it." Leo nods at me. "Really. It's unsettling."

Sierra shoves him for me. I press my lips together to bar a grateful smile.

"I'll have you know that I've loved weaponry since I was a young girl," I tell him. "Just a few years after Zenny came to serve and we met. I wish I'd caught interest sooner. We would have earlier taken care of the uncreative taunts the palace children unleashed: the freckled, spoiled princess and poverty-stricken tigress aspiring to be a female knight—both of which were orphaned. She and I eventually got on well because of it, though."

The memories flash across my mind with every word. "Especially because we were both angry at the world. Angry at authority for ruining our lives. We both saw a broken system, one that forced her to become a servant and keeps me under a cursed crown only I am allowed to wear..."

I don't know where the courage to expose these words is spouting from—but every one feels as if I'm shedding another patch of old skin. Relief... almost. At least a slightly lighter weight.

"And she supports you in this race," Sierra adds.

I hold my head to aid the remaining swimming sensation. "She knows that I would change things if I'd the power."

"Do you... not have the power?" Leo asks.

I pause. Perhaps I do. Perhaps I always did but preferred convincing myself otherwise; it's easier to pretend that I don't. Pretend that the councilmen are wrong. Pretend that my role in this world is irrelevant to the deaths of Meredith and Ambrose. Even Ithinor, in a removed way. Perhaps I've always pretended that I don't have power because otherwise it would confirm that my rule—my power—harmed and killed my loved ones. The only thing I do not have authority over.

Sierra places her hand on my back. "Are you all right?" she whispers.

Not as a physician. I've heard this question in this light before. As a friend.

"No matter what I do," I mumble, twiddling my thumbs, "I can't stop being afraid."

Afraid of assuming my position in full and the catastrophic consequences of it. Afraid of finishing this race, after all. Afraid of life. No matter how much I distract or lie to myself, underneath it all, I am still afraid.

Sierra's lips part as if she's about to reply. When no words follow, she looks at Leon.

He scoots a little closer to me. "Me, too. I was afraid when the portal opened. Terrified, actually, that these would be my last moments before I even had a chance to show Seavale who I've become. I don't think any of us have been able to escape fear during this—not even Ezra. I think we simply do it nevertheless. That's the wonderful thing about being afraid: it means you're about to do something incredibly brave. That's when it serves as my reminder of how much I truly have improved."

Sierra's smile grows. I sense either gratitude or pride in it, a story I have yet to hear behind it. If not for Zenevieve, I would be jealous of their friendship.

"If you will allow me the curiosity," I muse carefully, "have the politics between Seavale and Vineah ever threatened your relationship?"

With a shared glance at each other, they shake their heads. "No," Sierra replies simply, shrugging. "I've always felt more comfortable in Seavale ever since I arrived. Anything that threatened them threatened me. Vineah was where I lived for most of my life—but it was never my home."

"Did you leave solely to advise the prince?"

She takes a deep breath, her gaze falling to her lap. "It's... No. My family in Vineah..."

I immediately realise that I've overstepped. "Don't answer, I was only—"

"I don't mind," she assures, even meeting my eyes as if to

secure the words. "I used to have... an older sister. When my father passed, my mother and I discovered that she had had his will altered so that she would be the sole inheritor of his endowments. We only found out after a 'client' she had cheated found our home. She started a con business with the money my father had left behind for his family. The next morning... my sister was gone with every last cent my mother and I had."

I don't know why—but anger pulses through my veins as if Zenevieve's just told me for the first time how she wound up at the palace.

Despicable. I shove another hard lump down my throat. *Absolutely despicable.*

"I was always meant to replace my uncle one day as Leo's advisor," Sierra adds, "but now I had all the more reason to. Help the prince create a better world, one kingdom at a time."

I bite my lip to replace a nod. Their friendship reminds me all the more of mine with Zenevieve. I'm grateful that I've no reason to be envious, after all.

"That includes..." Leo begins softly, leaning forward to look at me better, "not aiding any kingdom that wants to invade another."

I recall his words to me the day Snowark and Seavale first collided: they were never going to accept. They only hadn't formally denied Vineah yet due to fear of retaliation.

"Thank you," I reply, as sincerely as my energy allows. I don't know if it means much, my gratitude or his gesture; I'm unsure how much any of this will matter when the race finishes. No matter *who* finishes.

"Ember," Zenny calls in front of us. "Are you still feeling all right?"

"Good enough to walk, if you believe me."

"I don't," she says, walking to us. She's right not to. Ezra tentatively follows, faithfully observant. "But if you mean it, walking is better than staying still."

"Then we'll leave the fire behind." Sierra stands. She and Zenevieve each offer a hand to help me do the same. A wave of dizziness threatens to push me back down, but I fight to conceal it. "Seeing as we have our supplies, at least."

Leo reaches out his hand towards me. "Are you sure that you don't need to rest—?"

No sooner than he speaks the forbidden r-word does a low growl rumble across the sky.

I cautiously look up, past the tree branches. It's an all-too-familiar sound. By the looks of Seavale's wary glances, it is to them as well.

Sierra's voice is low as if she's worried that the brewing storm will hear her. "Is that—?"

Lightning strikes a tree behind her at the edge of the clearing. She screams, jumping back as we yelp.

A raindrop pricks my nose. Another white bolt zaps a tree behind Leo. Raindrops race down as fire crawls from the tree's branches to the trunk. Lightning ignites a tree behind me.

The sky is setting the entire forest ablaze.

CHAPTER

"JUST HOLD ON"

Leo

ANOTHER BOLT OF LIGHTNING STRIKES DEEPER IN THE forest, in the direction we were about to take. Rain steadily descends over us, the tree fires reaching for the sky.

Fire—smoke. We need to run for Emberly's sake, but she can barely stand.

A tree too close behind me explodes into another bonfire. My courage is jolted awake; and I kneel in front of Emberly, my back facing her. "Get on!"

"What—?"

"You can't run, and that's what we need to do! Get on!"

I barely hear her weak, frustrated grunt as her small frame climbs onto my back with Ezra and Zenevieve's help. Standing, I bounce her to secure her position. I have to hold on to her all the more tightly because of the rain. She's a fairly decent weight with the armor and weaponry on; that tells me how much easier this would be if she weren't wearing any of it.

Run, run. There's only one place to run—the artifact must be our protection from the storm.

"Go through the forest and toward the main path!" I exclaim.

Another growl rips across the sky. We dart out of the clearing and farther into the forest. My strides are short but fast as I keep my hands secure under Emberly's thighs and pray that we don't slip on the ground sure to grow muddy soon. The cold droplets striking my face offer little respite from the exertion. Another lightning zap strikes a tree beside us, simultaneous with a bolt that lands just behind me. I jump and almost slip, and Emberly manages a yelp.

"I'm sorry, just hold on!"

"What do you think I'm doing, prat?!"

Her forehead falls onto my shoulder and her breaths deepen, unease violently swirling in my stomach.

Breaking out of the forest and onto the main path, the artifact pulls harder on me. Every breath now burns my throat as I desperately try to maintain it. A tree on the left side bursts into a thousand shards. None of us are exempt from a scream as I squeeze my eyes shut and turn my head, one piece flying by my face and another slicing my cheek open.

Emberly raises her head, her grip on my neck tightening. "What happened—?"

"Keep your head down!" I exclaim over the downpour, a hot sting radiating from my skin. Her forehead meets my shoulder again without question.

Warm trails of blood run down my face and to my neck, mixing with the rainwater. Fear ruptures in my chest when I realize that we're running toward a dead end: a giant, glowing tree sits ahead. A branch canopy stretches over it, so high that it leaves space between itself and the top of the tree.

If that tree is struck, we're all dead.

It has to be safe. There's no other way to go, and the artifact is definitely there!

Let this be over soon. Please.

Emberly's head picks up again. "Your cheek!" she cries next to my ear.

"I need to make sure we're safe right now! Keep your head *down!*"

I can't believe she can even see it—

Her grip tightens around me again, and it strikes me: her hands are catching the blood dripping down my neck.

I'm so sorry. I'll clean that as soon as—

"Don't stop!" Sierra shouts in front of me, Zenevieve just ahead of her. "Almost there!"

I see it more clearly now: the tree at the end stands triple the size of the flaming ones we run by now. A deep, light-violet glow radiates from its trunk and branches.

I force more strength into my legs, running harder to where I almost catch up to Sierra. The sky strikes the ground just behind me. Ezra yelps, but I no longer bear the strength to use my voice. Ezra pumps his limbs even harder. Sweat and rain drip down his face, just as with mine. It all mixes with the blood, all falling onto Emberly's hands. And yet, she clings to me as if for dear life. My heart skips another hard beat.

In a blink, we run off of the path and onto the grounds of the titanic tree.

Finally!

Firm, dry soil pads our steps. My chest and throat are alit with the fires of exhaustion and exertion, but adrenaline surges past both until we approach the gargantuan trunk. I slow, our breaths entangling in the air as the rain pours behind us. Just as I'm about to set Emberly down, the edge of a pit behind the tree catches my eye.

I take a few steps around the trunk. A small pool with crystal-clear water lies back here. Even see the distorted details of the sandy bottom are exposed.

Emberly sinks off of my back, panting furiously as she grabs her head and sits against the trunk. My vision blacks out in spots as I blink. A ringing assails my ears and head, the heat of Lavara pouring over my body. I'm drenched with sweat and water dripping down my limbs and torso. It's too much for my clothing to soak up; a bath in the pool is more than enticing.

We made it, I think with relief. *We're safe. I can't believe I found it in myself to manage that.*

Moments pass before our friends round the trunk as well, rapidly panting.

"Wow..." Sierra exhales, but I can't determine if it's from awe or fatigue. Most likely both. Along with her reddish-pink face, her messy bun has come undone amidst the hard running, unveiling her bust-length, chestnut-brown hair.

She raises her arms to tie it up again until her eyes widen on me. "Your—cheek!"

I reach a trembling hand up to the left side of my face, my arm itself paralyzed with exhaustion's ache. I wince at the sting upon contact. When I withdraw my hand, my fingers are tipped with blood. The salt of my sweat amplifies the sting of the open wound.

"It... it's fine," I say, clenching my hand into a fist. "Better than—man-eating pixies. It doesn't—"

Sierra is already weakly rummaging through her satchel. "You'll risk an infection," she manages. "Let me—clean it."

Her arm falls limp in her bag, and she leans against Ezra for support. He puts a frail arm around her, panting just as furiously.

"Let's rest," Zenevieve whispers. She stumbles to Emberly's side before sliding down. Her chest heaves, a few black coils sticking to her dark face. The shallowness of her voice tells me that her throat burns as much as mine does. "Would be—nice to be spared—a moment."

Black only swarms the edges of my vision now. I'm anxious to wash off the cut in the pool beside me, to bathe. But if I take even a step toward the pool right now, I'll fall straight in as if an invisible force had pushed me.

Wait. An invisible force...

"Emberly." Her name is nothing but a breath, my pants slowing. "Do—do you feel—the artifact?"

Now that we're at the tree, I can't understand what we're meant to do. Something still pulls on my chest. Is this tree meant to help with the main obstacle of this stage? What *is* the main obstacle? The storm?

Emberly opens her mouth to speak. Then, her eyes open more as they travel upward. Her delicate finger points up, and the four of us follow it. Glowing, violet specks dot the dense awning of branches and leaves. As they draw closer, the pull grows within me.

Ezra and Sierra grab their swords, Zenevieve abruptly standing.

"Pixies!" Sierra exclaims.

An army of a thousand man-eating creatures is descending straight in our direction. I shove down my terror and reach for my sword—

"Wait!" Emberly cries. She shakily stands, maintaining her gaze up above. "Don't, they're… they're not swarming."

She's right. If anything, the pixies seem as hesitant as we are: their descent remains slow as if *they're* afraid to draw too close.

We're trapped in a staring contest with them; both sides are too wary to make the first move. When the pixies remain peaceful, I allow my hand to drop from my sword. And the closer they draw, the pull in my chest reaches more and more for *them*.

"Wait," I say. "I think—*they're* the artifact."

"Exactly." Emberly's words pull my gaze back down, but she keeps her eyes on the others. "I think… they are what we're here for."

Sierra, Ezra, and Zenevieve remain guarded, their swords still drawn. The pixies land mere feet away, yet we're left in peace.

High-pitched chittering quivers across them as they gather above the area at the front of the tree. The five of us cautiously follow their lead. If they haven't ripped us apart yet, I want to believe that we're safe.

Rounding the trunk, two larger, glowing orbs descend from the branches. We tread toward them, the orbs glowing brighter than the other speckles suspended in the air. They soon take form in a shimmering wave of light: small persons no taller than my hand. Their crystal-like wings fade into nothing halfway down, beating like a hummingbird's. They radiate a regality that boasts their titles of king and queen of this realm.

They glide toward me and Emberly, motioning forward. She and I step closer to the trunk, somehow sharing the idea to curtsey and bow. Upon us rising, the king's and queen's bright, pale-violet faces beam. They turn to each other, exchanging silent communication, before they nod as though in approval of us. The queen rests minuscule hands on my forehead and places a kiss there, the king conducting the same for Emberly. While he returns to his original position, the queen floats down to my left cheek and repeats her kiss.

A cooling sensation spreads across the cut the shard of wood left me. My eyes narrow in confusion as the queen comes to hover in front of me again. I pull up my hand to my cheek, startled by the smooth skin. The cut is healed.

I smile, mouthing a thank-you to the queen.

It would have been wonderful to have you throughout the entire race, I can't help but think. I tighten my jaw at the memory. At the possibility that we could have lost less if...

No. Focus. Do not stop moving forward.

The queen flies back to meet the king at her original position. —*You are safe here,*— she whispers in my mind with a tender, motherly voice. —*We sense greatness in you both, hearts of benevolent intent for the sake of others. We will protect you as you rest for the final stage.*

—*Leon, be merry in your time with your teammates. Emberly may*

enjoy a fire with you all, as the Tree of Good will absorb the smoke and
purify the air. You may bathe and receive drink in the pool as well. The
water will cleanse itself. Your exhaustion radiates, so please rest in each
other's presence and strength. We will give you the key when you are
ready to proceed.—

Emberly and I exchange a glance as if to ask each other if we
heard the same voice. The king's and queen's forms mold back
into orbs, their glows emanating as they ascend back into the tree.
Their pixie kingdom takes its place among the canopy overhead.
The violet glow of the tree transitions to a deep color: a mix of
light blue and indigo.

Dry footsteps sound from behind us, and Emberly and I turn
around to face our team.

Zenevieve finally sheaths her sword. "They not only didn't
rip us apart, but Her Majesty *healed* Leo. I suppose we're safe, after all..." She arches a careful brow at Sierra. "Are you certain that
pixies are meant to be vicious?"

"According to my research on Magery," Sierra muses, adjusting her grip on her sword. "albeit that it was minimal... What
did they say?" she asks me and Emberly. "They *were* speaking to
you, right?"

"Yes," I reply, the queen's ethereal voice echoing in my
head. "The queen said that the pixies would protect us as we rest
and prepare for the final stage."

"The king as well," Emberly adds. "And this tree will protect
me from the smoke of a fire by purifying the air."

Sierra and Ezra only allow a glimpse of each other in response. I eye their swords with a strange opposition. "I feel... I feel
safe," I assure them. "We have their word."

They each note my glance at their weapons. With another reluctant look at each other, they finally sheathe them.

I can't help but notice that Emberly and I omitted the same bit: about the benevolence of our hearts. The greatness in us. It's as though speaking on it will somehow falsify the words.

"Well..."—Sierra exhales, reaching up again to tie up her hair—"then I suppose it's safe to establish camp and rest as much as we can manage so we'll be ready to finish this."

"Finish this"... Initially, my heart leaps over the words—but they leave behind something unsettled. What else did the king and queen say about—?

It falls on me like a brick. Emberly and I turn to each other in simultaneous realization: they said that we were to rest and prepare for the last stage.

"What is it?" Ezra asks carefully, his hand hovering over his pommel again.

I face him in agonizing defeat—because despite everything we've given and lost already... "Magery isn't the last stage."

CHAPTER

"YOU DON'T HAVE TO BE ALL RIGHT"

Emberly

I CANNOT AFFORD TO THINK ABOUT HOW WE'VE YET TO reach the last stage. That means we've more to run—more to lose. Right now, I'm quickly running dry of the strength I need to care.

It's as if we're trapped in a vicious cycle of torment. Magery being the last stage was meant to allow us enough relief to continue. Just as always, the relief is bitterly short.

Time doesn't stop. When night falls, a nearly black sky settles over the forest. Sierra and Leo build a fire near the Tree of Good. This time, the smoke doesn't even have the chance to reach my nose. It's been years since I've felt the warmth of a fire despite the cold land I grew up in. It's startling yet reaches an intoxicating warmth into my body.

We're able to wash our hands in the pool behind the Tree

before supper. Zenevieve and Ezra fetch a small deer. Deer is a Snowarkan delicacy and aren't native to Seavale, so morale increases at least somewhat. Sierra wants to maintain as much of the "preserved" food as we can with the snake jerky, which won't spoil; we freely feast on the deer.

I almost wish there were laughter to fill in the crackling silences around the fire—anything to fill it, really. But amidst the silence, amidst the rest, our minds are left to remember again. It's all the easier to when our greatest source of distraction is precisely what we're grieving. I don't even know if we're allowed to enjoy anything amidst Ambrose's mourning period.

A day. It has only been a day.

I miss his bright commentary—his smile—beyond my heart's ability to ache. That is just as well: I don't want to risk a smile. What it invites.

"I've always liked it when you smile." He said it lit up the rest of me. Meredith said it was lovely. Both of them knew why I don't allow such a wicked thing often, and both proved why shortly after saying—

Sierra speaks before my mind can spiral any further. "Did the pixies say when they will give you the key?" she asks across from me, finishing off a piece of meat.

"Once they deem us ready," Leo replies on her other side, twisting his own piece in his hand. "Which warns that there's another trial waiting here."

"If they want us to rest and guaranteed our protection, I don't think so," Zenevieve states beside me. "Even they sense our exhaustion. We've had no room for true rest since…"

A hard lump passes in her throat. My jaw tightens to cage

my own emotions.

Can't anything get rid of this?

Zenevieve shoves her last bite into her mouth. Standing, she dusts off her hands. "I'm going to bathe." Her dark eyes stay away from us as she grabs her satchel. "Leave me be."

She walks to the pool behind the Tree before any of us can spare a word. Upon the clanging of her armour falling to the ground, Sierra stands and takes Ezra's hand.

"It's a good night for a walk." She exchanges her glance between me and Leo. "Would... would you two like to join us?"

For some reason, the three of them turn their attentions to me. I lock my jaw and stare deeper into the fire. Why are they all staring at me as if I'll fall apart otherwise?

I close my eyes, angry at the realisation: *Because that's true.* Despite the weakness I blatantly exposed in Soilera, their eyes are the only reason I've yet to snap.

I don't know how to reply. A walk should mean distraction. Relief. But I think that relief's evanescence is what frightens me.

It won't be enough.

A presence fills the spot next to me. When I open my eyes, Ezra has taken Zenevieve's seat. Despite his intimidating, buff build and the fact that I have to look up at him, I don't feel threatened. Maybe it's because I've only ever seen his ferocity on a battlefield, but I think the part of me that processes fear has gone numb.

"Emberly..." The softness of his deep voice is as startling as the icy blue of his eyes. "May I tell you a story?"

I scoff to myself. "As long as it's not about a princess."

"It isn't." He takes a deep breath. "It's about my father."

Now he has my attention—especially when Leo's and Sierra's lips part in surprise. Leo said that Ezra's father passed away a few years ago. This must be an intimate part of his past. Why would he reveal—?

Perhaps Ezra knows how damaging his stare is; he finally takes it to the ground as he gathers his words. "I know it isn't quite the same thing—but growing up, I was very close to my father. He was my best friend—the reason I wanted to join Seavale's guard. He believed I'd become one of our best knights, and I wanted to give him the satisfaction of watching his dream come true. We trained on the beach every day and loved to go night swimming almost every night. Sometimes we hunted for shells in the sand to surprise my mother with. He even forged my very first sword..." A sombre silence overcomes him. "My world shattered apart when he passed from an unknown disease. Months before I was knighted."

Why are you telling me this? I almost snap, unsure of my own reaction. Does he hope to relieve me by discussing death, of all things?

He seems to read my thoughts and continues. "I was furious with the world. Part of me even regretted every memory I had with him—they only worked against me in my grief. And I wanted to lock my heart to the world because I thought it would protect me from the pain—"

"How is this meant to allow me any comfort?" bursts from my lips without my control. Every part of me knows that this story is reserved for those Ezra deems worthy to hear it, and only the cursed Ancients know why he's chosen me as such—but I want him to stop talking. I want him to leave with Sierra and Leo because my nose is stinging; my eyes burn; and I don't think my rope of sanity is strong enough to hold me up anymore, eyes or no eyes on me.

"It isn't," Ezra replies with a tenderness that weighs even heavier on me. His large yet careful hand rests on my back as he leans in. "It's to allow you relief in knowing that you are not alone."

I am *alone*, I want to snarl. *None of you understand why I've taken responsibility for his death. You do not know!*

"There is another side at the end of this, I promise," he tells me. "I know because I've been there. For now, you don't have to be all right—you don't have to be anything right now while you grieve."

Those words—*those* words ensnare my attention. Those words are what build an instant wall in front of the tears ready to help me unleash my anger the longer my mind processes them. Nobody has ever spoken them to me before. Nobody has ever expected—*desired*—nothing from me before. And there's a strange, bittersweet... relief in that.

It alleviates the pressure. Not the pain. Not the anger.

The fire blares its heat across my face. *I'm not alone in my experience of losing someone. Fine. But I am alone in the guilt that has accompanied every death. I can never escape that no matter how relentlessly I still try.*

Ezra awaits my reaction. My mind has never been so violently torn. I want to thank him for considering me as a friend to this degree—and yet curse him for daring to speak of death at all.

"Thank you," I force myself to whisper.

His selflessness is all the more transparent when he nods,

consolingly taking my hand. Sierra comes to rest hers on my shoulder.

"We won't be long," she says as Ezra stands.

Their footsteps fall to the soft, wet soil of the main path behind me. I'm left alone with Leo. For the first time in the time we've known each other, I don't know if I want him to talk to me or stay silent. I don't even know if my mind is beyond the ability to be distracted or relieved now.

"I'm envious of him," he says across from me. "His honour, his humility, his strength..."

Right. Silence, it is—

"I'd much rather trust him with my heir than myself."

The tears instantly retract back into my head. Grief melts into confusion, and I blink. I only match our eyes once I feel the burning red fade. "What?"

He softly scoffs, tearing his last chunk of meat into two. "Apparently, I'm an irresistible influence. Even on the morning the portals opened, I was dismantling a prank the castle boys had set up for the maids in the courtyard when Sierra came to tell me." He shakes his head. The fire lends his skin an orange hue that ignites his tan. "My children would be intelligent, that's for certain... Admittedly, I do sometimes miss the thrill of my past. I'm not sure I'd be able to restrain myself from imparting my best tricks. All I do know is that I trust Ezra with a child infinitely more than I trust myself."

So he *is* trying to distract me. He somehow knows that that is what prevents my mind from spiralling, not comfort. Too big a part of me is tempted to bite the bait; numbing myself is always easier when I'm distracted and impossible when I'm consoled.

"That is quite possibly..." I reply, "the first thing you and I may agree upon."

Leo's smile grows into a chuckle. "My protection with a sword is just about the only other thing I can provide—and that's only thanks to Ezra and how we trained together once he was knighted. It's also part of what gave me hope to save my reputation with my people. I often preferred pranks to lessons; and Ithinor received my princely responsibilities, which, as you can imagine... discredited my abilities as a ruler. Then Lavara attempted their invasion. I managed to earn the respect of the army that day, at least. It's a step."

I nod. "And the scar on... your chest. It proves you've loyalty to those you care about. Surely that's a redeemable quality."

His smile melts into... gratitude. "Thank you. That is the one trait I've always been able to boast about. Growing up in that castle, it often felt as though it'd be easier—safer, even—to discard loyalty. But that was also what allowed me to change, to start righting my wrongs. When it's acknowledged, I know my efforts weren't in vain. And..."—he swallows, exhaling softly—"I'm allowed to be proud of myself."

I'm envious of that. I'm envious that Leon finally achieved the person he desired to be no matter how many years it took. Meanwhile, I'm trapped in the same vicious cycles of my curse and character. And every time I try to break free of it, I fall straight back to the bottom.

"Well," Leon says with satisfaction, straightening in his seat, "I know one other thing: Ezra and Sierra's child will have the best uncle."

He's trying so fervently. As if he cares. He cares about my grief despite his own loss.

Why?

Well... he's always been this way, hasn't he? Trying to forge an alliance rather than kill his rivals, attempting to comfort me about Vineah's events, stepping first into the jungle temple on his team's behalf, trying to overcome his fear of tight spaces in Soilera for the sake of time...

The longer he offers me his smile, the clearer I see it: before me is Prince Leon, someone he had to grow into from the boy named "Leon". The stories of that boy align with the person I thought I was meeting during our first few days together. Despite it all, despite my prior judgment without speaking two civil words to the man, he instinctually saved my life when I almost fell off of the edge in Vineah. He comforted me yesterday after I lost Ambrose. He saved my life today when the smoke almost took it. He's making every attempt to keep my mind busy now.

Prince Leon is anything but a foolish boy. If anything, he is better than anyone I could ever be.

"I don't know what this team would do without you," I tell him.

His lips part slightly; he's surprised. A week ago, I would have been, too—but even my pride must bow for the sake of what he has done.

"And..." I catch myself saying next, but nothing in me stands in the way of the words, "if even I am thankful to have you as a teammate, then how much more should Seavale be to have you as their ruler. You're a good man, Leo. Your instincts have proven that over and over again."

His gaze falls to the soil before my last sentence can escape.

A hard swallow passes in his throat as his finger furiously taps his thigh. I think I've broken him.

"Thank you, Emberly."

Those three little words steal every last one of my own fluttering in my head. I don't know why they possess such strength right now. I don't know why, as he looks back at me with the kindest smile I've seen in too long, I want him to know how deeply I mean all that I said.

The softest pitter-patter whispers from the main path behind me. Leo looks over my shoulder. I turn around in my seat as he stands. He falls into my vision as he steps off of the Tree's grounds and onto the main path, holding out his hands.

His eyes return from the midnight-blue sky and warily land on me. "It's raining again."

I don't hear thunder or lightning this time; hopefully, that means Sierra and Ezra are safe out there.

"Didn't you say that rain is rare in Snowark?" Leo asks. I can see it now as the rain grows a little heavier; droplets lightly bounce off of his armour. "Don't you want to embrace this?"

"I'd rather not grow ill just before the end of the race," I reply dully. "You'd do well to follow my example."

"Seavalens adore the rain." He looks up at the drizzling sky with admiration, his eyes squinting against the drops. "Actually, my favourite thing to do—"

He stops himself, wiping his mouth with his hand. Then, he shakes his head.

"It certainly isn't finishing a sentence," I say, now intrigued enough to stand.

A soft smile graces his tan face. Instinct warns me to brace myself.

The prince extends his hand. "Dance with me."

I blink, pausing. "Did the pixies put something in the water, after all?"

That cursed smile grows. His hand remains outstretched. "I simply believe that this is a part of Seavalen culture you'll enjoy."

He's still trying.

Surely he's struggling the same way. I know he's grieving, too. Do his friends simply mean that much to him that their well-beings take priority?

I wouldn't put selflessness past Leon Wales for a second. And given how effortlessly words can cross the border of distractions into reminders, I'm encouraged to accept his invitation. There's just something about the Prince of Seavale standing in the rain and inviting me to dance that inspires me to step onto the path and take his hand.

He gently pulls me closer to him. My heart misses a beat. The air smells dustier out here. I can almost feel the droplets inside my nose as Leo's hand slides around my waist and rests on my lower back. His entire hold on me is firm yet mindful. The longer his gaze bores down into me, the more control I lose—the tighter I must hold on to him.

He's holding me. I don't know why the thought repeats so incessantly in my mind, affecting the very rhythm of my heart.

"Step to your right," he begins, "and then diagonally backwards to your left. Then step again to your right,"—he chuckles as we clumsily follow his instructions—"reverse it, and repeat. That's the Seavalen waltz."

My hair is already damp and water strolls down Leo's face,

but our attention is on our steps. Well, rather, it's on my dismal attempts at the steps. I spend three rounds fumbling, and Leo spends three rounds in increasing laughter.

What is this? I've never had trouble with rhythm before.

"As if you could master the Snowarkan waltz so easily, prat," I grumble. Water seeps between our hands. I hold on tighter. He reciprocates, jolting my heart again. "Why do you go *diagonally?*"

"To see the looks on first-timers' faces," he replies cheekily.

I take my hand off of his arm and shove his chest. The laughter that resounds from his lips as he tightens his hold on me, still waltzing, echoes in my ears. I'm envious of it.

A raindrop plops into my mouth. I yelp, startled. Leo's laughter embarks on another round and finally pulls mine with it.

At the beginning of the night, I didn't know if I was allowed even a smile. Yet here my laugh is, unabashedly attempting an escape. It doesn't feel right, yet I don't care.

Relief. Bittersweet relief.

Leo's smile softens as our dance becomes a simple, soft sway. Water drips off his hair, and rain coats his lashes as he looks down at me. Each drop strikes as a cool, wet prickle on my head. It's... enjoyable. And I can't stop staring at the prince. I can't stop holding on tightly to his warm hand, nor the swirl of nerves flurrying around in my stomach as he pulls me closer.

The rain dances all around us. Leo's hold allows me to fall into a swaying rhythm with him. He is smiling and reaching out a relief I don't think I've ever come to know. He is promising me that laughter is all right—maybe even safe—while my mind is desperately fighting otherwise. After all, he lost Ambrose, too. He mourns Ambrose, too. Yet here he stands with me, extending a moment of relief.

A soft clink chimes between us. We stop swaying and look down: somehow, we've gotten so close that our armour is touching.

We meet each other's gaze. Our faces are even closer. Every part of my being stills.

His eyes are so bright. Even in the night-time rain.

My heart hammers straight through my chest. Leo's face remains mere inches away, his breath intertwining with mine. He refuses to look away—until his eyes catch on my lips again. Mine instinctually follow suit with his.

What if I...?

He reaches up and brushes a drenched piece of my hair behind my ear. The touch sends lightning across my skin. He bends down and leans in until the tips of our noses are about to meet.

They graze each other. And no matter how many times I've learned, my heart surrenders completely.

Leo softly presses his lips against mine, his hands finding their place along my cheeks and jaw. My hands fall to his waist, rainwater dripping off his chainmail. Lightning crackles down my spine as I press against his lips in return. I've never done this before, and I've no inkling about him—but I know that none of it feels wrong. I know that my heart is now palpitating with a thrill I've been deprived of my whole life, one my mind yearns to explore. I know that Leo's lips are soft, warm, and inviting. They gently hold mine like his hands gently hold me. A perfect fit like a key in a lock. And I don't know why, but it's all the easier to ignore every part of me saying that I can't have this, that it will end. Because a bigger part of me is screaming its confession that it is exactly what I want. I want it. I want him.

We break apart, leaving our breaths between us. Leo gazes at me with the same stun that's struck my chest. Amidst that stun, though—amidst it is contentment. Something else I feel infecting me.

The back of his fingers brush against my cheek. "Hi, firefly," he whispers.

It's as if I'm hearing the name for the first time—in a new light. And I can't help but smile under it. This moment feels... wonderful. It feels like an embrace amidst a storm of dark clouds and acidic rain. It's relieving.

Leo's thumb traces my cheek down until it reaches my lips. His eyes dart between mine. Their blue offers me the limitless bounds of the sky itself. They offer everything I could have if—

His lips graze mine again, bordering on another kiss. He sighs, whispering, "You have the most beautiful smile."

I freeze.

Those dark storm clouds in my mind roar with thunder. Their rain starts to burns my skin. In an instant, my world falls through my fingers yet again.

"I've always liked it when you smile."

"There's that lovely smile. It's been a while."

No... No, I can't do this to myself again. I can't do this to him, I can't fill myself up just for everything to spill out when I lose—!

That's why my laugh didn't feel right: it was a warning that I was falling into the same trap again. And I ignored it. I blatantly ignored it for the sake of...

"Firefly?"

I step back at Leo's whisper. I can't afford that nickname anymore—what it makes me feel. The moment flashes in my memory a hundred times over. The brief joy, the fleeting... happiness. I'm wet and cold and about to start shivering, yet a thousand nerves are ablaze in my chest. My swallow is stuck. I'm stuck.

I know how this ends. I can't allow this to end that way, I... I can't even have this, either.

"Emberly—"

"No," I whisper. "No, this can't be again, I... Leo, you can't let this happen to me, please..."

"Let what happen?" he asks softly. "Are you all right—?"

I turn away. Every time I look up at him, he reminds me of everything I could have that I shouldn't, that I don't deserve, that I am cursed to be without.

But I want it more than I've ever wanted my happiness before. Why do I want it so much now? The drought has never been this severe. What has changed between now and then other than—?

I don't have the woman who kept me anchored or the boy who kept me distracted. And that's because I lost both of them for the exact same reason. I lost them after the same moments of relief and contentment.

I can't—I can't stand this anymore!

"Emberly—"

"Stop, p—please." I hold up my hand behind me. Leo's steps obey. "Please, Leo, d—don't."

I don't know what else I may do. I don't know if I've already begun the cycle and I'm about to lose him, too, nonetheless. I want to believe that it isn't too late: I can force myself away and detach and resume ensuring Snowark's security in the future of the Last Kingdom—

But what happens after today? Tomorrow? If we finish the race?

If he and Zenevieve don't survive it but I do?

I cannot escape this. I will never escape this.

Take the warning.

Zenevieve emerges from behind the Tree of Good as I walk back to the fire. I grab my satchel and insist on being alone. When she asks, I only tell her once that Leo hasn't anything to do with my demeanour. She doesn't believe me. I don't have the strength to convince her.

I kneel at the edge of the pool behind the Tree. I will not make the same mistake yet again, I will not further stain my hands. I can prevent this before it enters its third cycle—can't I?

I run my fingers across the surface of the water. Soft. It's physically comforting, causing a deeper ache for the emotional comfort. But no matter what I do—no matter what relief I find—it slips through my fingers and leaves me in more pieces than before. As if to remind me of my place. It's simple: I cannot escape any cycle that runs in a circle.

That moment of respite with Leo replays in my mind. All those moments with Ambrose. All those moments with Meredith. Everything I've found relief in has been stolen. Thrown over the edge, sunk to the bottom of the world. I don't want to live long enough to find what lies beyond the next door.

If all is doomed to fall... why do I continue to wait?

I'm not only afraid to wait for the good; I feel no purpose in doing so, either. Because if Leo wins this race... he'll ensure that Snowark lives. Snowark will be safe with him, especially with Zenevieve beside him. I know it.

I don't understand: the realisation should have been the key to unlock these weights around my wrists and ankles. I should feel a burden hardened by eighteen years of persistent torment release me at last. And yet, I don't. My burden is resolved, yet all I feel is... empty.

The next morning arrives slowly. Somehow, the emptiness is heavier. I finally find its name: a lack of need. My initiative has been honoured—which means that for the first time in my life, there's nothing left to fight for, nothing left to resolve.

Sierra kneels at the pool, washing our sleeping supplies. Zenevieve and Ezra have gone hunting for the next meal. I can't even feel the burning of my stomach despite my hunger only my logic is telling me is there. For some cursed reason, I still *want* to feel. Not this suffocation, but the smiles Sierra and Ezra and Leo and even Zenevieve can find amidst small moments of distraction. Amidst periods of respite with each other. But I know why they have that. I know why I can't.

Maybe there is only one way to cut myself loose from it for good. One way to a relief that can't be stolen.

"I'm taking a walk," I mutter, standing.

Leo looks up from the fire. He starts to stand. "I'll come with you—"

"No," I say. My feet itch to continue into the forest. "Alone—please. I need to... clear my head."

I walk away before he can reply.

I don't bother with the main path for long. Alone, I realise that I no longer need to be afraid anymore—not that we've encountered many threats on this stage. Walking through the dark cherry trees, I'm the only one making a sound. My hand instinctually rests on the pommel of my sword to prevent my arm from constantly hitting it. The cold metal ignites my memory, how many times I've wielded this sword—my weapons. How many times I've had to use them in this race. Memories of the monster fight on Snowark's stage ripple through my head. How long ago it all was. The ice cavern. The beast. Using the fire sword to protect Zenevieve, Ambrose, Meredith—

Meredith... Meredith, I'm so sorry...

A ragged breath skitters through my chest. I hold my head higher, passing the trees and bushes. The branches reach for me, scraping my armour.

I want to slap my past self. How could she be so horrendous? So selfish and childish, especially towards Meredith, of all people? As if she knew any better than Meredith did. As if Meredith weren't trying to help!

I deserved to lose her.

I wish I couldn't remember.

I mindlessly push away the trees' low-hanging branches amidst the cool, fresh air. The scraping against my hands feels... pleasant in a way. A pain other than emotional.

My hands no longer sting with the sunburn I earned on Lavara's stage. It finally healed. Ambrose and I were the only ones severely burned because we were so pale. I remember... he put me in my place that night. He told me exactly what I needed to hear. On Lavara's stage and Soilera's—

Ambrose...!

I slam my palms against the tree in front of me. A thousand trapped screams and cries rack my chest in gasps. Eighteen years of suppression and internal torment.

Ambrose was younger.

He had his entire life! Why him? Why is it never me?!

You were so terrible to him the entire time you knew him. You deserved to lose him, too. You complain about it, yet you deserve this existence.

I wish I couldn't remember. I wish I didn't have my entire life's worth of evil memories and reminders. I wish I *didn't* deserve this life; that would make it easier to accept that this will always be my reality. I would be able to breathe through it—but I can't breathe. I can't live. I cannot survive this.

I open my eyes. My dagger's silver pommel glints at me.

My hot palm rests on the cold metal. Relief.

My hand slides down to the black leather. I wrap my fingers around it. The blade smoothly slides out of its holder as I unsheathe it.

There is no sun today, either. I haven't seen one in quite some time now that I think about it. And yet, even with no sun, the blade winks at me now. It's smooth and familiar and comforting and... promising.

It would hurt—but nowhere near as much as every breath I take.

What if I were Rowena's final target?

I revel in the sensation of a swallow. Of my throat being intact, keeping me alive. Of how close I could be to falling off the edge. Just to know what it would feel like. To stop. To never remember or feel again. To eradicate the cursed stain that I am.

End it.

My trembling hand raises the blade to my throat.

CHAPTER 34

"A HOPE TO LIVE"

Leo

"**N**O!" I EXCLAIM, DARTING OUT FROM BEHIND THE tree I hid behind. "Emberly—!"

She jumps, whirling around with the dagger in hand but lowered from her throat. Her red, swollen eyes harden in fury once they realize that I'm the one standing in front of her.

"You despicable *prat!*" she screams, slashing the air with her blade. My heart twinges at the raw, grieving agony that racks her voice. "This has nothing to do with you, go back!"

I knew something was wrong the second she said she wanted to be alone to "clear her head"—how she had waited until after Zenevieve was gone to do so, like she was about to commit something her best friend would stop her from doing. Thank the stars that I followed her, that she's still breathing in front of me right now.

"You are part of my team," I tell her. "Your well-being has everything to do with me if it's in danger."

"You've NO idea what I—!"

"I *do*, Emberly!" I don't care what I must do or say—as long as she sees how desperate I am to keep her. "I know you're grieving, you've lost more than you can stand. But I promise—I promise—this isn't the solution—"

"You are the last person I want to see!" Her red eyes narrow as fresh tears flood them. The hand gripping the dagger shakes. "You think you know my burdens? You don't know how cursed I really am. You know nothing of how this is all my fault, the deaths of my loved ones are on *my* hands! And I will never be able to forget it! Do you know what it's like to live every day with the knowledge that you are cursed and you haven't an ounce of power to fix it? You can't mend your past mistakes because they're in the past, and you can't even mend your own future! Every smile you give, every moment of joy has a price, you are punished for it because you don't deserve it, leaving you with a future of desolation and despair! My happiness only exists if I'm to lose it, if I'm to be punished for it—and I can't stand an existence of falling into the same trap over and over again, of being happy just to lose everything!"

The pieces finally connect in my mind: *Is… is that how she feels about the kiss? It wasn't that she regretted it—she felt as though she didn't deserve it and it was just another trap…?*

She raises the dagger. My stomach lurches. "Why shouldn't I slash this blade across my throat right now? End my curse and my losses, cut it at the source?!"

I swallow hard. She's about to leap over the edge, and I need to throw everything I have in my arsenal to fight for her. Her hurt runs deeper than anything I can see just by looking in; I hope against hope right now that I have the ability to extend my blind hand and reach it.

"Emberly," I begin in the gentlest voice I can muster, raising my hands in surrender. I beg my words to accumulate faster—because I don't know what to say. The effects of the death curse were outside of our control; why does she blame herself so heavily for them? She has no power to control any of this, yet she feels responsible. Responsible for the one thing she doesn't have...

And yet, I don't know how else to phrase it: "It's not your fault. None of this—*none* of this is your fault."

She squeezes her eyes shut, her sweet voice succumbing to a high-pitched whisper. "Don't say that!" Her body trembles as the dagger lowers, her back meeting the tree she stands in front of. "He said that, he said that to me...!"

Her sobs bend her body forward, her waves falling over her face. She doesn't see me step up to her and take her hand with the dagger in it. At my touch, her fingers loosen their grip. She drops the weapon without a word; her voice has been silenced by the tears jolting her.

That arm slowly wraps around me as I pull her into my embrace. I lean my cheek against the top of her head. She trembles in my hold until a fierce, raspy inhale pierces the air. Every breath out is a guttural cry. And every one feels like a sword plunging into my stomach.

Don't cry. Be her strength. She needs your strength. Do not cry.
What do I say? How do I make this better instead of worse?

I close my eyes to cage the tears. Emberly's arms tighten

around me as she wails. I can hardly endure this myself. I can hardly endure the fact that she's so deprived of joy and feels as if she'll never find it. I can hardly endure the fact that I can't give her everything she needs right now to want to see tomorrow.

"I promise you, it's not your fault," I whisper. "Not one of them died at your hands. Not one. You are not the curse that killed them."

I regret the words as soon as they fall: she wheezes more furiously, her arms falling from around me and her knees buckling. I have to slowly kneel to the cold grass with her.

Why can't I know what to say? Why don't I know how to help her?

The minutes are excruciating. Softly swaying back and forth with her as she cries is all that alleviates the pain for me. I can only hope that it does the same for her. Her sobs finally start to give way to deep breaths, her hands balled into fists against my chest. Her body eventually grows loose but steady in my arms. All I can do now is simply hold her.

"I couldn't save them," she whispers with a raspy voice. Her head rests against my chainmail. "Why should I bother saving myself? What point is there in saving someone so undeserving of life, only ever destined for demise?"

She won't believe me if I tell her that she *is* worthy, and that's why I don't have an immediate answer. Every reason I can think of is selfish; it only keeps her here because her friends want her to be.

But I can't let her go. I can't allow her to think that she's beyond hope—

Beyond hope. That's why this hurts so deeply. I know this pain.

"I thought that about myself, too," I tell her softly. "When I was finally allowed to see Ithinor after I almost killed him, I thought I was beyond hope. None of Seavale's great leaders, let alone my parents, would have conducted something so foolish and childish. I wanted to abdicate the throne entirely, sever myself from myself in any possible way. I thought I was unworthy of help, of any and all hope to receive it. Yet Ithinor... Ithinor told me that he still believed in me. He knew I had more in me, I had better in me. I didn't even believe in myself, but I took the leap and trusted him. Now I know that we're never beyond hope—we only have to be brave enough to accept it."

"I'm not *worthy*," she cries. It feels like every ounce of strength she has is spent on those words. "You don't understand."

"I do, I promise." I rest my hand on the side of her head. "Out of all of Seavale, I was the person least deserving of the throne. I spent my entire life hearing it all: that I was a disappointment, the most unworthy to rule, a stain tarnishing the legacy of Seavale's great rulers..."

I hesitantly swallow as Emberly stills against me. Her breaths soften.

"I still don't know how to bring myself above those voices," I say, clinging to the hope that my words are traveling the right path. "I try every day but I never know if it's enough. I want to stop listening to them, disregard them and rule by my own—like you. You assert yourself when it matters and you don't allow the wrong voice to persuade you, and a kingdom needs that. *I* need that, firefly; and I don't have it. I fight those voices every day and I can never say for certain that I've won against them. But you inspire me to fight harder against it, to refuse it. Teach me. I need your help. I need you, Emberly."

I don't know where my last sentences stemmed from. Maybe they were spoken from a place other than my mind, somewhere that required no thought and only for me to feel—but I think I've spoken from the right place, because Emberly's breaths have steadied. Quieted. She stays in my embrace, allowing me to gently sway with her.

"Please," I say. The words feel safer now. "Teach me. To fight that voice, to rule like you. We need you."

"They needed me," she whispers. "They had a hope to live."

"And they died with the hope that *you* would live."

Silence. Her body freezes against me.

"Look at me," I whisper.

She shakes her head. "No—"

"Emberly." It is the first time I've ever allowed a beg to weigh down my words, but she needs it. She needs that anchor, to know that I'm willing to throw it down for her.

I hear her swallow before she leans away from me. Just enough to grant me her swollen, red eyes and shiny cheeks. Even her lips have intensified in color.

"You are not beyond help or hope." I give both of her eyes equal attention—to show her that they're just as beautiful as each other whether she's a warrior or allowing herself to crumble. "I'll be right here to help you find both. If it was there for me—I know it's there for you."

I explore every detail of her muted-green irises, carving out each curve and line and emotion trapped in them. They almost remind me of Sierra's green, but I admire how unique they are to just her. Emberly's green.

Another hard lump passes in her throat. "And if I'm punished again for being happy?"

I take in a deep, careful breath. She never loses my gaze. "Being happy... is a brave thing. It means you have something to lose, yes..." I brush her hair out of her face, tracing the same strands over and over. "But it also means you have something to hold on to."

My fingers continue rubbing her hair. She exhales, allowing me to release her and herself to straighten. Minutes pass before she stands. She denies my help, but that is just as well. I let her walk in front of me the entire way back to the Tree of Good.

Sierra excuses herself to find Zenevieve and Ezra once we arrive. I know that it's really because she saw the alarming redness in Emberly's face as we approached and knew that the last thing Emberly wanted was anyone else's attention during this state.

Taking our seats at the fire, I grant her space by staying across from her. The heat would be a satisfying warmth against the cool morning if not for the adrenaline and blood still flooding my face.

"Don't tell Zenevieve."

Emberly's whisper is so abrupt that I almost don't process her words in time. She maintains her gaze on the flames in front of her as if she's afraid to meet my eyes. "She would never understand. I could never face her if she knew that I..."

I nod. "You have my word."

I'm thankful that she doesn't leave us in the crackling quiet: "Then I will also have your word that you will never mention the event again."

She doesn't want to remember it. I more than understand that—but part of me can't prevent the protective instinct I feel over what I said to her, hoping she won't so easily forget it all.

"My word," I repeat.

I don't know if the silence is what she prefers, but my thoughts and memories threaten to spiral—threaten the idea that things will only worsen if I leave her in her own mind for too long.

Distract her. At the very least, distract yourself.

Only one other topic comes to mind, and I harshly scold myself for it; I can't ask about the kiss no matter how terribly I want to. I have realized in full what's happened in my heart regarding her; to deny it would be an ignorant lie. It was verified all the more to me when I almost lost her moments ago. Nevertheless, it's unchartered waters. While I want nothing more than to navigate them with her, that doesn't mean anything if she isn't willing to board the ship with me. And if I assume that she reciprocates, I don't doubt that she'll give me another scar with Rowena.

My eyes trace up to her own scar on the right side of her forehead. I can't ask about that, either; she deliberately told me to never mention it again. I also can't help but think that something so poignant is the last thing she needs to relive right now.

Mine, however...

It's an embarrassing story, but I'll be grateful if it can manage a simple smile out of her.

"Offer your best guess." I point at my left brow. "How do

you suppose I earned this?"

She raises her eyes from her hands outstretched toward the fire. The flames lend her irises a fantastic golden hue I've never observed in a pair of human eyes. They're aglow with amber, ablaze with the flames licking at the air. My full attention is ensnared yet again.

"The day Lavara attempted invasion, no?" she asks in an unfamiliar soft voice.

I force a chuckle, hoping to encourage the lighter mood. "If only the cause were so valiant. No, when I was fifteen, I was still trying to accustom myself to the idea of responsibility—becoming a better leader. Temptation earned the better of me one day, and I abandoned duties for a day at the tavern as a reward for 'behaving myself'. There, I accepted a challenge from a drunkard to... juggle the cook's knives for as long as it took the drunkard to down a pint of ale. One knife—slipped from my grasp. The rest is indelibly marked on my face for the rest of history."

She fails to conceal the start of her laughter, pressing her hand to her mouth as her shoulders shake. My heart beats a little lighter, especially when she closes her eyes and can only uncover her smile when it fades. "And all this time, I thought..." She closes her eyes again, the remainder of a giggle escaping her. "Thank you. That was almost as funny as the time Zenevieve and I swapped Whiny Winston's cottage cheese for spoiled milk."

"What?" The smile on my lips widens. "I *must* know more about this Whiny Winston."

"I would tell you—but spoiled milk is as sweet as sugar when compared to the taste he leaves in my mouth."

I nod, chuckling. "Understood."

The quiet between us shifts: softer, but still too reminiscent of recent moments. I pray that it's not cruel for her, that she hasn't been left to memories of her worst moments now that conversation has ceased. As her delicate features fall the longer we sit, my hope become more earnest.

Just as I open my mouth, she digs her sabaton into the soil and exhales. "When we were nine and ten," she begins quietly, "Zenevieve and I wanted to prove our rebellion to the council—that we weren't puppets to be controlled. We left for the south forest for a campout and challenged ourselves to stay for the entirety of the night."

Is this...? Is this the story of how she earned her scar?

Her eyes never leave her hands in front of the fire. "A small group of Vinean knights found us. Snowark and Vineah have been bordering on war since before I was born, so bringing in Snowark's princess was the ultimate prize for them. Zenevieve and I climbed a tree in an attempt to escape them. When I had to jump to the next tree, enter smoke sensitivity. That was the night I discovered I had it—or, at least, had developed it. Something of the sort. I fell from the tree because I was so dizzy, and cut my forehead on the rock I landed at. Certainly provided a lovely trinket from the night."

She slowly shakes her head. "Zenevieve somehow managed to save us. I know what she's capable of now; but to this day, I can't begin to grasp how she managed it back then. She's never told the story. I understand why. After that night, I demanded that she start formal training for the royal guard. Only by... only by Meredith's convincing was she accepted two years later."

"At *twelve* years old?" I ask, leaning forward. The youngest someone may be inducted in Seavale's guard for training is four-teen; evidently, the Snowarkan royal court provided an excep-tion just as we did for Ezra to be knighted.

"Knighted when she was almost seventeen." Emberly nods. "We certainly proved we'd the bravery for defiance—but our 'competence', as Winston called it, was 'inadequate' for the world that lay beyond the palace walls. Again... Meredith all but sold her soul working a case against the council that would allow me to resume timely training for my coronation as queen. Even the royal court trusted her input more than theirs."

So that's why she's afraid of heights...

Meredith truly was to her as Ithinor was to me.

Now I know the full weight of that story, of her experiences. And not only do I want Emberly to know that she truly isn't alone, but I catch myself feeling compelled to share my own scarred fears with her. It's fair—and I feel safe.

"You've probably noticed that I don't do well with small spaces—"

"Ezra told us the story." She lightly nods. "I understand."

"Ezra doesn't know how many times it happened."

My words grip her attention. She's never stared at me with such—compassion before. "You mean... it happened more than once?"

"A few times a year every year until Lavara's attack."

The worst eight years of my life.

If not for her sitting upright and wide-eyed at me, Emberly's stillness would greatly alarm me right now. Still, the last thing I want between us is silence; and she should know that I feel safe being open with her, too: "Sierra knows. That's part of the reason she's able to keep me calm. The castle determined that I had been so shaken by the first time that sending me down there every few months for 'reflection' on my role as a prince was wise. Surprisingly, they never locked me up as punishment for my pranks. Maybe they were afraid that I'd retaliate in some way and set the castle aflame."

After the treasury incident when I was eleven, it's the only plausible excuse that I can think of. But I don't want nor need their justifications anymore.

"Did they..." Emberly begins carefully, unmoving as though the ground beneath us will break, "forget that you were down there more than once, too?"

I press my lips tightly together, nodding. "Half the time. I was only ever remembered at mealtimes, when the castle realized that the prince hadn't arrived at the table yet. Every time they locked me up..."—my throat scarcely squeezes the words through—"I didn't know if I'd be in that cell for an hour or half a day."

A quiet all too long is absorbed by the crackling of the fire between us. It's thrown back into my ears and amplifies every second.

"That's terrible," Emberly says. Her furrowed brows tell me how deeply she means the words. "Truly."

"Forgive me, but... it's somewhat comforting to know that I wasn't the only one who grew up with a royal staff that wanted nothing to do with me."

She cocks her brows in thought, exhaling. "Perhaps Whiny Winston wasn't entirely inaccurate about me. After all, I've now a permanent mark of stupidity and rebellion on my face."

Defense rises in my chest. "Don't say that."

"What would you call it? Certainly *you* understand what I mean."

"Because that is how I earned mine, yes." That defensive instinct urges me to stand and move to the seat beside her. "But you're wrong about yours. That scar... completes everything your appearance already reveals about you." I brush a dark-auburn wave away from her face. "Your fiery passion,"—my fingers lightly brush her freckles—"your brilliant uniqueness,"—I trace her scar next—"your resilience and strength,"—I gently hold the side of her face—"your tender heart"—the back of my fingers brush down to her lips—"and the softness you manage to maintain that allows you to care. To feel with and for others. To love with that heart nonetheless."

I'm staring at her pink lips now. Glances become nonexistent as my eyes trace the defined shape of her lips until they move up to her stare. Her fierce eyes are ablaze with gold and green and everything that stirs within me everything I shouldn't feel for her.

But I do. I do, I do feel it for her. I know it by the fact that she understands me, she truly understands me, deeper than even Sierra does after less than two weeks of knowing each other. I know it by the rhythm my heart beats with when I stand by her, when I'm alone with her. I know it by how the world feels as open and free as the sky when she is beside me.

I know it by how I need her to survive this race. I need her to live even if I don't.

The words are beating with life and fire in my mind and heart. And yet I have to quench every spark of it for her sake right now. Despite how deeply it pains me that I can't express the care I want her to know exists for her, I will not put her under the weight of that right now.

"You can't say these things about me, Leon," she whispers with a solemnity that reaches her eyes.

"I mean them, firefly. Anyone who knows you would say the same thing."

"But *you* can't," she states, bringing down my hand. "You can't, you can't allow me to think that what you feel towards me goes beyond an alliance."

But what if it does? I almost make the mistake of blurting.

My words condemn me nevertheless: "Why not?"

Her eyes are an even, transparent mixture of resistance yet softness, as though a war is waging inside her for how she truly feels. "Because if you say it," she murmurs, "we'll both have to admit it."

"You don't have to admit anything," I whisper. "I would never—"

"You don't understand." She swallows, her eyes falling from mine. "I bear a different curse than you do. If I admit this, it becomes real. I won't be able to deny it anymore and protect my-self, protect you from my repercussions. You weren't even to know that I had a heart, let alone how weak it is; yet now you have me spilling out every one of my darkest secrets, you horrible prat..."

"Your heart is anything but weak—"

"I'm a curse, Leo," she says shakily, her hold on my hand tightening, "a cause of death—"

"Stop saying that." Desperate for her full attention, I take her face into my hands. "Listen to me. You haven't killed anyone. Nobody has died by your hands, whether deliberately or by accident or curse—"

"You don't *understand*—!"

A cacophony of high-pitched chitters ripples across the canopy overhead. The branch-and-leaf awning is dotted with the army of a thousand pixies again. Their panic is tangible as they sink toward us.

Emberly and I stand, gazes stuck on their purple amidst the deep-blue glow of the Tree of Good. Then I see it: the holes being poked into the purple covering. Glowing specks disappear one by one, fading into nonexistence.

The pixies are... dying?

"Leo! Emberly!"

I look toward the main path. Sierra, Ezra, and Zenevieve are sprinting back onto the Tree's grounds.

"We couldn't find a single animal," Ezra announces, panting fervently. "We thought it was because there was simply nothing in the area, but then the stage began—*disintegrating* around us."

"We ran," Zenevieve says, breathless and briefly glancing behind her, "but something isn't right! Are the pixies saying anything?"

"I don't think they need to," Sierra says gravely, gaze stuck above us. She looks back down, the saturation of her green eyes absorbing the purple and then just as quickly losing it as it gradually fades. "None of the other stages disappeared before we finished them, not even Vineah. If we're on the seventh one and being forced out of it to reach the last one—I think the remaining teams are already there. We're out of time."

CHAPTER

"SISTERS, YOU MIGHT EVEN SAY"

Emberly

A S IF THIS CURSED HEART OF MINE COULDN'T GROW even weaker. Now it pumps a burning fear all throughout my being as the realisation collides into me: we have to enter the final stage without knowing a thing about it.

In my current mindset, at that. Angry regret bubbles in me. This is precisely why I never tore down that eighteen-year-old wall: what I felt towards Leo was never meant to delve past attraction for this very reason. Because of his selflessness I so desire, his wit that challenges mine to levels past dangerous and admirable, how he sees past my every mistake and flaw and still wants to stay despite them—my mind is crumbling apart.

I'm not meant to be wanted by him. Yet I am. He wants me enough to save me from an attempt on my own life.

Leo wants *me* when I don't want myself. And that's become

my greatest weakness.

A lower-pitched chitter pulls my attention. The five of us look at the front of the Tree of Good to find the king and queen pixies descending. They motion for me and Leo to come forth and take our original positions in front of them.

Right—there are greater matters in front of me right now. My team are what matter most in this moment. That is the voice I must assert and listen to.

I stand in front of the king and Leo in front of the queen. They fly to the centre of the trunk, waving their hands in an arch. A sheer, violet light follows, a small portal swirling open. It fades and leaves behind a hollow the size of Ezra's hand. The king and queen reach inside and take hold of something small and bronze: the key.

Turning around, with their free hands, they motion for Zenevieve, Sierra, and Ezra to come forth and stand with us.

Why aren't they speaking to us like they did before? We're out of time and are not fluent in hand gestures!

The violet glow from above dims to half as bright. We truly must be at the end. My fear has never been allowed throughout this race, and right now is no exception no matter how violently my stomach is tossing and turning.

Leo and I meet the other's wary yet urgent gaze. His jaw is tight with what I must assume is fear of his own. At least, if he is just as terrified as I am right now, it would certainly make entering the next stage slightly more bearable.

We're doing something brave. That doesn't mean I have to like it.

I unintentionally reach out my hand the same moment he does. The sides of our hands meet just below the king and queen.

Before I can retract, they drop the key.

A blinding, white light opens in the Tree of Good. Our last portal. Its rim crackles with a deep colour, cyan and indigo blending together to create a storm of deep-blue lightning.

The king and queen pixies part like a double door, extending their hand out to the portal.

Leo allows me the key. I wordlessly accept it and drop it into my satchel before my curiosity can ask what word is engraved on it. I don't care. I may be running the race, but I am no longer playing the game.

The five of us share one final glance with each other.

"For Seavale," Sierra says, then leaning forward to meet my and Zenevieve's eyes, "and Snowark. No matter what."

"And Snowark"...?

She and Ezra step forward, hand in hand. Zenevieve squeezes my shoulder, pressing her head against mine.

"No matter what," she whispers. Then, she steps up behind Ezra and Sierra at the portal entrance.

At the edge of my vision, Leo looks up at the queen. My gaze meets the king's. He nods once at me, his arm still extended. His voice swirls and resonates in my mind: —*Let not your heart remain hard, Princess Emberly. In accordance with its obstinance, you are treasuring up for yourself wrath in the day of revelation.*—

I silently curse the fact: these nosy pixies were eavesdropping the entire time.

I swallow as Leo takes his first step towards the portal. I force myself to follow suit. The king's stare presses heavily on my back, the blinding light beckoning the five of us forward.

—*Your feelings are not your greatest weakness,*— the king says.

—Your resistance to them is.—

I lock my jaw. Not right now—not when my team need a fierce leader unfazed by circumstances or mental weight.

Thank the stars that Leo is the real leader among us all.

Stepping into the portal, the light overwhelms my vision for the last time as I squeeze my eyes shut against it. My team and I step onto a hard, white platform: I instantly recognise it as the one we landed on when we first began this wretched death trap. The glass dome still cascades over us, barricading us from the raging sea below. We're back to standing above the middle of the ocean.

I was with three Snowarkan members the last time I was here. Now I've only Zenevieve.

I should be grateful to still have her at all; that is how I force my focus back onto what is sure to become a battlefield in front of me. The air is as comfortable as it was in Magery, but that doesn't make it any easier to breathe right now. We five face five others: Vineah's brat, Luciana; her knight; her mage; Lavara's dunce, Amon; and his mage. They stand as one united front just as we do.

They've allied together. The two most ruthless leaders of our world are fighting us.

They have two mages, and we don't even have one.

"The pirate boy and ice princess made it to the end?" Luciana sneers in that knockoff of a Snowarkan accent. She pushes a long, auburn bang behind her ear, the rest of her hair in a dishevelled bun. She's lost the top half of her bronze armour, left with only the leg pieces and sabatons; two weeks ago, I would have had to stifle a laugh. She rests her warm-brown hand on the bronze pommel of her sword. As if she isn't afraid of us. Her muted-green eyes send their own sword through me. She knows the power she has over me. I loathe her for it. "How unfortunate that we never met during the race, Princess. I could have left you another pretty scar, and the two would have been best friends... *sisters*, you might even say."

Rage moves my feet before I can think. What surprises me is when Leo follows suit. That is the only thing that stops me from moving forward and decapitating the brat.

"You dare such remarks after *your* history?" Zenevieve snaps on my other side, drawing her sword. "Your kingdom attacked *children* that night! Two innocent kids spending a night in the woods! How could you possibly think yourself fit to rule the Last Kingdom?"

"Simple," Luciana spits. "For one, you were on our side of the forest. It was military."

"You tried to kidnap the Princess of Snowark," Zenevieve hisses.

Luciana's eyes glint at me. "No. We tried to take her home."

Instinct grabs my bow behind me and nocks an arrow. "I'd stop talking before my arrow decides for you, brat!" I shout, aiming straight for her unprotected chest.

But to my heavy dismay, her sentence has already stolen my team's defensive stance. Ezra's, Sierra's, Leo's, and even Zenevieve's eyes have all gravitated to me.

"What is that meant to mean?" Zenevieve asks Luciana. As if she could even consider that the wench is telling the truth.

"According to what my army described to me," Luciana begins, shifting her weight, "aren't you the girl who saved her that night? And here you are all these years later. Surely you're close. Has she ever told you that I'm only a few days younger than her?"

"No," Sierra says, stepping forward, "that's would imply that Emberly..."

My grip on my bow tightens. Some kind of resistance is preventing my fingers from releasing the arrow. Luciana isn't even intimidated by my aim on her. I am already in the snake's trap; the only way to set myself free is to cut off the head.

But—I can't. Why can't I bring myself to shoot? Why am I paralyzed, why am I under her control?

Then I realise that Amon and his mate have adopted the same smirk on Luciana's face. As if... they know.

She wouldn't... She couldn't have... Why would—?

For all things sacred and uncursed, shoot her! End this, now!

I can't. My fear—my shame that's built up over eighteen years and solidified into iron chains around my wrists—is stealing every initiative I have to retaliate. Those chains have never been heavier.

My shame—and my guilt. I can't take yet another life. Knowingly. Not with my own hands this time.

Luciana snickers at Zenevieve, unfazed. "All these years, and she never told you that we share the same father? Your little ice queen is a Vinean princess."

CHAPTER

"THERE WILL BE ONLY ONE"

Leo

MY BODY IS NUMB. I CAN'T FEEL THE WEIGHT OF MY bow and quiver hanging on my back or the presence of Ezra and Sierra behind me. Against every instinct of survival I've ever built, my stare is trapped on Emberly and her death glare at Luciana. I'm no longer staring at just the Princess of Snowark—but also the other Princess of Vineah.

The only other princess there has ever been.

She feels illegitimate and like she isn't good enough for Snowark— because she is illegitimate and not born entirely of Snowark.

Leaf-green eyes. The same warm-toned hair like Sierra's and Luciana's. Delicate features like Sierra and Luciana. A deep-rooted hatred for Luciana and Vineah...

"I'm a curse. I bear a different curse than you do."

Every piece has fallen into place.

There has never been an illegitimate heir recorded in history; the death curse always specified that the two monarchs of a kingdom must bear an heir to avoid their kingdom falling with them once they died. I suppose no one was ever brave enough to test fate and marry and conceive with another monarch—or anyone else, for that matter. Especially since a king or queen likely would have died by the curse once that illegitimate was born before they could bear an heir with their spouse...

...unless the two heirs were conceived at the same time.

But Emberly's mother—how could she—? Did she—?

And the King of Snowark... If Emberly wasn't his daughter, the death curse wouldn't have killed him. What happened to—?

How did Emberly or Luciana find this out...?

"Ember...?" Zenevieve whispers.

The voice ensnares my attention. Her open mouth and relaxed features tell me that she is just as stunned as I am.

Not even Zenevieve knew?

"You were right, Luci." Prince Amon's mage snickers. "This was well worth the wait."

A victorious grin beams across their faces—all except Luciana's mage, who remains stolid yet timid.

A deep part of my mind begs my body to move, to defend, to protect, to do absolutely anything but remain still—but a bigger part has already taken control. The stunned part. Revelation has infected my being. To my shame, pity accompanies it.

"How is that even possible?" Sierra asks. It is the first time since we met that she's completely dropped her feigned Seavalen accent.

Prince Amon groans, throwing his head back and running a

hand through his tousled, black hair. He hasn't lost a piece of his black-plated armor, and neither has his mage. "Who cares?" he says with an accent nearly identical to Emberly's posh one. "Show's over, I'd like to get on with what we came here to do!"

Luciana holds out her arm to bar him, never stealing her eyes away from a red-faced Emberly. I'm almost just as surprised that Emberly hasn't moved, either; she's still holding her arrow in its drawn position. It's a miracle she hasn't released it.

Her greatest enemy is the one person able to paralyze her. No wonder she was so determined to uphold every wall she's ever built.

"Nobody's read their history books, I see," Luciana says snidely. "Otherwise you'd have realized that tensions began between Vineah and Snowark soon after Emberly and I were conceived. The kings often visited each other's lands to maintain peace, seeing as we're neighboring kingdoms. After one such visit from the King of Vineah, the Queen of Snowark must have confided in her husband about the actions my father committed against her, because we've been on the brink of war ever since. While I don't agree with what my father did,"—a hungry malice glints in her eyes—"he certainly left me a lovely prize for the race."

Rage boils in me. *How can she speak so insensitively about something so—?!*

"And you haven't outgrown your stupidity, I see!" Emberly snarls, pulling her arrow back farther. "You were stupid enough to open your mouth, for one; and you were foolish enough to ally with a team that slaughtered their own teammates. I'd wonder why they haven't betrayed you yet, but I'm more grateful that I have the privilege of dealing with you personally!"

Save for Luciana's mage, they all laugh and turn to each other. "Amon is no different than when I threw my advisor over the edge of Vineah's stage," Luciana chirps, tightening her bun. "A strong ruler weeds out those too weak to stand, to be of any value. Amon and I plan on killing each other by the end of this. It's only a matter of who does it first."

We're dead.

"Right," Amon states with black eyes darker than Zenevieve's. He draws his sword as orange magic ignites in his mage's ash-colored hands. "Now that we've had our reunion, I'd like to claim my new kingdom."

With a speed that rivals Ezra's, his mage throws a ball of fire at Emberly. The attack seems to jolt us all awake, and Zenevieve only deflects it in time because her sword is already in hand.

That's why they wasted time telling us all of that: my mind is completely blurred. I can't... I can't believe—

Sierra shouts my name as she unsheathes her sword. Instinct ignites in me at the sight, and I try to shake away the shock still infecting me. I throw down my bow from my back and draw my sword. Emberly is still on her bow, and Ezra travels the circumference of the platform as Luciana shoots an arrow at me. I scarcely dodge in time and reach for my dagger in case. Ezra happens upon her, using his sword to fling her bow out of her hands.

Luciana turns to him, sliding out her own sword. She barely manages to hold her own against him, and I see part of the reason why: when Ezra lunges for her left side, she goes to protect her right before just managing to protect her left—and the opposite applies.

It's as though—

She can't tell her left from her right!

"Ezra!" I call to tell him just as a shadow looms over me.

I look behind me: Amon is lunging for me, his sword ready to swing. I brace myself, holding my own in front to parry. A malevolent grin carves his lips, shooting a bolt of rage through my veins: he wore that same wicked grin when Luciana was taunting us with the truth. He knew. Luciana *told* him, a secret that wasn't hers to tell; and it's nothing but a twisted game to him. A tool and weapon against his enemies. He doesn't care, he doesn't even care that—!

Amon gives a hard shove, pushing me down onto the platform. I open my eyes barely in time to see his sword raised to strike me. I'm able to roll away just as the blade falls onto the floor.

Focus! You can't be there for her if you're dead!

I'm just close enough to trip Amon as he raises his sword, but he only falters before swinging again. I'm on my knees when I block, using every fiber of muscle my anger and adrenaline provide me on pushing him back. I thank Ezra in my head a hundred times over for the excess training he always insisted on the last few years. While the shove is only enough for Amon to stumble a step back, it's the amount of time I need to stand.

He swings and swings again, and I counter with a block every time. My eyes are locked on his every move as memories flash through my mind.

"Lavara's men have begun swarming the front of the island!"

"Send me. I'll be the last man Lavara ever sees."

I was proud of that young man back then. I was proud of my

initiative. Right now, part of me desires to mark that same state-ment true today—but the other is ruled by a new voice now. A bigger voice:

"Your heart is your greatest strength. It will guide you. Your head will protect you. Act in one accord."

My heart... feels for Amon. It regrets that he doesn't know better. It regrets that he may have a better fate if he only knew.

That's why I can't bring myself to hurt him—but I can inca-pacitate him to make him listen.

He blocks my slash, a reverberating ring echoing in my ears with every clash. Based on the underhanded fighting culture of his kingdom I saw on that day, I know to calculate his every move, waiting for deception.

There: the malevolent grin as he lowers himself and swipes his sword close to the ground. I jump, narrowly avoiding the blade's edge.

"Your men tried that five years ago!" I shout.

His sharp, narrow features contort in rage. "I swore my re-venge on you that day, and I *will* have it!"

Every time he swings, I parry. That's the pattern until his swings slow and his breathing intensifies in ragged, heavy breaths. I step forward, raising my sword; and his grin returns.

I step back as he launches himself forward. My heart is al-most pounding too hard for me to breathe properly. If anything, the ache in my arms is threatening to debilitate them as Amon swings for my side. I deflect and spin, having to parry the second I come out. Sweat already drips down the sides of my face, but I've just about figured out Amon's pattern.

He takes his next swing, and I take mine to counter it. We're deadlocked, the steel meeting with a reverberating impact. I tighten my muscles against the force rippling through my arms. Determination and even a fire of hope for him burns in me.

"We don't—have to kill each other!" I choke out. "Me and Emberly, you and Luciana—!"

"There will be only ONE!" he snarls, pressing harder against me. "This has always been Lavara's destiny, you will not stand in the way of that again! Death to Seavale, to you all—!"

"Amon! Look out!" Zenevieve calls.

My mind also knows how to protect me from his refusal. It isn't that he doesn't know better; it's that he chooses otherwise.

Regret and fury now boiling in my blood, I wait until his black eyes dart in Zenevieve's direction behind him. The woman is running toward him with her mace.

He has no choice but to break the deadlock, whirling around. With a hard swallow, I thrust my blade through his back.

My chest heaves with breaths almost too big for my lungs. Zenevieve slows just before reaching us. I walk around Amon's body as he falls to his knees. His mouth is permanently stuck in a gasp as his sword falls from his hold. He collapses backward onto the ground, skewering himself along my sword.

I... I killed him.

Did I have to? Did I have no other choice?

"Thank you," I tell Zenevieve, panting and picking up Amon's sword. There's no time to unsheathe mine from his body.

As she remarks something that I can't hear amidst the cacophony of battle, I rise and note how far away from the edge we are. Turning, I realize that Amon has fallen in the middle of the platform.

Next to his body is a keyhole in the ground. A small, rectangular perimeter surrounds it.

I lean closer, my stare stolen. *What is this...?*

I look up to ask Zenevieve, as if she would know the answer; but she's already left to assist Sierra in a close call with Luciana's knight. Ezra is still engaged with Luciana, and that's when I urgently glance around for Emberly: she's shooting her last arrow at Amon's mage toward the edge of the platform. He grabs his sword in the time Emberly needs to switch weapons.

My feet sprint to her. I land between her and the mage, bring up Amon's sword, and block his swing. "Your prince is out of the race!" I shout, parrying another attack. "Do you really want to serve Luciana for the rest of your life?"

He glimpses Amon's impaled body. I push him back at his weakened resolve, tripping him with my foot.

I only manage one step when Emberly snaps, "I had him, you arrogant prat, I don't need you to fight my battles for me!"

"Normal people usually settle for 'thank you'!" I reply, turning around to face her. I wipe the sweat from my forehead and into my hair. "You should try it sometime!"

I almost curse the words, but a significant part of me is defensive over how she never confided in anyone to help her carry such a burden of a secret—not even Zenevieve. I now know exactly the weight she was carrying on Magery's stage. She's caused so much suffering for herself because she won't allow herself to—

Her eyes fall behind me and widen. Before I can turn around, someone flings me out of the way. I whirl when I find my balance, finding Sierra in my spot. She slashes at Amon's mage, locking swords with him until she manages to kick him back.

I run to his side, holding the sword high above his body. "You don't have to kill!" I exclaim, my breath almost beyond my control. "Fight *with* us instead of—"

"*Death to Seavale!*" he snarls, reaching for a dagger behind him. The second I see the blade glint in the sunlight, my hope plunges with Amon's sword into his heart and through his body.

Why? I ask myself in hollow thought. *Why do they want to kill? Why don't they want us to spare them, why are they making me do this?*

"You two!" Sierra snaps, pointing her bloodied sword at me. Emberly has already engaged in a battle with Luciana's mage. "Stop bickering like your kingdoms depend on it, because they do, and grow up!"

My eyes widen at Sierra's right arm. Her sleeve and gauntlet have been ripped off, and blood is streaming down her light skin like rain droplets against a window.

"Are you all right—?"

"Get back in and *fight!*" she exclaims, sprinting past me.

I turn around. My gaze snags on Luciana with her bow. She has an obsidian arrow pointed straight at Emberly as Emberly continues fighting Luciana's mage. His green robes sway with every spell he casts to defend himself against her sword. His back is to me while her back faces Luciana's sinister grin and arrow.

"EMBERLY!"

My feet pound against the hard floor. The mage turns his head to me as Emberly meets my eyes. Luciana's bowstring twangs. The arrow shoots through the air. My hands reach out, shoving Emberly away and into the glass dome. I take her place as a sharp, searing pang sinks into the left side my chest.

CHAPTER

"WITH ALL THAT I AM"

Emberly

"NO!" I SCREAM AS LEO FALLS TO HIS KNEES. AN ARrow pierces us in the same instant—except his is real.

It happened again. It happened again, all because of—!

I catch Luciana's eyes. In a blink, the resentment I've internalised for the last thirteen years shatters its own chains.

No. Vineah. You will pay for everything you've ever cursed me with!

I run to Leo's side. He gasps desperately, warning me to stay away. The sword he was wielding lies beside him. With a glance back up, I duck and roll into the glass dome just before Luciana shoots another arrow. It lands next to my sword, the obsidian arrowhead chipping on the ground.

How hard is this—?

Wait. Obsidian. Luciana shot Leo with an obsidian arrow.

I throw down my bow and quiver. My right hand takes my sword, Leo's in my left.

You will pay for EVERYTHING you've done to me and the ones I love.

The fact resonates in my bones: this is the day I avenge my parents.

My gaze locks on Luciana's wicked green eyes. She draws back another arrow. Sweat rolls down my face as I swat it away and then another, tracking the trajectory as she shoots. It's my left hand and then right and then left when she fires a third. If only my glare could shoot its own arrows: the girl would break through the glass dome, fall over the edge, and drown in the crashing waves below.

An arrow plunges into her side from somewhere across the platform. She cries out, faltering for only a second. I don't dare look over to see who shot her as her nocked arrow flies askew. In her distraction, I run the rest of the way to her.

She stumbles as she messily draws another arrow. A scream of vengeance and long-awaited revenge tears from my throat as I bend and use Leo's sword to trip her. Mine flings the bow out of her hands.

Luciana falls on her back. She cries out again and holds up her hands, blocking the sunlight from her eyes. It exposes the sweat on her light-brown skin. Her blood drips onto the pristine, white platform. Sinister satisfaction flares in my chest. A minuscule part of me twinges.

I stand over her to block the light. I want my sister to see me. I want my image to be burned into her mind and sucked down with her into the depths of hell, where our father burns.

Amidst the sun's rays, exhaustion and heat aren't all that rack my arms and legs. It's rage. It shakes Leo's sword in my left hand as I hold the tip against Luciana's heart. Right against her heart—she doesn't have armour protecting her torso. Vineah— my sister—is finally at my mercy.

And yet, my blade never breaks past her shirt. This vile woman just killed the man who saved my life—twice—and I can't run my sword through her. I can't bring myself to avenge him. My cursed regret—my wretched guilt—still controls my hands. They've locked up and thrown away my ability to wilfully take another life under my crown.

"You never committed anything against them."

If I kill her, I will permanently defile that. I'll become something worse than my greatest insecurity: the embodiment of it.

Death isn't the answer.

Another jolt of conflict bolts through my chest. It's as if Ambrose is speaking to me straight from his grave.

"We don't want to kill each other."

Leo has believed that since the beginning—that we don't need to slaughter each other to win this. Clemency has always been his priority. He even spared Amon's mage until the last second. For all I know, he tried to spare Amon.

But this poor excuse of a princess, of even a half-sister—!

"Let all that you do be done in love."

My lips tighten in anger, furious at my hesitation that won't release me. Because Luciana is the only blood family I have in this world. And I am hers.

We are the only monarchs in history who have ever had

that.

Your actions surpass your mind. Let them surpass your mind.

My jaw trembles, furiously fighting for the words to remain locked. But Leo, Ambrose, and Meredith have reached my heart to depths immeasurable whether I like it or not. I must maintain their honour—even if that means overcoming my resentment and pride.

"You just killed a good man," I hiss, forcing steadiness into my voice. I'm already sparing her deserved revenge; my tears are the last thing I will waste on her. "He believed multiple winners of this race possible. It is only his honour extending a final act of mercy towards you now. If not for him, you would have been dead minutes ago. You have one chance to stand up and fight with us, even stand as my family; or I can strike you dead with a single blow."

"That is precisely why he didn't survive to the end," Luciana sneers in strained breaths. A malicious smirk slides across her lips. "He was foolish enough to believe something like that."

I almost don't catch her last words before her foot trips me. My body flies backwards, and I drop my sword to avoid impaling myself with it.

Luciana overcomes me, and I raise my left hand. Leo's sword slides straight through her torso as she pushes a dagger into the right side of my chest.

The blade glides through my armour and punctures my skin as an arrow flies into Luciana's head. My and her faces mimic each other's in stunned agony, lips parted and eyes wide. I dare not a single breath against the blade slicing my chest open.

"EMBERLY!" a voice shrieks in the distance.

Zenevieve.

Luciana falls over me and rolls off. Her dagger falls from its sheath in my chest. It narrowly avoids my face as it clobbers onto the platform, landing beside my head.

It wasn't—too deep. But a dagger... I know it cut more than my skin. If... if my lung was...

Am I going to die here?

My wound stretches with every excruciating breath I take. The blue sky above me provides little serenity. Luciana couldn't plunge the blade even halfway in; Leo's sword stole her strength and stunned her before the tip even met my chest. She forced it through to pierce me.

My heart... I think in tired, trembling thoughts. *Why... why didn't she strike—my left side—my heart?*

Zenevieve reaches me in the space of two death-defying breaths, pushing Luciana aside. Tears mark their shiny trails on her black skin as her hands hover over me.

"Sierra!" she screams, sliding her hand under my head as she looks somewhere behind her. "Sierra, help!"

She's the only physician we have. If only Ambrose were here. If only—

The platform is swarmed by a fuzzy silence, save for Zenevieve's wails and Sierra's breathless tears. She soon appears at the edge of my vision. Metal steps accompany her.

Leo—?

Sierra drags Luciana's body farther away. Ezra carefully sets down Leo in her place.

His eyes that match the sky are open. He smiles at me.

"Leo," I whisper tightly. Zenevieve kneels at my right side.

"Firefly," he says with the same strained breaths. "Are—are you all right?"

I open my mouth as Sierra and Ezra kneel beside him. Luciana's mage follows behind. His brown hand runs through shaggy, dark-brown hair. As though he isn't meant to be our enemy.

"It's all right," Ezra begins, acknowledging my doubt, "this is Aspen. He wants to help you both, all right?"

He fought me before Luciana shot Leo! He—!

—never released an offensive attack. It was all in defence against mine.

I force my mouth shut. If Sierra and Zenevieve aren't being cautious around him now, I've no choice but to oblige their trust no matter what my mind tells me.

"Ember." Zenevieve's voice is gripped by an unfamiliar quiver as she slides off my armour pieces for my wound to be treated. "Don't you dare do this to me after everything! Don't you dare be so cruel to me right now!"

Zenny... I'm so sorry.

I keep my eyes steady on Leo. The arrow is still stuck in his upper chest. His left side—where his heart lies. It's about as deep as his wound in Vineah. Not as deep as his own, but his heart, if it struck his heart—

Sierra's words echo in my head. *If it were obsidian...*

No. *No, don't you dare.* I'll die faster if I think about it.

"Don't"—I gasp, my breath quivering as I choke out each excruciating word—"take out the arrow—until Aspen can help."

Leo swallows in place of a chuckle. I just know he would have chuckled if he could. "The archery—master would know."

"Stop talking!" Sierra demands. A glisten shines in her

wide, green eyes as her hand fervently searches her satchel. Her bun weakly droops behind her. "You need to save your breath and energy!"

I notice the bleeding slice on her upper arm as Zenevieve and Aspen remove my shoulder pieces—yet she hurriedly takes out her waterskin, instructing Ezra to wet any clean cloth he has in his satchel. She resumes her scouring in her bag as if she hasn't even noticed her own wound.

Wait. The six of us are here right now. No weapons drawn. No worry about those that surround us. We've done it: we've defeated our enemies. Leo and I made it to the end of the race.

This is it. I've made it to the end. And I need to make things right before I go.

"Leo," I whisper, allowing every tear I've ever trapped to swarm my vision, "I want to admit it."

Zenevieve comes to sit at my head and removes my breastplate. Leo's hand gently wraps around mine. He struggles just as much between his words. "I do, too. I've—I've fallen for you, firefly. Completely. Un-regrettably." He squeezes my hand. "Wholeheartedly."

"I've fallen for you, too, lion." I swallow hard, weakly squeezing back. "With—all that I am—and would have been."

The warmth of his hand—of his heart—lowers my mind into a place of peace. And the rest of me is ready to follow.

All too late, my mind processes the warm blood pooling on the right side of my chest. It sops my shirt, sticking to my skin and threatening to roll down my chest and to my neck.

I no longer have the strength to mind it. To mind anything.

I know I've made Leo proud—my people proud. In a way,

I've even avenged my mother and adoptive father, who took his own life the day I was born so as to protect my illegitimacy. To protect the fate and honour of Snowark. Now neither of their fates were in vain. And I can rest.

I allow my mind to dedicate Leo's eyes to its final memory. Aspen's healing magic pours into my wound with an instant, cool relief against its sting and my body's sweltering heat. Now I can tighten my hand around Leo's with a few more grams of strength—because his face is paling, too. I'm leaving just as Meredith did, and he's leaving just as Ithinor did. We won't be alone when we close our eyes.

A drop of sweat rolls down my face. I smile in full, gathering my strength for one more sentence: "Looks like we'll rule our kingdom together, after all."

I shut my eyes. The shouting of my name from my friends fades into the distance. Darkness envelops me in a comforting silence.

CHAPTER 38

"STAY WITH US"

Leo

"**E**MBERLY!" I GASP AS SIERRA GRIPS THE ARROW shaft. My heart pounds harder against my chest, and I can almost feel the tip of the arrow prick it with every beat. "No, wake up—!"

"Stop moving, Leon!" Sierra snaps, her cries saturating her voice. Zenevieve's sobs curdle the air with it. "This is an *obsidian* arrowhead! You'll further tear your wound, and I can't apply the tonic until you stop bleeding!"

Her cut on her upper arm is still dripping with her own blood, yet she is focused on me. That is the same care that I have for Emberly right now.

"Aspen, please—you're the only one who can save her!" I choke out, shaking Emberly's hand that has gone limp in mine. Her eyes stay peacefully shut, and there hasn't been a day that's passed that I've seen her so serene. And I want to shatter it if it means that she stays with me.

It's all right to be selfish this time. I will not let you die!

"I'll g—give her everything I h—have," Aspen replies in a shaky voice. The waves of his green magic intensify in his brown hands.

"I... I never wanted th—this." He speaks quickly despite his stutter and exhaustion. "All this bloodshed. Lu—Luciana would kill me like—like she did with Vera if I didn't prove my loyalty b—by running. Then I saw you all f—fighting for one another instead of against. I made m—my own choice of which side I wanted to be on. It's why I helped you k—kill Zax while you were busy with Ceres." His eyes meet Zenevieve's, which are red and overrun by her ceaseless tears. The waves of his magic flicker, and he immediately focuses on them again. "I'm glad."

"We're grateful for your help," Sierra replies sincerely. "Thank you for taking care of her while I tend to Leo."

She instructs Ezra on what to do for when she takes out the arrow. My heartbeat echoes all throughout my head. Before I can open my mouth and ask about Emberly, a searing, hard substance burns the edges of my wound as it slides out. I cry out, my hand squeezing Emberly's.

At least she can't feel it, because holy—!

"Stay calm," Sierra says, pressing a damp cloth to my chest. "You just need to hold on until Aspen can stabilize—"

She looks at him as if to verify. He doesn't look back. Instead, his gaze is frozen on Emberly. Sweat drips down his pale face as his magic grows sheerer.

"What is it?" Zenevieve demands to know.

He only swallows. My heart misses a beat as Ezra begins stripping my armor. I can't breathe through the block in my throat, and the rest of my mind has been rendered numb.

"I want to know what's wrong!" Zenevieve cries, reaching for Aspen until Sierra sharply scolds her.

"The only chance he has at saving her is if you let him concentrate his energy to where it's needed!" Tears are on the verge of my best friend's voice again as she and Ezra hurriedly pull up my gambeson. An unfamiliar, haunting anger hardens her words.

I suppress my every breath. *This isn't happening. Not to her, not to us.*

I force myself to look at Aspen. Sweat rolls down his face, and his lips are paling. Terror surges through my veins that his magic is costing him more than he can afford. My mind taunts me with the knowledge of it.

"Don't you dare!" Zenevieve exclaims, bringing Emberly's head into her lap. "You can't do this to me, I won't lose another sister, too!"

It can't end this way, I won't accept that! It can't be over for her!

Don't let her die, please. Please don't let her go. I know I'll survive this—but what good is it if the only place I can find her is her grave?

Sierra presses a cold cloth firmly against my chest. I squeeze my eyes shut—but not because of the burning agony under the cloth. Tears race down my face and drop onto the platform. Down my jaw and neck they stream, saturating my lashes and leaving behind cold trails of water and salt. My skin never has time to dry before more replace the old ones. I can't even recall the last time I felt tears on my face.

Aspen's green waves disintegrate, evaporating into the air.

He slumps over with fluttering eyes, and Zenevieve barely manages to catch him.

"Aspen!" Sierra cries, standing and darting to his other side. Ezra immediately takes the cloth and presses for her. "No, stay with us!"

I look beside me at an unconscious Emberly. She's deathly pale. Her hand is still limp in mine. I desperately squeeze it as if it'll wake her up.

No, don't, I whisper in my mind. *Please, please, don't. I was so close. We were so close.*

"Is she still alive?" Zenevieve cries. "Is she still alive, please!"

Aspen doesn't respond. His eyes are closed and body limp in Sierra's hold.

My heart pounds harder with every word that beats in my head: *He gave too much. He gave too much, he gave it all away.* We don't even know whether it was in vain.

"No," I whisper under my breath. "P—please..."

Zenevieve repeats the same cries to Emberly. Sierra reaches out to Emberly's wound with one hand.

"It's—it's closed," she says. She puts a hand under her nose, then conducting the same with Aspen. "They're both still breathing. But..."

When she looks up at the three of us, worry glazes over her eyes. A hard swallow passes in her throat. I shake my head.

No, I repeat a thousand times. Emberly's form blurs in my vision. My thumb rubs her fingers. Even unconscious, she has managed to steal everyone's eyes right now.

My wound throbs and burns as I helplessly stare. All I can do is stare. If I sit up, if I bring my face close to hers like I want to do, my wound will rip open and pour out my blood past repair. A dangerously large part of me doesn't care. I want to bow low to Emberly's face, to hold it in my hand again. Her freckles dot her cheeks and nose like the fireflies of the Magery forest. Like the stars on a clear night of sailing in Seavale. I want to kiss each one, embrace her if it means giving her every ounce of my life that she needs right now to survive this.

Please. Stay with us.

"Please, firefly..." I squeeze her hand one more time.

I remember that Sierra took a few minutes to wake up from her sword wound after being healed on Windale's stage. That is the only hope I have right now, it is all I have right now.

One minute passes. Aspen and Emberly never stir. The four of us hold our breaths as the seconds mercilessly continue. I anxiously await Emberly's eyes to flutter open, for her first gasp of life, for her to awaken.

She doesn't.

CHAPTER

Emberly

A VIVID TAPESTRY WOVEN BY MY MIND SWIRLS TOgether in my vision. Echoes of stone and its emitting cold wrap around me. My feet stand on solid ground. I reach out my hands. They land on the textured rock of a windowsill. Cold air nips the skin of my cheeks as I step forward. A whiteand-silver kingdom fades into view: Snowark.

Snow-topped, stone houses and buildings sit in the peaceful cold. Cobblestone paths cross through the kingdom in a grid pattern. Lanterns sit on every corner, unlit amidst the daylight.

The weight of a crown rests upon my head. It is a crown I have yet to wear; the princess's tiara is half this weight and doesn't wrap all the way around the head.

I raise my hands and press my fingers against the cold, ornate metal. I do not remove it. I can't. It sits too heavily upon my head. Doubt whirls in my chest, burning with insecurity.

I stand before you, unable to shoulder even the symbol of your majesty and power. An illegitimate bearing your honour. Yet you rest it on me nonetheless.

A breeze whispers through the window of the stone tower. It carries with it soothing voices of my memories. Zenevieve's teases, Meredith's wisdom, Ambrose's joy, Ezra's courage, Sierra's determination, Leo's love. Encouraging voices, laughing voices, strong voices that reflect the ruler I've always sought from myself if I could ever convince myself to fill those shoes.

"Your mind lies. Your actions surpass it."

"Had it not been for you, Snowark wouldn't exist."

"Teach me. To fight that voice, to rule like you. We need you."

"You were chosen."

I turn my head. Zenevieve now stands beside me in her silver armour. Her full lips are curved in a strong smile, black eyes radiating pride.

"You were chosen," she says again, "and now you are called."

How...? After everything I've failed in? Even keeping my own teammates—myself—alive?

I turn to her, ready to protest; but the tower around me swirls into a brighter, vibrant scene: a marketplace in the square. The villagers and subjects of Snowark surround me on the wide, cobblestone street, clapping and cheering. My name is repeated by a thousand voices. The cold has fallen to a tepid air. Snowark's flag, boasting its silver emblem on an indigo backdrop, hangs proudly from stone windowsills down the street. It reminds me of what has been built by generations before me—and what awaits my influence next.

All of this. How could they ever entrust me with all of this? They deserve a worthier leader—

The crowd in front of me parts down the middle. Leo emerges in his princely, dark-cyan–blue uniform. The golden crest of Seavale is patched on the left side of his chest. Golden epaulets broaden his chest. His eyes swim with an adoration and a love that transcend my words and belief. He takes my hand into his. The doubt I had in the icy tower threatens to sizzle away at his warm touch.

"You've earned your place, My Queen," he says, his thumb rubbing the top of my hand. "I would be honoured if you took it beside me."

My heart thrums with an anxiety that feels... abandoned by my previous fears. Each one is desperately trying to uphold its marble wall, terrified of taking the leap—of falling into the same trap again.

I open my mouth to protest again—until a familiar, tender hand rests on my left shoulder.

I turn my head: Meredith.

My heart leaps at the sight of her elegant, dark-brown bun and motherly smile. Another hand lands on my right shoulder. I turn my head: Ambrose, red curls and freckled face and all, beams with a familiar, child-like grin. The warmth of life itself emanates from their fingers as they both squeeze my shoulders. I have no place to hide my tears as I glance between them both, my hand shaking in Leo's.

"You can still overcome your mind," Meredith tells me in her traditionally soft voice. "It is never too late to act in love."

My mind stills. *Love towards all.* Including myself.

"Be the leader I always saw in you," Ambrose chimes, turning my attention to him. That familiar smile embraces my heart yet again. "She's always been in there, you know."

A gentle thumb reaches out and brushes a tear from my cheek. I look forward, back at Leo. A golden king's crown now sits atop his head. His grins warmly emanates a love that transcends my insecurity—because it's a love I never thought I would live or ever deserve to see. A love that assures me that I can do this.

None of them... None of them would ever lie to me.

Does that mean it's safe to believe them?

I step forward. Meredith and Ambrose release their hold. Upon my foot landing on the cobblestone, the street spirals together in the middle. Black swarms the world around me; yet my steps remain secure on an invisible, solid ground.

My vision fades to my reflection in an elegant, silver, full-length mirror. In her left hand rests a matching orb ornately designed with swirling Snowarkan carvings. In her right is a similar sceptre, a sapphire crowning its head. An indigo royal cape rests on her shoulders. It is lined with the white fur of the Snowarkan foxes. I've wanted to outlaw poaching them for such frivolous, selfish purposes since Meredith told me years ago that they became endangered just before I was born.

A silver crown adorns my reflection's head, decorated in sapphires, diamonds, and tanzanite. Queen Emberly stares back with power and resolution. Her muted-green eyes are unyielding in her determination and protection. Dignity despite the circumstances of her birth.

Forced to face her in full now, I see the difference that separates us. Why I am not the ruler in this mirror yet: I am a woman under the weight of her mind, but she is a woman under the freedom of her heart. And that is because she understands something about my birth right that I never have. Staring at me now in all that I could be, she is trying to show it to me: it is not a burden. If anything, all the more because of our origin, we bear the essence of a new chance. We hold the future in our hands, and we may mould it according to the righteous sovereignty we desire to uphold.

I am not a burden; I am an opportunity. A fiery beginning: Emberly Genesis.

Just as my parents promised me.

"You are only what you make yourself to be," she tells me—in the most authentic regality I've ever heard from myself. She holds out the orb and sceptre to me, her head held high. "Will you unlock me next?"

The key. I have the key. The woman in front of me is locked away and always has been, but I finally have the key.

This is who I've fought to be.

When I reach into the mirror, there is no glass to bar me. I take the orb and sceptre from my reflection into my own hands. I expect their weight, but they're as light as a key. Queen Emberly brings her hands to rest in front of her. Her lips beam with pride.

"As you desired," she says, the edges of my vision fading into a bright, white light, "so you've become."

White soaks the darkness, seeping into the mirror and absorbing its surface. The mouth of a portal beams open in the silver frame. A strong force—like the force of life itself—pulls me forward, away from the dark. With the orb and sceptre in my hands and my own head held high, I step into the light of the portal.

CHAPTER 40

"THE LAST KEY"

Leo

"**S**HE'S STIRRING!" SIERRA CRIES, SITTING ON EMberly's other side. Ezra jolts up from his spot next to her.

I knew it! my helpless excitement exclaims, watching Emberly's eyes flutter open. Zenevieve's cries instantly cease. *Come back, firefly, come back.*

Those Emberly-green eyes fully open, glimmering in the sunlight. Five voices chime together, encouraging her to awake, even Aspen, as exhausted as he is. Emberly gives a hushed moan as she slowly sits up, holding her head. I throw my arms around her armored-again torso, embracing her with my strength that's still rebuilding itself.

She yelps as a sting jolts through my own wound, and I realize my mistake.

"Forgive me!" I release her but hold her shoulders, catching my breath. "Are you all right? Did I reopen it?"

"It's fine, just—sore," she whispers. After a moment of recovery, she exhales, her eyes falling to the scabbing arrow wound on my chest exposed by my torn shirt. Her fingers graze the skin just below it. "Leo..."

With one look up at me, her arms wrap around me and she buries her face into my neck. Surprise and joy prickle my skin, warmth seeping across my chest as I embrace her.

The second she pulls away and looks up at me, I lean down. She already has the same idea, cupping my face and pressing her lips against mine.

No part of me regards our friends as I close my eyes and wrap my arms all the way around her. After Aspen regained consciousness, my hope was reignited for her even though there was nothing left to do about her wound, internally and externally. While he and Sierra worked together to close my arrow wound, hope was all I had left to hold on to.

Now I don't need hope because I feel Emberly's lips against mine. Even her kiss is a reflection of everything I adore about her and crave more of: her ferocity yet tenderness, her assertiveness yet fragility—how she melts into my hold yet stays firm in her own right. I take her lips into mine, and it instills in me my desire to show her how she is everything I want in my queen—every part of her, good and bad.

She breaks away, looking up at me. The wet trails on my neck grow colder as she asks, "Have you been *crying?*"

I breathily laugh, holding the sides of her face. "You've broken every last wall I ever built, firefly. And you broke my heart just now when you almost left us."

She narrows her sharp eyes. "As if I may help that I'm irresistible to even death!"

My grip on her face tightens, and I lean in close. "Never do that to me again. Ever."

She slaps my arm, wincing in pain. "You started it! Had you never sacrificed yourself like the arrogant prat you are—"

"Even when they flirt, they can't stop bickering," Ezra notes disappointedly, sitting on Sierra's other side. He shakes his head as she gives him an excited peck on the cheek, holding a tonic-doused cloth to her arm.

Emberly glares at him just as Zenevieve attacks her from behind. Her short, curly hair falls against the sides of Emberly's face; and Emberly sinks into her hold.

"I'm with Leo on this one," Zenevieve says in a tear-soaked voice. "Never do that again."

"He started—!"

Her grip tightens around Emberly, her smile widening. "Don't care."

"How is your wound, Emberly?" Sierra asks. She gestures to Aspen, next to me. "Aspen managed to close it, but how do you feel?"

"It's all right," she replies, nodding. "Sore, but—I'm not dying." She emptily chuckles, yet her grin beams. "I'm... I'm not dying."

Our stares fall onto Aspen, whose shoulders are still slumped with exhaustion. His brown face is slowly but surely regaining its color, drenched in sweat after everything he poured into Emberly—and a little into me to ensure my wound wouldn't reopen. Despite his deep breaths, his hands are balled into fists; and he stares back at both of us with a timid joy.

"You did it," Sierra tells him, wiping a stray tear from her cheek. She looks at Emberly. "He almost gave his own life in the process and passed out from exhaustion, but he was determined to come through for you both."

Emberly's brows furrow and lips purse, a "wh" sound escaping them. Then, she closes her mouth, a foreign shyness overcoming her features.

Zenevieve squeezes one of Aspen's hands, one arm still choking Emberly. "Thank you. I can never say that enough. You saved my sister."

He nods feebly, but Emberly's gaze hasn't left him.

"You saved my life," she says. "I was going to ask why you would sacrifice so much just for our sakes. But I'd rather you know that no amount of thanks will ever suffice. My gratitude is extended to you in full and more."

I've never heard her speak with such humility. An admiring pride swells in my chest, one that entices me to kiss her again.

"I've never encountered such... a strong mage before," I tell him, rubbing Emberly's hand with my thumb. I'm not even sure that Ithinor would have been able to manage what Aspen did.

"Lu—Luciana always believed that she would—would run the race," Aspen replies diffidently, fiddling with his fingers in his lap, "so she forced me to strengthen my s—stamina for a few years. But I believe in—what you all do. What you want. And I had to a—apologize for Luciana. The things she said..."

A terrible thickness swells in the air, one that emphasizes the pulse still thrumming under my closed cut. That same silence that forces us to remember. This time is all the worse because only one person is allowed to determine how we should interpret it, and she has yet to speak.

Instead, Emberly's eyes fall to the scuffed platform. I'm ready to comfort her when she raises her head. "I've accepted my origin, I'll have you lot know," she says, exchanging her attention equally with us. "No matter what the brat said, I am and always have been the Princess of Snowark."

"Why did you never tell me?" Zenevieve speaks with an unfamiliar softness. "Judgment was eradicated between us the day you learned of my childhood."

"It wasn't exactly something I wanted to remember," Emberly replies simply. "I suppose enough of me was convinced that if I managed to forget it—it'd no longer be true."

Too big a part of me understands that reasoning. My heart doesn't know if it should reach further out to her or continue letting her stand on her own two feet right now. She doesn't need anyone to hold her hand, but I still want to be her support.

"Did anyone know?" Zenevieve asks.

Emberly stills as if she is all too mindful of her injury. She struggles with the words before she finally says, "Meredith."

The twinge in my heart becomes a stumble: another piece has fallen into place. Now I know the true weight of Meredith's loss.

Emberly's gaze avoids us, kept with my hand in hers. "I was ten," she begins, "in the library for lessons. Meredith already knew of my distaste for Vineah after what happened in the forest,"—she glimpses Zenevieve behind her—"but I suppose the council's derogatory rejections of my rule had begun to break me by then. It had already been a particularly unideal day. After Meredith kept insisting that we study Vinean history despite my relentless resistance, my temper blurted the truth for me." Her exhale is shallow. She squeezes my hand. "Meredith being Meredith—her first instinct was to console me. Hearing how heavy of a curse it was for me to bear... that was the day she promised to help me become better than my origin."

Help to become better... Just as Ithinor promised me.

"Ember..." Zenevieve whispers. "I suppose I'm grateful that you didn't bear that alone for your entire life. If only I could thank Meredith personally."

My resolve keeps my words firm. "Well, now you're alive to rub Whiny Winston's face in it. You survived."

Emberly smiles. It's a beautiful, soft smile that lights up the rest of her face, even as she shakes her head. "I don't know how you lot did it."

"Especially since we had to tend to Leo's wound as well." Mischievous sarcasm laces Zenevieve's words. "So you were both foolish enough to sacrifice yourselves for each other."

Something like recognition and remembrance seems to ignite in Emberly, and she faces me. "You took an arrow for me."

I cup her face. "You avenged me."

The longer I stare into her eyes, the more I see flashes of everything we've endured to arrive here. The more I remember all the times those eyes stared at me with hatred, contempt, anger—devastation. Determination to make it through, to make things right. I remember everything we did—everything we had to do—every sacrifice we've made to sit right where we are. The lives we had to take. The lives we had to lose.

Yet nothing awaits us at the end.

The silence between us grows louder. It's... chilling. The waves continue lapping below the platform, but that is the only sound we're allowed. It's all the easier for my mind to reel in every memory, every second, of the last two weeks. And I don't believe for a moment that my friends are exempt from that. Even Aspen, serving such a wicked princess the entire time.

I drop my hand from Emberly's face, leaning back in my spot. "We did it." The words are empty, bereft of joy. They're merely truth, inarguable fact. I can't find the celebration I was so certain in the beginning would accompany them.

"We did," Sierra echoes softly, bringing down the cloth from her arm. I almost want to say that she's trying to convince herself of the words, and I can't fault her if she doesn't believe them. If anything, *I'm* afraid to believe them.

We've endured too much—have believed in so much—for it to all end so suddenly.

I glance around at my friends. They stare back at me and each other. I think Aspen receives the heaviest eyes out of the six of us.

"Is it really over...?" Zenevieve asks behind Emberly. "Just like that?"

"It can't be," Ezra replies. "I don't—I don't know. Every last kingdom was eliminated except—"

Emberly and I face each other. That's it. There are two king-doms left standing, and nothing has progressed yet. Which means...

"No." The word is firm on her lips. "We haven't endured all that we have to get here only to throw it all away by slaughtering each other! We'll unlock the Blasted Kingdom another way, even if I have to strangle the Mages myself—!"

"Emberly." Sierra and Zenevieve scold her, but I'm not sure that they entirely disagree with her; I certainly don't.

"What have we done all this for?" Emberly snaps. "We've lost and murdered and run and suffered, where is the prize we were promised after being *forced* to participate in this? What have we run around collecting a bunch of keys for if our ultimate objective was to kill?"

"Wait." The word falls from my mouth without my control, the realization mimicking it. "The keys. We forgot about the keys, that's why this isn't over yet. You're right, there must be a greater purpose to all of this. We wouldn't have needed to collect the keys otherwise."

Ezra hands me my satchel. I tentatively open it, my eyes widening at the glow: the bronze keys are *glowing*. A high-pitched, glimmering ring radiates from their shine. I reach in and grab Seavale's key. Upon my touch, the glow explodes into glittering dust. In its wake is a gleaming, silver key.

When Sierra gives Emberly her satchel, Emberly brings out Snowark's key—which turns silver in her hold as well.

Her brows furrow together. "Am I the only one who sees silver?"

"No," Zenevieve says in astonishment, reaching out a careful hand like the key will burn her if she touches it. "Do they all do that?"

We quickly establish an agreement: I take Windale's and Vineah's; and Emberly takes Lavara's, Soilera's, and Magery's. We both have copies of Seavale's, Snowark's, Windale's, and

Lavara's—the remaining of which disintegrate into a bronze dust in our satchels. That leaves us with only the seven keys we've selected, all silver and glowing in my and Emberly's hold now.

A word is engraved at the bottom of every head: "endurance" on Lavara's, "sacrifice" on Soilera's, "tenacity" on Windale's, "patience" on Vineah's, "bravery" on Seavale's, "vigilance" on Snowark's, and "humanity" on Magery's.

"A—are these..." Aspen begins timidly beside Zenevieve, "the Last Keys?"

"No," I muse, rubbing the teeth of Seavale's key. "There's only meant to be one. One for—"

I pause. The keyhole in the middle of the platform. That has to be for the Last Key, which means...

"Leo?" Sierra asks.

I look up at her and then back down. The keys are still glowing even amidst the sunlight. Why would they glow if...?

Collect all seven keys, and you will form the Last Key.

If these were formed by us touching them... if we collect all seven together, would that form—?

"I have an idea," I say, bringing Seavale's key closer to Snowark's. Just as I hoped, both glow even brighter, their shing resonating louder.

"That's it," Emberly says. She and I push all seven together. A vibrant, white glow ignites over them; but when it fades, they've fused together into one golden key.

"The Last Key." The word is a whisper on Zenevieve's lips.

Its gold glistens with an almost intimidating elegance, the ornate head mimicking the others exactly. There only lies a simple circle in the center, and its shaft is smooth without a knob to interrupt it.

Despite its beauty... part of me almost fears it.

"I know where this goes." I look at Emberly. "But if I'm right..."

She exhales. "I've wanted to end this race since it began."

I have, too. Especially if it proves that I don't have to kill my friends, after all. The longer we stay here, the longer we're trapped in a nightmare that rivals even all those years I spent under the castle.

I take the Last Key, reach out my hand, and help Emberly stand. She and I grunt with the pang of our injuries, but the keyhole in the middle of the platform is at the front of my mind. It's almost as though it has a pull of its own.

My gaze lands on Amon's body right next to it. It still lies with my sword through him, its bloodied tip facing the sky. Luciana's knight lies beyond him toward the edge. I know Amon's mage and Luciana remain somewhere behind me, but I can't bring myself to look.

We rid the world of entire kingdoms.

Emberly's fingers intertwine with mine, pulling my eyes down to hers. "It was self-defense," she whispers. "You committed no evil against him—any of them."

I tighten my lips. Then, I bend down and press a soft kiss to her head.

She walks to Amon's body and drags him by the arms away from the keyhole. Then she unsheathes my sword from him, wiping his blood on his black-plated armor. I almost see the girl who did the same thing on Vineah's stage after Ithinor and Meredith were killed—but the woman in front of me is different. Better.

Grown. She stands with a new purpose, a new fire—one she shares with me.

She returns, hands me my sword, and then allows me to sheathe it before kneeling with me. Together, we lower the key.

"Are you ready?" she whispers.

I nod. "I am now."

We turn it together, and a click echoes under us.

Veins of white magic travel across the glass dome over us, emanating brighter until the dome shatters into a thousand crystalline shards. They cascade into the ocean below, their shimmering lights dancing all around us as they fall. A whirlwind of magic erupts from the keyhole, the seven colors of the kingdoms swirling around in patterns as they travel throughout the air.

This is it. *This is really it*—

The white floor shifts. Gray veins of vibrant marble snake across its expanse, crackling into place. The now marble floor rises into the air, the swirls of magic surging through the sides to form towering walls. My jaw falls open as elegant archways, grand columns, and majestic corridors are formed amidst shimmering waves. Carvings and embellishments adorn the walls and corridors forming, my curiosity begging my feet to move.

Magic is building an entire—!

"Look!" Zenevieve shouts across the rising, creaking palace towering on all sides. She points at the open front doors on our left side just in time: the brightness of the blue sky begins to fade as an artistic ceiling climbs over us, forming a dome.

Ezra grabs Emberly's bow on the ground and I grab mine before we spring to the doors. I almost stop in shock as we run down the smooth and newly laid steps of the rising palace. They're forming too quickly for us to match its pace, and my mind is almost convinced that my foot will fall straight through each one. A crème, cobblestone path is already stretching out even farther when we reach the bottom of the monumental staircase.

My mind whirls as the world in front of me does. I've just about convinced myself that I'm dreaming as potted bushes glimmer into existence every few feet down the path we stand on. A large, majestic fountain bursts to life on the platform we ran down from, translucent water erupting from the middle column and winking in the sunlight.

Wow... Even the water seems alive, glimmering and flowing in such a hypnotic way that entices me to touch it as it did when I was a little boy.

Hesitation yet wonder burn in my chest as Emberly's eyes meet mine. The same thoughts seem to be running rampant in her mind: we've done it. We've unlocked the Last Kingdom.

And we didn't have to kill each other.

We never did.

Stunned, I walk back up the steps with our friends. Gardens embrace the front of the marble palace. Trimmed hedges and lively blooms offer an entire symphony of nature as we approach the top of the staircase. The palace itself stands three stories tall. It's intimidating if nothing else, a palace so large looming over and awaiting its rulers and staff. I can't prevent my mind from remembering how its throne sits for the victor of the Last Kingdom's race—one of which is me.

The world in front of me feels like a hallucination—even a lie my mind has conjured.

I arrive on the top step just as the seven swirls of magic land at the front doors. The six of us walk around the fountain, their figures fully forming: the seven Ancient Mages.

Anger surges through my veins. Opportunity knocks a hundred doors in my head, and I worry that I won't remember every one of them. Answers, vengeance, and even closure reside in these sheer projections of the Mages—and I will take it from them before they disappear this time.

Evidently, Emberly is thinking along the same lines; she takes a firm step forward, but I reach out and take her hand to stop her. Patience is all we have right now, especially if we're to receive answers. With one glance at me, she seems to understand and then steps back.

"Princess Emberly Genesis Whitaker of Snowark and Prince Leon Atlas Wales of Seavale," Vineah's green Mage announces in an ethereal voice, standing in the middle. She raises her arms and motions inside the palace. "We humbly invite you and your friends inside."

Emberly and I lock our stares with each other's again. Our friends wait for our lead.

My hand tightens around hers and hers around mine. The Mages turn and file into the wide double doors. Emberly and I follow suit with our friends, walking inside the palace.

CHAPTER 41

"VICTIMS OF THE WICKED AND UNLAWFUL"

Emberly

REGRETTABLY, EVEN AWE FLOODS INTO MY CHEST. The vastness of the foyer greets us as we step through the doors. Polished, marble floors stretch out like an ocean of pristine, grey-veined white. I quickly realise how the four dead bodies previously on the platform have vanished as if into thin air.

So magic does rid all impurities.

The sheer, colourful Mages' steps are soundless as they guide us into the palace, unlike our clamouring sabatons. Ezra still holds my bow and Leo his on their backs as we walk down the opulent hallway. Aspen timidly walks between Sierra and Zenevieve. The hallway seems to split the palace down the middle. Delicate crystal chandeliers suspended from the high ceiling hold seven candles each. Golden moulding crowns the empty walls. But I will not allow myself to appreciate any part of the creation from the seven puppeteers of death in front of us.

They guide us to a grandiose, imperial staircase at the end of the hallway. A dark, royal-blue carpet runner runs down the steps without a wrinkle in sight. A strip of gold lines each side.

Ironic how Snowark detests gold. And I'm fairly certain that this is where the Last Kingdom rulers are to reside.

I'm enticed to trace my fingers along the intricately carved, golden handrail as I climb the stairs. Even the banister is marble, ornately woven in patterns that sweep and swirl all the way up.

Arriving at the landing, a set of golden double doors stands metres away from the top of the stairs. I'm afraid the throne room lies behind them; where else would the Ancient Mages take the monarchs? We're certainly not travelling either hallway that stretches down beside us on both sides.

Lavara's red Mage and Magery's violet Mage push the doors open and allow the space to unfold into view. Tall thrones sit on a royal-blue platform at the back of the room. A matching carpet runner splits the room in half and streams all the way down to them.

"This is three times larger than Snowark's throne room." Zenevieve's words are unfamiliarly light and airy. Her eyes trace every detail carved in the walls and floor. "And you lot are privileged to sit under the sky itself."

I follow her gaze up. A vaulted ceiling reaches for the sky. Magnificently engraved depictions of allegories of strength and honour—like lions amidst fire—adorn it. Sunlight beams down through the glass dome atop with golden window grids uniting the panes.

My stare trickles down to the thrones. The Mages approach them. The high, velvet backrests rise to Ezra's sitting height. Most curious, though, are the banners that hang behind them: seven in total, each with the crests and palettes of the kingdoms.

The translucent Mages walk up the three steps to the platform, then turning around to face the six of us. Snowark's indigo Mage and Seavale's cyan Mage step to the edge.

"Princess Emberly and Prince Leon," Snowark begins in a regal voice I almost envy, "you have proven yourselves as true rulers by heart, not only by title, and stepped into your place as the sovereigns of the Last Kingdom."

Seavale gestures to us, then to himself, and then to Snowark. "You have honourably represented both Seavale and Snowark in the race to break the death curse. For that, the seven kingdoms thank you."

I step forward, ready to accept more than a pathetic thank-you. "Representation?" I sneer. "Is that what this was all for? To prove which kingdom was 'better'? And the audacity to *thank* us!"

"Ember," Zenevieve whispers behind me, driving me forward again. The harshness of my step, of even my resolve, tugs on my freshly healed wound. A sting zaps me, but fury is pouring over me. In truth, I'm ready to tackle the figures in front of me— if only they weren't already dead.

I plant my feet firmly in the carpet. "Being the ones who conjured the curse to begin with, who constructed the entire race, surely you understand its cruelty! Or perhaps you don't care since you had the capacity to build it to begin with! Do you know what we've lost to stand here right now? Are you aware that twenty-two people were sacrificed for your sick game? Our friends sacrificed themselves solely for us to survive! All for what? To see who was *the best?*"

Snowark speaks calmly with fluid, gentle gestures. "There is something you don't understand, Your Highness. When war broke out among the seven kingdoms, we knew the world would fall far from the balance it was founded on. We conjured the death curse to allow each heir to grow in their own ideas from their individual observations of their kingdom—rather than their parents pushing forth an agenda that would further divide and conquer. This would all be until the generation to unlock the Last Kingdom arose, for such a ruler able to unlock it would inherently prove that they possess the qualities and heart of a leader—not just a monarch."

"Is that your excuse?" I hiss. The arguments swirl in my mind. It desires for a memory of my parents to fire against their pathetic attempt at justification, anything more than the portrait that hangs in the Monarch's Hall of Snowark's palace. And simply because my mind has no such memory, it feeds my anger hot coals. "How much crueller should that be! Why were Leo and I 'chosen'? Why did that give grounds to sentence the others to death simply because they weren't born as the true rulers?"

Lavara steps forward in a calm demeanour. His gravelly voice replies, "My dear, neither of you were chosen for this role. It was you who chose to fit it when you were called."

I open my mouth, scouring for the right words. Padded footsteps whisper behind me, and Leo appears at my side. He scrutinises the Mages with scepticism. "The generations before us sacrificed their lives for the sake of bringing forth the next heir, all so that their kingdoms wouldn't fall. Why were none of them given the opportunity to run in the race?"

Yes! Exactly that!

Seavale speaks, keeping his hands folded in front of him. "The Last Kingdom was created by a pure magic. When darkness and malice threaten to consume goodness, it fights back. As darkness began to consume the world, anarchy and treachery loomed closer and threatened the good; and the seed of the Last Kingdom sensed it. It was created to blossom at just the right time. While the Kingdom didn't know who the final rulers would be, it knew when to call them forward. You two simply embraced your call."

"Why not the others?" Leo asks solemnly. "Did we ever have to kill them?"

Seavale bows his head. "Murder was never part of fulfilling this prophecy. It was added by those unfit to rule—those whose hearts were hardened by the world to the extent that upon being given the chance to accept goodness, they spat on it instead."

"Your hesitance to kill never went unrecognised, Prince Leon," Snowark adds, her voice kind as she gestures to him. "The innocence of your goodness spared you a heart darkened by murder. It even affected Princess Emberly to the extent that she offered mercy to her greatest enemy."

"You weren't supposed to hear that," I state, pointing an accusing finger.

No doubt they know of my and Luciana's true relationship. I can't help but wonder if they silently judge me for it or if they support me in my desire to forget about the entire matter. It's almost strange to have the brat's mage standing with us now—but in a way, Aspen has earned his place here for the same reason we have.

"This race was for you," Lavara says humbly. "All of you. For you to be given a chance to join together for the same great cause."

Vineah's Mage steps to the edge of the royal-blue platform. "Hence why the race allowed for multiple teams on the same stage. Strangely enough, you weren't meant to arrive at Vineah's stage simultaneously—magic was meant to send only one of you to aid Windale when it sensed that they lacked members. Nonetheless, when you did arrive, your first reaction was caution and maintaining mercy as a possibility. Windale, however, upon realizing your presence, immediately chose a dark and... costly path."

At least she speaks with sensitivity. That was a day that demanded my and Leo's strongest mental capacity.

It's a sheer miracle we never killed each other.

Soilera's orange Mage arrives on the edge next. "You possess character that the united kingdom needs," she says softly in a sweet voice. "It was your inherent disposition that brought you through the trial and the storm—precisely the rulers a united world needs to guide it."

"We desired to unify the seven sovereigns," Magery adds in a whispery tone, "but over the centuries, the notion was abandoned and soon tainted by generations who sought to be the sole victor of the race. Eventually, such was the legend that was ultimately passed down."

"And you never thought to clarify any of this?" my shaking voice asks. Urgency courses through me: a familiar pressure rests heavily against my eyes. I don't know if I possess the strength to control my composure when my entire life's worth of resentment and regret finally has a place to pour itself out. "Before the race? Before I lost more people I could bear?"

"Our magic was only unlocked with the portals," Snowark replies regally—almost motherly. "We announced in the beginning that you all would be racing as uniters of the land. We weren't to interfere in the stages once the race began. At times, it was devastating to witness—but your decisions were to remain in your hands alone."

I don't want to accept it. I can't accept it.

"My parents were good people," I whisper before I can stop it. Yet again, I catch myself imagining my father—the only man worthy of that title, the King of Snowark—taking his own life right after losing his wife and gaining her illegitimate daughter he was willing to adopt. I remember again that my mother kept me out of love—both of my parents did. And they suffered at the hands of this wicked curse. "They ruled with dignity yet humility, with the purest form of love there is to offer."

"And they were victims of the wicked and unlawful." Vineah's tone offers me compassion. "As were many of this curse. They may not have met the gracious end they deserved; but we can assure you now, Your Highness, they're in a place where their suffering is no more. They share honour and peace with those alike."

They're happy. Wherever they are that I may meet them in, in death, my parents are together and happy. At peace.

And I know my biological father is where he belongs as well.

Leo swallows hard next to me in the corner of my vision. Seavale nods a confirmation to him. His parents. Leo lowers his head. A soft smile graces his lips.

"Do you know?" I dare to ask, barely affording eye contact with Vineah and Snowark.

"Yes, my dear," Snowark replies. "And you are no less because of it."

"You are no less."

My mind recalls the moment Meredith said those words to me—just before her death. A warmth spreads across my chest that I don't feel worthy of. Leo gently takes my hand and lightly squeezes it. I can only squeeze back.

Vineah folds her hands over her stomach. "Have we answered your final questions?"

"Oh!" Sierra chimes behind me, startling me. For a moment, I blatantly forgot that our friends were here. "The stages! How in the world did they reset? I spent the entirety of the race theorizing how they worked, trying to ascertain an order if one existed; yet every theory I had seemed to be disproved."

Ever the curious cat. It is only because Aspen healed me to the extent that he did that I can stand here long enough to satiate our curiosities.

Windale's yellow Mage, as if his colour doesn't radiate joy on its own, beams with an unmatchable excitement. "Yes! Each stage simply reset upon the departure of the previous team. Otherwise, whether or not the main obstacle had been unlocked yet, two teams would have merely resided on the same stage. You may think of magic as an eraser here, as the stages *were* built by such. Enchanting, isn't it?"

"The pixies being an exception, of course," I say, arching a brow. "Surely they couldn't have been the main obstacle *and* the artifact."

484

Magery nods once. "They were. Their reputation was the obstacle, meant to encourage the monarchs to protect their team. There, the pixies—serving as the artifact—would reveal the key, acknowledging that a true sovereign was present."

Ezra's tone is curious behind me. "Interesting—considering they were hesitant to approach *us*."

"Before your team," Magery replies solemnly, "every other one assaulted them. They gave each one the key in hopes of stopping their attacks."

"Luciana m—made me shoot fire at them." Shame drowns Aspen's words. I'm tempted to turn around and console him after he wasted so much time serving such an insolent brat.

Interesting... The artifacts did *have a pattern: fire to ice, water to land, sky to root. What does that make magic to—?*

Humanity. That's why that word was on Magery's—

My breath falls in realisation. My hand rises to the wound under my armour. It's stiff, my skin slightly stretching. How close that dagger was to landing in my heart if Luciana had only struck the correct side. How quick she was to decide that she wanted me dead. How quick *I* was to seek her life in the name of vengeance— until my humanity shook me by the shoulders. A true sovereign maintains humanity.

Let not your mind judge you, but your actions. Let all that you do be done in love.

Meredith's words had taken root by the time we reached Magery's stage. I finally understand in full what she meant.

My heart rises in gratitude that I felt the pixies' pull before we could attack. Simultaneously, part of me twinges in anger at the other monarchs. It twinges in grief for the pixies who were, based on their fading away at the end of the race, nothing more than illusions of magic.

Who am I?

Wait. Illusions of magic, fading away, grief for those lost...

That's simply it: "If none of us were meant to die, why create monsters to attack us?" I ask, my voice rising with every question. "Why send us through terrains with a deadly threat at every other turn? Why did Ambrose have to die just because we chose the wrong tunnel in Soilera?"

A sombre silence engulfs the Mages. They glance at one another, all seeming to ask the other who will relay their next spew of information.

Finally, Snowark folds her hands over her stomach. "The terrains and obstacles were all meant to be overcome with the right amount of thinking, coordination, and teamwork, Your Highness. The quickmud was not our doing—that was a cruel spell Princess Cassandra of Soilera ordered her mage to cast to eliminate the other participants. The left tunnel was meant to lead you to a room that would require you to surrender your weapons in exchange for a passageway that would lead you to the right room nonetheless."

There was a wall at the end! I'm about to shout. And then I remember how far away we had been from the end—I realise the chance that I wasn't able to see if the tunnel broke off on either side to a new one.

That means Ambrose was killed by Princess Cassandra. He was killed... Meredith and Ithinor were killed by—!

My teeth instinctually grind together, my fists clenching tightly at my sides as I squeeze my eyes shut. An all-too-familiar rage burns in my veins, its acid deteriorating me from the inside out.

And then, in the space of a single breath out, my fists release. My teeth separate. Memories of Ambrose and Meredith amidst moments of happiness and relief flutter through my mind. Laughter and jokes. Friendship and strength. And I realise that people like them are in the same place my parents are at.

I stare after the thrones behind the translucent rainbow of Mages. It strikes me like a large bell: those thrones are for me and Leo. The other kingdoms' banners, those are our reminders of the power within unity, no matter how imperfectly it's executed. There could have been seven thrones in this room. There could have been...

"Then seven rulers—seven thrones—would have been possible?" I dare to ask.

"In a perfect world, Your Highness, yes." Seavale sighs sorrowfully. "But if this were a perfect world, there would be no need for such a race to begin with."

"Nonetheless, here you and Prince Leon stand." A proud yet humble smile graces Snowark's indigo face. "Ready to come into and fulfil your roles as the king and queen of the Last Kingdom."

The words ring in my ears as if I haven't spent the last two weeks preparing to hear them. I realise that I haven't; instead, I've spent the last two weeks steeling myself against any and all challenges that would prevent me from reaching the end for Snowark's sake. I've hardened my resolve in the name of survival. My final goal was to live for the sake of protection and vengeance—at some points, to find a reason to live at all—not once to rule.

With one look up at Leo, it seems that he has these same thoughts pulsating in his head: his eyes are mindlessly fixed on a nonspecific point. A hard swallow passes in his throat. His finger mindlessly taps his thigh. Somehow, though, a smile starts to stretch his lips.

I turn to face him when Zenevieve attacks me from behind. "Grab a horse!" she exclaims as I gasp from the sting in my chest. I don't think she hears me over Ezra and Sierra tackling Leo. "Send word to Whiny Winston and the rat colony that Emberly Whitaker won the race, and will hereby be crowned as Queen of the Last Kingdom!"

"Zenevieve, I'd like to cordially remind you that I was stabbed today." I stiffly hold up my arms, which reminds her to release me. "Second of all, say that q-word one more time and I *will* vomit on you."

She skips over to stand in front of me. Beaming cheekily, she has the audacity to bop my nose. "Vomit all you'd like, *Your Majesty*. It doesn't change the fact that it's true!"

That's it. I'm punishing her. It's finally time to let myself vomit on—

"Is that glare because you've landed a lifetime position by my side?"

My heart skitters at Leo's voice. "By my side" is definitely at fault for that.

"That would certainly make things easier," I reply. Sierra and Ezra fall back to stand next to a shy Aspen, whose green eyes have turned curious on us. Leo steps towards me. "You've mastered one other thing, Your Highness: shattering my resolve against you."

"Consider it me returning the favour," he says, looking down at me. He takes my left hand and raises it to his lips. Tenderness swarms his gaze. "Now, let's do this properly this time." He bows, placing a soft kiss on my knuckles. "It is a privilege to meet you, Princess Emberly."

Every beat of my heart booms across my torso. I suppress a giddy, breathy chuckle, tightening my jaw. "You *will* pay for that, you royal prat."

He rises from his bow, smirking. "I'd love a demonstration as to how."

That's it.

"With pleasure." I drop my hand, and Leo catches me as my body pushes him back upon impact. Just as I take his tan face into my hands, a Mage coughs.

Our attention moves to the line of them still standing along the edge of the platform. Leo's hold on me loosens, leaving inches of space between us.

"Pardon me for being so bold, Your Highnesses," Seavale begins, tilting his head, "but would I be negligent in my observations that your hearts have found themselves intertwined with the other's?"

I've fallen in love with the prat. Just say it.

"You'd be negligent to assume otherwise," I reply instead, smiling cheekily.

Seven grins gleam back at us. Vineah raises her arms, her sheer, green robes swishing with her every motion. "Then a week from this day, so shall commence the marriage of Princess Emberly Whitaker and Prince Leon Wales, who shall be crowned thenceforth as King and Queen of the Last Kingdom!"

CHAPTER 42

"THE PRICE FOR OUR FUTURE"

Leo

OVERNIGHT, THE SEAVALE AND SNOWARK CASTLE staff are sent for in strict confidentiality. They arrive as the sun sets, and the Mages conjure a shield of magic to prevent unauthorized guests threatening to swarm the path to the palace upon the establishment of the Last Kingdom.

Three days after, amidst the wedding preparations, Emberly and I are well enough to visit our new kingdom thanks to Aspen's healing magic and Sierra's care. Gazing out the window of our carriage as it rides through the cobblestone streets provides me a strangely peaceful excitement. White clouds dot the blue sky above, and crème-brick buildings line the streets. The buildings often stand two stories, covered with stone roofs.

All built by magic. Wow.

People from all seven regions roam the kingdom. I imagine

them forming dreams and aspirations and plans to move in. They all originate from different backgrounds, different classes; yet they gather now with joy and excitement right here in one place.

The carriage comes to a careful stop at the start of a main street, and the footman opens the door. Emberly takes his hand to step out first in a scarlet-red gown, her elaborate, silver tiara winking in the sunlight. I follow her, setting my feet on solid ground and offering my arm to begin our rounds with the people. The sun offers a comfortable warmth amidst the cool air, not a breath of suffocating humidity or parched dryness for miles around as we start down the street.

Emberly would never admit it, but I think even she is nervous to start a conversation with our subjects as we walk. Which is rather unfortunate for me, considering I was depending on her assertiveness to lead us.

I'm unsure whether to regret the thought as we approach an intersection and she whispers, "Your Highness."

Her gaze sits on the shaded right corner of the intersection. There, a man and woman in linen clothing are marveling at the crème building that stands tall in front of them. Their loose style of linen, neutral-colored clothing instantly exposes them as Seavalens. I don't doubt that Emberly knows it.

Searing-hot nerves swirl in my chest. "I don't know if I'm ready."

"You never will be," she tells me. "But right now will at least tell you how to move forward."

If only she weren't right so often.

With a deep breath, I force myself to look at the couple—at the same moment they turn around and find us standing in the street. Despite the storm of fear—and, for some reason, shame—inside me, I maintain the regal smile my title requires as we approach.

The woman curtsies, the man bowing. A kind breeze blows by my face, alleviate the fire of my nerves. The man's voice carries a startling tenderness as he says, "Your Highnesses. It's an honor to meet you both."

It is? almost falls off my lips, but I cage it in time.

"Our privilege," I reply, nodding. "Really—thank you for having an audience with us. May we know your names?"

The man, as tall as I am and whose large build mimics a smaller scale of Ezra's, gestures with a tan hand to himself and then the woman. "I'm Nikos. This is Rhea, my wonderful wife. Please allow us the honor of being the first to express our gratitude and pride, Prince Leon."

My shock almost succeeds in stealing my words this time, but my curiosity quickly overcomes it. "Please, forgive me—'pride'?"

"Pride," Rhea answers in a soft-spoken voice. Her curly hair is blond, which is rare in Seavale; but it's a brilliant complement to her warm, blue eyes. She's just taller than Emberly, almost as tall as Sierra. "May I have the privilege to speak freely, Your Highness?"

Terrified my words will condemn me, I only nod.

"The Ancient Mages appeared to Seavale and relayed Your Highness's journey in the race to the kingdom. For many, it was the verification of an answered prayer that their ruler would become one worth assuming the same crown His and Her Majesties wore. Your improvement never went unrecognized among those many throughout the last few years—but another many were skeptical and hesitant to trust the prince who—forgive me, Your Highness—originally had no incentive to change. Let alone in a race with no favor for him, all in the name of a kingdom he seemingly cared little about."

She reaches out her light hand before retracting. I quickly reach out my own to grant her my permission.

A tender smile touches her lips, and she accepts. "Your journey has redeemed you, Your Highness. Long before the race, but now your heart has exposed your true character in full. We're proud—honored—that we should have a prince who cares for us so deeply and with such loyalty."

I swallow a hard lump in my throat. I've dedicated the last five years of my life to earning those exact words from my kingdom's lips. Hearing them now, it isn't any wonder I feel so free: I think those words have unlocked the last cell I was trapped in for so many years.

A small hand rests on my arm. I look down and find the corners of Emberly's lips turned upward. Reassurance radiates from her sharp yet delicate features. I can even feel it in her comforting touch.

"His Highness has certainly come a long way," she says, linking her arm with mine. "I'm certain he appreciates those words more than you'll ever know."

"Your own acts of selflessness haven't eluded us, Your Highness," Nikos assures quickly. "You sacrificed much, and you avenged our prince when you thought him dead. We're grateful that His Highness has someone of your character to lead beside."

Emberly's features soften. I almost want to say that a shyness has overcome her, but I know her better. "Thank you. The prince and I do not take your kindness lightly."

"May your reign be long and prosperous," Rhea says, nodding at us. "We have hope in you both."

Despite our conversation, the words weigh heavily on me as we watch the couple travel farther down the street. Rhea keeps her arm linked in Nikos's and rests her head against the side of his shoulder. I estimate that they're around Ithinor's age—yet I can't stop imagining myself and Emberly in that same position in ten years.

That only allows me an even greater peace.

I've redeemed myself.

"Thank you," I tell Emberly. I'm grateful for the smile on my face, for the warmth it shares with the rest of me. "You were right. I think I lost hope that I would hear those words from Seavale one day. That was exactly what—"

When I look back at Emberly, she stands turned with her gaze set on the other side of the intersection next to us. Her smile is absent.

"Unbelievable," she mutters under her breath.

I follow her eyes. My stare lands on a group of middle-aged men in silver robes.

Something tugs at me in my chest. *They feel familiar, as if I know them from a story.*

Emberly scoffs. "Leave it to the councilmen to ruin a good moment no matter what kingdom they stand in."

That's *where I know them from...*

I eye them carefully, all too aware of the woman standing next to me. "Imagine if they knew about..." I exhale. "I'm grateful you had someone as honorable as Meredith to protect your secret from them."

She never steals her eyes away from the glaring group. "Why do you think they treated me so despicably over the years, lion?"

I jolt upright, facing her completely. "You mean... the council knows?"

Realization blooms in me. She's right: no wonder they so ruthlessly rejected her and her rule. If they knew she was illegitimate, and if the King of Snowark somehow did pass away nevertheless after she was born—

She grants me her full attention. "Winston was close to my father—the King of Snowark. Everything Luciana said is true and was written in the letter he wrote and then gave to Winston to give to me one day. The king knew I wasn't his daughter because he and my mother hadn't exactly been... *together* for some time due to their royal duties occupying them so incessantly. He explained his plan to take his own life by poison so as to create a natural-seeming death just after I was born. He desired to protect not only the image of Snowark, but my validity—had he not died, the people would have known that he was not my father."

Air is absent from my lungs as an arrow of truth strikes my chest: that's why she so adamantly believes she killed her parents. She's been shouldering not only the circumstances of the death curse, but also the fact that a man who wasn't even her father gave his life for her sake.

Just like Ambrose did.

Emberly continues as if she's spent her entire life relaying this story. "He told Winston to give the letter to me once he felt that I was ready. Winston blamed me for the king's death and shared the news with his herd so as to create a council against the princess who killed the true monarch—another reason they rigged the council selection ten years ago, to stay together. The truth was hidden to maintain the reputation of Snowark. I am a disgrace to them, unfit to rule their kingdom; so keeping me a secret gave them the perfect grounds to make me their prisoner... Winston gave me the letter when I learned of the death curse."

My mind freezes. "When you were five...?"

She nods.

My heart sinks into my stomach, thumping hard. Images of Emberly holding a blade to her throat on Magery's stage flash in my mind. Not one part of me regrets persuading her to live to see the next day, but the sheer weight of her mind from that morning has imparted itself onto me. I feel my own mind start to crumble under the merciless pressing of guilt, and I can't begin to fathom how the woman next to me has borne it for thirteen years.

"That's why I wanted so earnestly for Meredith to skip lessons that day in the library." Her gaze remains stolid. "The details I'd already read confirmed that the letter was true, not forged by men who resented me—such as how the King of Vineah 'mysteriously' fell with a heart attack the same day I was born."

"Why would the king reveal any of that to you," I begin, a light breeze coming to relieve the hot anger in my cheeks, "if not for the purpose of provoking your guilt, just as the councilmen did?"

To my relief, she smiles. "I'm only able to believe it now: he and my mother truly loved me. Enough to not only want me despite my conception, but to want the truth for me. For me to

497

know my full heritage one day if I chose to. He wrote that they desired for me to know that I had just as much fire to rule with as Snowark's previous rulers—that I could symbolize a new beginning out of my origin. That's why they made..." Her shining green eyes bounce from the cobblestone street up to mine. "My name."

I arch a brow. "Your name?"

She speaks it slowly: "'Emberly Genesis'. That was their— final gift to me, as my father wrote it. But despite how many times I read his words... the council knew how to eradicate my faith in them."

They knew exactly what they were doing to a five-year-old girl.

My gaze feels sharp enough to cut a diamond as it settles on the councilmen standing across the street. They're snickering at us.

The man upfront must be Winston. I can feel it.

"I may not have been ready," I tell Emberly, "but something tells me you are."

"I have been."

I offer her my arm. "After you, Your Highness?"

"Right again, lion," she says, linking her arm with mine.

The group's judgmental glares have yet to move away from us. They're challenging us to walk to them—as though walking to us admits their concession to our rule.

I brace myself. Instinct warns that they're worse than Emberly has ever managed to express.

"Your..." the bald man at the front begins reluctantly as we approach, resting his hands on his distended belly, "Highnesses."

"Still unsatisfied, Whiny Winston?" Emberly asks sweetly.

His brown eyes narrow, his pack behind him exchanging expressions of disgust and disturbance. "'Whiny'—?" he begins, swallowing the rest of his words. "We only made the journey to see the fuss. Imagine our surprise upon hearing that you emerged victorious in the race for the Last Kingdom. Of course, all fell into reason when we realized that His Highness from Seavale pulled you through it as he did."

My brows furrow with Emberly's, but she continues for us. "What leads His High and Mighty to this conclusion?"

Winston peers down at her. "We can't imagine that your temper allowed you an easy journey."

Anger tightens my throat as I start to speak; but Emberly doesn't even spare me a glance as she holds her hand up, stopping me. Instead, a curious mien rests on her face. "You're right—it did not," she replies. The light breeze dissipates, leaving us in a warm atmosphere that intensifies under the sun's rays. "I suppose that is why the monarchs competed with their chosen teammates, is it not? And if such is the case, then rejecting your initial selection for my team truly was the right course of action."

My pride can't possibly swell more than it already has.

"Interesting that you raise the matter," Winston says with a stolid expression. "We hear that the royal advisor has become a Lady Cathridge of Seavale, the mage a Spellster Oliver of *Vineah*, of all kingdoms. What ever became of Lady Prim and Spellster Walsh?"

Emberly's hand falters. She lowers it. "They committed their sacrifices for the sake of the Last Kingdom during the race."

"Ah." A wicked malice glints in Winston's brown eyes. He seems to suppress a smirk from his round, pitiful face. "In other words, two more lives have yet again been lost to your illegitimate rule."

That's it—

"No," Emberly states quickly. Then, she slows, bringing her hands together in front of her stomach as she recollects herself— reminding me to do the same. "That is two more lives that were encouraged enough by my rule to lay down all that they had to bring forth the coming kingdom. Two lives who loved me and our world enough to pay the price for our future."

"Something we can't say of you, from the sounds of it," I remark, wrapping my arm around Emberly's waist. "Please excuse us, gentlemen. The future queen and I must—"

All twelve members of the council scoff and jeer. Against every corner of my mind demanding otherwise, I can't help but retract under the harsh scrutiny and judgement of their glowers.

"'Queen'," Winston spits, holding his chin high above Emberly. Instinct awakens in me, one that entices me to reach for my sword: his eyes have darkened, and his scowl now boasts its presence. As though he's ready to unleash something of his own without boundaries. "You may run a thousand races and send hundreds more to their deaths under your illicit rule without shame, but no misbegotten shall ever be my queen! And none of your wretched, ignorant sheep will think so, either, once they learn what a unmentionable abomination their 'sovereign' truly is—!"

I push Emberly behind me, gripping the handle of my sword and peering down at Winston. "Is that a threat to the future queen?"

"Not a threat, *Your Highness*." His eyes stare back up at me with daggers just as sharp. "Every tongue will know the truth. She'll be dethroned before the end of next week. That is a promise."

"Are you even aware of—?"

"Leave it be, Leo," Emberly commands, pulling me back. I'm grateful that I'm not the target of the death glare she wears right now. "A rat doesn't starve when you always leave it cheese."

I lock my jaw for her sake. Perhaps my own as well—I've just redeemed myself in the eyes of my subjects, and I won't allow someone at the bottom of the food chain to steal that from me.

I take a brief glance around. We've already a few eyes on us. *Do not retaliate.*

Emberly takes my arm, and I turn on my heel. We begin our stroll down the main street. Eventually, I hear the council start in the other direction.

My blood bubbles in my veins. An anger so intense that I'm unsure how to calm myself grips my being.

"I don't understand," I say, finally allowing my hand to release my sword at my side. "*That* is what you've endured all these years, and you never... Not once did... You still—"

"I see someone is due for a review of the alphabet with Sierra once we return to the palace," she says, keeping her head high. "If the future king is illiterate, I'm not sure how the kingdom will fare at the news."

She's deflecting again. Something isn't right.

"That's exactly it," I finally manage, nodding at passing subjects. Each one bears a kind smile that I want to become further acquainted with, but an urgency burns in my chest right now. "Would they really commit treason for the sake of dethroning you?"

"They would certainly attempt it." She scoffs, holding up the skirt of her slender, red gown as we step down the sunny incline of the street. The carriage trails softly behind us. "Particularly because their 'rumors' are true. And if we were to punish them for sharing it, how much worse should it seem on our account."

Some would understand, but would enough declare us as unjust rulers who silence opposition?

"So much for a council meant to be knowledgeable on legal matters," I whisper. "They can't dethrone you on grounds of conception. It's prejudice and—"

"I don't care about their ridiculous threat in terms of my position. No law in any of the kingdoms would allow it, and they're quite aware of that. Winston was grasping at straws. It's..." She exhales, softly shaking her head. "I don't want it publicized any more than it has been."

On the platform, she confessed that she had accepted her origin. Now, though, I realize the chance that that meant she had accepted there was nothing in her ability to *change* her origin. Accepting that others would sooner or later uncover it, however...

"We'll discuss it with Sierra," I finally say, taking her hand. "Don't worry. You aren't alone in the matter anymore."

It takes her a few seconds to convince herself of it; she only takes a deep breath and nods.

"I'm proud of you, firefly," I say, which earns a curious gaze from her. "Despite their display, you spoke—fairly wisely to them. In the face of their implications, their threats... even when they spoke that way about Ambrose and Meredith."

A sight for the seven kingdoms appears on Emberly's lips: a sheerly shy smile. She shrugs. "Surely you of all people don't need the reminder, lion," she says. "I've grown. You three taught me too much for me not to learn."

CHAPTER

"THE LAND OF THE NEW COVENANT"

Emberly

A S IF THE COUNCIL WEREN'T ENOUGH CAUSE FOR UN-
necessary worry—Leo and I return to the palace that afternoon to find the Vinean Court awaiting an audience
with us.

Thankfully, they only came to formally acknowledge me in
my offer of mercy to Luciana; the Mages have spent the last few
days relaying the races' events to the kingdoms. Evidently, it was
never mentioned to the Vinean Court, either, that Vineah had
two princesses. Leo and I decided to withhold the truth; it no
longer mattered.

Meeting personally with Vineah's surprisingly humble leaders did allow me the realisation of my misplaced anger. All these
years, my hatred boiled against Vineah. All these years, I sought
a vengeful closure with "them". I should have first seen it with

Sierra—but the people of Vineah are generally good, just as those of Snowark. I see now that I was never able to blame who was directly at fault for what became of my parents. The kingdom of Vineah suffered under my resentment as a result. This afternoon, though, I released them from my chains—as well as myself. I've also Vinean blood running in my veins, and that fact isn't deserving of my shame.

I'm proud of the queen I'm to become in only a few days. Every day, I work harder to earn her honour.

That night, I follow Leo down the elaborate, wide hall where our separate bedchambers reside. The red dress that hangs down my figure hugs me comfortably—almost consolingly. After all... three days simply isn't enough time to recover from the race. Not in any reality would it be. That is the one matter no one has yet to discuss. As if the topic itself is cursed. Leo and I are just about completely physically healed thanks to Sierra and Aspen— though a terrible scar will be left in my wound's wake—but my mind threatens to regress beyond my control every day. Every time the world around me grows dark, every time I blink, I see it all: the race, my history, both combined in nightmarish tapestries in my mind. Though, the burden grows slightly easier when I'm with Leo: he is the only participant of the race who bears identical burdens, identical losses, to me. That understanding, the mere presence of it, helps me breathe in the outside world, in reality. He helps me recover every moment I'm not visiting my mind.

In front of my bedchamber doors, he slows behind me. "Firefly."

I turn around. The clicking of my heels, which add several deserved inches to my height, fades to echoes down the hall. Leo has my attention captured to a greater extent than he should: he's dressed in a princely uniform similar to the one from my dream on the platform, but with a royal-blue doublet this time. His eyes that match the shade of the daytime sky radiate a warmth and love I never thought I'd live to see.

His smile is tender as he looks down at me. "You are absolutely stunning."

I cross my arms. "If you start your sappy speeches now, I'll move back to Snowark."

The prat grins, taking my hands. "Then I will follow and marry you there."

"'Marry'—?"

My mouth falls agape as I remember.

Leo's face falls. "You forgot. You *forgot*?"

"I've spent the last eighteen years preparing to either marry when I'm old and thirty or be killed by the race we somehow managed to escape. Forgive me if my union to Seavale's own royal dunce temporarily escaped me."

He cocks his slit brow. "Tell me you're joking."

"Listen, prat, as if the transition has been *smooth sailing*!"

He gently pulls me closer to him. "If I can't make terrible jokes, then neither can you."

"Really?" I ask flatly. "What does His Royal Prat-ness plan to do in retaliation? Sounds like a lot of complaints and *Wales* to me—"

He moves his hands to my waist and wriggles his fingers. Laughter bursts from my lips in a helpless, high-pitched glee, my body writhing. I try to step away, but he wraps his arm around me. I beg him to stop, turning in a final effort to escape. He pulls me against him, his other hand releasing my waist and coming to rest on his arm.

I stand with my back against him. His chin rests softly on my head, and I exhale. Crystal chandeliers hang every few metres apart from each other down the opulent hall, their candles aflame. Spotless windows invite the cascading rays of the setting sun in. The grey veining of the marble floor is exposed in full detail amidst the light.

I helplessly sink into the warmth Leo radiates from behind me. No armour stands in the way this time to mask our humanity that lay underneath it when we were running the race. Now we only have each other. From now on until death, we will have each other.

"A few days isn't enough," I whisper before I can realise that the words are on my tongue. But confiding in Leo allows my heart to feel—and that allows my heart to heal. "To recover. A week won't be, either. Sometimes I wake up from nightmares of all the worst moments—Meredith, Ambrose... of you, this time with the arrow *in* your heart. I don't know how it missed you..."

Leo stands upright, encouraging me to turn around. "You will never wake up from a nightmare alone again once I'm your husband. You have my word now and every day."

"Do you not dream of it?" I whisper. It almost feels as if the question will raise up another race.

"Every time I close my eyes." He raises his hand to my cheek, his thumb gently rubbing it. "Sleep has become my sworn enemy; and the less of it I receive, the more often I close my eyes to rest, the more often I blink—the more I see flashes of it all. The more I replay Ithinor's death, the more I crawl through the tight spaces,

I see you on the ground of Soilera's stage after Ambrose sank, I stare at you dying next to me on the platform—"

My throat tightens. A shine glistens in Leo's eyes, followed by a stray tear down his cheek. I use my thumb to wipe it away.

"I see it a thousand times a day," he whispers. "And the only hope of solace I have at the end of the day is remembering that out of it all came you. Out of my darkest curses came the greatest blessing that doesn't even belong to me yet still chose me nevertheless."

"You wanted me. You wanted me when I couldn't stand my own existence."

"I *want* you, Emberly." He cups my face. "I want you now and for the rest of my life."

I feel a blush radiate from my cheeks. My fingers wrap firmly around his. "I want you, Leo. I want you as my king, my husband, and my best friend."

His stare intensifies. Then, he nods.

"Then you deserve a proper proposal," he says. "Not an announcement by a group of mages. You deserve to know that I meant every word of what I said in Magery, firefly. You deserve someone willing to prove that they aren't ashamed of you, someone willing to shout their pride of you from the tallest mountain in all the seven regions—because you unlocked parts of me that I thought were long gone with the curse, and I want the world to know that."

I swallow down the wave of joy that overwhelms my being. It still feels tricky to allow that in. Now, though, at least hope is there to offer a safer landing for it.

Leo's thumbs rub my cheek. "You reminded me—you

showed me—what it means to love and be loved, to understand and be understood, beyond friendship. You are more than my friend and ruler—you are part of me, someone to share my future with. I love you, Emberly. And I have only one last question for you."

I dart my blurring vision to the windows beside us, to the brightness of the setting sun. It does nothing to satiate the tears pricking my eyes. Looking back up at Leo, I decide that I don't want to hide any part of my heart from him—let alone when he's pouring his out unto me.

His kneels on one knee, both of his hands holding mine. "Will you marry me?"

A breathless laugh helplessly escapes from me. Sniffing, I squeeze his hands. "Yes. Yes, lion, of course."

He springs from the ground with a bright grin. Time dissipates as his hands cup my face and he bends down, pressing his lips to mine. They're soft and inviting and safe, igniting my memory of our kiss in Magery. My longing surrenders unto him, his hands falling to my waist. His lightning bolts down my body. I can finally feel his touch directly, not through the barrier of my armour.

This time is different. This time, I can throw myself into Leo's hold, melt into it and know that I'll return to the surface. Rather than crumble in the aftermath of happiness, my heart throbs with a joy that swirls all throughout my chest. And I don't feel the need to run away from it, but run straight into it.

Breaking away, Leo connects our foreheads. His cedar-like musk inflames my senses. His fingers tighten around my waist as his breath tickles my nose, fresh with the peppermint tea we were served after dinner. "You have me unable to wait to call you my wife," he whispers, pushing a piece of my hair behind my ear.

"I certainly can." I scoff. "They expect us to name the kingdom in a few days, and I've already asked the Mages: we can't name it 'The Last Kingdom'."

He chuckles. "I know. I asked them, too."

That certainly isn't comforting. "And they truly haven't seen the mistake in crowning *us* as their rulers?"

Amidst acquainting ourselves with the kingdom, recovering from much more than physical scars, and preparing a wedding, I can't quite say that naming a brand-new kingdom made it to the front of my mind often the last few days. What single name suits all seven regions whose titles reflect their individuality and distinct nature?

"I've got it," I say, using my hands to gesture a grand title. "'The Final Kingdom'."

Leo freezes as though I've actually provided the answer to our prayers. Then, he blinks. "It truly is a blessing that you'll have me to help you make decisions—"

"Prat!" I exclaim, slapping his arm. "The least you can do is pretend."

"Another time—when we aren't facing a deadline mere days away."

I fall against the frigid marble wall beside my bedchamber doors. "What does His Royal Wise-ness suggest, then? We've supposedly united everyone under one crown, but how does one name capture the essence of such individuality combined?"

"I don't think we should complicate it as such," he replies curiously, folding his hands together. His brows furrow in thought. "Actually, I think a name that swirls all seven regions into one defeats the purpose of the Last Kingdom to begin with."

I arch a brow at him, crossing my arms. "How do you suppose that?"

"We would be combining the single trait we all have in common—our part in the Last Kingdom—but it would remain to ostracise each region's distinctiveness along with it."

I'm not sure that I entirely agree with him—or even understand him. The imminence of our wedding and coronation, however, leaves no room for argument right now.

"Then what does the royal lion propose?"

He snickers. "I just did—"

With one slap of his arm from me, he shakes his head and looks out the windows in front of us. The sunlight is cascading through the glass and drenching the floor in its glow. It temporarily distracts me in the idea of its warmth until Leo speaks again: "A name that reflects the purpose. What it was always meant to represent so that no one ever misconstrues its legend or twists it into a wicked lie again."

That, I can agree with... It's certainly a worthy premise for a name to be founded on. But it isn't as though we can name a kingdom "Unity" or "Unified" or "Together"—

I cringe with every "name" that enters my mind.

"It's not working yet," I say, glimpsing Leo.

He takes my hand again. "We're close to it... I can feel it. What does the coming of the Last Kingdom truly mean?"

I exhale. "Unity, of course. The breaking of the curse. A new world for all... almost a new agreement, of sorts, for how things will be from henceforth."

He hums curiously. "Like a promise that with the new world comes a new order, something better than the old. A royal covenant, almost."

It strikes me. I straighten, reaching for his arm. "'Covenant'. 'Covenant', I like that... Something reflective of not only our union, but our dominion as a covenant—the one between the Last Kingdom and the world, between us and our people now. The promise we make to them for a better world as long as we all have the desire to uphold it."

I can almost see the gears turning in Leo's mind. "And something that promotes our modesty," he adds, standing from the wall. "Emphasises that we're a land that's been humbled by its past and its mistakes."

The words and letters are tantalizing my mind. A land built on the foundation of its covenant...

"'Covenaan'," I say in realisation. "The land of the new covenant."

Leo's smile breaks into a grin. "I think we've just named the Last Kingdom, firefly."

Another weight lifts itself from my shoulders. I exhale. Covenaan. The King and Queen of Covenaan. It sounds fitting in my mind, and it flowed off my tongue moments ago. I think this is it, the true title of the Last Kingdom.

"Perhaps we've a proper chance at a great rule, after all." I allow myself to share Leo's smile in full; I tell myself that it's all right. It is safe now. I am brave enough to be happy, to welcome these precious opportunities. I no longer want to be afraid of what I may lose; I want to embrace everything I have to hold on to.

I walk into Leo's hold. My body relaxes against him, a foreign calm—security—settling in my chest. For the first time in my life, my heart beats with life and hope for the future instead of dread. Leo has unlocked that ability in me; he unlocked the unwritten chapters of my story. I thought it had already been written down years ago upon discovering the cause of my parents' deaths—upon being silenced by the ones who had stolen authority in Snowark—but here I stand with my fiancé and our greatest soldiers now. The course of it all changed upon the opening of that portal almost three weeks ago.

Now my every step carries a new purpose, one that I wholeheartedly accept. It's time to write a new story.

CHAPTER  44

"THE GOOD NEWS"

Leo

THE NIGHT BEFORE THE WEDDING IS ANOTHER COLD one as I approach Emberly in the back of the palace courtyard. She stands at a small patch of red roses planted in plush soil, a circle of smooth stones rimming them. Next to the circle are two others like it: one with three orange marigolds planted instead, the other with dark-purple irises. Fireflies dot the sky, illuminating patches of Emberly's dark-auburn waves cascading down the silk of her royal-blue–and–silver gown. Her head stays down as I approach.

"Come here," I whisper, resting my hands on the textured fabric around her arms. I lean my head against hers, keeping my voice soft, my mouth just above her red-tipped ears. "It's cold again tonight. You shouldn't be out here without your cloak. You'll wake up sick tomorrow of all days."

Her chest expands with a deep breath, her head staying down.

"Is something wrong?" I ask.

She kneels down, and I come to her side to follow. She presses a kiss to two fingers before placing them on the frontmost stone of the circle around the roses. "I've become better, Meredith," she whispers. "If you can see me right now, I hope I've allowed your legacy to act through me. I've finally learned the blessings of acting in love, and I have you to thank for it." She turns her head to the light-orange marigolds. "And don't believe for a second that I will ever forget what you did for Covenaan, Ambrose. We've ensured that your family—your parents and all four siblings—are provided for and will be from now on. Just as your honor will be as well. We've plans to convert the old palaces into accessible schools for the regions. I know you would have enjoyed reading to the children."

She presses a kiss to her fingers before pressing it to one of the stones around the marigolds. "Happy birthday."

I close my eyes in bittersweet remembrance. Ambrose's eighteenth.

Happy birthday, Ambrose. Nobody could distract me from the world better than you.

It is no easier enduring his loss—but we're stronger doing so now than we were a week ago.

Emberly stands, taking my hand into hers as she walks to the grave on the far left: the dark-purple irises. We stare down at the flowers. "My only regret is that I never had the opportunity to know you, Ithinor. If Leo is any reflection of your guidance and character, it truly is a tragedy."

Her eyes look up into mine. "He would be so proud of you, lion."

A happy storm flurries in my chest as I smile, squeezing her hand.

We step back. Emberly's eyes sweep across all three graves. "Generations will know what you three did for us and Covenaan."

I place a gentle hand on her lower back, the silk cool against my skin. She nestles into my hold, wrapping her arms around my torso. We release a quiet sigh, memories of Ithinor and Ambrose flowing through my mind. I wonder about the memories of Meredith that are likely going through Emberly's head right now, anticipating the lifetime I have with her to hear about the woman who influenced her in the same way Ithinor influenced me.

"I hope it lasts," Emberly whispers as she turns away, facing the entrance to the palace on the other side of the courtyard.

"What do you mean, firefly?" I ask, walking with her on the light soil. Our plant-lined path is illuminated by the glowing bugs. The night air blows a cool breeze as we walk under a clear, dark sky. It's as if the night is foreshadowing the perfection of tomorrow.

Her hand tightens in mine. "I'm unused to the idea of living in a curse-free kingdom," she replies. "Even more unused to the notion that—a life so beautiful exists for me."

I bring her hand up to my lips as we come to a stop. "We made it, firefly. We are the first of the New Covenant according to the Ancient Mages themselves, and we will be the first to live to raise our children. We've started what will succeed past the old boundaries. We're seeing to it every day. And..."

Her eyes, a jade green amidst the glowing fireflies, meet mine.

"...you *will* see the eyes of our firstborn open."

A smile graces her precious lips, a blush rushing into her light cheeks. "You can't say such things when we've an audience, prat."

I glance at the guards stationed at the open double doors of the back entrance. I smirk. "They'll have to accustom themselves to it if they plan to serve the king and queen for long."

She rolls her eyes. "All right. It's my turn, then."

I grin. "What's that?"

"When we do bear an heir, you'll make a brilliant father, Leo. Even if you impart a few tricks."

I helplessly bite my lip. I know she means it, as much as she meant what she said following this conversation in Magery.

She arches a brow at me. "Well?"

I lean down for a kiss. My fingers caress her face as I take her lips into mine, her hands finding my cheeks. I provide another gentle peck before breaking away, allowing her to lead us farther down the path and closer to the back entrance. The guards remain stationary and stolid, but I offer a smile nevertheless. They finally, subtly return it before we walk through the doors and onto the illuminated marble floors.

"Your Highnesses," the servants say, bowing or curtseying as we pass under the chandeliers. Emberly and I offer our courtesies in reply. I've never seen her so happy and for so long.

I wait until the servants continue past us in the vast, opulent hall to lean in for another kiss. "I'll see you tomorrow, My Queen."

"I would if I were you." She places a hand on my chest just before I can meet her lips. "I know where they hid Rowena."

Our smiles meet, melting into a soft kiss. Just as I reach for her waist for a final embrace for the night, a familiar, sweet voice urgently calls from down the hall, "Your Highnesses!"

We reluctantly break away, and I press my lips together in disappointment. Slipping my arm around Emberly's waist, I straighten and turn around with her. Sierra briskly walks toward us in a silver gown from the other end of the hall. Zenevieve and Ezra, whom Sierra is recently engaged to, walk behind her on either side, their swords swinging in their sheaths as they do.

"News, Sierra?" I ask.

Her bun is now an organized, elegant mess, two wavy, chestnut bangs framing her fair face. It's a strange—but admittedly refreshing—difference. "The advisory council has devised an emergency rerouting of the royal tour set to begin next month."

My brows furrow. "Why?"

"Despite the Last Kingdom's rise," Zenevieve begins, resting her dark hand on the silver pommel of her sword, "they've just received word of the despair that's broken out amidst certain areas across the seven regions. The people are worried about the rule to come and the futures of their dominions. Part of them are going so far as to say that the Last Kingdom's rule is unjust."

"And those in fear are unable to travel here to receive word directly," Ezra adds, his grave voice contradicting the courage in his icy-blue eyes. "So many have flocked here that not many remain to inform them on what's happened, let alone what lies ahead."

It's strange—I expect a well of disappointment, of even fear;

but instead of dread, instead of doubt for how I am to manage the future, there's... hope. I listen to my friends' words with hope—in my ability, in my rule with my queen. A knowledge that I won't be doing this alone.

With one glance of agreement at Emberly, I look back at our friends. Determination lifts my lips into a smile. "Then we'll just have to tell them the good news."

EPILOGUE

"NONE OF IT WAS EVER IN VAIN"

Emberly

DEAR MEREDITH AND AMBROSE,

My only regret is that neither of you will ever read these words for yourselves after the future you both valiantly gave yourselves for—but I'd like to relay them to you nonetheless.

Against my previous belief and judgment, Snowark helped unlocked the Last Kingdom, along with Seavale. A week after, it was formally announced as "Covenaan" at my and Leo's wedding and coronation. It is a reflection of the new world we've stepped into, the new agreement between the king and queen and their people: to have better hearts for a better world.

Leo and I returned from the royal tour yesterday. We made productive rounds across the seven regions despite opposition and even minor resentment from certain areas. It's been six months since we accepted our roles as King and Queen of Covenaan at the altar, yet we *already face a mission worth a thousand lifetimes...*

Meredith—how I long to start my days under your guidance as I used to. The last instruction you ever gave me was to let all that I do be done in love. That included allowing Seavale a chance, which began as the most excruciating yet became the greatest decision of my life. I adhered to your wisdom to the best of my ability throughout the rest of the race. Since then, I've come to accept that moments of weakness are not evidence of my inability or illegitimacy; rather, they are reminders of my humanity—of how even Rowena was forged in fire in order to become her greatest. If I can only endure the fire, my weaknesses shall become my strongest steps towards betterment. Under the weight of my weaknesses and the impression that I hadn't any power to escape them, I lashed out in a childish attempt at obtaining whatever control I could. You saw through that and persisted in helping me become better, showing me what the heart of a true leader looks like. I cannot change the girl you handled when you were alive, but I can promise that the woman you raised shall faithfully continue in the footsteps you inspired for her.

Until your last breath, you were the only one in my life who knew me entirely—all of me, in mind and heart and darkest secret. And you loved me in full regardless. You guided me amidst my most insufferable hours, and you mothered me when I was unlovable. You led me so that I may lead Covenaan. Thank you.

Ambrose, you will be glad to know that your big sister Zenevieve is now Co-Captain Lathrop of the Royal Covenaan Guard, along with Co-Captain Ezra Everguard. They would do well with your smile and charm. We all would. After all, part of the reason I chose you for the race was to upkeep my morale. You served your true purpose in life well: blessing those around you with the purest form of your heart under every circumstance. If only I still had you with me—you would have known just the right way to alleviate my daily strains.

I never appreciated that fact in full with you, yet your faith in me was eternal. You believed in me to a perilous extent. I repeat your words from that day to myself every day. Take heart in knowing that they are part of the reason my steps are so strong and purposeful now.

Leo and I both work hard to honour your memories, to become the rulers you both saw in us long before we ever saw them in ourselves. I miss you both dearly—but from now on, we may all rest with the knowledge that none of it was ever in vain.

With love,

Emberly Genesis Whitaker-Wales

Leo

Dear Ithinor,

I don't know where to begin. Much has happened in the last six months, let alone since I lost you...

Emberly and I spent the first month of our marriage preparing for the royal tour, and then the next few months traveling Covenaan—the Last Kingdom that Seavale and Snowark unlocked in the race—and the seven regions under it. I couldn't help but think of you during every diplomatic meeting. Part of me still expects to find you by my side, and then when I turn my head... The realization becomes a little easier to endure each time, but the weight never lessens. After everything, it may sound boyish of me—but I regret that you were never allowed to see me fulfill the duties you raised me to accomplish.

I wish you could see the progress our world has made. Snowark and Vineah have reached a respectful acknowledgment of each other and promised to uphold peace when they may amidst minor infractions. Witnessing the destruction that resentment is capable of, not to mention the monstrosity of Vineah's previous king—who, we discovered, was truly a sinister and wretched man—has sensitized the two lands to the storms of wickedness. Therefore, the Covenaan Court, headed by me and Emberly, is to address any substantial cases beyond domestic reconciliation.

Such peace may likewise be said of Seavale and Lavara. In fact, Emberly and I aided the two in accomplishing a vital trade negotiation: water is a scarce and precious resource throughout most of Lavara, but Seavale's mages are able to purify the water that our ships will deliver to the areas of the region unable to easily receive it. In turn, Lavara is rich in minerals and even new spices that Seavale desires in order to stimulate the island's economy.

That was the change that was most difficult to accept that you weren't present for... You were there when Lavara tried to invade and almost started a war with us; you deserved to be there as we finally achieved resolution after five years. But it's all right. I choose to believe that wherever you are, you can see the imprint you've left on me—and my rule.

I wish I bore only good news. Of course, however, opposition remains in a part of every region. Unfortunately, Soilera, Windale, and Magery have yet to see peace, either. But I had only the best example of persistence growing up, and Emberly and I are earnestly working toward the negotiations and treaties. Much must be understood between the three of them, and even more must be forgiven. Neither is easy, even for me in my outside perspective; but your advice has certainly been useful amidst trying to settle the wars.

Emberly is insisting that I come to bed—we have an early morning tomorrow with their ambassadors. But I promise, Ithinor, that now I can proudly claim the progress I've made since your passing. Your pride in me is no longer in vain. I will never forget that you are the one I have to thank for who I am today. You are the one who established my foundations. You never stopped trying to unlock the man I had trapped in a cell out of fear and even resentment. Thank you for seeing that man within the foolish little boy, even all those years ago. Thank you for never giving up on him—for helping him grow into someone to be proud of.

With all my mind and heart,

Leon Atlas Wales

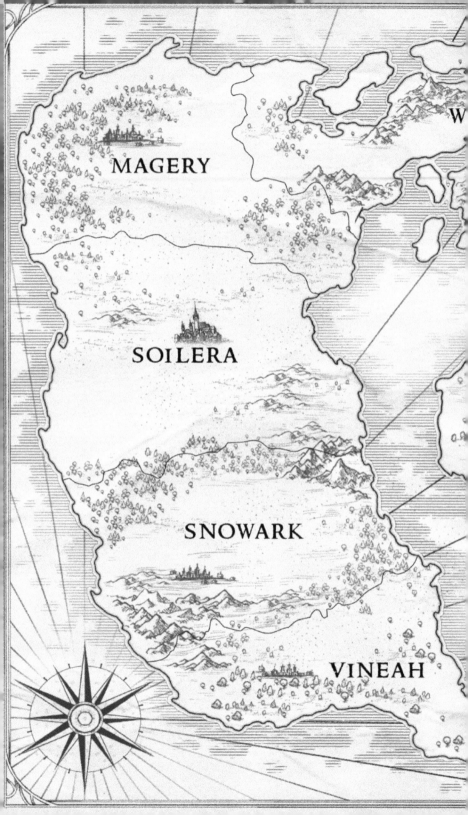

BOOK PLAYLIST

CREATED BY @_BOOKS.WITH.EMMA ON INSTAGRAM

1. "Live Like Legends" – Ruelle
2. "Ends of the Earth" – Lord Huron
3. "Savior Complex" – Phoebe Bridgers
4. "Ribs" – Lorde
5. "Year of the Young" – Smith and Thell
6. "The View Between Villages" – Noah Kahan
7. "Seven" – Taylor Swift
8. "Fourth of July" – Sufjan Stevens
9. "Wasteland, Baby" – Hozier
10. "My Tears Ricochet" – Taylor Swift
11. "Traveling Song" – Ryn Weaver
12. "when the party's over" – Billie Eilish
13. "Hold Back the River" – James bay
14. "Can't Live Without You" – Owl City
15. "War of Hearts" – Ruelle
16. "Genesis" – Ruelle
17. "The Fruits" – Paris Paloma
18. "Last Man Standing" – Livingston
19. "Not Another Song About Love" – Hollywood Ending
20. "Phoenix" – Cailin Russo, Chrissy Costanza, and LoL

~✺ ACKNOWLEDGEMENTS ✺~

I did not write this story alone. I will never be able to stress that enough.

Velo—it all started when you shared your personal fanfic plot with me. Thus was born the idea of a world's kingdoms running in a death race for a key that would unlock an ultimate kingdom. I didn't know it at the time, but that single idea would change my life. Thank you *so* much for being brave enough to share something so personal with me that night.

Signe, Bryce, Emily, McKenna, Paris, Amelia, Emma, Grace, and MC—my alpha and beta readers... needless to say, THANK YOU. Especially for constantly putting up with me coming back to ask you questions and to help me solve story crises. This book would have gotten nowhere without any of you.

Mike Diener—now you have TWO books where you have a paragraph in the acknowledgements. You will ever know the extent of what you did for TKC. You read an extremely problematic draft and built with me the concrete foundations of the final story. Thank you for the constant mentorship and boundless patience as I not only tried to work through this story, but also my identity as a writer and author.

Bryce, you need a paragraph of your own, too. You dedicated *literally* almost as many hours into this project as I did—and you dedicated *literally* just as much care about it. If every author had a friend like you, there would be a lot more books in the world. It's a bittersweet thing. You were a beacon to me on so many days, so many nights, throughout so many weeks and months. "Thank you" will never do my gratitude justice, ever—but thank you.

My Kickstarter backers, YOU GUYS made this physical book happen. That is an indisputable fact that will hold up in court. Seriously, I need you to know that. Thank you infinitely for believing in this project with me. Your faith stretched miles further than you could ever know.

Finally—to the One Who chose me to write this story down. A good friend helped me realize that You chose me because You knew I wouldn't give up. You knew I would stop at nothing until this book was released. And You not only knew that I wouldn't give up, but also provided everything I needed to continue: strength, discipline, rest, even finances. In the midst of my emotional breakdowns, storms of doubt that were so powerful that they made me physically tremble, fear that crippled my very appetite, You supplied me. You sustained me. It was an honor to bear this story and grow with it—an privilege to run with these characters in the greater race for life and the coming Kingdom. Thy kingdom come, and Thy will be done on Earth as it is in Heaven.

THANK YOU, KICKSTARTER BACKERS!

YOU DID MORE FOR THIS BOOK THAN YOU WILL EVER KNOW.

Abby Johansen

Adeline Minett

Alexander

Alexandra

Amelia E. Clawford

Amelia Spowart

Chloe Grace

Elsa (Sarah)

Elsa L. Singer

Emma Shirley

Franchesca Caram

Hannah Gaudette

Jessica J. Lewis

Jimmy

Joan Willows

Justise Briones

Kyle

Lauren D. Fulter

Lorelei Jensen

Maria Mejia

McKenna Rowell

Megan Astell

Nichole Christian

Paris Kaufman

Sarah

Savannah Stenson

Savannah-Rose Roussos

Sera Amoroso

Signe Wikström

Stephanie Crachiolo

Thomas Orosco

ABOUT THE AUTHOR

Ariana Tosado is a 21-year-old author, musician, and content creator for young adult audiences. She started pursuing her passion of writing novels in middle school. Growing up in sunny California, transferring to multiple schools throughout her childhood left her seeking her own sense of identity. Tosado found solace in her writing projects in high school. Today, she's homed her focus on the *Emmalynn Atera* series and her music.

Tosado aims to create relatable and encouraging content through her Instagram account and YouTube channel. She hopes to be able to continue her passion and love for writing through her books and lyrics. Find her on her website, www.arianatosado.com.

MORE FROM THE AUTHOR:

Our Mistaken Identity (The *Emmalynn Atera* Series #1)
The Hunter in the Room (The *Emmalynn Atera* Series #2)
No Memory Unturned (The *Emmalynn Atera* Series #3)